LEARNING TO SWIM

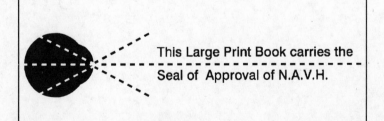

This Large Print Book carries the
Seal of Approval of N.A.V.H.

LEARNING TO SWIM

SARA J. HENRY

THORNDIKE PRESS
A part of Gale, Cengage Learning

GALE
CENGAGE Learning·

Detroit • New York • San Francisco • New Haven, Conn • Waterville, Maine • London

GALE
CENGAGE Learning®

LIBRARY OF CONGRESS CATALOGING-IN-PUBLICATION DATA

Henry, Sara J.
    Learning to swim / by Sara J. Henry.
        pages ; cm. — (Thorndike Press large print peer picks)
        ISBN 978-1-4104-5525-3 (hardcover) — ISBN 1-4104-5525-4 (hardcover) 1. Women journalists—Fiction. 2. Boys—Crimes against—Fiction. 3. Large type books. I. Title.
    PS3608.E5796L43 2013
    813'.6—dc23   2012039315

Published in 2013 by arrangement with Crown Publishing, a division of Random House, Inc.

*To my dad, who taught
me how to read,
and made sure I always
had plenty of books.*

■ ■ ■ ■

PART I

■ ■ ■ ■

"Swimming is a sport that is
not natural to everyone."
— *from a Learn to Swim blog*

CHAPTER 1

If I'd blinked, I would have missed it.

But I didn't, and I saw something fall from the rear deck of the opposite ferry. It could have been a bundle of trash; it could have been a child-sized doll. Either was more likely than what I thought I saw: a small wide-eyed human face, in one tiny frozen moment as it plummeted toward the water.

I was on the late afternoon ferry on Lake Champlain, the big one that takes an hour to reach Vermont. It was overcast and misty, one of those in-between Adirondack days just before summer commits itself, and I'd pulled on a windbreaker because of the occasional chilly gust of wind. I was the only one out on deck, but the closed-in lounge with its narrow benches and tiny snack bar makes me edgy. And I love watching the water as the ferry carves through it. Today the water was calm, with no other boats out except this one's twin, chugging stolidly in the opposite direction.

What I did next was a visceral reaction to those small eyes I thought I saw. Without conscious thought I vaulted onto the railing I was leaning against, took a deep breath, and dived.

It's amazing what you can do if you don't stop to think. The coldness of the water seemed to suck the air out of my lungs, but instinctively I curved upward, fluttering my feet.

In the weekly mini-triathlons in Lake Placid where I live, I'm always one of the last out of the water. The closest I'd ever come to underwater swimming was picking up my hair clasp at the bottom of a friend's pool, and that had taken two tries. And whenever I see a movie with scenes where the hero has to swim through a long, narrow passageway, I always try to hold my breath. I never make it.

But I was in the lake, committed, and surging strongly underwater. By the time I broke the surface, I'd traveled more than a third of the way to where I'd seen the thing go in. Both ferries had gone onward, in their opposite directions. There was no one in sight. No shouts of alarm, no ferry slowing and turning about.

I kept my eyes fixed on the water ahead, and saw something bob up, too far away. My stomach gave a nasty twist. Then I swam, harder and faster than I ever had in a mini-triathlon with middle-aged tourists coming up behind me.

When I reached what I thought was the right spot, I took a deep breath and dived. The water wasn't clear but not exactly murky, sort of a blurred translucence with a greenish cast. I didn't get very far under, and had to try again. This time I saw only a few flat, colorless fish skittering by before I had to come up for air.

Gasping for breath, treading water while I sucked air, reason began to creep in. I wasn't just cold; I was close to numb. I was alone in a very deep lake twelve miles wide, diving after what could be a bag of garbage somebody didn't want to pay to haul to the dump. I was none too sure I had enough strength to get to shore. But I dived once more, and this time something led me straight to it.

It wasn't a bundle of trash. It wasn't a doll. It was a small boy, arms entangled in what looked like a dark sweatshirt, straight dark hair floating eerily above his head. For one awful moment I thought I was looking at a corpse, but then I saw a small sneakered foot kick weakly. By the time I got close enough to grab a handful of sweatshirt, I'd been without air far longer than I'd ever managed to hold my breath watching underwater scenes in movies. My throat was convulsing in an effort not to suck in water instead of the air that wasn't there.

The boy turned toward me, looking at me with those wide dark eyes I hadn't imagined after all. Then they slowly closed. I started upward, dragging him with one hand, swimming with the other, kicking as hard as I could.

It was endless. My ears were ringing, my body a marionette I was directing with an inner voice: *Keep swimming, keep swimming, keep swimming.* I no longer felt cold, and my throat had stopped jerking. I began to wonder if I had drowned. But I felt a dull pain in the arm clutching the boy, and I wouldn't, I thought, feel pain if I were dead.

I kicked on, and sensed rather than saw light above: either Heaven or the surface. In a burst of motion we emerged, the boy bobbing up beside me. I gulped in so much air it hurt, and shook water off my face.

The boy was limp, entangled in the sodden sweatshirt, and I couldn't tell if he was breathing. I struggled to get the sweatshirt off over his head and tried to thump his thin back. I'd taken CPR, but it was several years ago, and no one tells you how to do CPR when you're treading water in a deep, cold lake.

No response. I pulled the boy toward me, put my mouth over his and blew, turning to suck in air — once, twice, three times. Now I was feeling almost furious, at fate or irony or whatever had put me in this cold water with a thin dying child in my arms. I'd found him, and damn it, he needed to start breathing.

The boy coughed, spewed forth a gush of water, then opened his eyes. *"Yes!"* I whispered, "yes, yes, yes!" and I think I shook him a little. I might have cried if I hadn't learned a long time ago you can't cry and swim at the same time.

Now we had to get to shore, which looked a lot farther away than I'd ever swum in a mini-triathlon.

I've read that drowning victims are likely to drag you under and you're supposed to tow them with one arm around their neck so they can't grab you. But I knew I'd never make it swimming with one arm. I pushed his hands under my belt, and squeezed them into tiny fists.

"Hold on," I told him, looking into the dark eyes, and he seemed to understand.

The swim to shore wasn't dramatic, just grim. There's a formula that predicts how long you can survive in cold water before hypothermia renders your brain foggy and your arms and legs useless, and it was probably a good thing I couldn't remember it.

This is the part of *Rescue 911* you never see — the long, slow, dreary stuff. I did the crawl; I did the sidestroke. In my head I sang a slow dirge from Girl Scout camp: *Mandy had a little bay-bee. Had that baby just for me.* Stroke, breathe. *Mandy, oh, my Mandy oh, my Man-dee mine.* Stroke, breathe. *Baby made my Mandy cry. Cried so hard she soon did die.* Stroke, breathe. *Mandy, oh, my Mandy oh, my Man-dee mine.*

At one point the boy's hands slipped from my belt, and I spun and grabbed him as he was sliding under. He opened his eyes halfway and looked at me dully. I cradled him in my arms as the water sloshed around us. "Just a little farther, just a little farther," I pleaded, and his eyes flickered. Now maybe I was crying, but I was so wet and cold I couldn't tell.

I could see details of the shoreline, rocks and a big tree that seemed to beckon to me, and damned if we were going to drown this close to land. I yanked the drawstring from my windbreaker hood, pulled one of his hands underwater, and lashed it to my belt. We swam on, in awkward tandem.

We had been carried well past the ferry dock, and reached shore in a rocky area. I swung my feet down to feel for bottom, and there it was, sandy and shifting and at tiptoe length, but there it was. I yanked my belt loose to free the boy and pulled him toward me, hoisting him to my hip. I staggered as we came out of the water, him clinging to my side like a baby orangutan, and sat down on the first big rock I came to.

We sat there for a moment in silence, sucking in air, both of us shivering. My inner voice was saying *Thankyouthankyouthankyou,* but to whom or to what, I don't know. I was strangely conscious of the hardness of the rock I sat on and the fact that I was no longer being rocked by the water.

The boy stirred, and turned toward me, his dark hair plastered around his thin face. For the first time, I heard him make a sound.

"Merci," he whispered.

CHAPTER 2

He was thin and pale, with a slightly snub nose and huge, long-lashed dark eyes with deep hollows under them. He was small, maybe five or six years old, wearing a snug, long-sleeved striped pullover and jeans. He watched me placidly, then sighed like a tired puppy and laid his head against my chest.

I felt a rush of emotion so strong it jolted me. For one crazy moment it seemed this boy was mine, sitting here in my lap, delivered to me by the lake.

We sat there awhile, my arms around him — how long, I don't know. Water, clouds, sky, and shoreline seemed like something out of a movie, and time had a different dimension, as if it were thick and moving slowly. Suddenly I was aware of the breeze against my cold skin and wet clothes. "We'd better get moving," I said, shifting him from my lap onto his feet. The instant he stood, warmth began to dissipate where he had pressed against my body.

I squeezed water from my ponytail and wrung out my windbreaker. The boy still wore his sneakers, and I still had on my sports sandals, so light I hadn't wasted time unstrapping them when in the water. I held out my hand. *"Viens,"* I said. I grasped his small cold hand, and started clambering over the rocks.

This was like a dream, a bad one. Walking felt like trying to slog through quicksand. After a few minutes the boy started to cough, then gag, and fell to his knees and threw up lake water on the scruffy grass we'd reached by then. I held him by the waist as he retched, and wiped his mouth with the sleeve of my windbreaker.

I thought of my Subaru in the parking lot, with the bag of emergency clothing and sleeping bag I've carried since a sudden snowstorm left me stranded overnight in a friend's chilly cabin. In the Adirondacks, people say, *If you don't like the weather, wait five minutes.* I'd moved here to cover sports for the local newspaper, and discovered that you can be at a baseball game on an April afternoon enjoying the sun on your bare arms, and by the fourth inning have snow falling on you.

By the time we reached the road, the sky

had begun to darken and the mistiness had turned to a light drizzle. I pulled up my windbreaker hood and plodded on. When the footsteps beside me began to lag, I swung the boy up onto my hip. *Right foot, left foot.* A car surged past, and not until I watched it disappear did it occur to me that I could have tried to wave it down. "Gotta get to my car," I thought. "Gotta get to my car." I heard the words before I realized I was speaking aloud.

Now I could see the parking lot and my blue Subaru where I'd parked at the back so I could exit quickly. My brain cleared enough to realize the significance of the fact that nothing was going on. Like the curious incident of the dog in the night-time in the Sherlock Holmes story — curious because the dog had done nothing.

There was no hubbub at the dock. No police. No Coast Guard. No frantic parents of a small French-speaking boy who had disappeared off the side of a ferry. If it hadn't been for a small wet child clinging to my side, I could have convinced myself I'd dreamed the whole thing.

The boy began to shake, in tiny tremors.

Keys. I slapped my pocket. *Damn.* My key ring apparently was now on the bottom of Lake Champlain. But Thomas, the guy I've been dating, had given me a hide-a-key box I'd stashed under the car, primarily because I knew he'd ask me about it. It had seemed an odd gift, one that suggested I couldn't take care of myself. And I at least halfway wished I was the sort of person who received less practical presents.

But right now I was grateful it was there. I groped under the car and found the little box, far back atop the greasy undercarriage. With cold fingers I fumbled it open, then unlocked the car and pulled the bag of spare clothes from behind the front seat. I swung open the hatchback door and lifted the boy to the edge, where he sat, legs dangling, watching me.

Now I was remembering some French. I'd studied it at university, and living this close to Montreal, where people can get irate if you try to speak English to them, I practice with CDs from the library, reciting French phrases and getting odd looks from people in nearby cars.

"Comment t'appelles-tu?" I asked him. Something flickered in his dark eyes. Then they were empty again, unblinking and carefully blank.

"Je n'saispas," he murmured, running the words together. He didn't know his name.

"Tu ne parles pas anglais?" I asked. He

shook his head. No English.

I rooted in the bag, passing over a sweat-shirt similar to the one that had been wrapped around him, and pulled out a T-shirt that had shrunk too much for polite wear and an Adidas jacket with a broken zipper.

"Lèves les bras, s'il te plaît," I said. He obediently raised his arms, and I peeled off his wet shirt. As the shirt came off, as if watching a miniature movie I saw myself in the lake yanking that sweatshirt over his head, and could see clearly what I'd blocked from my mind up until now: the sweatshirt sleeves, wrapped around his body and tied in a tight, dark, wet knot.

On that long swim to shore I'd imagined a set of parents for him: a well-dressed and attractive man and woman who had left him peacefully napping in the backseat of their late-model car — something boxy and safe, a Volvo, perhaps — while they'd gone up to the lounge for a cup of coffee, never suspect-ing their child would slip out of the car and fall overboard. I'd imagined them at the dock, surrounded by police and Coast Guard and dive team, mother frantic, tears rolling down her cheeks, father gruff and angry in his grief and fear, both of them hysterically grateful for their son's safe return.

But the dock was empty. No parents, no police, no Coast Guard. And I could no longer pretend I didn't realize that someone had tied a sweatshirt around this child and thrown him in the lake to drown.

CHAPTER 3

I began to chatter, as I would to a dog that was injured or scared, a mix of English and French, whatever I could think of. I pulled my old T-shirt over the boy's head and manipulated his thin, white arms into it and then into the jacket, as if I were dressing a doll.

I pried off his soggy sneakers and pulled my heavy wool socks up over his jeans to anchor them, my fingers thick with cold. I had no shorts or pants that would fit him, so I wrapped a towel around his bottom half and carried him to the passenger seat. I pulled out the fiberfill sleeping bag I've carried since the night I spent shivering in my friend's cabin, and tucked it around him. He didn't say another word. I didn't let myself think.

No one was around, but I was so cold I wouldn't have cared if the entire Saranac Lake football team had been watching. I yanked off windbreaker and T-shirt in one quick motion and pulled on the hooded sweatshirt, then stepped out of my shorts and into a pair of old track suit bottoms. The dry fabric felt wonderful against my skin. I tossed our wet clothes in the back, jumped in, and started the engine. The boy seemed even smaller with my sleeping bag fluffed around him, and he just watched me. As if waiting to see what I would do next.

The car engine hummed. I cranked up the heat.

What do you say to a small boy who has just been tossed off a boat and isn't crying or telling you what happened? *"Je m'appelle Troy,"* I said at last. I hadn't realized how tense he was until he made a tiny movement of relaxation, one I sensed rather than saw.

"Trrroy," he repeated softly.

It's an odd name for a girl, I know. My sisters had suitable southern belle names of Suzanne and Lynnette, but by the time my brother and I came along our mother had run out of child-naming energy. So our father named us after characters from his favorite mysteries — Simon from The Saint series by Leslie Charteris, and me from the Ngaio Marsh books about a policeman and his wife, Troy. I liked the character I was named after: slim, thoughtful, graceful, a talented painter and a watcher of people. Although I've always wondered if my mother would have liked me better if I had been a Christina or a Sharon or Jennifer.

Not in a million years did I believe this boy didn't know his name. He just didn't want to tell me.

"*Qu'est-ce que s'est passé sur le bateau?*" I asked.

He gave a little shrug, but didn't speak. It didn't surprise me. If he had wanted to tell me what had happened on the ferry, he would have told me by now.

"*Tes parents?*" I asked.

I don't think I'd ever seen such a completely blank expression on a child's face.

During college I'd volunteered two afternoons a week at an emergency children's home, where police and social workers dropped children off, sometimes in the middle of the night. One thin blond girl named Janey had begged me to adopt her. I'd tried to explain that nineteen-year-old students couldn't adopt anyone, let alone a nine-year-old — but when you're desperate for a happy home, you keep asking. I kept having to tell her I couldn't. Each time she returned to the shelter, she was increasingly hollow-eyed, thinner, and more withdrawn.

Staffers at the center weren't allowed to tell us details of children's cases, so I could only guess at what was going on at home. And then she was gone. Maybe she went to foster care or a group home, or her family moved away, out of the reach of Social Services. I never knew what happened to her.

For years, whenever I'd catch sight of a thin blond girl, I'd look to see if it was her.

Our breath was fogging the car windows. I tried to force my brain to work. The ticket seller booth was empty. The passengers were long gone; the boy's ferry was probably halfway back to Vermont. The ferries had no passenger list; you just paid your fare and drove or walked on. But the police could meet the boy's ferry when it docked and ask for descriptions of anyone who had boarded with a small boy.

My cell phone was dangling from its charging cord where I had forgotten it — which was the only reason it wasn't sitting on the bottom of the lake. It wouldn't pick up a signal here, but there was a pay phone just uphill, next to the Amtrak station. I pulled the car closer and took a fistful of change from my ashtray, gesturing toward the phone so the boy would know what I was going to do. As I leaned against the phone stand, I leafed through the pages of the phone book, my cold fingers turning more than one page at a time.

People don't want to believe bad stuff — they work hard at not believing it. They don't want to think that teachers can be demons, that priests abuse children, that the apparently pleasant boy next door could be systematically molesting all the neighborhood girls, one by one. They ignore the evidence as long as they can.

If I told authorities an adult-sized sweatshirt had been tied around this child like a straitjacket, they would smile pleasantly and tell me I must be mistaken, that the arms had simply been twisted or tied around his waist. Because that sweatshirt was now at the bottom of a four-hundred-foot-deep lake, I couldn't prove anything.

And this boy was clearly not going to tell them what had happened.

I gave up leafing through the phone book and called Information, thumbed in change, and punched in the number for the Burlington police. When a woman answered, I said distinctly, "Someone threw a small boy off the ferry from Burlington to Port Kent. Less than an hour ago. He's age five or six, dark hair, brown eyes, thin, speaks French."

Questions squawked from the receiver. I ignored them and repeated what I'd already

26

said. I didn't have any answers, other than my name, and I wasn't about to tell them that. Next I called the police in Elizabethtown, which I knew had a police station, told them the same thing, and hung up.

I looked over at the boy, watching me through the windshield.

I got in the car. "Let's get going," I said, gesturing for him to fasten his seat belt. He freed his arms from the sleeping bag and obediently clicked the belt into place. As I pulled out of the parking lot my wheels gritted on the gravel.

A few miles down the road my phone gave that beep that says it's back in cell tower range. I glanced at the car clock. I had been on my way to Burlington to see Thomas, to go to a piano recital he'd wanted to attend, and he'd be wondering why I hadn't arrived. I picked up the phone and hit his speed dial.

"Tommy, it's Troy," I said, working hard to speak clearly through my fatigue. "Look, I'm really sorry, but something came up, and I can't make it."

A moment's silence, then he said calmly, "Okay." His careful lack of reaction annoyed me — it's not always easy dating someone this determinedly understanding.

"Look, I can't explain right now," I said.

"But I'll call you tonight."

Another pause. "Are you all right?"

"Fine, I'm fine." I tried to sound re-assuring. Thomas would be sitting on the sofa in his apartment, sandy hair neatly combed, looking like a Lands' End model in his crisp khakis and button-down shirt. Diving off the railing of the Burlington ferry was not something I wanted to explain to him, not now and probably never. "Talk to you later," I said, and clicked the phone off.

I looked at the boy. "Men!" I said. He smiled faintly, and I felt a little twist inside me.

We were approaching Keeseville, where I could turn south for Elizabethtown and the police station. I thought about it; I really did. I envisioned us traipsing inside in our motley clothes, damp and bedraggled, me trying to explain, insisting someone had tried to drown this boy, then watching him being carted off, never knowing where he was being taken or what happened to him.

But I wasn't going to let him be sent back to whoever had tossed him off the ferry like an unwanted kitten. I wasn't nineteen any-more.

What I didn't admit to myself was that I was already beginning to think of this child as mine. I'd found him, I'd saved him. I

wasn't about to hand him off to a stranger.
I passed the turn and headed for home.

CHAPTER 4

I pulled into my parking spot in front of the house. The boy had sat quietly during the forty-mile drive, waiting when I'd gone into a small store for hot chocolate, then clasping the cup in both hands, drinking in tiny sips. Neither of us had spoken.

"We're here." I gestured at the house. *"Ça, c'est ma maison."* I'd rented a room here when I'd first arrived in Lake Placid, and when the speedskater running the place moved on, I bought the furnishings and took over. I rent out the extra bedrooms to athletes in town to train and people who end up here because they love the lakes and the mountains and the ski trails. Some are here a few months; some a year or more. We share the living room and kitchen, and everybody does their own dishes. If not, I put them in a paper bag and set it outside their bedroom door. They catch on pretty fast.

My family would consider this place a dump, but I like it. And I have a houseful of guys willing to go biking, running, or dancing, so I have company when I want it, and escape to my rooms when I don't.

This is a part of my life Thomas finds unendearingly irregular, although he's far too polite to say so. He's too reserved to let me know that my athletic male roommates make him uneasy, and I'm too obstinate to let him know I have a hard-and-fast personal rule against house romances. Which I was tempted to break only once, but that's another story.

I walked around the car and opened the passenger door. I reached over the boy to click open his seat belt and pulled off the sleeping bag and towel to free him. He glanced at the ground and then at me, wanting to know if it was all right to walk in his sock feet. I nodded. He put his small hand in mine, and stepped carefully up the porch stairs in the big wool socks.

The front door was unlocked, as usual. I'd given up trying to get the guys to lock it. All too often one of them would forget to take a key when going out for a run or a bike ride and would end up climbing on the fuel tank and through the downstairs bedroom window. I'd installed individual locks

31

on the bedrooms, but I was pretty much the only one who used them.

Two of the guys were in the front room watching TV and eating pizza from a box on the battered coffee table. The smell made my salivary glands tingle.

I leaned into the room. "Zach around?" I asked.

"Nope," said Dave, without looking up. He was a quiet guy, a kayaker working at a local sports shop. Zach, who had been here the longest of the current batch of roommates, had my spare room key. I motioned to the boy to sit on the bottom of the staircase and went up to Zach's room, where my fingers found my key on the nail in the back of his closet.

On the way downstairs, I kept my hand on the fat rounded banister to steady myself, then took the boy's hand and led him through the kitchen and up the narrow private staircase into my rooms. I use the outside room as an office, and my bedroom is at the back, with a tiny bathroom to the left. My own little suite.

The small fingers gripping mine were cold, and I was chilling fast once out of the heated car. My wet ponytail had soaked the back of my sweatshirt, and my underwear and bra had soaked through, so I was pretty damp.

"I think a hot bath is next," I said. I couldn't remember the French word for *bath,* and the boy looked blank. I led him into the bathroom, turned on the faucets, and squirted in shampoo to make bubbles. Without hesitation he shrugged off the baggy jacket onto the floor and held his arms up for me to pull the T-shirt off, as if this were routine, as if he were used to a parent saying *Time for your bath* every evening. We struggled to get his damp jeans off, and finally he sat on the bathroom floor and pushed at them while I worked the narrow cuffs over his bare feet and pulled. I would have had him bathe in his underwear, because I wasn't going to ask a small child I didn't know to strip, particularly since my brain recognized the possibility that a thrown-away child could have been abused. But he matter-of-factly pulled off his briefs and reached for my hand to steady himself as he climbed into the tub, as if he'd done it a thousand times.

His body was thin but unmarked. I handed him a soapy washcloth, and he started running it over his arms. I didn't know if he could wash his own hair, but it seemed safer to do it for him, so I squirted shampoo on my palm and gently rubbed it in. He held his head back for me to rinse it, and as I poured clean water over his head, water ran down my arms, soaking the sweatshirt. Suddenly I was nearly shaking with cold.

"Will you be okay for five minutes? *Cinq minutes? Je vais aller dans l'autre salle de bains.*" I pointed downstairs and pantomimed showering, and he nodded. I ran more hot water into the tub so the water would be warm enough for him, then grabbed a towel and clean clothes, leaving the bathroom door ajar.

I stepped carefully down my stairs, which had been built by someone who didn't comprehend rise-run ratio — they're so steep and narrow there's barely room for your foot. Once I'd slipped off and bounced painfully down the last few steps on my tailbone. Now I hold on.

The smell of the pizza from the living room beckoned. If ever a day called out for splurging, this was it. From the front hall I dialed Mr. Mike's across the street, reading the number from the flyer taped to the wall. The two guys in the living room were intent on Vanna White, who was spelling out a phrase that even to my fuddled mind seemed obvious. "Dave, would you get my pizza from Mr. Mike's in ten minutes?" I asked. "I'll leave the money under the phone. You can have whatever I can't eat."

"Sure," he said, without looking up.

Male athlete roommates don't know the meaning of the word "leftovers." Sometimes I'll smell pasta in the middle of the night, and if I roll over and look through the vent in my floor, I'll see one of the guys cooking, too hungry to wait for morning.

I shampooed vigorously to erase any lingering reminder of my lake swim, and then did it again. I yanked on my clothes, not taking the time to comb out my thick hair, and headed back upstairs.

"You okay?" I called out softly as I approached my bathroom. *Comment ça va?*

He was stretched out, head resting on the sloped back of the old tub, thin limbs just visible through the water. He looked as he had in the lake when I first saw him, eyes closed, more dead than alive. His eyes sprang open, with a flicker of fear that receded when he saw my face. I felt a pang of something like pain.

"Guess you're waterlogged," I said, as matter-of-factly as I could. I pulled the plug and wrapped him in a towel as he stood, and as I lifted him out he seemed incredibly small and frail. I began to gently towel his hair dry. Of course part of me wanted to blurt out, *Who did this to you? Why would someone throw you off a ferry?* But I didn't think he would answer, and neither was I ready to know.

I pulled an old rugby shirt over his head to use as a nightshirt. It fell past his knees, making him look like the youngest kid from *Peter Pan.* I rolled the sleeves up and drew my comb slowly through his hair. He just watched me.

We heard Dave call my name. "Back in a minute," I told the boy, holding up one finger, and went downstairs for the pizza. I balanced a carton of milk and two plastic glasses on the steaming box and climbed back up.

"I hope you like pizza. *Tu aimes la . . .* pizza?" Pizza must be a universal word, like McDonald's, because his face brightened. I hadn't realized how hungry I was until I took a bite, and three slices went down fast. The boy ate delicately but quickly, and we were just starting to slow down when we heard footsteps and then a clatter on the stairs. His eyes widened and he stopped mid-chew, pizza slice gripped tightly in his small fingers.

"It's okay. *C'est mon chien.*" I barely got the words out before Tiger erupted into the room. She's half German shepherd and half

36

golden retriever, and because having a golden retriever is sort of a status symbol in Lake Placid, I say I'm halfway there. Mostly she looks like a shepherd with a retriever-shaped head, a little rotund from being fed too many pizza crusts by too many room-mates. Now she was very excited and very wet.

Zach poked his head around the railing of the stairwell. "Can I come up?"

"You're already up." My rooms are off-limits to the guys, but the rules never quite pertain to Zach. He lives in Lake Placid year-round, cross-country skiing in the winter and biking in the summer, eking out a living at odd jobs. He's tall and rangy, with a stammer he hasn't quite overcome.

"Not really," Zach said, grinning as he bounded up the last few steps. He was wearing running shorts and shoes and a T-shirt that looked like it had been used as a paint rag. "Only part of the way. Say, wh-wh-who's this?"

"A friend, visiting tonight." The boy had scooted closer to me, eyes wide.

"Pl-pl-pleased to meet you." Zach stuck out his hand. The boy shyly let Zach shake his fingertips. "Hey, pizza!" Zach said, and took a slice. Without warning, the whole tableau — boy, pizza, dog, Zach, room —

shifted and shimmered as if my vision were blurring or the whole scene about to disappear, like a faulty *Star Trek* holodeck program. As if this were a safe ending I'd dreamed up while in the lake struggling to hold my breath, wondering if I were alive or dead.

After what seemed a lifetime I heard Zach say something and laugh, and with an almost tangible *ching,* I shifted back into the here and now. Tiger had shaken herself and sent water droplets flying.

"So Tiger took a swim." I grabbed a towel to start rubbing her down.

"Yep, after we went around the lake. Hey, I thought you were going up to see old Thomas."

"He's not old," I said automatically. "I was, but this young man is spending the night instead."

Raised eyebrows. Zach knew something was up but didn't ask. The boy was tentatively reaching out to touch Tiger's black fur. I was suddenly exhausted and no longer hungry. "Hey, Zach, would you take the rest of this down to the guys?"

"Mmm," he said, gracefully gathering up the box and the milk carton, and stuffing most of another slice in his mouth as he disappeared.

"Thanks for watching Tiger," I called out. I heard a muffled reply.

The boy's eyelids were drooping. "Are you sleepy?" I asked. *"Tu veux dormir?"* I led him to the bedroom, and convinced him to set the half-eaten slice of pizza on the bedside table. I pulled down the covers on my bed, and he crawled in, Tiger jumping up after him. Some people think it's barbaric to let your dog sleep with you, but I like that warm body snuggled in the curve of my knees. My dog, my house, my rules. One of the many reasons I'm single.

In the bathroom I spread the contents of my wallet out to dry on a towel, tossing out the wet business cards. Now I remembered I had to call Thomas.

Sometimes I wonder what Thomas sees in me. I'd met him late last summer when he was in Lake Placid for a running race, and he pretended not to care that I wouldn't commit to dating just him. Not that guys were lining up to take me out, but you never know. He's a history professor at the University of Vermont, and the most methodical and organized person I've ever met. He would never do anything on a whim, like diving into Lake Champlain. Nor would he understand what had compelled me to do so.

So I didn't tell him. I said an emergency had come up and I had had to turn back to babysit someone's son. Which was true, sort of. Anyone else might have asked for details, but not Thomas.

The conversation ended awkwardly, as it always does. I know Thomas wants to say "I love you," but the natural response would be "I love you, too." And I don't, which I'm sure he knows. I can't lie about it, and he knows that, too.

Something's missing, and I don't know if it's him or me. He's smart enough that I don't have to limit my vocabulary around him. We both like to run and bike and cross-country ski, and, well, all his parts are in good working order. At times I think I should end the relationship so he doesn't keep hoping it'll turn into more. But I would miss him, I think. So I do nothing. And feel more than a bit like a cheat at times like these.

I went down my creaky stairs to shut the door that closes off my stairwell. As I clicked the deadbolt, my brain went into replay, seeing the boy falling, me diving in, the long swim, the dreary walk, as if on a tiny screen inside my head.

If you threw a child in the lake, would you stay to watch him drown? Could anyone have seen me rescuing him? Like an icicle moving down my spine, the next thought arrived: *If you threw a child in a lake and knew he survived, would you come looking for him?* I tried to reason it through. But because I couldn't imagine tossing a kid off a boat in the first place, trying to work out the subsequent thought process was futile.

The boy was curled up in the bed where I'd left him, facing the wall, with Tiger next to him. The bedroom window was open a few inches, as always during the months with no snow on the ground. But if someone banged a ladder against the side of the house to try to get in, I'd hear it. Or Tiger would.

As I brushed my teeth I scowled at my reflection in the wavery mirror. My face was haggard, with dark shadows under the eyes. I don't know when I'd last needed sleep this badly. I had to concentrate to keep the toothbrush moving.

I tiptoed into the bedroom and eased into the bed. I pulled the covers up and settled down on my side, back to the boy, Tiger between us. I closed my eyes and was just about immediately halfway to Never Never Land.

"Trrroy," came a quiet murmur beside me.

"Mmm," I said, too tired to turn over.

"Je m'appelle Paul."

I lay in silence for a moment, hearing the small sounds of his breathing. "Okay, Paul," I said at last. "Sweet dreams. *Fais de beaux rêves.*"

CHAPTER 5

I woke abruptly, in the same position I'd fallen asleep. Sunlight was streaming in the window, and the dust in the air seemed to dance on the windowsill. Tiger was standing beside the bed, giving me that look that said I was sadly neglecting her. I peered at my bedside clock: 8:47. I never sleep this late. I'm a roll-out-of-bed-at-7 kind of girl. Or earlier.

For a moment I wondered if I had dreamed it all: the drive, the ferry, the child, the swim. Maybe I'd never left the house to go visit Thomas. I pushed myself up on my elbows and turned and saw the small body, facing me, sleeping hard, curled into a tight ball.

Troy, what have you done? I could almost hear the words, an inner Jiminy Cricket. What the voice should have been saying was *Troy, who are you?* I'd woken up yesterday as one person and today as a different one.

This person had dived from a ferry and rescued a child and brought him home with her. Troy Chance didn't do things like that.

But I had.

It seemed to make sense at the time. I could hear someone saying this in earnest explanation: a driver who convinced herself that she hadn't really hit someone, that it was just a bump in the road or a wild animal, and it wasn't safe to stop. Or a woman who took home a baby she found in a pram outside a store, because clearly she could take better care of it than the person who left it alone.

I could wake this child now and walk him to the police station a block away and explain that I hadn't been thinking clearly yesterday — that the coldness of the water, the length of the swim, the shock of finding a child thrown away, all had robbed me of the ability to think rationally. They'd believe me. This was a small town: people knew me and liked me. I'd been the sports editor of the daily newspaper; I'd covered their kids' baseball and hockey games, soccer tournaments, and track meets, put their photos in the paper, spelled their names right. I'd be a hero for rescuing a child, and not reporting it right away would be swept under the rug.

But I had known what I was doing.

I had saved a boy someone else had thrown away, and had made the decision not to turn him over to authorities, not to risk him being sent to a bad foster home or returned to the person who had tried to drown him. I'd found him and he trusted me, and I'd made the decision that he needed to be with me. For now.

Sitting there propped up in bed, I watched the boy sleeping, his body moving slightly with each breath.

It wouldn't sound rational to anyone. I knew that. But neither had it been rational to have been on deck on a gray misty day — or to have believed what I saw was a child, or that I could find him in the murky water. Or that we could survive that long cold swim to shore.

But we had. And maybe I wasn't meant to blithely pass him on to someone else.

I eased myself out of bed and bit my lip not to groan. I wouldn't have thought swimming could cause such pain; I felt a million years old. The boy didn't stir. I hobbled out to my office and clicked my computer on before heading down to let Tiger out. As she gratefully relieved herself on the grass, my brain inched into gear. *Maybe the boy's parents hadn't been on the ferry.* Maybe

45

someone had snatched him — like the young Las Vegas boy I'd read about who had been abducted by drug dealers and abandoned — and then dumped him into the lake.

But what if his parents or guardian or stepparent had done it, but claimed someone else had? Susan Smith had claimed that a carjacker had taken her car with her two small sons, but she had been the one who had driven them into a lake to drown. If I saw a tearful news clip, would I be able to tell if that person was telling the truth?

I didn't know.

I shook some food into Tiger's bowl and climbed back upstairs. The boy was still sleeping. I sat at my computer and opened my browser.

If this child had been snatched by someone and dumped, the story would be all over the news, and it would be safe to let him go home. I should have checked last night, but my brain simply hadn't been working. I'd be guilty of letting his parents endure a sleepless night, but I could trot out the *too tired, too cold, too confused* excuse. Which would be true.

Tiger climbed the stairs and wandered into the bedroom, and the bed creaked as she jumped on it. She was staying close to the boy.

I pulled up Google and searched *missing boy Vermont* and *kidnapped boy Paul,* then a variety of combinations. I found a depressing 2006 story of a mother who had drowned her eight-year-old son in Lake Champlain near the Canadian border, but that was all. The Burlington newspaper had nothing, but I emailed the news desk asking if they'd had any report of a missing French-speaking boy, using my anonymous eBay email address. Montreal was less than a hundred miles from Burlington, so I checked the newspaper there. Nothing. If frantic parents were pleading for the return of a beloved child, I couldn't find them.

I Googled *missing children,* then searched MissingKids.com. I found the missing children's website for the RCMP, the Royal Canadian Mounted Police, and entered Paul's name, gender, and eye and hair color. *Records found: 0.* I searched again, using no parameters other than gender, and came up only with two brothers, neither of whom resembled Paul in the slightest.

Then I looked up the Lake Champlain ferry website, and from the schedule saw that Paul's ferry should have passed mine roughly midway in the lake, not a mile or two from shore. Maybe mine had been late or his early, or both — but otherwise, I never would have seen him fall. Five minutes earlier or later, and one small boy would have drowned.

I'd been hearing small noises from my bedroom, as if the boy was moving around. I went to the doorway, and it took a moment to register that the bed was empty. No boy, no dog. For a moment I couldn't breathe. I saw the window was open a few inches, just as I'd left it. For a split second I wondered if they could have crept past me while I had been engrossed in my research, but even I'm not that oblivious. Boy and dog had to be somewhere in the room, and there were only two options: under the bed or in the closet. My eyes went to the bedside table where we'd left the half-eaten piece of pizza. Okay, missing boy, missing dog, missing half slice of pizza.

"Paul," I called out softly. "Paul, where are you? *Où es-tu?*"

A whine from Tiger. I eased back the hanging sheet that served as a closet door, and there was Paul crouched in the corner, one arm around Tiger, his other hand gripping the gnawed pizza slice — looking as if it were perfectly normal to hide in a closet with a dog and a piece of pizza. I knelt, a careful distance away. "Good morning,

Paul," I said, keeping my voice steady. "Would you like some breakfast? *Veux-tu prendre le petit déjeuner?*"

He shifted but seemed unsure what to do. I snapped my fingers and Tiger obediently came toward me. "Did something frighten you?" I asked Paul. *"Tu as peur?"* No answer. "Paul, sweetie, come on out," I said, opening my arms and letting a little emotion into my voice.

He wouldn't look at me, and I waited a long, long moment. Finally he moved into my arms. I could feel the frailty of his limbs; I could feel his heart beating; I could almost feel his fear and confusion and loneliness. I hadn't known you could form an attachment to a person so quickly, so atavistically. Had my sisters experienced this when their children were born? I realized I would do anything to protect this child. *"Je ne te blesserai jamais,"* I whispered to him. "I will never hurt you. Never."

And I knew I wouldn't be marching this boy down to the police station, not today, and possibly never.

CHAPTER 6

The boy was looking thoughtfully at the slice of old, cold pizza he was holding, as if considering eating it. Time for breakfast.

Even if I had run his clothes through the washer and hung them up to dry last night, they'd still be wet. I searched through my dresser and pulled out my snuggest Lycra sports shorts and tiniest T-shirt, and knotted two bandannas around his waist to hold up the shorts. They came halfway down his legs like baggy pantaloons, making him look like a tiny pirate. I turned him to let him look at himself in the mirror on the back of my bedroom door. His mouth twisted with amusement, and for a moment he looked like anyone's kid, playing dress-up.

I led him by the hand down my narrow stairs into the kitchen, where he seemed to think a picnic table with a plastic-coated checkered tablecloth made a fine dining room table. He emptied his bowl of Cheerios and looked at me wide-eyed, like the hungry orphan in *Oliver!* I know my Dickens — both movie and novel — and correctly concluded he wanted more. We negotiated: more Cheerios if he would give the half-eaten pizza slice to Tiger.

I watched him munch his cereal, and hoped if he had any food allergies he'd be smart enough to turn down whatever he was allergic to. While he was finishing his second bowl, I retrieved our wet clothes from yesterday and dumped them in the portable washing machine. I wheeled it to the kitchen sink, attached it to the faucet, and switched it on.

What now? I could try to coax Paul into talking or I could do more research to see if I had missed anything. We headed upstairs and were just stepping into my office when my phone rang. I jumped, and Paul scurried into the bedroom.

It was my brother, Simon.

"Hey, kiddo, what's up?" he asked. I don't think being eleven months younger warrants being called kiddo, but I let him get away with it. Most of the time. Simon had managed our family much better than I had: he had obediently gone to Vanderbilt, where our father teaches, and majored in pre-law. But when he was supposed to be sowing wild oats on senior spring break he'd slipped off to take the police exam in Orlando, and after graduation had accepted a job there, thereby managing to do exactly what he wanted after being comfortably supported through university. After the initial shock, everyone decided this was a singularly clever way to acquire experience before law school, and Simon lets them think what they want. What they don't know is that he's quietly building a second career as an artist, selling a few pieces here and there, and has no intention of going to law school.

But when I landed a scholarship to Oregon State and wanted to skip my last year of high school, it was Simon who calmed our mother and convinced our father to sign the admission papers — although I would have forged them if I'd had to. So if anyone comes close to understanding me, it's Simon. He'd known I'd had to get away. Just as he knows I need to live in this mountain town more than a thousand long miles from Nashville.

"Not much," I said. "Work, dog, house. Rode up Keene Valley. Hiked Algonquin." I'd taken Simon up two of the Adirondack mountains; I hadn't yet summited all forty-six, but I was marking them off, one by one.

He laughed. "Hey, it's a tough life you

lead up there in the boonies."

"Yeah, well, have fun down there while you can, before it gets so hot you can barely breathe."

"At least we don't have black flies."

"No, just cockroaches so big they fly." I hesitated a moment. "Hey, Simon, what do you do at work if you find a lost kid and no parents show up?"

He answered without hesitation — like me, he can switch gears quickly. "Basically it gets publicized until a relative appears or you track them down. Like that kid abandoned in a shopping center out west. Or that little girl in New York found wandering the streets after her mother was killed by her boyfriend. She was in the papers and on TV until she was identified. What's up, Troy?"

"Mmm." There was a lump in my throat. "Just an article I'm working on." This didn't have to be a lie — I *could* write an article about missing kids, abandoned kids, kids tossed off ferries. I made noncommittal noises and slid into small talk. Simon told me he had two paintings appearing in a local show; I mentioned an article I'd sold to *Triathlete* magazine.

I caught a movement out of the corner of my eye. Paul was standing in the doorway of the bedroom. I put up a finger — *one minute* — and told Simon goodbye, and as I hung up I thought of something to try.

I patted the sofa, and Paul climbed up beside me. I pulled a photo album off my bookshelf and opened it. First I showed Paul pictures of me and Tiger, then a photo of Simon. *"C'est mon frère,"* I said, and asked if he had a brother or sister. He shook his head. A dog? Another shake, with a little frown that made me think he had wanted one but hadn't been allowed.

I flipped to photos of our parents and the house we grew up in. Paul began to shift uneasily, maybe guessing where I was heading. But instead I asked where he went to school. This he answered.

"Je ne vais pas à l'école." No school.

Time to ask him where he lived. *"Où habites-tu, Paul?"* I tried to make the question sound casual. He frowned and shrugged. *"Tu habites avec tes parents?"* I asked next. At this he became visibly agitated and shook his head. He either didn't live with his parents, or didn't want to answer.

I looked at him, clownlike in the baggy T-shirt and shorts. He needed some regular clothes — and maybe being around other kids would help him relax. And although I would never have admitted it, maybe I needed to talk to someone.

I picked up my phone and speed-dialed my friend Baker in Saranac Lake. *"C'est mon amie,"* I told Paul. *"Elle a trois jeunes fils —* three sons." I'd met Baker when she had filled in temporarily at the newspaper during someone's maternity leave. Her first name was Susan, but she'd been called by her last name ever since working with several women who shared the same first name. Now she remains Baker, despite having acquired a large burly husband, a new last name, and three small sons.

Her husband answered.

"Hey, Mike, it's Troy. Is Baker around?"

"She's here somewhere." He was almost shouting over the background din. "She's playing Indian chief with the tribe. Hang on a sec."

Baker was breathless when she got to the phone. If she thought it odd that I needed to borrow some of her oldest son's clothes, she didn't say so. "I suppose you'll explain this when you get here," she said dryly.

"Yup. I'll be over within the hour. Do you need anything?"

"Nope, unless you've got an Algonquin chief's outfit. See you."

Paul was frowning, looking worried.

"We're going to go visit my friends. To borrow clothes," I told him. *"Pour emprunter des vêtements."* He seemed wary, but didn't protest. I put my driver's license and cash in my jeans pocket, leaving my still-wet wallet behind. Paul's sneakers were damp and a bit shrunken, but I pulled them on his bare feet and tied the laces. He and Tiger watched me hang our wet laundry on the line behind the house, and after putting Tiger back in the house we were off.

It was slow driving along Main Street. Lake Placid hosted the Winter Olympics twice, in 1932 and in 1980, and tourists seem to think this is an Olympic theme park and that the townspeople are part of the scenery. Of course they have no idea most locals don't go anywhere for vacation because they can't afford it at North Country rock-bottom wages. Or that the 1980 Olympic Village is now a prison camp, and that being a prison guard is considered a great job here because it pays so well.

I do love this area — I've lived here nearly five years now. You can walk your kayak to a clear lake for a paddle before breakfast and hike up a mountaintop after lunch. Saranac Lake has a spectacular Winter Carnival, with an amazing ice palace and a parade the whole town turns out to watch no matter how cold it is, and Lake Placid has the best July 4 fireworks I've ever seen.

I'd come here as sports editor on the daily newspaper in Saranac Lake, covering three area high schools and two community colleges, plus all the Lake Placid events: horse show competitions, boxing, luge and bobsled, biathlon, ski jumping, and more — and community sports: softball, bowling, dart tournaments, sled dog races, and ice fishing. On a small paper the editor is the editor, writer, photographer, and layout person — you're it, the whole department. After spending too many nights sleeping on the couch in the newspaper office because I didn't have either time or energy to drive home, I'd known it was time for a change.

Now I do freelance writing and editing and some computer and website consulting. I write press releases for the area chambers of commerce and theater reviews for the paper, and sell articles about sled dog races, rugby tournaments, three-day canoe races, and ski jumping to magazines like *Southwest Spirit* and *Scholastic Scope.* It's not a huge income, and it's sporadic. But my expenses are few, and I like the freedom. It had suited me fine.

I had the feeling that was about to change. And maybe it already had.

CHAPTER 7

Once out of Lake Placid, it's about twenty minutes to Baker's house.

Baker is just this side of plump, sort of a heavier, freckled, younger Maura Tierney, with a round friendly face that spells Mom, apple pie, and meat loaf. The corners of her mouth twisted at the sight of Paul's odd outfit, but she just led us to the stack of clothes she had set aside. Paul shyly picked out a Batman T-shirt and jeans, and I helped him change. The clothes were slightly big, but he seemed to like them, and gave Baker his wistful half smile. She popped a construction-paper headdress on him and pointed him toward the backyard where the kids were playing. He looked at me with a mixture of eagerness and nervousness, and I gave him an encouraging nod. "I'll just be inside," I called out as he took a step toward the play set. *Je serai juste là, à l'intérieur . . . dans la maison de Baker."*

Baker gave me a look.

"Uh, he doesn't speak English — did I forget to mention that?" I asked as I followed her back into the house.

She shrugged. "Doesn't matter. Kids all speak the same language." Through the kitchen window I could see Paul being coaxed up a slide by a pigtailed, overall-clad kid with a dirty smear on her cheek, one of the neighbor's daughters. "He'll be fine," Baker said. "What, are you adopting a French-Canadian kid?"

I shrugged. "I found him. Literally. In Lake Champlain."

She stared at me for a long second, reading more in my face than I wanted her to. "Okay, you're staying for lunch. We'll eat first and then I'll feed the horde." As she made sandwiches I watched Paul through the window, going down the slide and then marching around and climbing back up to do it again.

"So tell me," Baker said as she plopped tuna sandwiches and carrot sticks on the table, with a Coke for her and iced tea for me.

"Mmm. I honest-to-God found him in Lake Champlain. I was on my way to see Thomas yesterday, and I saw him, well, fall in from the other ferry."

She stared at me. I took a sip of iced tea and made a face. Too strong, as usual. Nobody in the North Country knows how to make iced tea. Most of them think it comes from a jar of powder from the grocery store. I was lucky Baker brewed it for me. I pushed my chair back, the skittering sound loud in the sudden stillness, ran tap water into the glass, and swirled the ice around.

"You just happened to have a portable raft with you, or what?" Baker asked. Sarcasm does not become her.

"No, I swam and got him and then swam to shore."

More staring. "Troy, you can't swim worth a damn."

"I'm not that bad," I protested as I sat back down. "I don't like swimming in groups and I sort of veer to one side. But if I concentrate, I do okay."

She picked up her sandwich and took a bite. "Okay, he fell in the lake. You got him out. So why do you still have him?"

Dead silence. It was difficult to say aloud, and it took a moment to get the words out. "I'm pretty sure someone threw him in."

Another friend might have exclaimed, but Baker wasn't made that way, and she knows how tough I like to pretend to be. We chewed our sandwiches.

"Did he say so?" Baker asked.

"No. He won't talk about it. But no one was at the dock looking for him, and he had . . . there was . . ." I cleared my throat. "He had an adult's sweatshirt tied around him, the sleeves knotted around his arms."

Baker thought about this. "Did you call the police?"

I nodded. "Etown and Burlington. I didn't give my name. But Paul wasn't talking, so he wouldn't have told them anything. And I'd pulled the sweatshirt off him, so it was at the bottom of the lake." I clinked my ice around in my glass and took a long drink. "I think he'll calm down soon and tell me who he is and what happened and where he's from, and then I can decide what to do. He's just starting to talk."

She stared at me a moment longer. North Country people are known for their reticence and staying out of other people's business, but even Baker couldn't let this go. When she spoke, her voice was mild.

"Troy, you can't just keep a child. He has parents somewhere, parents who are bound to be looking for him."

"Maybe. Maybe not. Maybe they're the ones who threw him in the lake." My voice almost cracked. "And I don't want him being sent back to them."

She watched as I drank more tea, and then I spoke again. "When he tells me what happened, then I'll know what to do."

For a moment I thought she was going to pull maternal rank and say, *"Are you out of your mind?"* But I could see her working it out, considering the possibilities and the risks: *parents who don't get their kid back immediately* versus *child may be sent back to people who tried to kill him.* At last she nodded. Paul's safety was most important.

And I think we both knew that a kid who had simply been scooped up and dumped overboard would have been screaming for his mom and dad. And this kid wasn't.

"So is he Canadian?" she asked.

"Probably — but he hasn't spoken enough for me to tell." To me Canadian French sounds more slurred, but probably that's the street version. Québécois say theirs is the purer form of French, because after the Revolution everyone in France switched to a more common form of the language. Which makes sense, considering that all the aristocrats had been beheaded.

The back door opened and the herd came thundering in. They were thirsty, they announced, and needed Kool-Aid. Paul separated himself from the group and came to my side. I felt his forehead, damp with sweat. Baker calmly handed out Kool-Aid, and Paul drank deeply, leaving a purple stain around his lips. She set out a stack of cut-up sandwiches and carrot sticks and dumped potato chips into a bowl, and the kids fell on the food. Paul looked at me for permission, and stood next to me as he ate, slowly and with great precision. I put some potato chips on a napkin for him, and he ate them delicately.

"I think I'd better get this guy home. He may need an *n-a-p.*" I was suddenly worried I'd let him overexert himself.

"Kids are tough," Baker said, reading my mind. "Listen, be careful, and keep me posted. And if you need me, just shout."

"Okay." I stood, picking up the bag with my clothes and some extras Baker was lending us. "Paul, say goodbye and thank you. *Dis* 'goodbye and thank you.' "

"Goodbye t'ank you," he said, to my surprise. He glanced longingly at the plate of sandwiches, and when I nodded he took two more pieces, one for each hand.

Baker had reminded me that small children aren't supposed to ride in the front seat, so I buckled Paul into the back, doing my best to explain why. It felt odd to have him back there, as if I were a chauffeur, and I didn't like not being able to see him beside me. We drove through town, and just after we turned right onto 86, heading toward Placid, a rattly, rusty station wagon passed, going the opposite direction. *What a piece of junk,* I thought idly. I noticed its out-of-state plates, and wondered if someone had driven down from Québec just to take that ferry, just to dump a child. If Paul had been living in Vermont, surely he'd be able to speak English.

I looked in the rearview mirror at Paul, his head slumped against the side of the car. He had fallen asleep as soon as we were out of town. Suddenly I had a new worry. He'd had a long dunking, swallowed God knows how much lake water, and walked in wet clothes after an exhausting swim. I hadn't the vaguest idea how that could affect a child who seemed none too robust to begin with. Water in the lungs? A bacterial infection from the lake water?

I glanced at the clock. My friend Kate is an ER nurse, and soon would be heading to her shift at the Saranac Lake Hospital. I gave her a call. No answer, but I left a message asking if she could stop by. We had scarcely gotten into the house when I heard her lilting tones in the front hallway. "Anybody home?"

Why I end up with friends who look like

models, I don't know. Kate is tall and slender, with flowing auburn hair and a wholesome wide-eyed look that tends to drive men nuts. She's had more than one stalker, which can be awkward in a small town where everyone knows both stalker and stalkee. Last summer a tuba player from Albuquerque who was here to play in the summer symphony had fallen madly in love with her from across the room. It was quite a nuisance and rather annoying to me, who has yet to be fallen in love with from across the room.

Kate's also a by-the-book kind of girl who follows regulations, dots every *i,* and crosses every *t.* She would have no doubt that a stray boy should be reported to the authorities, and although I might be able to dissuade her, she wouldn't be happy about it.

So I told her Paul was the son of a Canadian friend and had taken an unexpected fall into the lake. I let her think it was a fall from a canoe into Mirror Lake, two blocks away, and that I would rather avoid the expense of dragging him to an emergency room that wouldn't honor a Canadian health insurance card. Although I never said any of that, just hinted at it.

She believed it all, so readily that I felt guilty. But while she may be a trifle gullible,

Kate is a competent and caring nurse. She put Paul at ease, while peppering me with questions: *How long had he been in the water? What had I done for him? Had he been eating and sleeping?*

She popped an old-fashioned thermometer into his mouth, thumbed his eyelids back to look at his pupils, peered into his ears, and pulled up his shirt to listen to his heartbeat.

"He seems fine," she announced. "He's probably tired. And maybe he hasn't been eating enough; he's a little thin."

Paul, who had sat quietly during the examination, looked at me. "She says you need to eat more," I said, deadpan. *"Il faut que tu manges beaucoup de bonbons et de gâteau."*

He looked confused for a moment and then let loose a short high trill of laughter. A wave of happiness bubbled up in me, so intense it startled me.

As I showed Kate out, I remembered what Baker had murmured as I'd left: "Don't get too attached to this kid, Troy." She thinks my boarding house scenario results from sublimated maternal urges, that I love acting as house mom to a brood of roommates, although they're only a few years younger than me. I tell her, tongue-in-cheek, that I just enjoy having so many hunky guys around. But it's true that I'm the only one of my sisters unwed and childless, and true, I thought, that I had fallen hard for this kid.

I looked over at the boy, perched on the bottom of the staircase, watching me with those long-lashed dark eyes that had seen things no child should ever see — like maybe the face of the person who had toppled him into the lake. I felt a surge of a fierce emotion I couldn't put a name to.

"Well, let's get started on the medical treatment," I said. "*Aimes-tu la glace?* You like ice cream?"

His eyes lit up. "Let's go," I said, opening the front door. "They've got your name on an ice cream cone up at Stewart's."

CHAPTER 8

There are advantages and disadvantages to having a Stewart's only 144 steps from your front door. It's handy to dash up for milk or eggs, but too easy to indulge in ice cream, especially when it's on sale.

After careful deliberation, Paul pointed at the container of strawberry, and I took my usual, chocolate peanut butter cup. He licked his cone tidily, while Tiger looked at us imploringly. But even I draw the line at sharing ice cream with a dog, although I'm pretty sure one of my friends buys Tiger her own cone when I'm not around.

"It's good, yes?" I said to Paul. *C'est bon, la glace?*" He nodded, his tongue chasing melting droplets. In the afternoon sun outside Stewart's with our cones, it seemed a perfectly normal day with a small boy who just happened to be visiting me.

But if I was going to feed him ice cream, I thought, I should get him a toothbrush.

"Tu veux venir au magasin avec moi?" I asked, gesturing up the street. He nodded again, and we walked the few blocks up to the drugstore on Main Street. Tiger waited outside patiently, earning *ooohs* and *ahhhs* from tourists who apparently don't have dogs where they live. At least not fancy shepherd-retriever mixes.

I bought a toothbrush and a comb for Paul, and then we walked on to Bookstore Plus. There we poked around before selecting a copy of *Harold and the Purple Crayon* and a pack of Uno cards, which would work even if you didn't know any English. On the way back to the house I nodded at people I knew. Suddenly the small grip on my hand tightened, and I looked down. Paul's face had turned white. Belatedly I realized that the group of people we'd just passed was chattering in French — so many tourists from Montreal come here that I hadn't noticed.

I whisked Paul into a little alcove in front of a collection of tiny stores, Lake Placid's version of a mall. I knelt and pulled him toward me. *"Paul, est-ce que tu connais ces personnes?"* I asked.

He was trembling, but shook his head. No, he didn't know those people.

"What's wrong? *Qu'est-ce qu'il y a?*

Qu'est-ce c'est le problème?" I asked.

He mumbled something I couldn't make out. I looked at the people walking away from us. Everything about them spelled tourist: clothes, gait, how they were talking and laughing.

I looked down at Paul. Instinct said to get him back to the house. I held his hand firmly as we marched past the post office, high school, town hall, through the kitchen and up my stairs. Paul climbed up on the sofa and curled in a tiny knot in the corner. I sat across from him in my captain's chair.

"Paul," I said, *"c'est important que tu me dises si tu connais ces personnes."* You must tell me if you know those people.

He looked up and shook his head again, eyes glistening. *"Non, non, je ne les connais pas, pas du tout."*

He didn't know them. Okay. Maybe he'd just recognized the Québec French. *"Est-ce que tu habites au Québec?"*

Silence. A tiny shrug that could mean yes, could mean no. And then he burst into tears. I took him in my arms and held him as he cried.

"Paul," I whispered, *"Paul, où sont tes parents?"*

He burrowed deeper into me. After a long

pause, he answered.

"Ma mère est décédée," he said in a high-pitched voice. *"Et mon père veux rien savoir de moi."*

His mother was dead, and his father did not want him. In the next instant he was crying, deep wrenching sobs I didn't know could come from someone so small. I didn't ask if it had been his father on the ferry with him. I didn't want to know, at least not yet.

In a moment he lifted his tear-streaked face and began to babble, torrents of French so fast and slurred I could pick out only a few words. I was crying myself by that time, and held him and rocked him. Some tiny presence of mind led me to reach across to my desk and flick on the little tape recorder I use for interviews.

As he calmed, he began to speak more slowly. Gradually the story came out. He had lived in Montreal with his *maman* and *papa,* he said, until one day some men had taken him and his *maman.*

When, he wasn't sure, because it had gotten fuzzy in his mind. It was before Christmas, because he had been promised a new *vélo,* a red one, and had never gotten it. He'd woken up in a big car, no, a van, and had been sick, and when he'd awakened again he was in a small room with no windows. He'd heard men in the next room and heard the voice of his *maman* and a bang, like the gunfire he'd heard on television sometimes. Then the men had told him his mother was dead, and if he didn't do as they said, they'd kill him, too, and he had cried and cried.

Sometimes he'd sleep very hard, and when he woke up he'd be sick again. Once he woke up in a different room, a smaller one. He had a soft ball and some comic books, and one of the men gave him a bag of little plastic toy figures. If he was quiet and lay near the door, he could hear the television, usually in English but sometimes French. They'd leave food in his room, boxes of cereal or doughnuts, cracker packets and apples, and at night one of those meals on a plastic plate from the freezer or sometimes a box of McDonald's food with a toy. Most nights he'd get a little carton of milk. If he cried or tried to get out of the room, they would smack him. He had started to dig a hole in the wall beside his bed with one of the little plastic figurines, hiding the hole with his pillow.

Then he had slept hard and remembered being very sleepy, under a blanket, and then being picked up, something wrapped tightly around him, and then falling, falling, falling, unable to move his arms.

"Et puis vous êtes revenue pour moi," he said, his face brightening. My eyes filled with tears and my chest tightened until it hurt. Yes, I had come for him, and pulled him from the water, and saved him. I hugged him, probably too tightly.

Could he write his name? I asked. Of course, he nodded proudly, of course he could. He was, after all, six years old. I handed him a pad of paper and a pencil and he laboriously wrote, *Paul Dumond.*

"Et ton papa et ta maman?" I held my breath.

He thought a moment, and then wrote *Philipe* and, after a few tries, *Madline.*

Philippe and Madeline Dumond. Montreal.

So I had names, and a place.

Chapter 9

I think I'd expected Paul's story to trickle out in bits and pieces, gradually revealing a bit more of the puzzle until it became a neat tidy package and I could calmly decide what to do. I suppose I had hoped he was simply a child no one wanted.

In my wildest imagination I wouldn't have come up with anything like this.

I was itching to start researching, but Paul needed to be calmed. So I moved to the computer and slid in a simple two-player game I'd found in the five-dollar bin at Staples, one with funny little characters that scurry down halls and up and down stairs, grabbing prizes and avoiding traps. Paul snuffled and blew his nose with the tissue I handed him, then climbed onto my lap. He began to tap at the keys, and we chased down bad guys as if our lives depended on it. After his tears dried I got out a coloring book and crayons, plus markers and old computer paper, the kind with the punched-out sides made for a tractor feed.

"Il faut que je travaille maintenant." I nodded toward the computer. *"Je dois écrire à l'ordinateur."* He seemed to understand that I needed to work, and began pulling crayons out of the box. I guess if you've been kept locked up in a room for weeks on end, coloring seems like a blast.

It took only seconds to locate a Canadian online phone directory. I found plenty of people named Dumond in Montreal and suburbs, including three Philippes, with addresses and phone numbers. Then I checked Montreal newspapers for Philippe Dumond, Madeline Dumond, and a few alternative spellings of each. I knew that women can't automatically change their last name in Québec when they marry, but can use their husband's name socially.

I found nothing in the archives for the *Montreal Gazette.* I began searching archives of Montreal's French-language newspaper, *Le Journal de Montréal,* from last fall.

Then I found something: Madeleine Dumond mentioned in a brief article on a social page. I couldn't translate the whole article, but it said she had chaired the event the previous year. The words that jumped out were *"Mme Dumond est l'épouse de Phi-*

lippe Dumond, président de l'Agence Dumond." Wife of Philippe Dumond, president of the Dumond Agency.

I glanced over at Paul, busily crayoning. I searched other Montreal-area publications, including a glossy monthly magazine, *Montreal Monthly,* and in less than a minute got a hit — a photo.

It appeared first as a ghostly image, then the pixels filled in until three people were smiling out at me, a frozen moment in an apparently gala evening.

Madeleine was the central figure: head thrown back, smiling gracefully. She had gently waving honey-colored hair, high elegant cheekbones, dark eyes, and a wide Julia Roberts mouth. She was dressed chicly, a trifle daringly compared to the other woman in the picture, in a silvery snug dress cut across one bare shoulder. The caption read, "Yves and Geneviève Bédard and Madeleine Dumond at the Spring Festival of Arts dinner."

I looked at the photo. I looked for any resemblance to Paul, with his dark hair and thin face. I tried to imagine this woman holding Paul, combing his hair, hugging him, tying his shoes, walking him to school. I couldn't. But neither could I imagine her kidnapped and dead.

I saved the photo, and moved on to searching the *Gazette*'s archives. I found a few mentions on the business page about companies whose marketing was handled by the Dumond Agency. Then I hit the jackpot: a tiny blurb in the business section that said the agency was moving to Ottawa.

Back to the *Ottawa Citizen,* where I found two small articles, one on the company's move and another mentioning an account it had just landed. In years past people might have assumed Dumond was moving out of Québec because of the risk of it seceding from Canada, which would be somewhat like Florida or California pulling out of the United States. Once the vote for separation had been razor close — 49.4 to 50.6 percent — but since then the separatist movement seemed to have died down.

I found nothing about a kidnapping, missing wife, missing child. *How could this have been kept out of the news?* The police could keep it quiet in response to kidnappers' threats, I suppose. And picking up and moving 125 miles would certainly let you dodge unpleasant questions about absent wife and child. I glanced at Paul, still busy coloring.

My brain was going down a path I didn't want it to. Most people don't make such major life changes a few short months after a tragedy. I supposed Paul's father had given up hope of wife and child returning; I supposed the walls of the home they'd shared would haunt him. But that little voice in my head asked, *How could you abandon it so quickly? Wouldn't you want to stay in the home you'd shared, on the tiny chance they would return someday?*

Unless, of course, you knew they wouldn't.

In Nashville in the late 1990s, a lawyer named Perry March had killed his wife, apparently after she threatened to divorce him and take their two small children. He got away with it for a decade, until his father confessed to helping him dump the body. And in a notorious Washington, D.C., case I'd read about, a former Motown recording engineer had his ex-wife and disabled son killed, along with the son's nurse, so he would get the child's huge trust fund. The killer apparently consulted a how-to book called *Hit Man: A Technical Manual for Independent Contractors.* The surviving family sued the publishers, who lost.

Paul had turned to a new page in the coloring book and begun filling in the characters in bright colors. He was a neat crayoner, staying carefully inside the lines.

I couldn't locate a home address for Philippe Dumond in Ottawa or suburbs, but found an address for the downtown business, with phone and fax numbers. For one insane moment I thought of sending a fax: *Dear Mr. Dumond: Are you missing someone?*

I flicked off the computer and moved to the sofa. I admired the pages Paul had colored, and read *Harold and the Purple Crayon* to him. Which he liked so much we did it twice more. Fortunately, it's a short book.

I'd almost forgotten about the play I was due to review that evening for the newspaper. I usually ask Baker or Kate along, but tonight I'd take Paul.

I ran a bath for him, setting out clean clothes from the ones Baker had loaned us. His own had dried, but they were too small, and I didn't want to put him back in them, anyway. When he emerged from the tub, his wet hair was hanging down past his eyes, several inches too long.

Time for a trim, I thought. I draped a towel around Paul's shoulders and perched him on the edge of my desk, explaining with a combination of French, English, and gestures that I wanted to *couper* his *cheveux* with my *ciseaux.* I've been cutting friends' hair since high school — nothing fancy, but I can do a decent simple cut. He seemed agreeable, so I got out scissors and comb.

His hair was full and straight, but long and uneven. I combed and snipped and layered, and when I finished, his face didn't seem as thin and he didn't quite have that abandoned, neglected look. "Very nice. *C'est beau,*" I told him, and he smiled shyly. He hopped down and without prompting held the dustpan as I swept up the hair. Someone had trained him to do this, which didn't seem to fit with being a child someone would throw away, a child wearing too-small clothes that were gray from wear.

On the way to Saranac Lake we zoomed through the McDonald's drive-through, which I disapprove of on several counts. Fast food and drive-throughs seem to represent a lot that's wrong with this country: fatty, salty, cheap food delivered while you sit in your fossil-fuel-wasting, pollutant-spewing vehicle. But it wouldn't kill me to do it once. I hesitated before ordering a Happy Meal for Paul, not wanting to remind him of the ones he'd gotten in captivity. But he seemed pleased with the brightly colored carton and cheap toy, and not at all traumatized.

Damn. Damn damn damn. Time to shut off my brain.

Going to the theater that evening was probably the best thing we could have done. It was a Larry Shue play called *The Foreigner,* by a local theater group founded by a couple who had left Off-Broadway. The play features a timid Englishman stuck in a lodge in Georgia for three days, introduced as a foreigner who knows no English. I wouldn't have thought we could have laughed so hard. I'm not sure how much Paul understood, but the exaggerated dialects and facial expressions required no translation. Or maybe it was just emotional release. He nodded off in the car on the way home, and I walked him upstairs, steered him into the bathroom, pulled off his sneakers and jeans, and rolled him under the covers. He was instantly asleep.

I was yawning, so I detoured down to the kitchen to make a cup of coffee, using the paper-towel-as-filter drip method. Then I sat down and started typing: *What can you say about a play that has you laughing out loud minutes after it starts?* I hammered out a thousand words, printed it, edited it, then emailed it to the editor at the *Enterprise.* Then lay awake long into the night, thinking.

I woke early, plans made. Before Paul

stirred, I slipped out of bed and fired up my computer to print some business cards. I packed a few things and made a quick call to Baker before waking Paul. Then a trip to the corner with Tiger, Cheerios at the kitchen picnic table, a note asking Zach to watch Tiger, and we were off to Saranac Lake.

CHAPTER 10

"This is crazy, Troy," Baker said flatly. "You're going to go up to Ottawa to find Paul's father, and then what?"

I didn't say anything.

She turned from the kitchen sink and faced me. "Okay, you kept Paul until he was comfortable talking. Probably you found out a whole lot more than the police would have by now. But now you know who he is. You know he was kidnapped. You know his mother was murdered. You know he has a father. Troy, you have to report this."

I could hear the *tunk, tunk* of her quartz-powered wall clock. The house was quiet. Her two oldest boys had left for school, and we'd stashed her youngest son and Paul at Holly's, across the street.

I was trying to formulate words, figuring out how to explain something that wasn't entirely clear even to me. Finally I started to speak and, God help me, my voice cracked and a tear slipped down my cheek. Baker stared at me in something approaching horror, as I'd put my head in my hands and narrowly avoided outright sobbing. She'd never seen me cry. She'd never even known I could cry, she told me later.

I finally got it out, more or less lucidly. I'd thought about it long into the night. Maybe Paul's father had nothing to do with this kidnapping or his wife's death. Maybe there was an innocent reason for his moving to Ottawa and for the lack of news coverage. But maybe he had everything to do with it.

Maybe he had wanted to get rid of wife and child without the expense of a divorce. No muss, no fuss, no alimony or child support. If he had arranged all this but it couldn't be proved, Paul would be turned over to him. Just like the children of the Nashville lawyer, Paul would grow up with the man responsible for his mother's death.

Baker listened. She'd not only made a whole pot of Earl Grey, but was drinking some, too. Apparently emotional crises merited hot expensive tea instead of the Red Rose brand she used for my iced tea.

"I can't let that happen," I said. "I'm not having him go back to someone who could harm him, or who killed his mother." I took a deep breath. "But I think if I see him, if I look him in the eye when I tell him, I'll know if he had anything to do with this."

What I couldn't say was that something had made me see Paul plummet off the ferry; something had led me to him in Lake Champlain and had let me swim long enough and hard enough to save him. Surely when I saw his father, I would know if he had been responsible for any of this.

"And if you think he was involved?" Baker prompted.

"Then I'll show him a photo I'm taking along of one of my nephews when he was that age, and say that was who I found." Paul's father would tell me I was mistaken; I'd express regret and leave and come back to Paul.

"And then I'll keep him," I said. My voice seemed to echo in the kitchen. The quartz clock was clicking away the seconds. "If I can get away with raising him here, I will, but if not, I'll move somewhere and start over with a new name." Never mind that I would be acting as judge and jury; never mind that the culprits would never pay for what they had done. This child would be safe.

I was showing Baker more of myself than she'd ever seen and admitting to things I didn't want to admit. But a tiny part of me was aware that opening up like this was the only thing that could sway her into watching Paul while I went to Canada. There's a fine line between sharing and manipulating, and part of me knew I was dancing close to that line — like a kid deliberately crying hard over a broken window so Mom won't get mad. But I didn't tell her about Janey, the little blond girl at the children's shelter who had begged me to adopt her, and who one day was just gone.

Maybe I was manipulating her, maybe not. Sometimes I think Baker sees into my skull, past the bones and into my brain. She probably had a pretty good idea what was going on.

She looked at the clock and then at me. "If you're going, go."

If I were a hugging kind of person, I would have hugged her. I brought in the bag I'd packed for Paul, and we walked over to Holly's so I could tell Paul I was leaving for a day or two and that he would stay with Baker and Mike.

He clung to me, his eyes glistening. *"Ne partez pas,"* he whispered. *"Ne partez pas, je vous en prie."* Please don't leave.

"I have to, Paul. *C'est nécessaire.*" And maybe my eyes were glistening, too. "*Ce n'est pas pour longtemps. Seulement un jour*

86

ou deux. One or two days. No longer."

But I had to go, and I couldn't take him with me. He'd be fine here.

CHAPTER 11

Now I was driving north to Ottawa, trying hard not to think about Paul's face as I'd left.

It was a crisp spring day, the sky clear and a more vivid blue than I've ever seen anywhere. Trees were coming alive after the long winter, shooting out sheaves of green. You could see gaps in the tree line where acid rain had killed off trees, but the air still seems fresh and clean.

Did I know that what I was doing was risky? Of course I did. But so was jumping off the ferry, which had saved one small boy's life.

I had built a comfortable world for myself here in the Adirondacks: rental house, rotating roommates, freelance work, family a thousand miles away, a sort-of boyfriend, friends but none I really confided in. Baker was the closest, and I'd let her see more of me today than I ever had. It was a simple and safe existence: no mortgage, no lease, no steady job, no committed relationship. Not a whole lot at risk.

It had seemed like a pretty good life to me, and I thought I'd been content.

But from the moment I sat on the rock at the edge of the lake with Paul on my lap, I'd felt a bond I'd never experienced. Something had changed for me, as if a switch had been thrown. I had taken responsibility for this small person, and now life from before the ferry seemed in the distant past.

I had distilled it down to two things: If Paul had a father who loved and deserved him, I would turn him over. If he didn't, I was keeping him.

I'd brought along my voice-activated tape recorder and business cards I'd printed this morning with a fake name and fake address. Baker would most likely tell her husband, Mike, a slimmed-down version of the truth, that Paul was an abandoned Canadian boy and I'd gone to try to find his father because it was simpler than involving the authorities.

I'd dressed with care, assuming the closest I could to a businesswoman persona: cord slacks, pullover, Eastland leather shoes, and black linen blazer on the seat beside me. I'd braided my hair into one long neat plait down my back. Not precisely the image of corporate success, but I figured the blazer would make it work.

I hadn't figured out how I would get in to see Dumond, but I had plenty of time to think on the drive. It's about eighty miles to the Canadian border, and the route meanders through small towns so undeveloped that if it weren't for modern cars and a few scattered Subways and Burger Kings, you could imagine it was decades ago.

When I spotted a FedEx drop box, I had my plan. I doubled back and opened the bin at the top of the box where labels and envelopes are stored. I was in luck: it held international labels as well as U.S. ones. I grabbed a label and envelope and addressed a label to Dumond, scribbling to obscure the first name and inventing a Boston address for the return. I slipped a note inside the envelope, sealed it, and inserted the label in the plastic flap. And drove on.

Now I was at the St. Regis reservation and passing the Akwesasne Mohawk Casino. The parking lot was nearly full, and I could see a bevy of plump white women wearing fanny packs making their way inside, heading for the slot machines. To me gambling on reservations is Native Americans' joke on white Americans. We pushed them onto the least desirable land possible, and now flock to their casinos to gamble our dollars away.

Payback.

Gas is always cheaper on the reservation, so I stopped at the Bear's Den to tank up. While a tall jean-clad Mohawk man with dark close-cropped hair pumped the gas, I headed for the restroom.

The border crossing at Cornwall was a brief stop while an inspector glanced at my passport and asked a few rote questions. Apparently I fit no profile, because as often as I've crossed this border, I've never had my car searched or been asked more than the perfunctory questions: *Where are you going? How long are you staying? What is your citizenship? Are you carrying any liquor or cigarettes?* Once in a while they'd throw in *Are you carrying more than $10,000?* and I'd have to work hard not to retort, "Do I *look* like I'm carrying more than $10,000?" Apparently you can import ten grand without reporting it, but not a penny more.

Up highway 138, onto the Trans-Canada Highway, into Ottawa, exit into downtown. Traffic was smooth. My heart was thumping, my mouth dry.

It was comfortably before lunchtime. First

step: Check to see if Dumond was in. If not, try in the afternoon, then maybe crash with people I knew in Perth and try again tomorrow. I found a parking space and then a pay phone. I thumbed in some of the Canadian change I keep in my car console.

"Dumond Agency, Colette speaking," a pleasant voice said.

"Hello," I said. "This is Doris Felton calling for Philippe Dumond." I expected the stilted or bored *May I ask what this is concerning?* that you get from most businesses in the States, but Canadians are friendlier and less suspicious than their American counterparts. Or maybe I'd succeeded at sounding confident enough to be convincing.

She replied, "Certainly, just one moment," and as she clicked off, I hung up, figuring they'd think the call had gotten disconnected. I'd found out what I wanted: Dumond was in his office. It was possible she had been shuffling me off to an assistant, but that was a risk I'd take.

I'd tucked the FedEx envelope into the black canvas Lands' End satchel I use as a briefcase. As an afterthought, I ripped it open. Dumond would be more likely to glance inside if the envelope was open, and I didn't want it sitting in a pile for hours.

On the paper inside I'd written: *I may know something about your son, Paul.*

I breathed deeply, hitched the satchel up on my shoulder, and walked briskly toward his office building. If the entrance was keypad- or entry-card-operated, I'd slip in behind someone on their way in.

No keypad, no problem. The directory listed the Dumond Agency on the third floor. I stepped into the elevator. Deep breaths. I leaned against the brass railing and switched on the voice-activated tape recorder in my pocket. A drop of sweat trickled down my side.

I would, I thought, be facing one of two possibilities. Either Dumond would be clearly innocent, ecstatic with the news that his son had been found, and we would alert the police and arrange a happy reunion.

Or — and this was trickier — he would give off guilty vibrations, be evasive or insincere, or not admit his son had been kidnapped. Then I'd say I must be mistaken, show a photo of boy-who-is-not-Paul, offer apologies and leave, giving the fake business card if pressed. And make sure no one followed me to my car.

All too soon the elevator doors opened. And I was facing the glass doors of the office, with their heavy black raised lettering.

I learned a long time ago that if you can't be confident, pretend that you are. I whisked in to greet the woman at the receptionist's desk, and went into my spiel, sliding into the Canadian accent I automatically use when I'm up there. I'm no Meryl Streep, but Canadian English is easy. You enunciate a little more clearly, flatten your *a*'s, pronounce your *o*'s a bit differently. And say things like *zed* instead of *z, runners* instead of *sneakers, laneway* instead of *driveway.*

We'd gotten this FedEx envelope delivered to our office, I explained, where we had a Phyllis Dumond, and she'd accidentally signed for it and even opened it before seeing that it wasn't hers. My boss was worried that we'd accepted someone else's delivery, so she'd sent me over with it, and could she possibly check with Mr. Dumond to see if it was his?

"Of course." She smiled in sympathy at my rolled eyes about my demanding and completely imaginary boss. "I'll take it in to Mr. Dumond right away." She disappeared with the envelope, returned, and within a ten-count — *look up, accept envelope, open envelope, read note* — there he was.

Even I could tell he was wearing Armani, which on some people looks like a baggy suit, but on him looked like, well, Armani.

He was tall and lean, his face sharply angled and his hair thick and dark, worn longer than most businessmen — a perfect match for the elegant woman I'd seen in the photo. Only a slightly crooked nose kept him from being impossibly handsome. He spoke to the receptionist, and his gaze locked on me as she motioned toward me. A nearly imperceptible hesitation, a moment of indecision so slight I nearly didn't see it, and so brief I didn't have time to think what it could mean. Then he was the consummate businessman, moving smoothly toward me.

"You brought this envelope for me?" he asked pleasantly, in smooth, cultured tones, without a trace of French accent. "May I ask when it was delivered?"

I cleared my throat. "Actually, it's from me. It's not from FedEx."

For a fraction of a second the scene seemed to freeze, him with half smile and envelope in hand.

"Then I'd like to speak to you," he said, eyebrows slightly raised. "In my office?"

I nodded dumbly. My heart was thumping so fast he had to be able to hear it. Where was the intuition I'd been so sure would tell me if he was guilty? Surely an innocent man would be more emotional, not cool and collected, as dispassionate as if inquiring about a dry cleaner's bill.

I followed him into his office, passing offices where I could see people working, and registering the thick carpet underfoot. His office was exactly as I would have imagined it: rich cherry furniture, champagne-colored carpet, shelves heavy with books, brown leather armchairs.

I never saw him move. I heard the door close and suddenly I was flattened with my back against the wall, almost lifted off the ground, his hand hard up against my throat, gripping firmly, his hip pressing lightly against mine. His face was so close I could smell the crispness of his aftershave, see the small pores on his face, feel the palpable fury that shimmered between us. His words were slow and harsh, almost whispered into my ear: "Tell me where my son is."

CHAPTER 12

For a horrible moment I thought I was going to pass out or, worse, die here in this man's impeccable office. It seemed as if I couldn't get in enough air to make a sound, but I must have managed enough of a squeak that he realized he was slowly choking the life out of me.

He let go and whirled away, took two steps to his desk and propped himself on it, his back to me, breathing heavily. I leaned against the wall and rubbed my throat and breathed deeply. Air, as much as I wanted — stuff you take for granted until you suddenly can't get enough of it. My ears were ringing. It was curiously like how I felt when I'd surfaced in Lake Champlain with Paul.

When he turned back around he was once again the cool businessman, in perfect control, hair back in place. "If you have harmed my son, I will kill you," he said, almost pleasantly. "If this is a hoax, I will probably also kill you."

We stared at each other a long moment. If this was innocence, it wasn't what I expected. If it was guilt, it was terrifying.

"May I have some water?" I asked, my voice catching. He made a small violent movement, but restrained himself. He gestured toward a fancy watercooler in the corner. I walked to it on unsteady legs, ran water into a mug that sat nearby and drank, for once not concerned about germs. I carefully set the mug down and turned back to him. He was watching me unblinkingly.

I realized my entire plan had been absurdly naïve. I'd been insane to think I had the ability to face down either raw evil or deep anguish. Dumond either was responsible for his own wife's death and his son's near-death, or had suffered a life-shattering tragedy. And I had no idea which.

Time ticked by. I forced myself to breathe steadily. "Okay," I said. "I've found a boy who may be your son."

"Let me guess," he interrupted, lip curling, French accent slipping through. "You need a cash deposit to remember where my son is. For this I get perhaps a small clue, but to remember exactly where he is you will need more cash, eh?" He nearly trembled with rage.

"No, no, no," I said. "You don't understand," and God help me, my voice cracked again. I go years without crying — in public, anyway — and then I'm about to turn on the spigot for the third time in two days.

It stopped him for a moment, halted a tirade that I sensed had barely started. He abruptly gestured at a chair, and in that moment I thought I saw something besides rage: a flicker of despair, a deep sadness.

I sat, warily, on the edge of one of the leather chairs. I thought of a small boy, waiting for me, trusting me. Needing a parent who loved him.

"I've found a boy I think is your son," I said. "But before I tell you where he is" — I held up my hand as he moved involuntarily — "I need to know what happened."

He stared at me. "What do you mean?"

"How it happened. How Paul disappeared." My voice rose. "Why there was no newspaper coverage. And why you're here instead of in Montreal."

He eyed me, gauging the advantages and disadvantages of humoring me, of telling his story. At last he did, flatly and with little expression, leaning up against the edge of his desk.

He'd come home from work one afternoon to find his wife and child gone, along with her car, and a scribbled note saying she was going on a holiday. She had taken breaks before, especially during the winter, but had never before taken Paul. But the nanny had had the day off, and he assumed it had been spur of the moment. Some clothing and jewelry and her laptop were gone. He'd called their condo in Florida and then her friends. Nothing.

A few days later a neighbor wandered over with a misdelivered envelope that had sat in their mailbox while they had been out of town. It was a ransom demand with a deadline that had passed, threatening to kill both mother and child if he went to the police or failed to pay.

Paralyzed, he waited. Next a packet arrived at work. He'd obviously not cared about his wife, the note said, and she was dead, but he had another chance to get his son back. It included a Polaroid of a frightened Paul, perched on a chair in a room he didn't recognize.

He'd followed directions, leaving a bag of money near a park bench. Next came another note with a new photo, demanding more money. He paid. No Paul. Another demand, another photo. Now he went to the police, who orchestrated a fake payoff and staked out the drop site. No one showed. Three days later another demand, threatening to send Paul home in small pieces. Against police advice, he followed payoff instructions with as much as he could raise. Nothing. One more demand, but by this point he knew it was futile, and turned it over to the police. And then it all stopped. No more ransom demands, no more mysterious packets. Nothing — as if nothing had ever happened, as if wife and child had never existed.

He told neighbors that Madeleine and Paul had gone to Florida for the winter; the police had kept the story quiet. If any journalists had learned of the kidnapping, they had cooperated. Finally he sold the house and moved to Ottawa. One letter was forwarded from Montreal from someone claiming to have Paul, but with no contact info. He kept a Québec private investigator looking, with a standing offer of a reward. Nothing.

He recited it dispassionately, as if telling someone else's story, and then looked at me.

"You think you know where Paul is," he said, without expression.

"Do you have a picture of him?" I asked.

Barely shifting his weight off the desk, he pulled out his wallet, opening it to a snapshot of a dark-haired boy perched on a rail of a boat, laughing into the camera. He was younger and plumper than Paul, with a carefree look I'd never seen on Paul's face.

But it was him, without a doubt.

This was when I had to decide. I had a natural antipathy to anyone as attractive, polished, and wealthy as this man, and he'd given me a first-hand example of his frightening rage. But what swayed me was the very flatness of his tone as he told the story, as if his anguish was so intense he had to keep it tightly bottled up. I could not imagine him harming his child.

I took a deep breath, and made a decision that would change lives, for better or for worse. "Yes," I said. "He's with a friend of mine in upstate New York. I found him two days ago."

It seemed that the world should shift at this point, but Dumond didn't blink. "How?" he asked.

The question caught me off guard. I wasn't ready to trot out the ferry story: it was too involved, too unlikely, too traumatic. I didn't know how to answer. He repeated it: "How did you find him?"

"He was on the ferry coming into Port Kent," I said carefully, and that part was true. "He was alone, and told me he had

102

been kidnapped."

His eyes narrowed. "Why do you think it is my son?"

This wasn't going at all as I had expected. I hadn't considered his doubting me. "He says his name is Paul Dumond. And that his parents are Philippe and Madeleine Dumond, from Montreal. He says he was taken before Christmas."

A long silence. Then he asked, "Where has he been?"

"I don't know. The ferry was coming from Burlington, Vermont, but they could have driven from anywhere."

"And his mother?" The question was casual.

My throat tightened. I hadn't considered that I would have to tell this man that his son had heard his mother being shot. I wished I could lie and say I didn't know, but I'm a terrible liar. And he needed to know. "Paul says . . . Paul says she was shot soon after they were taken."

Dumond raised an eyebrow, but gave no other reaction. "He saw this?"

"No," I whispered, "but he says he heard it."

He stood suddenly. He had made his decision. I could be a lunatic or a criminal; I could be playing a horrible hoax, but he had

reached a decision: he would go see the boy
— now. We would go to New York, in his
car. I would leave my car here, in the garage
under the building. He had no intention of
letting me out of his sight.

"Don't you want to call the police?"

"Later. First I need to see the boy."

Spending three hours in a car with Paul's
father hadn't been in my script. But I could
see his point: he didn't want to run the risk
of my getting away from him. And he was,
after all, the person I'd decided to turn Paul
over to.

"All right," I said after thinking it through.
"But you need to call the police, tell them I
said I found your son, and that you're going
to go see him."

We stared at each other. But on this I
wasn't giving in. I was all too aware that I
could be making entirely the wrong decision about a man who may have plotted the
murder of his wife and child. With deliberation, he picked up his desk phone. As he
punched in a number that he read off his
cell phone I could see the wedding band on
his ring finger. He pushed the speakerphone
button and I heard voice mail kick in.

Dumond shoved a pad of paper and pen
at me, making a writing motion as he spoke.
"Yes, this is Philippe Dumond and I have

spoken to you about my son's kidnapping last winter from Montreal. I am with a young woman whose name is" — I'd figured out what he wanted and hastily printed on the pad — "Troy Chance, from Lake Placid, New York. She says she found my son at the ferry station in the New York town of Port Kent, day before yesterday. We are traveling to New York State now so I can determine if this is my son." He rattled off his cell phone number, hung up, and stood.

I followed him out of the office as he spoke briskly to his secretary, and then he strode beside me to my car, waiting with barely restrained impatience as I scrabbled to move map, water bottle, and other odds and ends from the passenger side. I'd never realized how much stuff I travel with. He directed me curtly into a slot in his underground garage and waited while I got my things. As I rummaged in the glove box for my ID and phone, I slipped the tape recorder out of my blazer pocket and into the compartment. If the worst happened, someone would find the tape of our conversation. Like the schoolteacher from New Jersey years ago who had recorded her conversations with her teenaged carjacker, trying patiently to talk him out of killing her, but failing.

He silently ushered me into a black Mercedes a few spaces over. Awkwardly, I sat in the leather seat and buckled up.

"What about —" I started.

"What?" he asked sharply, as he backed the car out.

"I thought maybe . . . shouldn't you, well, take along something of Paul's? I mean, he's been gone for a long time. Does he have a favorite toy, a teddy bear or something?"

He looked at me as if I were crazy. But I could remember Paul saying his father didn't want him. Maybe the kidnappers had told him this; maybe he'd just assumed it because his father hadn't come and rescued him. But having a tangible reminder of happier times couldn't hurt.

Again he made a quick decision. We veered away from downtown and toward an elite area with winding roads and stately homes of diplomats and a few embassy compounds, with private homes mixed in.

We stopped at an elaborate Tudor home nestled behind a tall wrought-iron fence with a hedge thickly entwined. The gate swung open when he fingered a gadget in his car. He parked in front of the house and ushered me in front of him, through the heavy oak door and across the polished floor of the hallway.

He moved fast. He punched off an alarm, then stalked down a corridor. He paused to pull down a soft black bag from a hallway closet, and continued down the hall and into a room. I followed, tentatively. From the doorway I could see a child's furniture: oak bunk beds with matching dresser, desk and chair, rocker, and toy box. Otherwise the room was bare, with a row of stacked boxes still sealed with movers' tape. Dumond moved to the boxes and ripped four or five of them open, one after another. In silence he rooted through them, grabbing a stuffed bear, a truck, and action figures and cramming them into the bag. I didn't say a word; I scarcely breathed. My throat tightened. Here was Paul's childhood, boxed away, carefully moved into a new room. Waiting for the boy who had spent the last five months alone in a tiny room.

As quickly as he'd started, Dumond was finished. Back down the hallway, up a short flight of stairs to what seemed to be a loft area. I sat on the stairs to wait. He reappeared a few minutes later with a packed leather bag.

"Let's go," he said, and we strode in silence across the shiny hallway, our heels clicking on the marble, and climbed into the Mercedes.

Chapter 13

"Does he speak English?"

"What?" I asked, startled. We'd traveled in silence the first half hour. He had no idea if I was telling him the truth. If he was innocent, he wouldn't want to get his hopes up that he was about to see his son. If guilty, he was probably working out how best to get rid of me. I was working hard not to consider the second option.

I felt as if I'd suddenly stepped into a movie without having seen the script. Had he been involved? I hoped the hell not. Was I doing the right thing taking him to Paul? I hoped the hell yes. Was I in danger? I had no idea. The Ottawa police knew he was with me, and knew where we were headed. But either way, this man was going to take one small boy out of my life forever.

He grimaced. "This boy you say is Paul."

"No. At least not much. Did your son . . . ?"

"He speaks a little, but we spoke French at home." I knew that most Québec schools didn't let kids study English until third grade or so. Which seems to me a tad exclusionary, especially in a country that's officially bilingual.

Silence for a few moments.

"Is he healthy?" he asked.

"He seems fine. I had a friend who's a nurse look him over."

More miles in silence. We zoomed past an exit, and I could see McDonald's arches in the distance. My stomach rumbled. I had a packet of peanut butter crackers in my bag, but I couldn't picture myself pulling them out and crunching them down in this car with its spotless leather seats.

He drove well, checking rearview mirrors regularly and changing lanes smoothly. It was at least a quarter hour before he spoke again.

"How did you find me?" When he wasn't angry, his English had no trace of an accent. It's not uncommon for Canadians to be flawlessly bilingual, especially Québécois who move in both anglophone and francophone worlds. Although some never learn English, and others have a heavy accent.

"Paul told me your names, and I searched on the internet until I found your company and its address. I mean, I assumed it was you."

"You live in Lake Placid."

"Yes," I said. And then, because talking, however inanely, seemed better than sitting in silence for the rest of this three-hour drive, I told him where I'd grown up, where I went to school, about working for the newspaper, and what work I did now. I'm not usually a rambler, but something had to fill this silence. He asked no questions. Neither did I.

Suddenly I thought of Baker — I needed to let her know we were on our way. I didn't want to be left sitting tensely with Dumond in their driveway waiting for them if they had gone out. And I owed her some warning: *Hey, Bake, I'm about to arrive at your house with Paul's father, who I'm hoping like hell didn't have anything to do with the kidnapping.*

I pulled out my cell phone and gestured with it. "I should tell Baker that we're coming."

"Baker?"

"My friend that Paul's with."

He thought a moment and then nodded, pulling a cell phone out of a cradle I hadn't noticed. "Use this one."

Fine by me. He'd have a record of the call,

but since I was taking him to Baker's, it hardly mattered. I punched in the numbers. Baker answered.

"Bake, it's me. How's Paul?"

"He's fine," she said mildly. "The boys are home from school and teaching him all kinds of naughty slang. Did you talk to his father?"

"Yep. I'm in his car. We've crossed the border, as a matter of fact."

Silence for a moment. "So you're coming down here. And you've decided he's not the bad guy."

"Yep and yep. I mean, yep, I've decided, pretty much anyway."

"Should I expect squad cars to descend on us?"

"No, he just wants to see Paul for now. I wanted to give you a heads-up. We'll be there in about an hour." What I wasn't saying was *In case I've guessed wrong and this man is a homicidal lunatic, have Mike on hand and the kids tucked away safely.* But Baker was smart, with a mother's instincts. She'd probably send the boys to Holly's. And Mike was an Adirondacker — he hunted, had more than one gun, and knew how to use them.

Dumond watched as I carefully put the phone back in its slot. "Who is this Baker?"

"She's a good friend of mine, in Saranac Lake. She's got kids, and Paul likes them, so he's fine with her." I was starting to babble.

"She has been keeping Paul?"

"No, he's been at my house; I just left him at Baker's today while I went to see you."

We were quiet the rest of the way, me speaking only to direct him at intersections. By the time we pulled into the driveway Dumond was stiff with tension, and I could hear my heart pounding.

Then we were out of the car, Dumond at my side, gripping my elbow, his fingers tight on my arm. Baker was in the driveway, moving toward us with a slight frown, her eyes worried, her very posture telling me something was wrong. She glanced at Dumond and then spoke to me.

"Troy, he's gone." I felt as if I'd been punched in the stomach. A harsh exclamation, a sudden movement from the man beside me. I ignored him.

"What do you mean, gone?" The words were thick in my mouth. *Oh God, oh God, oh God,* ran a little voice in my head. *Please tell me that Child Services got him or he's in the hospital. Please please please . . .*

She gestured toward the doorway, where sturdy Mike was standing, looking like a lumberjack in his jeans and plaid shirt, their sons lined up in front of him, his hands on the shoulders of the two youngest. "They were playing Sardines outside but then they couldn't find Paul, and finally gave up and came and told me."

I knew Sardines was a hide-and-seek game: when you found the first person hiding, you squeezed in, until the whole group was squished in together and only one left searching.

Dumond whirled on me and began to spout a torrent of French so furious I was glad it was too fast to understand. Midway he switched to English, just as fast and almost as angry. "What game are you playing that you bring me here and pretend you have my son? How dare you . . ."

I jerked my arm free and faced him. "Look," I said hotly. "You have to believe us. Paul was here; he's your son, he has to be. How many Paul Dumonds have been kidnapped from Montreal? Why would we make this up?" He was staring at me angrily, and I remembered something I'd tucked into my satchel. I grabbed it and pulled out the paper where Paul had written his and his parents' names, and held it out. "Look, he wrote down his name and your names. He wasn't lying and I'm not lying."

Now I was almost shouting. His eyes and posture told me he wasn't buying it, any of it. Baker had stepped away from us and re-appeared, silently pushing something into my hand. I looked down, and saw a small digital camera. "Mike Jr.'s," she said. "They took pictures today."

I lifted the camera and looked at the viewing screen. Baker's middle son, Rick, was grinning a toothy grin, with Paul beside him. I turned to Dumond and silently held out the camera.

He took it and looked down at it. He looked at it a long time, then across the driveway at Rick, wearing the same shirt as in the photo. Now I saw what I'd been looking for and what did, at last, put an end to that horrible am-I-doing-the-right-thing doubt. His face was etched with agony, so stark and pained it made my stomach jolt.

"Yes," he said. "This is my son."

CHAPTER 14

Mike strode forward and introduced himself. "First thing to do is contact the local police," he said. "I'll call Jimmy Dupuis down at the station and he'll have everyone keeping an eye out, even the Staties."

Dumond nodded. Mike normally stays in the background and lets Baker manage things, but when action is required — like when Mike Jr. took a baseball to the forehead and spouted blood like a geyser — he moves, and moves quickly.

We plugged the camera's memory card into their computer; I selected the best shot of Paul's face, cropped out the other kids, and printed copies. Mike emailed one to his friend at the police station. They couldn't do an AMBER Alert, he told us, because we had nothing to suggest that Paul hadn't just wandered off. Holly and her husband, Tom, appeared, and she herded the kids into the living room to watch a movie.

Mike shook out a map of Saranac Lake onto the kitchen table. "Phil and I will drive this section of town." He slashed red crayon lines up and down streets. "Tom and Holly will drive this section." He marked off more streets with a blue crayon. "Troy can search the immediate area on foot and check with neighbors. Susan will stay here in case Paul comes back, and she can alert all of us if anyone finds him."

For a moment I wondered who Susan was, before I remembered it was Baker's first name.

I searched for over an hour, knocking on doors and peering into backyards. *Excuse me, have you seen a small boy about this size, who looks like this?* I was trying not to panic or despair, but I saw only three possibilities: Paul had gotten lost, Paul had run away, Paul had been abducted. One, two, three. None good. After I'd circled the neighborhood, I stopped back at the house for a bathroom break. My head was pounding and my gut felt hollow. The kitchen door creaked as I came in, and Baker looked up from the kitchen table.

"When did you eat last?" she asked.

"Mmm. Breakfast." She pointed, and I pulled out a chair and sat. Within minutes she had a toasted cheese and tomato sandwich and a cup of steaming Earl Grey in front of me.

My fear, one that I kept probing at like a sore tooth, was that I'd tossed away the miracle I'd been handed — of having saved Paul's life — by leaving him to be snatched again. I had to struggle not to envision his body in Lake Clear or one of the other nearby lakes. How simple it would be to stop to pretend you're looking at the view and slip a small bundle into the water. This time they'd be sure he was unconscious or dead first.

Baker spoke as if she were reading my mind. "It's not likely that someone took him, Troy. The other kids would have seen someone, they'd have seen a strange car. And someone would have had to follow you here this morning; you'd have noticed them."

She's not inclined to platitudes, but that's what this sounded like. I shook my head. "I can't imagine him just wandering off, Bake. He's stuck close to me ever since I found him. He wouldn't feel safe enough to go off on his own. And he had no idea where I was or what I was doing."

Baker shook her head. "Well, maybe he did." She took a sip of tea, involuntarily grimacing. She probably would have preferred a shot of Jack Daniel's — I always bring her back a bottle when I visit Tennessee. I assume you can buy it here, but she seems to prefer it from closer to the source. "When I was talking to you on the phone, the kids came into the kitchen to get something to drink. It never occurred to me that Paul could understand me, or that —"

I finished the sentence. "That he'd run away from his father." I chewed a bite of sandwich as I thought. "I don't believe Dumond had anything to do with his son being kidnapped, but I'm not sure that Paul knows that. No telling what the kidnappers said to him. And his father not coming to rescue him would seem like abandonment to a kid."

I never should have left Paul. What I should have done, I wasn't sure. I'd stopped being entirely logical the moment I'd dived into the water.

The phone rang, and we both jumped. Baker grabbed it, spoke a few terse words, and returned to the table. "That was Mike. They're heading back here for coffee."

I let the tiny hope fade that had formed when the phone rang. I pulled one thought from the tumbling mass in my brain. If Paul had been snatched, we couldn't find him. But if he'd wandered or run away, we could.

And to have evaded us this long, he'd have had to find somewhere to go.

"Baker, do any of the kids around here have a hideout, a clubhouse or anything? Something they might have told Paul about that he could have thought would make a good hideaway?"

"Maybe," she said, frowning. "Let's ask them."

In the living room the kids were intent on *Free Willy*. The whale was about to sail over the wall to escape to the ocean, so we politely waited until he leaped, and then hit the Pause button, freezing him just before he splashed down on the other side.

"Hey, guys," Baker said genially, "we need to talk a little." Seven solemn sets of eyes looked at her. "You know that Paul's missing, that he may have wandered off somewhere or gone to hide." Her tone was amiable. Seven solemn nods. "What we need to know is if anybody may have mentioned something about a cool place to hide or a fun place to explore, that maybe Paul thought he'd check out."

It took a while to convince them that they weren't in trouble, but eventually Mike Jr. and Holly's older son, Jack, admitted they'd mentioned a scary cave on the hill behind Jack's house, and, well, maybe bragged about having explored it and how it was much too hard to find and much too scary for anyone younger than them. By now Tom and Holly had returned, and Holly joined us while Tom poured himself some coffee in the kitchen.

"But Paul doesn't understand English," Holly protested, pushing her hair away from her face.

"I think he knows more than we realize," I said. "I think he can understand a lot. And kids are good at communicating."

Baker had already assembled a row of flashlights on the counter, and was piling up jackets, because the sun was beginning to sink and it was cooling off. Suddenly I thought of something. I jumped up. "Tiger. I'll bet Tiger could find him." I grabbed the kitchen phone and dialed. I was in luck — Zach was home and so was Dave, with his car. They'd be right over. I rattled off directions.

Mike and Dumond strode into the kitchen while I was on the phone, arriving like the next set of characters in a play. It was clear they had no news, and I could see Baker relaying to them what the kids had told us. As I hung up, Mike nodded. "I figured that'd be the next place to search anyway," he said, wiping his brow. "There is an old cave up there, but the opening's pretty small and it's hard to find. He could be anywhere up there, so we'll have to cover the whole hill."

Baker looked over at Dumond, still in his brown Armani, now slightly bedraggled. "Do you have any other clothes?" she asked.

He blinked. "A few things, yes. But . . ."

"You're going to need something sturdier than that, and shoes that won't slip."

He started to speak again, then turned and headed out to his car for his bag. The clothes I had on weren't fancy, but they were the best I had. No point in ruining them. "I'll change, too," I said, and ran out to get the bag with the clothes I'd brought in case I'd needed to stay over in Canada.

In Baker's downstairs bathroom I pulled on jeans, T-shirt, and sneakers. When I came out, Dumond had changed to khakis, a button-down shirt, and soft leather lace-up shoes. Scrambling around on the hillside would probably ruin these clothes, but at least they were sturdier. And less expensive.

Baker insisted that everyone gulp mugs of coffee and eat sandwiches while she filled a thermos and gathered supplies. Then I heard the sound of Dave's rattletrap old Pontiac, and ran to the door. The car doors opened and bodies piled out: Tiger, then

Zach, Dave, and Patrick — young, muscular, full of energy, wearing sweatshirts and faded jeans, almost like a uniform. I ran to meet them and they surrounded me, a warm protective ring, not quite touching me, but close.

"Sixteen minutes, flat," Dave said proudly, shaking his shaggy hair out of his eyes. Patrick balanced on the balls of his feet, bouncing up and down; Zach gave my arm a little punch.

"Hey, don't w-w-worry," he said. "We'll find him."

We walked in silence to Holly and Tom's house, armed with flashlights. The sky was starting to dim and we could feel the incoming chill. Holly shooed all the kids inside, where her younger sister was waiting to watch them. Baker set up a base at the bottom of the hillside with a lawn chair, spare flashlights and batteries, first aid kit, thermos, blankets, and air horn. She'd rounded up these things with so little effort that I could only assume that households with three small boys keep them stashed away for emergencies. Dumond was restless, impatient to get started, but waited for Mike's instructions.

Two neighbors Holly had called joined us. We'd sweep up the hill in rows in pairs,

Mike said, and try to cover every inch of ground and every place a small boy might take shelter. Dumond teamed with me, which somehow I'd expected.

I'd had Zach bring over the clothes Paul had worn yesterday, and Tiger obligingly sniffed them. I had no idea if she knew what I wanted, but she can track an invisible squirrel across a field and find a peanut that's rolled under a couch, so maybe she could find a lost little boy on a steep, overgrown hillside.

For the next hour we plunged through dense underbrush, Tiger scooting under thick bushes and tree branches we had to battle through. Sometimes I got down on my hands and knees and crawled, holding the flashlight in my teeth, with the light shining crazily off to the side. Sometimes I had to call to Tiger to wait. Sweat was trickling down my back despite the coolness of the evening. I was very aware of Dumond's presence. I was praying silently, over and over, *Please let us find him, please let me have been right about his father. Please please please.* Now Tiger was sniffing at the ground, following a scent, and I hoped we weren't painstakingly tracking a deer or a squirrel. We seemed to be zigzagging, and occasionally I'd catch sight of a bobbing light from someone else's flashlight. So much for Mike's plan of careful linear searching.

Then Tiger plunged ahead, into a thick bramble, woofing. I knelt and played the flashlight ahead of me. I could see a tunnel-like opening in the brush, about the diameter a small child could crawl through, too small for either of us. Tiger dived in. I strained to hear. Was she nudging, licking, greeting a small boy? My pulse quickened. Dumond's hand was gripping my shoulder. He didn't speak — maybe he couldn't. What could you say when you might see the son you thought you'd lost forever?

"Paul, Paul," I called softly. "*C'est Troy. Tu es là?* Are you there?"

Silence. I called again, "Paul, please come out. *Il n'y a rien de dangereux ici.* You are safe. Please come out. Paul, Paul, come on, sweetie."

Beside me, on his knees, Dumond didn't move, but I could feel the pressure of his fingers on my shoulder. A tiny rustle, then another. The grip on my shoulder tightened. A small figure appeared, slowly, crawling through the tiny space, and then we could see Paul's face, tear-streaked and more than a little grimy, with Tiger close behind, as if she was herding him out. I held out my

124

arms and he scampered the rest of the way and fell into them.

"Vous êtes revenue," he squeaked. *"Vous êtes revenue pour moi."* You came back for me. I could feel Dumond beside me, shaking in tiny tremors.

My heart did that funny twisting thing again. I clung to Paul. I could feel the breath going in and out of his body, in unison with my own. *"Chéri, chéri, chéri,"* I whispered. *"Tu es fou de te cacher.* You are silly to hide like this." Dumond must have moved or made a sound, because Paul lifted his head and saw him. Paul's small body tensed in my arms. I turned his face toward me. *"Paul, ton père est ici. Il était inquiet pour toi. Tu lui as beaucoup manqué."* Your father is here; he is worried about you; he has missed you a lot.

In the glow of the flashlight, Dumond's face was haggard, naked with emotion so raw my stomach turned over. Now Paul was trembling a little. I gave him a nudge, and then he was in his father's arms, and Dumond was murmuring French so fast and low I couldn't understand a word. Paul was saying, *"Papa, Papa, Papa,"* over and over. They were both crying, the dark heads close together. I backed away and sat against a log. I was drained. I'd reunited a father and

125

child; I'd lost a child who was never mine. I'd filled a hole in Dumond's life, but had carved one in mine. Only now did I realize how intense had been my dream of keeping Paul, protecting him, loving him, watching him grow up.

It was a long trek down the hill, Dumond carrying Paul, me playing both flashlights in front of us. At the base, Baker was waiting, ever-patient, calm and ready. I fell into her arms wordlessly. Guess I forgot I wasn't the hugging type. Baker held tight and patted my back once, before releasing me to give the air horn a blast. She knew what I'd found, and lost again.

She turned to Paul. "Hey, little guy," she said. "You sure gave us a scare." She ruffled his hair and snuggled a blanket around him, still in his father's arms. People began to straggle off the hill, weary but ebullient. We stopped to collect the kids from Holly's house, and trekked back to Baker's house together. Mike called the Saranac Lake police to report we'd found Paul, and Dumond made a call, I suppose to leave a message with the Ottawa police.

It was a crazy celebration: eleven adults, most of whom hadn't known each other before, plus eight kids, crammed into Mike and Baker's kitchen area. We were tired, dirty, and nearly giddy. Baker kept the table filled with sandwiches, chips, cookies, beer, and soda, and I think even she was amazed at how much my housemates ate. I had to tell three times how Tiger had found Paul. Paul, ensconced in his father's arms, piped in with bits of French and English mixed together that made everyone laugh. Mike and Zach had found the cave and Zach had squeezed in, but found nothing other than a few drink cans and empty chip bags. Mike Jr. and Jack strutted around, proud that they may have helped find Paul by telling about the cave, never mind that their tales had probably enticed him to go cave hunting in the first place.

No one knew why Paul had hidden himself up on that hillside, that far from the house. When we'd asked if something had scared him, he'd just shrugged. Maybe he had been looking for a great hiding place. Or maybe he had been worried about seeing his father. It didn't matter now. Dumond sat with his arms lightly around his son. He was deeply fatigued but looked years younger, a different man than the one I'd met that morning. Finally Baker took her youngest son off to bed. Holly's two youngest had already fallen asleep on the sofa.

I stirred and looked at the wall clock:

10:15. Unbelievable that I'd just left this kitchen this morning to head for Ottawa. "I need to go home," I said, into a momentary silence, and stood. I looked at Dumond, across the table. "You can stay at my house." I was too tired to make it sound gracious.

Dumond nodded. Zach, Dave, and Patrick hopped up to leave, grabbing sandwiches on their way out.

We loaded our bags into the Mercedes and tucked Paul into the backseat with Tiger, where he promptly fell asleep. I directed Dumond out of town and into Lake Placid, along Main Street and into my parking space. Never had my paint-peeling, ramshackle house looked so good. Dave's car was already there, motor pinging the way old cars do after they've been shut off.

Carrying his sleeping son, Dumond followed me up to my bedroom. I set down Paul's bag and pulled down the covers so Dumond could lay Paul in the bed. "You guys can have this room," I said. I nodded toward the outer rooms. "The bathroom's outside there, and there's another bathroom downstairs, off the kitchen."

He glanced around. "This is your room. Where will you sleep?"

I tugged a sleeping bag down from the top shelf of the closet. "On my sofa, out there," I said.

He nodded, grimacing an apology at taking my bed. I was so tired that standing upright was a huge effort, and I was almost swaying on my feet. I turned to leave just as Dumond moved toward me. He put his right hand out and grasped mine, his skin warm against mine. "Thank you," he said.

The contact of his skin on mine felt like a conduit, an opening into my soul. Suddenly I wanted to cry, long and hard. I wanted him to wrap his arms around me while I cried until I couldn't cry any longer. I wanted to cry for Paul and for all the things I'd ever lost or never had. If I had looked at him I would have lost control. I muttered something, broke his grip, and left, pulling the bedroom door closed behind me.

By the time he came out to go into the bathroom, I'd brushed my teeth, washed my face, kicked off my sneakers, zipped myself into my sleeping bag, and wiggled my bra off from under my clothes. I closed my eyes to pretend I was asleep, and when I opened them it was morning.

CHAPTER 15

I looked at the window without recognizing it, and squinted to see if the curtains had the cartoon character pattern of my childhood curtains.

Sometimes I think that when you're in a deep sleep you regress into your past, and wake up with your psyche in an entirely different place and time, before you've made it back to the present. This morning I'd made it to about age eight, a relatively uncomplicated time.

Sounds came from downstairs: a shrill boy's laugh, a man's deeper tones, and a slightly higher voice punctuated by a stutter. My brain slowly identified them: Paul, Dumond, Zach. The window came into focus: chipped paint, the curtain I'd made from a sheet, the old glass that looks grungy even after just being washed.

Across the room my bedroom door stood

open. I was alone. Even Tiger had deserted me.

I lay there a moment, and when I stirred, it hurt in a way I'd never hurt before. Deepwater swim one day, sit in a car six hours, and then crawl around in underbrush. My body wasn't taking well to this new regimen. I regretted not having taken a hot bath last night.

I wriggled out of the sleeping bag and padded into my bedroom for clean clothes. The bed was neatly made, Dumond's bag nowhere in sight. I stumbled back to the bathroom. I pulled the plastic shower curtain closed and stood under the spray with my eyes shut, for once not caring if I drained the hot water tank.

I'd found Paul's father; I'd delivered Paul safely. My adventure was over, and I had to reset. I had to block this mix of tumultuous emotions and move back into my safe, sane existence.

I had no idea how.

The anemic spray of the shower was beginning to run cool. I stepped out and toweled dry, moving slowly. Combing out my hair seemed impossible, even with my wide-toothed comb, and I gave up. My hair is so thick and curly that snarls just look like more curls, so it doesn't much matter. I pulled on jeans and polo shirt, and headed downstairs barefoot, carefully holding the railing.

As I stepped out of the stairwell, faces looked up from the picnic table. Paul was almost bouncing, eyes shining, his face alive and bright in a way I couldn't have imagined.

"Troy, Troy, Troy!" he chirped, as he untangled his legs from the bench. "Goot morning!" He ran toward me and wrapped his arms around my waist, and I automatically hugged him.

"Hey, hey!" Zach said, teeth flashing in a grin. "We're all t-t-talking English today."

"Good," I said, almost dourly. My vocal cords felt as if they hadn't been used for a year. "I don't think I remember any French."

Dumond sat at the table, hair damp, wearing a T-shirt and warm-up suit I recognized as Zach's. "Good morning," he said pleasantly. "Zach was kind enough to lend me some clothing, and keep Paul company while I showered."

"So I see." Somehow he seemed right at home here, not out of place as I'd felt in his fancy office, his stately house, his expensive car. This annoyed me.

"Troy, Troy, come zee my things," Paul

begged, pulling at my leg. *"J'ai beaucoup de choses, beaucoup de jouets.* They are from *Papa,* from my *maison."* He looked up at me, face bright and happy. Overnight he seemed to have turned into a normal kid, nothing like the thin pale wraith I'd held on my lap on the shore of Lake Champlain. Kidnapped, mother murdered, tossed off a ferry to drown, lost searching for a cave — apparently all that was behind him. He had toys to show me, a whole bagful, and that was what was important.

I glanced at Dumond, who smiled rue-fully. I let Paul pull me into the living room, where he had laid out the truck, the fat teddy, the action figures. Paul was making a complicated demonstration involving a little plastic man I wasn't quite following when Dumond appeared and handed me a steaming mug. "Zach says you drink coffee sometimes. We weren't sure how you took it."

The hot mug felt good to my hands. I took a giant swallow. On the rare occasions I drink coffee I drink it with milk only, and this was loaded with sugar, but I didn't care. I could feel it infusing life back into me, as if my brain cells were realigning.

Dumond perched on the arm of the couch, an indiscriminate nubby gray-brown fabric useful for hiding soda spills and pizza stains. We watched Paul play. Here sat the man who had slammed me against a wall yesterday. Here, playing happily on the floor, was the boy who had been kidnapped and almost drowned. And here was Troy, in the middle of it all. It was surreal.

Paul was still grimy. "Paul, have you had a bath?" As soon as the words left my mouth I realized this wasn't my concern anymore. But Dumond didn't seem offended, and when Paul looked at me blankly, I pantomimed scrubbing. It was one thing to talk to Paul in my rusty French; it was another to trot it out in front of his fluently bilingual father.

Paul shook his head, and looked at his father imploringly.

Dumond laughed, a deep delighted laugh, and stood up. "No, Paul, Troy is quite right. *Il faut que tu prennes un bain.* You're overdue for a bath."

We climbed the stairs. I started the water running in the tub while Dumond helped Paul undress. I went to get clean clothes from the ones Baker had lent us, and when I returned, Paul was in the tub, splashing his plastic men in the water. Dumond was sitting on his heels, leaning against the wall, watching his son.

"Et voilà, des vêtements propres, ici," I said,

showing Paul the jeans and T-shirt. "I'm putting them here on the toilet." He nodded, bashing the little figures in the water and making sputtering, crashing noises. Dumond closed the door part of the way behind us, and followed me into my bedroom.

He sat on the end of my bed. "How did you find him?" he asked. I think he knew I hadn't just found an abandoned boy on a ferry. I sat against the wall and told him all of it: Paul's fall from the ferry, my swim to reach him, bringing him here. I know I tell it flatly; I scoot past the grim parts. But a father, I expect, would live every moment no matter how you told it. Something flickered in Dumond's eyes when I told him about the sweatshirt that had been tied around his son's arms, but he didn't speak until I was done.

He shifted where he sat. "So someone threw him off the ferry."

I nodded. "I think so."

"And he has been kept prisoner this whole time."

I nodded again. "He said he was moved once, to a different place."

We sat in silence, until Dumond spoke suddenly. "You saw no one?"

"No, I just saw Paul fall toward the water.

135

I never even looked up at the deck — I kept my eyes on where he went in. When we got back to the dock, that ferry was on its way back to Vermont."

"So you got him out of the water and brought him here." His tone was even, but I don't think I imagined the blame behind his words. I flushed. I looked down. I studied a tiny spring from a ballpoint pen that had somehow rolled between the gray painted floorboards.

The words were thick in my mouth. "I probably should have gone to the police," I said. "Or the hospital. But I didn't think anyone could do anything right away — and Paul was wet and tired and I wanted to get him warm and dry . . ." My voice trailed off.

He started to speak again, but Paul interrupted from the bathroom, calling, "Papa, Papa." Dumond moved toward the doorway, and I stood. *"Papa, est-ce que je dois vraiment me laver les cheveux?"* Paul asked plaintively.

Dumond forced a laugh. *"Mais oui.* Of course you must wash your hair." He turned toward me, once again the crisp efficient businessman. It amazed me how quickly he moved from one persona to another. "I'd like to make some calls and my cell isn't working well here. May I use your telephone? I'll reimburse you, of course."

"Sure." I nodded toward the phone on my desk. Only then did I notice that the message light was blinking. "Just a sec," I murmured, and went over and pushed the Play button.

Hello, Troy, came Thomas's pleasant tones. *Just calling to see how things are going. Please give me a call.* Damn. He'd be wondering why I hadn't called him back.

Dumond paused, hand over the phone. "Do you need to use it?"

I shook my head. Thomas would be at work. Not that I felt like talking to him anyway. Dumond picked up the receiver and began punching in numbers.

As I helped Paul rinse his hair and dry off and get dressed, I could hear Dumond, calling his office and giving instructions; speaking in French to someone named Claude; getting a doctor's referral and, with calm insistence, making an appointment; and speaking with someone I assumed was the Ottawa police. Then he called someone else, speaking in voluble French, fast and emphatic, then slower and calming. He was just hanging up as we emerged from the bathroom.

"His nanny, Elise," he explained, eyes on

Paul. "She has been with Paul since he was a baby, and she came with me from Montreal, as my housekeeper. Now she can be a nanny again." I couldn't help but wonder if he was romantically involved with the nanny; he'd hardly have been the first.

Paul handed me the comb I'd bought him, and I ran it through his wet hair. Dumond watched, and I could see him noticing the worn lettering on the T-shirt and the faint grass stains on the jeans. "They're Mike Jr.'s," I said, a bit defensively. "Baker and Mike's son."

Dumond nodded. "*Paul, mon p'tit,* could you please go show your toys to Zach? *Veux-tu montrer tes jouets à Zach? Je pense qu'il veut les voir.* We will be down in a minute." Paul nodded, and walked carefully down the stairs, holding the railing as I'd shown him.

Dumond watched him go, and looked at me. "I want to head back to Ottawa today."

I nodded. Of course. Paul would go home to Canada with his father. My life would go on, minus one small child I hadn't known a week ago. "Did you want to see the police here?"

He shook his head. "No, we'll do that in Ottawa, tomorrow morning. The kidnapping took place in Canada."

"But the ferry," I pointed out. "That was in New York." State lines, I assumed, ran through the middle of lakes.

"I'd rather everything be coordinated by the Canadian police. They can work closely with the Montreal police; they can speak French with Paul; we'll be in our own country. It will be better for Paul to be home."

He stood. I felt the razor, cutting me out of their lives. Paul would remember the woman who rescued him, but to Dumond I was forgettable, expendable. It was a not unfamiliar feeling.

"I'd like to buy some clothes this morning before leaving, for Paul and myself." He gestured at the track suit he wore, smiling slightly, and I couldn't help but smile back. Of course he wouldn't be comfortable driving across the border in a borrowed track suit. Nor would he want to wear yesterday's crumpled Armani.

In the living room, Zach was delighting Paul by pretending not to understand how the bucket loader worked.

"So you turn this crank like this?" Zach fumbled with the truck.

"Non, non, non!" Paul declared, and with great deliberation showed Zach how to move the bucket arm up and down.

From the doorway, Dumond cleared his throat. "Paul, *mon fils,* we need to go shopping."

"*Shop-ping?*" Paul looked up, inquisitive. "*Pourquoi?*"

"Because you need some new clothes, my son. And so do I." He turned to me, "Do you know where to go?"

"The Gap on Main Street would probably have everything you'd need. If not, there are other clothing stores up there."

"Do you need to work, or can you go with us?"

"Um, no, don't have anything I have to do right now. Just a sec," I said. I ran upstairs for shoes and socks. On the way back down I realized I was ravenous, and stopped in the kitchen to slather peanut butter on a slice of bread to eat on the way.

CHAPTER 16

It's a quick walk to the Gap, about halfway up Main Street. Two boys from the track team I used to cover ran past, waving at me. As we passed the high school I pointed out the outdoor speedskating oval where Eric Heiden won his five gold medals in the 1980 Olympics, and then the arena where the U.S. hockey team had defeated the Soviets in the Miracle on Ice, en route to winning gold. Dumond nodded politely. Maybe he'd seen it before, or maybe he was, like me, underwhelmed by skating rinks where something exciting happened a long time ago. And a Canadian wouldn't likely be impressed by U.S. skating and hockey victories.

In the store Dumond quickly selected jeans, a pullover shirt, and a cotton sweater, emerging from the dressing room with Zach's warm-up suit in a neat bundle. The young clerk was ogling him as if he were a rock star. "I'd like to leave these on," he told her. She fell all over herself setting aside his price tags and the warm-up suit, and we went to the kids' floor downstairs.

I'd thought he'd get Paul one or two outfits, but Dumond apparently didn't do things by halves. He quickly acquired a stack of clothes. This was going to run into hundreds of dollars, even at a discounted outlet store. I shifted on my feet. "You know you may have to pay taxes on this at the border, and duty on anything not made in the States," I told him. I knew that Canadians here fewer than forty-eight hours get only a fifty-dollar exemption, although it was possible that children's clothing was exempt. Of course Paul had been here a lot longer, but Dumond wasn't going to announce that to border agents.

He shrugged. "We're here; we might as well get it now." He watched Paul eyeing a new jacket in front of the mirror. "I don't think many of his old things at home will fit."

Of course not. Paul had been gone since December — more than five months. Kids grow. Somehow I hadn't thought of that.

At Bass, across the street, Dumond selected leather shoes for Paul, and then at Eastern Mountain Sports he bought a duffel bag to hold all the new clothes, and Paul admired his new shoes as the clerk rang up the purchase. From the time we'd left my front door the whole expedition had taken just over an hour. Amazing how fast you can shop when you don't look at prices. Paul was wearing one of his new outfits, and now I was the worst dressed. But one of the reasons I like Lake Placid is that everyone dresses casually, so I fit right in.

We walked back to the house in silence, Paul skipping along between us, holding our hands. The sun was bright and it was one of those beautiful Adirondack days that make you grateful to be alive, a segment of life you want to hang on to forever. I could almost pretend this was real, that I had a partner and small son and was out for a walk with them.

On the front porch Paul turned to his father, his face creased in a frown. *"Est-ce qu'on retournera à Montréal?"* Are we going back to Montreal?

The porch swing creaked as Dumond sat on its edge. *"Non, nous allons retourner au Canada, mais pas à Montréal. J'ai acheté une nouvelle maison à Ottawa."* Not to Montreal, but to Ottawa, a new house.

The furrow between Paul's eyebrows disappeared. He emitted a burst of French too fast for me.

"Oui, oui, c'est vrai," Dumond said, pulling his son to him for a hug. His eyes met mine. "He says he is happy that we have moved, because now the bad men will not find him."

A lump grew in my throat. Paul had not, after all, shucked off what had happened to him. Of course not. This was no TV movie of the week, happy endings in two hours or less. This was real life, gritty and painful. He had a lot of adjusting ahead: new life, new city, new house. With no mother.

"I'll get his things together," I said. I went up to my rooms and stuffed the clothes he'd worn when I'd found him into a Gap bag, along with the things I'd bought him and, as an afterthought, my crayons and coloring book. I'd had them since I was a kid, but they'd only remind me of him. I wondered if Dumond would let me come visit, but it was, I thought, more likely he'd want his son to put all this behind him.

As I turned toward the stairs, Dumond was coming up. I held the bag toward him, but he didn't take it.

"I'd like you to come with us," he said.

I blinked, not understanding. Suddenly I remembered my car was in Ottawa — of course I'd have to go get it. "Oh, right, my car."

"No, I mean I'd like you to stay with us awhile, in Ottawa." I couldn't hide my surprise. "Yes, we have Elise, the nanny, but Paul has gotten very attached to you, and I think it will help him adjust to have you with us."

I stared at him.

"It's a big house," he said, meeting my gaze. "You can bring your dog. And I'll compensate you for your time."

I shook my head. "No, no. It's not that. I can do most of my work wherever I am." A moment ticked by. My brain raced. Me with Paul and his father, in Ottawa. Surely it would be better for me to break with Paul now — a clean, sharp pain, back to my solitary life. But I knew I wasn't going to.

"All right," I said. Dumond nodded, as if he'd expected nothing less. Maybe he hadn't.

It took less than ten minutes to pack: laptop, clothes, passport, leash, dog food, Tiger's rabies inoculation certificate, and my little digital Canon. No room for my bike, but I could survive without it for a while. While Dumond carried my bags out to the car, I speed-dialed Thomas's home number, knowing he wouldn't be there. The coward's way out, but you can't always take the high road.

"Hi, it's me," I said to the recorder. "Everything's fine; I'm . . . um . . . I'm going to be out of town for a few days, but you can reach me by email and I'll, well, I'll try to call." I hung up guiltily. Thomas deserved better than this. Thomas deserved the girlfriend I was unable to be. Next I called Baker, who wasn't home either. Another easy out. She'd already done her best to talk me out of going to Ottawa once and might try again. I told her answering machine I was going to Ottawa with Paul and his father and would call later, and would get the borrowed clothing back to her when I returned. I stuck a note on the fridge for Zach and locked the door to my rooms.

Paul and his father were waiting by the car, Paul apparently having assumed all along that I was going with them. In his bright new world, of course the woman who rescued you and delivered your father to you accompanied you to your new home. Paul hopped into the back, with Tiger beside him on an old comforter. Dumond drove smoothly out of town, remembering the turns without my prompting him.

In an odd way it felt right, sitting here in

this car, leaving Lake Placid behind, listening to Paul murmur to Tiger in the backseat. Like I was heading to a new adventure.

At the border Dumond told the customs inspector that we were returning to Ottawa after visiting Lake Placid. She glanced at our passports and Tiger's rabies certificate. Dumond told her he'd bought some children's clothing, and she waved him through. We pulled into Canada and stopped in Cornwall at a Harvey's for burgers and fries, the image, I suppose, of a happy little family. Soon after we left Cornwall I fell asleep, and didn't awaken until we exited from the Queensway into Ottawa.

■ ■ ■ ■

PART II

■ ■ ■ ■

"The more relaxed you are the
easier it is to stay afloat."
— *from a Learn to Swim blog*

CHAPTER 17

It felt more than a little odd to be climbing out of the Mercedes at the Tudor house I'd arrived at with the same man just over twenty-four hours ago. Like the old Bill Murray movie *Groundhog Day,* where you're doomed to live the same day over until you get it right. Here we were again, this time bringing home the missing child.

Maybe this time everything would be fine.

The sound of our car doors closing behind us was sharp. I was acutely aware of our footsteps crunching against the flat stones of the driveway, of the leaves of the trees around us fluttering in the breeze. Paul was clinging to his father's hand, with Dumond leaning over, speaking to him as they walked toward the house. The door opened and in the doorway I saw a spare sixtyish woman, gray hair pulled back, her entire body radiating anxiety. Paul pulled his hand free from his father's and ran into her arms. She was mouthing his name, over and over. Her face broke and tears streamed down her cheeks.

So much for my notion that Dumond could have been involved with the nanny-turned-housekeeper. She looked up at us as we reached them. *It was a mistake to come here,* I thought. She was Paul's life, past and future. I was the interloper.

Dumond spoke. "Elise, this is Troy Chance, who found Paul for us. Troy, this is Paul's nanny, Elise."

The woman released Paul and pulled me to her in a rough, hard hug. I sensed an enormous amount of emotion, so much she was barely keeping it contained. She didn't say anything and didn't look me in the face, but I knew it was because her feelings were so intense. She turned back to Paul and began chattering in rapid-fire French. They headed off together — toward the kitchen for cookies and milk, I supposed, likely the first line of treatment when lost boy returns home. I felt a pang of something uncomfortably like jealousy.

But this was his nanny, his father, his home. What I had given him had been great compared to being locked up in a room for months, but nothing like the life he was supposed to have.

When I turned to Dumond I saw something flicker across his face, and knew that what I was feeling was infinitesimal compared to his pain. Watching your long-lost son marching away with the nanny without a backward look must be the moment when you long to erase the long hours and late nights at work, wish for an Etch A Sketch moment when you shake the box, erase everything, and start over.

But now he had that second chance — with his son at least.

As their footsteps died away he spoke: "Elise has been with Paul since he was born."

I made an *Mmm* noise to try to convey *That's great* and *I understand.* He spoke again. "She's always blamed herself for Paul being taken. She thinks if she had been there that day she could have protected him."

I blinked, envisioning the tiny nanny trying to fight off kidnappers. "But she couldn't have —"

"I know," he said, picking up my bag. "But logic doesn't come into it. I know all about that. Let me show you your room."

Tiger and I followed him. We passed Paul's room and reached a spacious room with large windows and sunlight streaming

153

in. It had a queen-sized bed, light wood floors, and Shaker-style furniture. Just what I might choose if I earned ten times what I did. "I think this has everything you might need," Dumond said, waving vaguely toward an attached bathroom. I could see it was equipped with hair dryer and bottles of lotion, like a fancy health spa.

"Make yourself at home," he said. "If you need anything, ask Elise — you'll find the kitchen to the left of the front foyer. I'm going to show Paul around the house, and we'll have dinner in an hour or so."

I'd assumed he would take Paul straight to the police station, but he'd planned that for after a visit to the doctor tomorrow morning. Dumond was, I think, used to getting his way. I sat on the bed and bounced once or twice: a firm mattress, just what I like.

Okay, this was awkward. But there's no handy guide for introducing your motherless five-months-kidnapped son to a new life. Although maybe step one would be *Have the person who rescues your son come home with you to help out.*

I looked around the room. I like staying in guest rooms and hotels, nesting in miniature, setting up my things in a new space. I unpacked everything and set my laptop bag near the desk. This took about five minutes. I folded the comforter from the car beside the bed, where I could pretend Tiger would be sleeping instead of with me. She sat on it, watching me.

Sitting here seemed too Jane Eyre-ish, too much like a governess awaiting a summons. New Troy wouldn't hide away meekly — she would open the door and step out of the room. So I did.

I passed Paul's room and stifled the urge to unpack his bag of new clothes. *Not my house, not my kid.* This would have to be my inner mantra while I was here.

I wandered into the living room and dining room, which were tastefully furnished, but too austere for me. I perched on the leather sofa: comfortable, but cold. I wondered if Dumond's wife had picked out this furniture. I saw nothing remotely personal: no piles of magazines, no photos, no knick-knacks. But maybe they would be too-painful reminders of missing wife and child.

Then I found the library, which I loved instantly: built-in bookshelves, a fireplace of rounded stones, and stuffed sofa and chairs you could disappear in. I walked the length of the shelves, running my fingers along the spines of the books. They were new and old mixed in together — fiction, nonfiction,

English, French. I saw a French version of *The Count of Monte Cristo,* a book I'd fallen in love with around age twelve.

So the house did have some personality — and presumably its owner did as well. Greatly cheered, I wandered on. I found the state-of-the-art kitchen I'd expected, with a marble-topped center island and rows of gleaming pots and pans overhead. Elise, busy at a mixing bowl, looked up.

"Troy," she said, the *r* sound making it clear she was a native French speaker. "Your room is good, eh?" It's the uvula, the little thing that hangs down the back of your throat, that lets French speakers make that trilling *r.* For us English-speakers, it just hangs there uselessly.

"Oh, yes, it's great," I said quickly. "It's wonderful."

"Would you like anything? A snack, something to drink?" she asked, setting the spoon down.

"No, no, I'm fine. I was just — Paul's father told me to look around."

"It's a very nice house. It will be a good home for Paul." Her next question caught me off guard. "Where Paul was, where Paul was kept, was it very bad?"

My throat tightened. I had no idea how much Dumond had told her about Paul's

156

captivity or what he wanted her to know. I sat on a stool before I answered. "I don't really know. I mean . . . he told me only a little, but, no, I don't think it was very nice."

She dumped the dough on the counter-top. "Paul will be happy here. He will forget the bad things."

I didn't know what to say. Yes, Paul probably would be happy here, but he would never forget the bad things. I saw her eyes were bright with unshed tears, and realized she knew all this. "Yes," I said gently. "He will be happy here."

She shoved at the dough. "Paul likes you."

I shrugged. "I was the first person he met. I think he would have liked anyone."

"No. He likes you especially. He told me you saved him." Her voice broke. I blinked, my throat tight. She looked up from the dough she was assaulting, and somehow her look said *We are in this together.* I had rescued the child she loved.

I stood. Suddenly I wanted to see Paul and his father. "I think I'll go find the guys."

"They are up in Monsieur Dumond's room, I think." She nodded in the direction of the spiral staircase I'd seen yesterday.

At the base of the stairs I called out, "Hello?"

"Troy!" Paul answered. *"Viens! Jouons à*

157

l'ordinateur."

My sneakers squeaked on the metal steps. As I reached the top Dumond called out, and I could see the two of them in an attached room at the back of a large bedroom. I walked past furniture similar to that in my room, with darker bedding and a moody painting of a seascape. Then I was in an office with a built-in desk that stretched the width of the room. Paul was playing Tetris on a computer with a huge flat-panel monitor.

"Regardez, Troy," he exclaimed, bouncing on his chair. *"C'est mon jeu préféré!"*

Dumond, in a chair off to the side, caught my eye. "Yes, Paul always liked playing this game on my computer," he said. I watched Paul maneuver the colorful falling blocks as they came faster and faster, eyes intent on the screen, fingers poised on the keyboard. If you're fast enough, you can line the blocks up into a tidy wall. One misstep, and your wall has holes you can never fill.

A discreet beep sounded from Dumond's pocket, and he pulled out his phone and glanced at it. He excused himself and stepped out of the room.

When I turned back to Paul, a small silver-framed photo on the far end of the long desk caught my attention. I could see it was

Madeleine, with a younger and smaller Paul laughing into the camera; she was laughing as well, one hand holding down that honey-blond hair to try to keep it from being blown in the wind. I felt abrupt nausea: it seemed I was trespassing, here in this room with this woman's family.

A minute later Dumond reappeared. "I must make some business calls," he said apologetically. I stood up quickly. "Perhaps — would you mind? Paul might like your help setting up his room."

"Of course," I said. "Paul, sweetie, let's go unpack some of your things. *Paul, viens avec moi, s'il te plaît.*" His gaze was locked on the screen and the little falling blocks, but as soon as my words penetrated he flicked off the game and followed me. I wondered if he had always been this obedient, or if this was how an abducted child would act — a little too eager to please.

There was so much I didn't know.

CHAPTER 18

The sun was sending shafts of late-afternoon light across Paul's bedroom, seeming to welcome us as we stepped across the threshold. Paul walked around the room slowly, running his hand along each piece of furniture. He knelt beside one of the open boxes and began pulling out toys and inspecting them, as if greeting each one: *Hello, this is Paul, and I am back.* When he'd emptied the first box, he moved on to the next and began pulling out clothing.

I sensed another presence and turned to see Elise in the doorway. She smiled shakily. "I wasn't . . ." she said in a low voice. "I wasn't sure if any of his things would fit him. But we brought everything from Montreal."

I flashed to an image of the two of them, father and nanny, packing Paul's clothing and toys into boxes that might never be opened. Of course they couldn't have gotten rid of them, just as they hadn't been able to unpack them. Maybe years later they would have donated them or moved them to an attic. I wondered if Madeleine's things were packed away as well, in boxes stashed in a closet in Dumond's room.

"It's okay," I said softly. "It's good he has them all, even if they don't fit. Later he can get rid of things if he wants."

The pain in Elise's face was stark. "I have been with Paul since he was a baby," she whispered.

"I know. I know." My throat caught. She stared past me, tears welling, then murmured something about dinner and left.

Paul looked up. "How's it going?" I asked. *"Comment ça va?"*

He nodded solemnly and turned back to the box of clothes. Next he opened a box of books and began to thumb through each one. The room was starting to look like a rummage sale in progress. I moved closer and gestured at the bookcase, and Paul began handing me books one by one to place on the shelves.

"How goes it?" Dumond asked from the doorway. I jumped.

"Salut, Papa, je mets mes livres sur l'étagère," Paul replied, without looking up.

"No, I think it is Troy who is putting the

books on the shelf," Dumond said, smiling. "And I think it is only polite to speak English when Troy is here. *Nous devrions parler anglais quand Troy est ici.*"

Sitting back on his heels, Paul shook his hair out of his eyes and smiled at his father. "Okay, Papa. I try." Surrounded by piles of clothes and toys, he looked like any child in a messy room. It seemed impossible he had been gone so long.

Paul returned to the box of books, rooting through it as if looking for something in particular. Dumond picked up a toy car, and idly spun one of the wheels. He watched his son stash toys in the closet, in a dresser drawer, but none in the big toy box. Maybe it was Paul's way of defining his space. Or hiding his toys so no one could find them.

And then it was time for dinner.

We ate in the fancy dining room; Elise served but didn't eat with us. It made me think of old Agatha Christie novels, where nearly everyone had servants. But no one objected when Tiger tucked herself neatly under the table.

Paul emptied his bowl of rich vegetable beef soup and ate two steaming, buttery rolls. Apparently Elise had been transferring her unused nanny energies to cooking. When the main course arrived — salmon, with broccoli — Paul stared at his plate, then looked up unhappily. He shifted in his chair.

"Paul, what is it?" asked Dumond.

"Papa, I cannot eat," he whispered. *"Je n'ai pas faim maintenant. Est-ce que je peux le garder pour plus tard?"* A lone tear ran down his cheek.

A silent, frozen moment, broken by the rasp of Dumond's chair on the floor, and then he was at Paul's side, turning his son toward him and cupping his face in his hands.

"Paul, of course you can save it. There is no reason to be sad. Elise will understand that you are full," he said, and repeated it in French. "Let's take this to Elise in the kitchen and ask her to wrap it up for us." He picked up the plate and led Paul toward the kitchen.

I picked at one of the rolls on my bread plate, appetite suddenly gone.

Dumond came back alone and sat down. "Elise is going to help him get ready for bed. I should have realized that he isn't used to large meals. But I don't understand why he was so upset."

I twisted in my seat, figuring how to explain this. "He's been gone a long time; he wants to please you."

He frowned; he wasn't getting it.

I tried again. "Look, the kidnappers made him think you didn't want him. They probably told him you were angry with him or didn't like him. They do that — tell kids their parents don't want them, or that they're dead." I've read the grim articles; it's hard to miss them.

Dumond shut his eyes. I imagined he was seeing Paul locked up, wondering why his father didn't come rescue him. Because at six, you think your father can do anything.

"Does he believe I didn't want him, that I wasn't looking for him? That I wouldn't have given anything to get him back?" His voice was harsh, a mix of anguish and rage.

I blinked back the moisture gathering in my eyes. "It's what they told him," I whispered. "That's all he's known for months. And kids always think that bad things that happen to them are their fault."

Dumond sat for a long moment. "You have no children." Not quite a question.

"No." I wasn't going to discuss my sisters' children, needy kids at a shelter, other kids I'd known. Or tell him that I understood Paul a little better than he did right now, that the Paul he'd gotten back wasn't the same child he had lost months ago and in some ways never would be again. Although maybe he knew.

He picked up his fork. "I'll tell Paul those men lied to him, that I never stopped looking for him. And I'll have the pediatrician recommend a therapist, psychologist, whatever he needs." Dumond ate a few bites before speaking again. "And you, what did you think?"

I blinked. "What do you mean? Think about what?"

"When you located me. You could have telephoned me, you could have asked the police to contact me. Instead, you came to Ottawa."

The salmon that had seemed so delicious suddenly was Styrofoam in my mouth. I swallowed with difficulty. "I didn't know if I could trust you."

He looked at me, eyebrows raised.

"I didn't know . . . if you were involved somehow." He looked shocked, and I wished I hadn't decided to be this honest. "It can happen," I blurted. "It has happened. People want out of their marriage, don't want to pay alimony, whatever. They arrange to have a spouse gotten rid of, or kids, too."

Dumond stared at me. "Look, I didn't know you," I said, my voice rising. "And my brother's a cop; he tells me stories that would set your hair on end."

We finished dinner with no more conversation. The broccoli was cold, but we ate it anyway. We skipped dessert and walked to Paul's room, Tiger padding after us.

Paul looked well scrubbed, his damp hair combed neatly. He was wearing one of his new T-shirts with snug stretchy pajama bottoms Elise must have found among his old things. Pajamas were one thing I hadn't thought of getting him, probably because I don't own any — I sleep in a T-shirt and old gym shorts, or sweats if it's cold. I gave Paul a hug.

"Sleep tight, cowboy," I said. "I'll see you in the morning. *Je te verrai le matin.*" He surprised me with a tiny kiss on my cheek.

Dumond replaced me at Paul's side, tickling him and then leaning over and whispering in his ear. Paul smiled sleepily, happily. Dumond settled himself next to Paul on the small bed and looked up.

"I will stay until Paul falls asleep," he said. I nodded and turned to go. He was Paul's father; I was a pseudo-temporary-nanny. It was to be expected.

Dumond's voice stopped me at the door. "Troy, thank you."

I looked back at him, next to his son, the two dark heads close together: Paul's eyes

166

closed, angelically young and relaxed; Dumond looking tired, but at peace. Maybe I didn't belong in this scene, but I had helped bring it about.

CHAPTER 19

Morning was a semblance of normalcy, or at least what I assume is normal in a household with a small child and a housekeeper. We ate steaming oatmeal and French toast and sipped fresh-ground coffee, which was astoundingly better than the stuff I made with my paper-towel-drip method. I'd always been scornful of the allure of money, but I was fast seeing the advantages.

The dose of reality came when Paul perversely decided to wear some of his old clothes and squeezed into a snug long-sleeved polo shirt and jeans so tight he could barely fasten the top snap. Elise called me into his room and we consulted *sotto voce*, Paul close to sullen and looking mutinous. I knelt and put my hands on his shoulders.

"Paul," I said, looking into his eyes, "these are nice clothes. But I think your papa will feel bad if you don't wear some of your new things." I repeated it in French, as best I could.

He looked dubious, then squirmed. The jeans had to be cutting off circulation around his small middle. His face brightened. "New pants, same shirt?" he asked, making his eyes wide.

I nodded. "That's a very good idea," I said, handing him a new pair of jeans. Elise and I stepped out so we wouldn't witness his struggle to peel off the old ones.

Dumond blinked at the sight of the too-small shirt, Paul's thin wrists showing, but just reached in the hall closet and pulled out a light jacket. "Get your jacket, Paul — *va chercher ton veston,*" he said matter-of-factly, and Paul ran back to his room for his new windbreaker. Dumond winked at me, and put his hand on Elise's back, murmuring something near her ear.

In the crowded waiting room I read old copies of *Ottawa* magazine, learning more than I wanted to know about people I hadn't known were Ottawans: Dan Aykroyd, Mike Myers, Alanis Morissette. I flipped through battered copies of *Highlights* for the Goofus and Gallant cartoon. Gallant was polite and good and neat; Goofus was sloppy and rude. But he had mellowed from the naughty fellow I remembered, and was

169

now only mildly ill-behaved.

I was trying hard to ignore the fear churning inside me: that Paul had been sexually abused, which was why the kidnappers had kept him so long. I expected it was what we all feared. I was nearly desperate enough to pick up a copy of *Marie Claire* when they emerged, Dumond's arm around his son's shoulders, Paul sucking a lollipop. "A clean bill of health," Dumond said. As Paul stepped into the elevator, Dumond moved closer, squeezed my shoulders lightly, and said the three magic words in my ear: *No sexual abuse.*

My face must have shown how much this had been eating at me, how I had needed to know. I hadn't expected this insight and compassion from Dumond, which shows what a reverse snob I am. Because someone is rich and attractive and successful, apparently I think they can't be human. Which made me feel pretty small.

As we drove to the police station my stomach was in knots. Now I'd have to explain officially why I hadn't taken Paul straight to authorities.

Paul looked up from the backseat when we pulled into the underground parking area. Dumond turned off the ignition and twisted around to face him. "Paul, we are going to talk to the police so they can catch the bad men who took you," he said, and repeated it in French.

Paul looked blank, a look I recognized as his *hear no evil, see no evil* face. When things are happening you can't understand or don't want to deal with, just shut down. It may not be the best way to deal with things, but it works. With a pang I realized the petulance over his clothes this morning had been the most normal six-year-old reaction I'd seen from him.

"It's okay, Paul," I added. "No one will hurt you, and your papa will be right there."

Paul looked uneasily at me. Dumond forced a laugh. "Yes, the policemen will be very nice to you and if they are not I will bark at them, like Tiger. *Arrrrf! Arrrrf!*" Paul's lips twitched. "And I will be there," Dumond said as he swung the car door open.

God, we were winging this, I thought as we walked in, Paul clasping our hands. He was trusting us, but he was still scared, like a dog you've rescued from the animal shelter. Every time we went somewhere he was, I think, a little afraid he was going to end up back in his prison.

At the front counter Dumond asked for the detective he'd been talking to.

"What's this in reference to, sir?" asked a policewoman in a crisp blue uniform, a slender black woman with precise British intonation. One of the things I like about Ottawa is the apparently seamless mix of nationalities and races. Although of course Canadians have their own biases.

"The kidnapping of my son, last year, whom we have now found." Dumond was holding Paul's hand firmly.

The woman blinked, probably wondering if a set of nutcases had just wandered in.

"Detective Jameson should be expecting us. I told him we'd be in this morning."

Another polite blink, a polite smile. This woman wasn't stupid. This was important, or at least more than she could handle. "Just a moment, please," she said, picking up the phone and murmuring into it.

Almost as soon as she had hung up, a man appeared. His suit was rumpled without quite being wrinkled and his hair looked as if he had a habit of running his fingers through it. He shook Dumond's hand, murmured a greeting, nodded at Paul. Then he turned to me.

"This is Troy Chance, of Lake Placid, New York," Dumond said. "She found my son, Paul. Troy, this is Detective Jameson."

His pale eyes assessed me, impersonally,

coldly. My stomach did a loop-the-loop. Now I couldn't ignore what I hadn't verbalized even to myself: to a policeman's brain, this didn't look good. Because I hadn't gone straight to the police, I must be involved. *Cherchez la femme,* so to speak. Only I was the *femme,* and here I was, walking straight into the spider's web. To mix a couple of metaphors.

Jameson nodded at me, and led us down a hallway. He paused at an open door and said, "Miss Chance, if you'd wait here, please."

I gave Paul's hand a little squeeze as I released it, and knelt to give him a quick hug. "I will see you in a little while," I told him. *"Je te verrai bientôt."* He clung a half beat longer and tighter than normal. Just when I was starting to think I was going to have to pry him loose, Dumond gently tugged him away and swung him onto his hip, a comforting arm loosely around him.

"We'll see you soon, Troy," he said cheerily.

The room was as institutional as you'd expect: table, metal chairs, a bookcase with thick uninviting tomes, a cabinet with a fat padlock. I sat in one of the metal chairs. I fidgeted. I inspected my fingernails. I thought about trying the door. I considered getting a dusty book from the shelves and reading about Canadian jurisprudence.

This is the warm-up time, I figured, to get you ready to confess or so uncomfortable you'll talk freely. *But all I have to do is tell the truth,* I reminded myself. I hadn't done anything wrong — not much anyway.

The door swung open and two neatly dressed and crisply groomed men stepped in, one Caucasian and the other dark-skinned and shorter — Pakistani, I thought.

The basics were simple: name, age, citizenship, address, occupation. Although after I answered "freelance writer" to the job question, their pause prompted me to babble, "I write for magazines, mostly sports magazines, some airline ones, and I do some work for the local newspaper."

"Do you live with anyone, Miss Chance?" This was the Pakistani policeman.

"Well, yes, I have several roommates." Then I had to list them — and because Dave had just moved in I couldn't remember his last name, so made something up rather than admit I didn't know. Then their occupations, which sounded more than mildly bohemian even to me. Zach paints houses and does yard work. Ben is a waiter. Dave works at a sports shop. Patrick seems not to work at all, but has an amazing talent for scrounging free meals, free lift tickets, free concert passes. It probably didn't help that right now all the roommates are guys. So much for sounding respectable.

"Is one of these men your partner?" the shorter man asked. They'd told me their names, but I'd forgotten them. I looked at him uncomprehendingly.

"Partner, boyfriend, lover," snapped the other, in the first show of impatience I'd seen.

Okay, gloves off. I sat up straighter. "No. I'm dating Dr. Thomas Rouse, a professor at the University of Vermont in Burlington."

I'd been incredibly naïve not to have realized I'd be considered a suspect. I'd expected to get reprimanded for not reporting the near-drowning right away — and figured the New York police could charge me with something — but none of this. Never mind that I'd thought of several horrible ways Dumond could have been involved; it was a shock that anyone could imagine equally grim scenarios for me. Me, whose worse crime is a tendency to jaywalk and reuse unpostmarked postage stamps.

The detectives were far more polite than, say, *NYPD Blue* detectives — no Andy Sipowicz screaming, threatening, or table-banging — but they were thorough. And tedious. Apparently if you ask a question enough times, *ad infinitum,* people eventually tire and tell the truth: Did you rob the bank? *No.* Did you rob the bank? *No.* Did you rob the bank? *Oh, okay, I did.* They kept asking the same questions over and over, particularly about the leap off the ferry.

You jumped off the ferry?

Yes, I jumped off the ferry.

Why did you jump off the ferry?

Because I saw Paul go in the water.

How did Paul go into the water?

Apparently someone threw him in.

You jumped off the ferry?

And of course they wanted to know why I hadn't immediately gone to the police. There was no easy answer to this, and I wasn't going to trot out sad stories of abused children I'd known or bad foster homes I'd heard about. No point in sounding like an Oprah show. So I stuck to the basics.

I was tired. We were cold, we were wet. I wanted to get home.

I wanted to let Paul get comfortable before we went to the police.

I thought it'd be better to find his father first.

As soon as I located his father, I went to see him.

I didn't call his father because I was afraid

he'd think it was a hoax.

I told my story, over and over. The policemen wrote down ferry schedules and names and phone numbers. They asked if I swam competitively, and I nearly laughed aloud, thinking of the Monday night triathlons. They were polite, but seemed to think it impossible to survive the chill waters of Lake Champlain as long as we had. They were probably right, but here we were, alive and well.

By now Elise's hearty breakfast seemed a long way away. I was beginning to feel dizzy. "Could I have some coffee?" I asked.

They glanced at each other. "In a little while," Tall Cop said.

Suddenly I'd had enough. I scooted my chair back from the table, and the skittering noise on the floor made them jump. "No," I said, surprising even myself. "I would like it now. Coffee, double cream. And something to eat, please."

They seemed taken aback by my defiance, but brought me coffee and a doughnut that tasted like a stale Krispy Kreme, a particularly greasy kind I thought you could get only in the South. I ate it, and drank the coffee with its awful fake creamer — this was Canada; they should be getting their coffee and doughnuts from Tim Hortons.

Maybe they did, but kept the good stuff for themselves.

Then they started again, more insistently.

They asked more about how I made a living. What was my monthly income? No pension and retirement plan? Finally they went off, presumably to call Baker, consult Jameson or whoever was interviewing Paul, and check my bank account for fat deposits. Then back they came, to ask me the questions all over again, with various permutations. When had I met Philippe Dumond? Why had I disliked Madeleine? How much was I paid? I answered steadfastly and calmly, but I was beginning to understand how false confessions happen. *Yes, yes, I did it all, just shut up and leave me alone!*

For extra credit in university I'd taken a psychological test called the MMPI, the Minnesota Multiphasic Personality Inventory. Among the hundreds of questions were occasional bizarre ones, like *Do you ever feel you have a band of intense pain around your head?* or *Have you ever had a desire to kill someone?* Occasionally a question was repeated, to make sure you weren't answering randomly, the examiner told me later. This felt like that test, but longer and more intense, and I couldn't quit and go home whenever I wanted.

Suddenly something in me said, *This has gone on long enough.* Perhaps I hadn't used the best judgment, but I had, after all, risked my own stupid life to save Paul. I straightened up. "Gentlemen," I said, "I've answered all your questions, several times. Now I would either like to leave, or make a phone call."

I refused to speak again. Perhaps, I thought as they left the room, I should have asked for a lawyer from the start. But it seems that only guilty people demand a lawyer right away. On *Law & Order,* anyway. I never once realized I could have called the U.S. embassy — it's easy to forget Canada is a foreign country.

The door opened. Jameson walked in, expression blank, carrying a squat black telephone with cord dangling. He plugged it into an outlet in the wall, put it in front of me, and pulled out a chair and sat.

"The phone." His voice was flat, his face expressionless.

He seemed to be daring me to ask him to leave. But I wasn't in the mood to play games, and didn't care if he overheard me. I pulled my card of important phone numbers out of my wallet, and hoped my brother would be at his desk.

I punched in the numbers. "Simon Chance, please. Troy Chance calling." Because I was calling him at work, Simon would know it was important. Then I heard his voice: clear, decisive, hugely comforting.

"Troy, what's up?"

"Simon, I'm at the city police station in Ottawa, Ontario," I said. "I found a young boy in New York, who turned out to have been kidnapped. I returned him to his father here, and now police have been questioning me for several hours."

Pause. Simon was remembering our earlier conversation. He'd be pissed off, but he'd forgive me. "Have you been charged with anything?"

"No. At least they haven't said anything. But I'm tired and hungry and I've told them everything I know, and I want to leave."

Another pause. "Is there someone there I can speak to?"

I held out the phone to Jameson. "My brother would like to speak to you." His expression didn't change, but he took the phone.

Having a brother who is a policeman, a young and undistinguished one in the States at that, shouldn't make much of a difference, but it did. Simon spoke volubly and Jameson answered tersely, but when he handed me back the phone his manner wasn't quite as cold.

"Troy," Simon said, "listen, how soon do you need me there?"

"Look, Si, you don't need to come up —"

"Where are you staying?"

"I'm with Paul, the boy, and his father, at their home here in Ottawa."

A half-beat pause. "Give me the phone number there and I'll call you with my flight information. I've got frequent-flyer points and plenty of use-or-lose vacation days. It won't cost me a dime."

I recited Dumond's name and phone number. I owed Simon, and if that meant tolerating him swinging into Protective Big Brother mode, so be it. And to say that I was out of my comfort zone would be putting it mildly.

Jameson met my eyes as I clicked the receiver into place. "You can leave now, but we would like to talk to you again."

"Fine. I'm not going anywhere." I was exhausted.

On the way out of the room Jameson turned abruptly, pulled a card from his wallet, and scrawled across the back with a fat black pen. He handed it to me. "If you think of anything, call me. The office number's on the front, home on the back."

I blinked, confused.

He repeated, looking straight at me, "If you think of anything, if there's anything I need to know." I was too tired to try to figure out what he meant, and slid the card in my wallet.

CHAPTER 20

Dumond and Paul were waiting on the thinly padded chairs in the lobby, Paul playing with a little plastic figurine.

"You shouldn't have stayed," I told Dumond. I glanced at the clock on the wall — it was later than I had thought. "I could have called you or taken a bus."

Dumond looked at me as if I'd said something incredibly stupid. Maybe I had.

"Troy, *regardez,* from McDonald's," Paul said, waggling the toy, a character from a recent animated movie. One more thing for him to catch up on — you can't fit in with other kids without knowing every popular movie character, especially ones with Happy Meal status.

Dumond gave me that wry *What's a father to do?* look. Hey, if my kid I hadn't seen for more than five months wanted to go to McDonald's, we'd go to McDonald's. As we pulled out of the parking lot Dumond called

Elise to tell her we were on our way.

"How was it?" he asked me, after he switched off the phone.

"Okay, just tiring." I closed my eyes for a moment, aware that Paul could hear us. "And repetitious." The car moved silently through the thickening traffic. I opened my eyes. "Oh, my brother, Simon, is probably flying up."

"Your brother?"

"Yeah. He's a policeman, in Orlando. I called him for some advice, and he decided he wanted to be here. Probably just for a day or two." He didn't press me. We were both tired. And hungry. Somehow I doubted Dumond had eaten anything at McDonald's.

The smell of dinner cooking when we stepped into the house was enormously comforting. Paul threw himself to the floor to hug Tiger, then ran off to the kitchen to greet Elise. It would take him a long time to take all this for granted, I thought. If he ever did.

Dumond followed, I assumed to tell Elise the results of the visit to the doctor.

There were three of us now: father, nanny, rescuer, all here to protect and support Paul. Maybe there had been other supporters, back in Montreal, or maybe no one else had been let into the loop because of the kidnappers' threats. Or maybe Dumond was the type of person who liked to march on alone — not that much unlike me.

Which was about all the insight I could handle for one day.

Elise had made a stew and homemade whole-grain bread, and served Paul small helpings he could easily finish. He was tired, eyelids drooping, and Dumond sent him off with Elise to get ready for bed.

When I went in to tell him good night, he was pink and fresh from his bath, and his hug was tight. Less than ten minutes later Dumond joined me in the library for dessert and coffee; Paul had fallen asleep in the middle of his bedtime story.

Dessert was homemade blackberry pie topped with whipped cream — the real stuff, not the gunk that squirts out of a can. I nearly groaned when the first mouthful hit my taste buds. We ate in silence until Dumond spoke. "So tell me about your brother."

I finished my last smidgen of pie. "Simon — he's a year older than me. He's a little worried and he has some vacation days, so he wants to come up." I didn't want it to sound like Simon was suspicious of Philippe, although of course he was.

"If I had a sister, I'd do the same," he said easily. "Of course he'll stay here."

"Thanks." I was relieved. "If I know Simon, he'll be here soon."

"That's fine. I have to take Paul back to the police station tomorrow to work with a sketch artist on pictures of the kidnappers."

"He saw their faces?"

He nodded. "Apparently they wore bandannas when they came in his room, but he said if he lay on the floor and looked under the door he could see them across the room. And once the lock didn't catch and he got out and saw them both briefly."

I asked the question that had been nagging at me. "Are the police worried they may know he survived, and track him down?" I had found Dumond easily; they could, too.

He shook his head. "They doubt that anyone could have seen you rescue him because of visibility and the distance between the ferries. If we were still in Montreal, they might see that Paul is back. But here it's not likely."

Not likely wasn't particularly comforting. And eventually word would leak out. Someone would ask Dumond about his family; Elise would let something slip. The kidnappers were presumably from Montreal, not outer space.

"Of course we can't hide him away, but we'll try to keep it quiet until the kidnappers are found," Dumond said. "They wanted him to work on the sketch today, but I thought he'd had enough. He was tired and worried about you — he kept asking where you were."

I made a face. "I was worried about me, too — they seemed to think I was involved. But all they had to do was call Baker or my roommates or even ask Paul. The worst part was the ferry — they had a lot of trouble believing I dived off the ferry."

"Yes," Dumond said, sipping his coffee. "That was the part I didn't believe either."

"That I dived off the ferry?"

"That you could see him that far away, that you could swim that far, that you'd take such a risk when you weren't even sure it was a child."

I looked at him wordlessly. He smiled, crinkling his face. "Paul tells us you appeared from nowhere to rescue him, like magic — he thought you were an angel, or a mermaid, like Ariel, except that you had legs instead of a tail. And now that I've met you and your dozens of roommates and your Baker friends, yes, I believe you would dive off a ferry because you might have seen a child fall in the water."

It was hard to remember I had found this man intimidating. I grinned. "I don't have dozens of roommates. Only four, sometimes five."

"And all male."

"Right now they are. Sometimes I get a female, but guys are easier. Messier, but easier."

He raised his eyebrows. "Guys leave more stuff lying around and don't wash their dishes, especially the younger ones," I explained. "But women either want to be in charge or want to be friends. Or both."

"What's wrong with that? You're friends with Zach."

"Yeah, but with him it's easy. If I come home and I'm tired and don't want to talk, I go to my room and he doesn't care if I ignore him. But a female roommate always wants to know what's wrong and if you're mad at her, or what's going on."

Dumond laughed. "Yes, well, you've captured the essence of marriage right there."

As his laughter died away, we fell silent. For a moment, I had forgotten that this time last year he had had a wife and Paul had had a mother, and this seemed unforgivable.

188

He cleared his throat. "I haven't properly thanked you. For saving Paul. For diving off the ferry and rescuing Paul like an angel mermaid," he said, with a semblance of his former whimsy.

"Ça n'est rien," I said. *It's nothing.* No one could understand that I'd made no conscious decision to save Paul, that I'd followed a compulsion too strong to resist.

His eyes moved to mine. "You saved his life, at the risk of your own. You could have died. You both could have died." We sat in silence. "And I am also sorry," he added.

My confusion showed. "For what?"

"For yesterday, in my office." I was still confused. He grimaced and reached toward me, touching his fingertips to my throat.

I had to refrain from leaping in my seat. His touch felt like a jolt of static electricity. I'd almost forgotten the incident in his office, and now I felt it all again: the crackling intensity, the frightening intimacy. I couldn't speak or move. The air around us seemed to tighten. I could hear his breath, almost feel the rhythm of his pulse. He took my hand loosely, not quite holding it, not quite shaking it. It was a struggle to breathe normally. *Remember this man is not your type,* I told myself. *Remember he recently lost his wife. Remember he is so far out of your league it isn't funny. Remember, remember, remember.*

I'd broken my habit of falling for unsuitable men. I really, really had.

"Don't worry about it," I said, speaking through lips that seemed to have thickened. "I'd have done the same to someone I thought had kidnapped Paul. Maybe worse." My pulse was thudding. I pulled my hand gently away, breaking the spell. Cinderella back to earth.

"I should go," I said. "It's late." His eyes flickered, stirred. He stood when I did, the connection broken as if it had never existed. We'd stepped back from the precipice we'd been on. Or at least I'd been on.

I walked down the hall, wondering with every step if being sensible was always the best thing. Maybe sometimes you should just grab at the brass ring without considering all the possible ramifications.

But when a small child was involved, you couldn't.

CHAPTER 21

I was snuggled in bed with Tiger at my feet when a thought swam into my consciousness and crystallized into something cold and unpleasant. Detective Jameson, the card he'd handed me, his saying, *If you think of anything; if you need to talk to me.*

Was he suggesting that Philippe was involved? And that I knew something about it?

It took a long time to get to sleep. Even on this really firm mattress.

At breakfast Philippe seemed perfectly normal. No sidelong glances, no taps on my arm to accentuate a point, no casual brushes against me. Whatever seemed to have sparked between us last night had been one-sided or momentary, or both. This was good, I told myself. Falling for Philippe Dumond would be insane. Look at what happened to Jane Eyre — although Mr. Rochester did have that small problem of secret-wife-gone-mad hidden away.

But I was, I realized, now thinking of Philippe by his first name instead of his last. And managing to completely forget Thomas back in Burlington, the sort-of boyfriend I'd never been able to make myself fall in love with.

I winked across the table at Paul, who responded with a wan smile. Yesterday would have been too much for any small child, I thought, let alone one who had been locked away all those months.

While we were finishing our coffee — I was fast getting hooked on this stuff — a phone rang distantly, and Elise appeared with a handset. "It's your brother," she said, smiling as she handed it to me. Count on Simon to have already charmed her.

"Troy, I'm on my way. I'm changing planes in Atlanta now." He rattled off airline, flight number, and arrival time.

His tone dared me to complain, but I wasn't going to. "Okay, I'll be there," I told him, and handed the phone back to Elise.

"Simon's getting in late this morning," I told Philippe, realizing as I said it that my car was still in the parking garage at his office.

"We have to leave soon; we could drop

you off at your car, or Elise could take you closer to the time you need to leave." Elise nodded, and Philippe added, "Elise, Troy's brother will be visiting for a few days, and I thought we'd put him in the small study down the hall." It seemed a bit lord-of-the-manor, but I was fast realizing that it was sort of a game the two of them liked to play.

"Would it be all right if I plugged my laptop into your modem upstairs?" I asked. My laptop is so old it doesn't have built-in wireless, and my plug-in card had broken.

"Of course. But you're welcome to use my computer."

"I'd love to." I'd been itching to get my hands on it since I'd seen it.

"I'll get you set up." He put down his napkin, and I followed him upstairs. As the computer booted up, he noticed my instinctive frown. "Yes, it's been running a bit slowly lately, and freezing now and then," he said.

"You probably just need to clear out the registry and defrag," I said, and it was clear from his expression that I might as well have been speaking Greek. "I can do a few things that will help."

He agreed, and handed me the pad of paper and pen I asked for before he left. I like to write down everything I do to computers, just in case things go wrong.

It was odd to be there alone, and I more than halfway wanted to drape something over the photo of Madeleine across the room. But as soon as I sat at the computer I relaxed. *Someday,* I told myself. Someday I'd treat myself to a powerful new computer with a beautiful big monitor.

First I set a Restore Point, which I named *Just in case.* To me System Restore is the most valuable function in Windows — if things go completely blooey, you just restore your computer to before things went wrong. But you do have to have a Restore Point set.

Next I ran a hardware system check, updated and ran the virus program, and downloaded and ran a free program called Advanced System Care to clear out spyware programs, fix broken registry links, and solve other problems. I deleted several unused applications running in the background; they could still be opened, but wouldn't be needlessly soaking up RAM. I opened Outlook Express to compact the folders — me, I'd switched long ago to Mozilla Thunderbird — and noticed a second identity called Julia. *An assistant? A girlfriend? House guest? Feminine alter ego?* I pictured Philippe as a cross-dresser, and laughed out loud.

Defragging takes a while — it's basically reorganizing stored data so it can be accessed more quickly — so I'd do that last.

What I wanted to do now was research.

First I ran a search for *abducted children,* and up popped page after page of children, abducted in the U.S., Italy, Japan, Belgium, Austria, and countries I'd never heard of. Some of the children had escaped or been rescued; most had not. It shouldn't have shocked me that there were so many.

But I wanted specific knowledge, so I searched for *psychological results child kidnapping.* The screen flooded with child custody cases, so I searched again, this time excluding the word *parental,* then clicked through and started reading sections of books on Amazon.com.

In *Kidnapped: Child Abduction in America,* I read about the psychological power of kidnapper over victim, and learned it's easier to track a stolen car than a stolen child. In *Children Who See Too Much,* I read about Californian children kidnapped on their way to summer camp in a school bus and buried underground for sixteen hours. Afterward the younger kids would hide whenever they saw a school bus, and had trouble imagining the future — something the author called a *sense of foreshortened future* or *pervasive pessimism.* Which seemed to be a fancy way of saying *knowing the world is a scary place and not being sure tomorrow will come.*

Of course Paul would be having some of these same feelings.

I wanted to download my emails, so I plugged my laptop into Philippe's modem, and the first email to hit the screen was a *Hi, Troy, hope everything is well* from Thomas.

Crap. I didn't want to face this now. But even I couldn't disappear for days without explanation, so after a few false starts I wrote that I'd found a Canadian boy, returned him home, and was staying to help him settle in. Short and simple. Leaving out *death-defying rescue, kidnapped from Montreal,* and *mother murdered.* I also emailed my parents that I was out of town, in case they happened to call, which wasn't likely. I didn't mention that Simon was coming up.

And now it was time to go. I checked the route to the airport on MapQuest, set the hard drive to defrag, and went to tell Elise I was ready for her to drop me at my car.

Simon's plane was six minutes late. He strode down the corridor briskly, a small black duffel and briefcase slung over his shoulder — no dorky roller bag for him. He was tall and thin like me, with a patrician nose like mine, unlike the button noses of our mother and sisters. He wore his dark blond hair in short curls that drove women crazy, and somehow innately knew how to choose clothes that looked good on him. Today he wore crisp black jeans and a cotton pullover.

I threw my arms around him and hugged, tighter and harder than usual. We were more of a *hug hug pat pat* kind of family on those rare occasions when physical contact was required. He pulled back to look at my face. "You okay?"

"Yep." Of course you're not going to announce in an airport corridor, *I'm crazy about this intense little boy, the police seem to suspect me, and his father is . . . oh, never mind.*

"Let's get something to eat; I'm starving," he said cheerfully.

"You're always starving," I told him, but drove to a Great Canadian Bagel. Because when you're in Canada it's just wrong to go to Burger King or Wendy's.

Simon chose a carrot pineapple bagel with cream cheese, which seemed a revolting combination. But I put crunchy peanut butter in my oatmeal, so I guess I can't judge.

He let me elbow him aside to pay with loonies and toonies from my stash of Canadian change.

Because the one-dollar coin has a loon on the back, Canadians call it a loonie, so when the two-dollar coin came out it of course became a toonie — Canadians do have a sense of humor. They also figured out that people change only when they're forced to. In the States, dollar coins failed because we didn't have the sense to simultaneously phase out dollar bills.

"Tell me everything," Simon said as we sat down.

I did, step by step, and he didn't speak until I stopped. "You saw no one on the other ferry?"

I closed my eyes and took myself back there, on the deck, feeling the boat moving, seeing the small body fall toward the water. I almost shivered. I shook my head. "All I remember is seeing him falling. That's it."

Simon had his eyes narrowed, which meant his law enforcement brain was ticking. He's as analytical as I am, but better at compartmentalizing it. He finished his bagel and was neatly folding the paper it came on.

"The Ottawa police are handling this?"

I nodded. "The Montreal police are officially in charge, but now they've pretty much handed the investigation off to the local guys. I know they can pull in the RCMP, especially if they think the child has been taken out of Canada, but in this case they apparently didn't."

"Do they think Paul was kept in Burlington?"

I shrugged. "I don't think they know. He said most of the television he heard was in English, but that could be anywhere."

Simon pointed at the menu board. I followed his gaze. "Bilingual," he said succinctly.

It took a moment, and then I got it: the McDonald's meals Paul had gotten while held captive. I said aloud what Simon was thinking. "If he was kept in Canada, the stuff printed on the box would be in both French and English."

He nodded. I hadn't thought to ask Paul this, but surely the police had.

"So do they have any leads?" Simon asked.

"Don't think so. They tried to suggest I was involved, but after they talked to Paul I assume they gave up on that."

"I'm sure Dumond is on their list — the first suspect is always the spouse. Plenty of people try to get rid of their spouse or ex-spouse and sometimes kids, too, in one fell swoop."

I shook my head. "I was there when Philippe saw Paul for the first time in Saranac Lake, Simon. You can't fake that kind of emotion."

"Being crazy about his kid doesn't necessarily mean he didn't arrange to have his wife kidnapped. Maybe the kid wasn't supposed to have been taken. Maybe the wife wasn't supposed to have been killed. He could have set up a kidnapping, fake or real, and things went wrong."

I must have looked aghast, because Simon softened his tone. "I'm not saying that's what happened, just that those are possibilities. Does Dumond talk about his wife?"

"Not much," I admitted. "Just the bare essentials." I didn't mention that there seemed to be no trace of her in the house; he'd see that soon enough.

"And the body was never found?"

I shook my head.

"Any other relatives in the picture? Girlfriend?"

I shook my head. "Not that I know of."

"What about the nanny?"

"Elise? She's Mary Poppins, only in her sixties, and French. She's devoted to Paul; she'd never put him at risk."

"They managed to keep this out of the news?"

"Yep."

Simon drummed his fingers on the table-top, thinking aloud. "The kidnappers got rid of the mother right away, because she was harder to keep captive — they'd probably planned to kill her all along. They kept the child to send proof of life, and demanded ransoms until Dumond stopped paying."

"He couldn't keep it up forever." I knew I sounded defensive. "And by then he was convinced Paul was gone."

"No, of course he wouldn't keep paying, and they knew that. They just wanted to get as much money as possible. But then they kept Paul, what, a month or more after Dumond stopped responding?" He nodded toward the car, and as he dumped his trash I pulled out my keys. In the car he asked quietly, "Do you know if Paul was sexually abused?"

I shook my head. "The doctor said no."

He thought. "Then who knows? They hid their faces, which means they hadn't originally planned to kill him. Maybe they planned to sell him and it fell through. Maybe they were going to try for more ransom, but they thought police were clos-

201

ing in, so they dumped him."

I winced.

"Definitely cold-blooded," he admitted. "Especially when they'd kept him alive so long. Do the police think they may come looking for him?"

"Not unless someone learns that Paul is back. But they're assuming the kidnappers were from Montreal."

As I started the car he asked, "Do the folks know you're here?"

"I emailed them I'm out of town, in case they call."

Although we both knew they wouldn't.

If not for Simon, I would happily have assumed I was one of those switched-at-the-hospital babies brought home to the wrong family. We were both unplanned — our sisters had been eight and ten when Simon arrived. But Simon was the male heir that completes the southern family, and he was attractive and outgoing and personable and more than competent at all the things he was expected to do: football and baseball, Scouts and Cotillion.

By the time surprise number two, me, arrived less than a year later, the baby novelty had worn off. Judging from the pointed reminders my mother made to new mothers, my conception had resulted from the belief that you can't get pregnant while nursing. Apparently, you can.

If either Suzanne or Lynette had wanted a baby sister, let's just say I wasn't it. I hated the frilly, fussy clothing they and my mother chose — I buried one particularly hated outfit in the backyard — and instead snagged Simon's clothes as he outgrew them. I wouldn't play with Barbies and their pointy heels and tight outfits. I tagged around after Simon and his friends when I could, and read and rode my bike when I couldn't. I didn't do Cotillion. I didn't do Junior Miss. I didn't go to school dances or football games.

What I did was bury myself in books, discover bicycle racing, outscore everyone at my high school on the SATs, win a scholarship to Oregon State, and skip my senior year of high school. Which pissed off my family, who expected me to live meekly at home and go to Vanderbilt, where our father is a physics professor. But Vanderbilt reimburses part of faculty children's tuition at other schools, and my scholarship and part-time jobs covered the rest. Otherwise, besides health insurance and occasional plane tickets home (and twenties my dad slipped me when my mother wasn't looking), I've been supporting myself since

I turned seventeen, soon after I arrived at university.

I don't go back to Nashville often.

We drove in silence, Simon's brain working on the case and mine wondering how this weekend was going to go. My brother had never visited me at someone else's house, let alone in the aftermath of a kidnapping.

In the driveway I rolled down my window and punched in the code Philippe had given me. As we waited for the gate to open I could see Simon surveying the house.

A low whistle. "Nice digs, Sis," he said, raising his eyebrows. I made a face. I hadn't mentioned that Philippe's income level far exceeded that of our usual circle of acquaintances. But kids and wives of poor people don't often get kidnapped, I suppose.

CHAPTER 22

Elise chatted animatedly as she showed Simon his room, apologizing for its size, although it wasn't exactly tiny. At least I didn't get bumped from my room in his honor, which my family would have done.

Paul and Philippe arrived soon after, looking weary, Paul with a pinched look on his face. I automatically reached for him and hoisted him onto my hip, and just as automatically he rested his head on my shoulder. Philippe gave a tiny Gallic shrug that meant he didn't know what was wrong, didn't want to talk, or would tell me later. And I realized from a fleeting expression on Simon's face that the three of us were acting very much like a family unit.

I made introductions, and Philippe and Simon shook hands with that slightly formal air guys have when they're sizing each other up.

So you're the suspicious policeman brother

of the woman who rescued my kidnapped son.

So you're the father of the kidnapped child whose wife was murdered and who my sister has known less than a week.

It's tough enough to have family meet your friends in normal situations. Apparently I like to load the deck.

"Paul," Philippe said, putting his hand on Paul's shoulder. "I think Simon would like to see your room."

"Maybe set up that racetrack in your closet," I added, swinging Paul to the floor. "Simon likes those."

"Sure," Simon said, perfectly willing to pretend he adores toy racetracks. There's a reason he can manage our family so well. Paul looked at us uncertainly, but when we smiled encouragingly he led Simon down the hall.

"Paul didn't do very well with the sketch artist," Philippe said once they were out of earshot. "He kept saying he didn't remember what the men looked like, although they came up with something eventually. They had to coax and coax to get him even to look at the computer screen. And finally he started crying and wouldn't stop."

"I guess he just wants to forget about them." It was, I figured, a normal reaction for a six-year-old.

"I know, but it's frustrating, and I hate to see him so upset." He grimaced. "I'll ask the psychologist about it at his appointment this afternoon. I have to make some phone calls for work. Are you okay for now?"

I nodded, and headed down the hall to Paul's room. Simon was on the floor operating a car and making sound effects from deep in his throat, with Paul lying on his stomach watching. They offered me a turn, but I declined, and watched them play until Elise called us for lunch.

Elise had outdone herself: crisp green salads and tiny delectable homemade pot pies with flaky crusts. Simon had no trouble eating despite the bagel he'd polished off not long ago.

"Do you know anything about home security systems?" Philippe asked Simon as he finished his pot pie.

"Sure," Simon replied affably.

"Would you mind taking a look at mine?"

Simon nodded. This, I figured, was guy code to go off to talk — fine by me.

Philippe ran his fingers through his son's hair as he passed. I looked at Paul and patted my lap. "Why don't you come sit here awhile?" I asked, and he climbed up and curled against me. "Did you want to go with your dad and Simon? *Veux-tu aller avec ton*

207

père et Simon?"

He shook his head. I rubbed his back rhythmically. "You know you're going to go talk to someone this afternoon?"

"Mmm."

"It won't be like talking to the policemen. This will be a nice woman in a nice place, for no more than an hour, and you won't have to talk if you don't want to." I translated into French.

Paul stirred. "*Pourquoi?* Why talk?"

"It might make you feel better. You might want to talk about things you don't want to talk to us about. Maybe this person can help you not to worry about things — about the bad men."

He said nothing. "You know you're safe now," I whispered in his ear. "Your papa won't let anything bad happen to you." He let out a long sigh and snuggled closer. I held tight, wishing I could make his world bright and clear again. Wishing the kidnappers would be caught and locked in a small room for a very long time.

After a few moments he squirmed around to look at me. "You go, too?"

"No, your father will take you. *Seulement ton père.* I'll stay here with my brother, so he won't get lonely. But you'll be back soon. And maybe you could get your dad to get

you an ice cream cone — *un cône de glace.*"
His eyes brightened at the words.

When Philippe and Simon returned, Paul
announced, "Papa, it is necessary that we
buy ice cream," and threw me a look that
was almost smug. God, I loved this kid. I
loved the spirit that had him working his
dad for ice cream this soon after he got
home.

Philippe laughed. "A conspiracy. Certainly, we can have ice cream when we go
out, but Elise will be unhappy with me if
you have no room for dinner."

After they left I led Simon to the library,
and he ran his fingers over the spines of the
books, just as I had. "This is a nice place,"
he said.

"Yeah, nice. More like stupendous. So
what did you guys talk about?"

"Locks and things. He wants to make sure
the house is safe, so I was telling him things
to do, little changes to make."

"So you just talked about locks?"

"Maybe not all. Maybe I asked him what
his motives were toward my little sister." I
made a face. "Seriously, Sis, what's going
on?" His tone was somber.

"Nothing. Nothing at all. I'm here because
of Paul. I found him, he trusts me, and Philippe thinks it will help him to have me

here." He gave me a look. "Simon, the man's just gotten confirmation that his wife is dead. He's just gotten his kid back. And look around." I waved my arm. "People like him date movie stars or beauty queens, not someone like me."

I said it without rancor, but Simon had been there in high school. Guys had liked me just fine when they needed help with calculus or English papers, but for dating they headed for the pert girls who wore makeup and knew how to toss their hair. Things had improved somewhat since then, but men still had a tendency to steer, like lemmings, toward glamour and a certain something I didn't possess. I'd been out with Kate and her friends enough to know that when I was with them I was invisible to male eyes.

"Mmm," he said, wisely not commenting. "How long are you going to stay?"

"It depends on how long Paul needs me and what the psychologist says. Probably until Paul gets into school, gets into a routine."

Simon looked at me. "You aren't his mother, Troy. And you can't fix everything."

"I know." My voice cracked. "But I can't . . . I can't leave him yet."

Simon started to reply as the speakerphone at the gate buzzed, and we could hear Elise scurrying to answer it. She appeared moments later, looking worried.

"What is it, Elise?"

"It's a policeman. At least, he says he's a policeman. He says his name is Jameson and he wanted to see Monsieur Dumond. I wasn't sure if I should let him in." She was wringing her hands, the first time I've seen anyone actually doing this.

I followed her. In the viewing screen I could see a dark car outside the entrance and a man behind the wheel who looked like Jameson. I motioned to Elise to buzz him in. He got out of the car, as rumpled as yesterday and now seeming quite irritated. Probably not at all what Elise thought a policeman would look like.

I swung the door open.

Jameson's mouth tightened at the sight of me. "Miss Chance," he said, without expression.

"Detective," I replied, equally tonelessly. I'd have preferred open suspicion to this deadpan demeanor. "Philippe and Paul are out right now. Did you want —"

He interrupted, waving a large brown envelope. "I brought these sketches by for him." His gaze swung behind me, where I could sense Simon was standing.

I stepped back awkwardly. "This is my brother, Simon Chance, from Florida," I said. "Simon, this is Detective Jameson of the Ottawa Police Service, whom you spoke to on the phone."

More hand-shaking, more male taking-measure. Elise, flustered that she'd left a genuine police officer waiting, herded us toward the library and brought glasses of iced lemonade on a heavy lacquered tray.

"When did you arrive?" Jameson asked Simon.

"Just flew in a few hours ago. Can you tell me how the investigation is going?"

A small shrug. Jameson sipped lemonade slowly, deliberately, and set the glass on a coaster. "We've sent the sketches to the Vermont and New York police, and of course the Montreal police and the RCMP. The Vermont and New York police both considered Miss Chance's phone call a prank, although they did report it to the ferry offices in Burlington."

I worked hard at not squirming.

"I was curious," Simon asked. "The Mc-Donald's meals Paul got — were the bags or boxes printed just in English or also in French?"

For a beat I thought Jameson wasn't going to answer, but he did. "He says it was

English." Which meant that Paul had been kept in the States, most likely in Vermont.

"No leads from the original investigation?" Simon asked.

Another shrug, which could mean *No, nothing* or *Nothing I want to talk about.* Jameson asked Simon about his work, and they slid into general police talk. I've overdosed on this brand of conversation around Simon and his law enforcement pals, so I tuned out and was thinking about Paul at the psychologist's when Simon nudged my knee.

Jameson was speaking. "How long are you staying?" he asked me, almost exactly as Simon had.

"It depends on Paul," I said automatically. "It depends on what the psychologist says."

Something in my gaze must have satisfied him. He grunted slightly and stood. "Please give these to Monsieur Dumond." He held out the envelope. "He can call me if he has questions." He shook Simon's hand, and then mine. His hand was unexpectedly rough, his grasp strong and brief. His eyes were pale, like wolf's eyes. "You have my card." It wasn't a question. I nodded.

Simon looked at me after Jameson left. "What was that all about?"

"I think he thinks I'm going to have an

epiphany and realize that I saw the kidnappers, or find out it was actually Philippe."

He nodded at the envelope. "What's that?"

"Sketches of the kidnappers." Simon neatly lifted the envelope from my hands and was opening it before I could protest. "Simon, I don't think —"

"Ahhh," he said, smoothing the sketches out before him on the coffee table. "Your typical computer-generated sketches."

I looked at them. My first thought was that they were of androids, because they didn't look human. I've read that these sketches aren't supposed to look like a specific person, but just remind you of someone enough so you'll make the connection. But these looked especially strange, with dark brows, jutting jaws, thin mouths.

"Hmm," Simon said, disappearing and returning with the sketch pad and soft pencils he carries in his briefcase. He drew quickly, with intense concentration, and I knew not to try to talk to him. Soon he had a collection of drawings of faces with softer jaws, longer noses, wavier hair, and other variations.

I got more lemonade and watched Simon, and finally he laid his pencil down. "There, we'll see if Paul can tell us which ones are best."

I looked at him.

"What?" he protested. "You know no one will ever be able to identify anyone from those other sketches."

"I know. I just . . . it's hard on Paul to look at these faces, to remember them."

We heard a noise at the door, and Simon scooped up the drawings and tucked them inside his sketch pad.

Paul ran and hugged me, and shook Simon's hand when his father prompted him. Philippe gave me a discreet thumbs-up as Paul hugged Tiger, telling us in a mix of French and English about his ice cream cone, pink like the one he had in Lake Placid, a very small one, so he could eat dinner and keep Elise happy. I followed Philippe to the kitchen, where he poured himself a glass of water.

"Paul was quite comfortable with the woman. We met together first, and then he met with her separately. Apparently he opened up quite a lot."

"Philippe, I . . ."

As my voice trailed off he looked up sharply. I started again. "Detective Jameson brought by copies of the sketches for you. But Simon has drawn some others — if, that is, you think Paul can handle looking at them. To pick out the best ones."

He thought about it. "I think he can. He told the psychologist about the men, and how he wants them to be put in jail. Let's ask him."

Paul surprised me by agreeing, and sat on my lap as Simon brought out the sketches, his only sign of agitation the tightness of his small fingers on my arm. He looked over the first set with great deliberation, one after the other, and then pointed at one. *"Comme ça,"* he said. "With a thing on the face."

Simon whipped out his pencil. "A thing? Like this?" He penciled in a small dot.

"More," Paul insisted, and when the dot grew to resemble a good-sized mole, Paul nodded. In the second set of drawings, he pointed decisively at the fourth one. *"Plus de cheveux,"* he said critically, and Simon smoothly penciled in longer hair.

"How about colors?" Simon asked, and I translated. Paul pointed to the hair: *"Noir. Et le nez, rouge."*

"Paul has colored pencils in his desk," I murmured, and Philippe went to get them. Simon broke open the pack and began to add color, penciling in reddish veins on the nose, coloring the hair, and making changes as Paul directed, first on one picture and then the other. Philippe watched. At last Paul closed his eyes.

216

"Je suis fatigué," he said crossly.

"So you should be tired." I hugged him. "You've done a lot of work today. And you're probably hungry, too, because it's nearly dinnertime." I lifted him off my lap and took him off to wash for dinner.

After dinner Philippe put on a Jim Carrey movie about lost pets and jungle animals. To me it seemed painfully juvenile and not at all funny, but the guys found it hilarious, even my intelligent, discerning, artistic brother. I went off to bed, leaving the three of them chortling at the movie.

I had planned to read, but couldn't keep my eyes open. I knew Simon would be soaking up everything there was to take in here, and wouldn't talk to me about any of it until just before he left on Sunday. In some ways Simon is very predictable, which can be annoying, but also comforting.

It meant I could stop trying to second-guess everything and could switch off the part of my brain that kept nattering questions at me: *What is Jameson thinking? Why does Paul never mention his mother? Why does no one talk about Madeleine? Why did Philippe choose to move to Ottawa?*

At least for now.

CHAPTER 23

I slept hard — it was, I think, the first time I'd relaxed since I'd found Paul. By the time I got to the breakfast table the guys had filled their plates and were deep in discussion about window latches. I helped myself to a fluffy waffle and strips of bacon, and smiled at Paul, who seemed to get a little worried if someone wasn't participating in the conversation.

Then I caught the words *Canadian Tire* and *Home Depot.*

"What?" I said, in the tone that means *Did I hear that right?*

"We want to go pick up a few things for the house, some things Simon suggested," Philippe said. The three of them looked at me expectantly. Apparently the male desire to roam the aisles of giant hardware stores is independent of age, financial status, or nationality.

"Oh, no," I said, lining up sliced strawberries on my waffle. "You aren't dragging me along." To me this is the definitive gender difference — this and the Three Stooges. I hate wandering Home Depot searching for a particular screw or fixture, just as I have never found anything remotely funny about the Stooges.

The three of them grinned. "You'll do just fine without me," I said. "I can do computer stuff."

They were clearly eager to be off, Paul delighted to be included in this guy fix-it stuff. I tousled his hair, and my eyes met Philippe's. He nodded to acknowledge what I was trying to say: *Be careful and don't let him overdo it.* I lightly punched Simon on the arm as he passed, which meant *Watch out for Paul, and don't say anything embarrassing about me.*

I was glad Paul was going out in a normal visit-Canadian-Tire sort of Saturday, but the ordinariness of going off to hardware stores seemed strange in a way I couldn't quite define. Of course keeping him cloistered at home couldn't be good for him. Of course he would be safe with his father and with Simon, who pretty much automatically scanned every situation for possible threats.

Maybe I just didn't like seeing Paul going off without me. *Not your kid.* I was going to have to keep reminding myself.

I finished my waffle, and vaguely thought about calling Thomas. The thought made me uneasy, which probably meant I should do it, my theory being that almost always the choice that makes you the most uncomfortable is the one you're supposed to do.

It couldn't have gone much worse. I had forgotten about giving the police his name, and he'd gotten a call from them. At least I had emailed him the basics, but even Thomas couldn't manage to be completely phlegmatic about this.

"Troy, you don't know anything about this guy," he said, letting some asperity creep through his normal reserve. "You don't know how he might have been involved in this. This could be dangerous."

I'd waited a four count, then said, "I've got to go now. I'll talk to you later."

I had thought it would be a relief to have Thomas drop his careful indifference, but it wasn't. He had stepped out of the bounds of our carefully structured relationship, and I didn't like it.

I didn't want to hurt Thomas, but . . . *but you want to keep him as a safety net,* said that unpleasant inner voice. *You aren't ready to give him up yet.*

I hate these moments of self-realization.

I called Baker, who knew that something was up for me to call her from Canada, and told her about Simon's visit and about Thomas. "He seems almost jealous, which doesn't make sense. I mean, I live with four guys, for Pete's sake. And he doesn't know that Philippe is, well . . ."

"Gorgeous?" Baker said.

"Well, yeah, and all the other stuff."

"Like, rich? The Mercedes and the Armani and the hundred-dollar haircut?"

"Baker, you don't have any idea what his haircuts cost."

"No, but I'll bet they do."

I was silent. Baker's sister was a hairdresser who had worked in New York City, so she was probably right.

"But Elise is here. And Paul."

"Yes, there's Paul, and that may be what scares Thomas the most. That's the one thing he can't compete with, and he knows it."

I knew that Thomas didn't want children, and clearly I did. And here I was with a real live child and his real live father.

I told Baker I'd keep her updated, and went up to use Philippe's computer. I checked my Twitter account, then found more books on kidnapped children and looked up the nearest branch of the public library.

Then a little demon in my head made me wonder who had used that "Julia" identity I'd found in Outlook Express, and wonder if Philippe had had a girlfriend — maybe in Ottawa, which could be why he had moved here. Or maybe an assistant had used the computer. I could take a quick glance at email headings to see if they were work-related. So I opened Outlook Express, and clicked on the Julia identity.

But it asked for a password.

This was my downfall. It was a challenge that completely shut off the emotionally aware part of me and sent my brain into problem-solving mode. Instead of thinking *This is private, back off,* my brain said, *Aha, something to solve.* Without a twinge of guilt — because at this point it just seemed an intriguing puzzle — I tried the name of Philippe's company, its address, Philippe's name, and a few other possibilities.

Then it occurred to me that Philippe's wife could have used this computer back in Montreal. This alone should have caused me to push back from the keyboard, but it didn't. I tried Paul's name, alone and in combination with what I guessed was his birth year. *Madeleine* didn't work, but I hadn't expected it to — almost no one is that obvious, especially when they've gone to the trouble of setting up a password. Then I tried it backward: *enieledam.*

It opened the program, like the door to Aladdin's cave sliding open. Emails flowed onto the screen, one after the other, seemingly faster and faster. I watched, frozen. I could see enough of the subject lines flashing past to see that this had indeed been Madeleine's email account. The first messages coming in were months old, but then more recent ones started dumping on the screen. My heart hammered. How could Madeleine's friends not *know she was dead?*

The download stopped at last. My mouth was dry. That voice in my head told me: *You are sitting at a computer used by Philippe's dead wife.*

There were dozens of unread messages, dating back to July, long before the kidnapping. Why would Madeleine not have read or downloaded her messages for all those months? Could she have disappeared before Dumond said she had?

For a long moment my brain was blank, and then I got it. I've done this myself: begun to use a new computer without deleting the email setup on the old one. Madeleine either hadn't known or cared that her email program had been set to leave messages on the server — or that they would merrily download here if someone signed on.

Of course she had had no idea that someone else would open her account. Or that she would die and that Troy Chance would come along and sit at the computer she had shared with her husband, and randomly, rudely guess her password.

I stared at the screen.

I'd like to say that morality took over and kept me from reading any of the emails, and maybe it would have. But I heard voices downstairs. I switched back to Philippe's identity, and closed the program.

And clattered down the stairs, pretending as hard as I could that I hadn't just seen a dead woman's emails.

CHAPTER 24

The guys had found the special door locks Simon had suggested, brighter outdoor bulbs, intricate window latches. Paul seemed fascinated — maybe it was good for him to see the house being made more secure.

I watched them opening their packages, but standing around and handing people screwdrivers isn't my idea of a good time. I like fixing things, not watching other people do it. So I went for a quick run through the neighborhood, past the stately homes. Tiger was delighted to be out in the fresh spring air. I concentrated on putting one foot cleanly in front of the other and tried to not think about what I had just done. I was breathing hard sooner than I should have — too much of Elise's cooking, too little exercise.

When I got back, the guys were setting out a tray of sandwiches, sliced veggies, and cookies Elise had left us before she went out. We ate in the kitchen perched on stools while Simon explained the virtues of the new locks. I tried to seem interested, like he does when I talk computers or bicycles. Tiger sat near Paul, who dropped pinched-off chunks of sandwich when he thought no one was looking.

We'd decided to do some sightseeing downtown after Paul took a short nap. Paul followed me to his room without protest, but seemed subdued. He was on overload, I thought — Simon's visit and the Home Depot trip had been too much for him. His lip quivered as he perched on the edge of the bed.

"What's wrong?" I asked, concerned. *"Qu'est-ce que c'est le problème?"*

He burst into tears. Instinct told me this wasn't just a fatigued child who didn't want to take a nap. Something was horribly wrong. I folded him into my arms, murmuring to him as he cried against my shirt. I whispered questions; he choked out answers in French. It took me a while to comprehend.

Then I knew that the last prescribed nap Paul had taken was in Montreal, where he had gone to sleep a happy little boy in a lovely home with two parents and a nanny who adored him, and had woken up a prisoner in a small room far from home.

And he was afraid the same thing would happen here.

I took his face in my hands and told him he was safe here, that his father and Tiger and those new locks would never let a bad person in. When he calmed a little I went to get Philippe. I thought he might be upset that Paul had told all this to me and not to him, but he wasn't. Maybe it had been easier to tell me in French because I didn't understand it all — like talking in a confessional to someone you can't see.

Philippe told Paul much the same as I had, and that if he wanted to read instead of nap, that was fine. Some of the tension began to leave Paul's small body as he leaned against his father.

I pulled some books from the bookcase and looked questioningly toward Tiger, then the bed. Philippe nodded. I patted the bed and Tiger jumped up. I motioned to her to stay, although she seemed to know when she was needed.

We just told Simon that Paul was overtired, because neither of us wanted to talk about this small child being terrified that kidnappers would scoop him up during his nap. I went back and sat with Paul until he fell asleep, then Philippe took my place.

When Paul awoke we headed downtown to admire what looked like miles and miles of brightly colored tulips on the grounds of Parliament Hill. Philippe let Paul pick up a few petals that had dropped. I knew the story, but Simon didn't: During World War II, Princess Juliana of the Netherlands had been evacuated here and had given birth in a hospital room temporarily declared international territory. So in appreciation the Netherlands ships over hundreds of tulip bulbs every year, and Ottawa has its Tulip Festival every May.

From Parliament Hill we walked over to the locks on the Ottawa River at the beginning of the Rideau Canal. They were a small boy's dream — Paul was fascinated watching them opening and closing and the boats sinking along with the water level. I couldn't help scanning every face around me for any resemblance to Simon's sketches, not that it was logical that kidnappers from Montreal would be here. But I looked, and probably Simon and Philippe did, too.

Then we stopped at a chip wagon to buy poutine, which roughly translates to "mushy mess." It's thick french fries and white cheese curds with brown gravy poured over it, which you wash down with cold Pepsi guzzled from the can. It sounds awful, I know, but it's delicious. I laughed as I saw Simon's tentative expression turn to bliss. We explained to Paul that, no, you couldn't buy poutine just anywhere, and this was the first time poor Simon had tasted it.

Fortunately Philippe had told Elise not to cook dinner, because none of us could have eaten. By the time Paul had his bath, his lids were drooping. We tucked him in, and he sleepily accepted a hug before settling down with his father for his bedtime story.

Back in the library, Simon looked at me intently. He gently pulled at a handful of his short curls, which sprang back as soon as he released them. I couldn't read the expression in his green eyes.

"What?" I said. "What, what, what?!"

"They're nice people, Troy. This is a nice place."

But not my people and not my place. He didn't say the words, but they rang in my head. "Simon, I know," I said heavily, as we heard Philippe's footsteps coming down the hall. "This is only temporary."

He gave me a look that said, *Just be sure not to forget that.*

CHAPTER 25

We had dessert in the library, thick chocolate cake topped with fresh raspberries, and sipped red wine, which curiously enough went well together. Philippe told us about his marketing business and some of his clients: a brewery, a printer, a bank. We talked about the school Paul might attend, an English-speaking one so he would become fluent, and I told Philippe about a program that would let him access his work files from home.

In many ways it seemed like a pleasant evening with friends. But Simon's policeman's brain was hard at work, with some protective brother mixed in, and Philippe certainly was aware of it. With two less socially adroit people it could have been disastrous. Instead it ran just below the surface, like two movies showing simultaneously, one barely visible under the other.

Then Philippe played his face card. "Paul's

psychologist told me that Troy makes Paul feel safe, because she rescued him, and said it would be a big help to him if she could stay a few weeks." Philippe glanced at Simon and then at me, and I answered the question before he asked it.

"Of course," I said.

Simon's body language signaled nothing — one of the great things about my brother. Yes, staying here longer would disrupt my life and make it all the harder when it was time to leave. I knew it; Simon knew I knew it, and wouldn't point it out. Having a brother like this almost makes up for the rest of the family.

Philippe visibly relaxed. "That would be great. Whatever you need, I can set it up — a cell phone or anything else. You can use my computer, or I can get a desktop for your room."

"I can just add a Canadian calling plan to my cell phone. I can use your computer when you're out, if that's okay." I had one magazine article started I could finish from here. I should be looking for new assignments, but I always kept some savings in reserve.

"Of course," Philippe agreed. "I'll work from home whenever possible, but often I have to be in the office or meet with clients."

"Do you regret leaving Montreal?" Simon asked.

The question seemed abrupt, but Philippe shook his head. "Too many memories. In a way it might have been good for Paul to be in his old neighborhood and school, but people would ask a lot of questions. Here we can skip all that and start fresh. School officials will know his mother died, and that he's been away and missed school, but not much else. Eventually the news will come out, but it won't hit as hard as it would have there."

It was odd to hear it in such bland terms: *His mother died. He's been away and missed school.* But it fit with Madeleine seeming so absent from this house, with her almost never being mentioned.

Simon asked, "Do you mind if I ask you some questions about the kidnapping?"

"Not at all."

I took this as my exit cue. Simon could ask more probing questions in my absence and Philippe could talk more freely, and I didn't want to hear more grim details at this point. Simon would fill me in, probably just before he left tomorrow. I gathered our dishes, took a book from the shelves, and told them good night.

■ ■ ■ ■

After a leisurely breakfast Simon said his goodbyes, delighting Elise with a hug and shaking Paul's and Philippe's hands. We had left time to do some sightseeing downtown before his flight, and just as I was about to give up and go into an absurdly expensive pay lot, a parking slot on the street magically appeared.

We strolled around looking at old buildings, then Simon spotted a poutine wagon and insisted on buying some. I passed — as tasty as it is, it can be a little like lead in your belly. Two days in a row is too much for me.

We sat on a nearby bench. "So," I said, swiping a fry from his carton. "What do you think?"

Simon took a swig of his icy Pepsi. It was, he pointed out, the absolute perfect counterpoint to the greasiness of cheese and potatoes and the saltiness of the gravy. He thought before answering. "You have a good cop on the job here. Jameson's a lot smarter than he lets on, and he's going to keep digging on this."

"Okay. But what do you think? Like, what do you think of Philippe?"

He gave me that grin that makes me want to smack him sometimes. "What do I think of Mr. Tall, Dark, and Handsome?"

I punched his arm. "He can't help any of that. So don't hold it against him."

Simon ate a few more cheese-covered, gravy-soaked fries before continuing. "Here are the things that police are going to stick on. First, the misdelivered ransom demand seems like a ploy, like Philippe moved the letter to a neighbor's mailbox so he could miss the deadline and not notify the police right away."

He held his hand up as I opened my mouth to speak. "It could be real. When John Paul Getty was kidnapped, one of the ransom demands was delayed for weeks because of a mail strike." He went on, ticking off points on his fingers. "Second, why keep Paul so long? Kidnappers who are in it for money either usually kill the victim right away or release them when they get the ransom. The psychos or pedophiles keep the kids forever, or until they get too old. These guys asked for multiple ransoms, but then kept Paul more than a month longer before deciding to get rid of him.

"Third, cops are well aware husbands take extreme measures to get rid of wives. Scott Peterson, Perry March from Nashville, and so on." He paused a moment. "There is a brother, and I'm sure the police are taking a good look at him as well."

I was startled. "A brother?"

Simon nodded. "Philippe told me last night — his wife had a brother she was close to, who still works for Philippe."

Paul had an uncle, living here? Working in the office I'd visited? I didn't know which surprised me more: that this uncle hadn't rushed to see his long-lost nephew or that Philippe hadn't mentioned him.

We sat in silence for a few moments before Simon continued. "Philippe seems a little guarded when he talks about the kidnapping. Maybe he's just tired of talking about it, and maybe he's well aware he's a prime suspect. But my sense is he's holding something back. Maybe he has an idea who was behind the whole thing. Maybe his lawyer has told him to be careful what he says. Maybe he just feels bad that he assumed Paul was dead."

He drew a deep breath. "Or maybe he instigated the whole thing, without meaning to. When he was angry or upset or drunk he could have said to the wrong person that he wanted to get rid of his wife — and someone carried through. Or he hired someone to snatch her to scare her, and they killed her and blackmailed him. It's happened more than once."

"But Paul —"

"Maybe Paul wasn't supposed to be part of it. Maybe they weren't supposed to take him, but they screwed up, or turned on Philippe. The thing is, bad guys are very unreliable, and very, very greedy."

I opened my mouth to speak, but nothing came out.

"In a way it doesn't matter, Troy," he said gently. "Paul is home, with his father. He can build a new life. Maybe that's what's important."

I looked at him in disbelief. "But . . . but Madeleine?"

"But someone killed her and someone has to pay for it?" Simon's voice was calm. "Lots of murders are never solved, Troy. Lots of people get away with it, especially when no body is found. Maybe the kidnappers will be caught; maybe they won't. Maybe Philippe will be cleared; maybe he won't. This may be as good as it gets, and he may have to live with that."

The words he didn't say rang in my head: *But can you live with it?* We sat in silence.

"It's a tough situation, kiddo," he said at last. "I know you have to see it through. Just be careful, very careful." He put his

236

arm around my shoulders and rumpled my hair. "Keep me posted, and keep safe."

We drove in silence to the airport. I gave him a quick hard hug at the curb, and then he was gone.

I'd expected Simon to give me an idea of what to do — or at least put things in black and white and reassure me that the bad guys would be caught. Instead, he seemed to be telling me this was one big gray mess with no clear answers, and I was on my own.

I didn't believe Philippe would have done anything to harm Paul. But could he have planned a fake kidnapping, plotted to have his son's mother killed? It was true he seldom mentioned her and didn't have photos of her or her possessions scattered about — but no two people mourn the same. Some keep their dead spouse's coat hanging on the hall rack the rest of their lives; others pack up everything the next week and clean house like mad. People cope in different ways. I knew that.

I got back to the house almost too soon. It seemed strange to use the garage door opener Philippe had given me and park next to his Mercedes as if I lived there. He was moving boxes around in the back of the garage, and waved me over. I looked down into a long box he had opened and saw a child's bicycle, brand-new, shiny red and black. I could hear Paul's voice telling me he'd been promised a *vélo* for Christmas but hadn't gotten it.

"Paul's bike," I said into the cavernous silence.

Philippe nodded. "I got it for him for Christmas. Just in case."

We gazed down at the bike, me envisioning Philippe going out in the middle of Christmas season to buy a bicycle for a child he had no real hope of ever seeing again, Philippe probably seeing Paul locked away, missing Christmas.

I broke the silence. "Are you going to give it to him now?"

"I'd like to. But I don't want to upset him."

I shook my head. "I think it'll make him happy. You could ask the psychologist. But if it upsets him, you could just put it away."

Philippe could drive himself crazy the next few weeks, months, even years, wondering if something might remind Paul of the kidnapping. But maybe the bad memories shouldn't be buried — maybe they should be allowed to surface and erode away, bit by bit.

After a moment Philippe lifted the bike

out. It was a top-of-the-line kid's mountain bike with gears and caliper brakes, with handlebar dangling and front wheel, saddle, and pedals still in the box.

"I can put it together," I offered. "I used to build bikes at a bike shop." He blinked, but I think he was learning not to be surprised by me. He found the metric open-end and Allen wrenches and tube of grease I asked for, and watched as I assembled the parts, connected the brakes, adjusted the gears, and tightened the headset. I did have him pump up the tires.

When Paul got up from his nap, Philippe led him to the driveway, where we'd set the bike. Paul's eyes widened and he ran his fingers over the bright red paint. At a nod from his father, he hopped on. My eyes were a little shiny, but I was snapping away with my camera, so no one noticed.

The bike was almost too large, and Paul had to be shown how to use the hand brakes, but he clearly knew how to ride. So it wasn't that magical moment when a kid first successfully balances on a bike, but it was still big. An array of emotions ran across Philippe's face. Maybe he was thinking of Paul's mother missing this moment.

So maybe this whole recovery process was

going to be trial and error. No one could predict how one particular child was going to react or adjust to a new life. But it seemed that a shiny new bicycle could help fill one hole in a small boy's life.

And I imagined we'd just erased Paul's fear of napping forever.

For dinner Elise made a stir-fry with lots of vegetables, probably a nutritional counter-measure to the poutine we'd had yesterday. After she went off to her apartment at the back of the house, the three of us watched *Wallace and Gromit: The Curse of the Were-Rabbit.* I thought it odd, but it must have been perfect for a six-year-old, because Paul loved it, watching cuddled in the curve of his father's arm.

Tomorrow I'd take the sketches to Jameson at the police station, and Philippe would take Paul to visit his new school, both of which made me vaguely uneasy. Here Paul was safe, and we could spend cozy evenings watching movies. Here I could stash away memories of feeling like part of a family.

Tomorrow would be a return to real life. I wasn't looking forward to it.

CHAPTER 26

At breakfast Paul was almost too excited about the school visit to eat. Philippe wasn't doing justice to Elise's pancakes, so maybe he wasn't as calm as he had seemed to be. Me, I thought too much was happening too soon for a small boy who had lost his mother and been confined for five months. But Philippe wanted Paul in a routine as soon as possible, and he was the parent, and I wasn't. I wanted to take a quick run before heading to the police station, so I didn't eat, just filled a plate and set it aside for later.

It was a clear morning, and Tiger and I ran smoothly for about two miles. Running doesn't calm me as much as biking, but life seems easier afterward. I ate my warmed-up pancakes and sausages in the kitchen. If Elise hadn't been there, I would have eaten them cold, wrapping the pancakes around the sausages. She was whisking around like a happy wren in an apron, marinating something for dinner and preparing pastry to be filled with fruit.

"Did Paul like school in Montreal?" I asked, wondering how he would do with new kids and new teachers, struggling to speak English.

Elise nodded, rolling out pastry dough. "Yes, he liked it very much. He had good teachers and many friends."

"Did his school friends come over a lot?"

"No. No, Madame Dumond did not like so much to have the children over. Too much noise and fuss. But I would often take him to the park, where other children played, or to a friend's house."

I blinked. This was a surprise. Me, I'd want my kids' friends over as much as possible, so my kid wasn't watching R-rated movies, breathing secondhand smoke, or wolfing down Pop-Tarts or Pizza Pockets at someone else's house. But some people don't care for other people's children, or are prone to noise-induced migraines. Or maybe Madeleine hadn't quite been the involved, engaged parent I'd imagined. Which was an odd thought, but it could partly explain why Paul didn't seem particularly to miss her.

After a quick shower I scanned Simon's

sketches so we'd have copies. I clipped Simon's card to the originals and stuffed them in an envelope, then checked the route on MapQuest.

Walking into the police station was more than a little unnerving, especially since the same crisply put-together police officer was at the front counter. Sort of that *Groundhog Day* feeling again.

"I need to drop this off for Detective Jameson," I told her.

"Your name, please?"

"I don't . . . it's Troy Chance, but I don't need to see him; I just need to leave this."

But she was already speaking into a phone, and Jameson was there before I could decide to drop the envelope and leave. He looked at me, brows raised.

"It's some drawings." I gestured with the envelope. "My brother did some new ones based on the others. With Paul's help." Jameson took the envelope and waggled his head for me to follow. I opened my mouth to protest, but he was already disappearing down the hall.

His office was smallish and astoundingly cluttered. He moved a box off a chair for me to sit, then sat behind the desk and opened the envelope. Without speaking, he spread the drawings out and studied them, first one and then the other. He pointed at the mole and looked up.

I nodded. "Paul told him to put it there."

"Your brother didn't suggest it?"

"No, Paul did. He said the man had a thing on his face, and he told Simon how big to make it."

Jameson grunted and stuffed the drawings back in the envelope, and looked at the clock on the wall. "Let's go to lunch," he said abruptly. He scribbled something on a notepad, tore the page off and paper-clipped it to the envelope, and stood up.

I opened my mouth to say, "No, I've got other plans" or "No, I need to leave," but I wasn't fast enough. He whirled around, touching my elbow lightly to lead me out. At the front desk he handed the envelope to the woman, and then we were outside. I blinked in the sunlight. "My car's over here," he said, gesturing.

"I don't . . ." I said, but he was opening the car door for me. I gave up and got in. We rode in silence and ended up at a restaurant in the ByWard Market, an area packed with galleries and cafés and outdoor vendors selling fruits and vegetables and crafts. It was a trendier restaurant than I'd expected; I'd pictured Jameson as the meat loaf and potatoes type. He pushed a menu at me and we ordered.

I drank the water the waitress brought us. We sat. Damned if I was going to open my mouth first. Finally, he said, "Is your brother still here?"

"No, he flew home yesterday."

Dead silence. "Paul?"

"He's good. His father is taking him on a school visit."

"Are you working up here?"

"I'm finishing up a magazine article," I told him, wondering why he was asking. I couldn't work in Canada without a visa, but freelancing to the States wouldn't count.

"What do you write for?"

"Sports magazines mostly, some airline magazines, some newspapers."

"Pay well?"

I shrugged. "It varies. Some magazines pay a lot more than others."

Our food arrived — a black bean burger for me, a regular one for him. I got most of mine down before he spoke again.

"So you've known Dumond how long?"

I had to think a moment. "Since Tuesday, so almost a week."

"And you're comfortable staying there?"

Was my room comfortable? Was I worried about staying with a man whose wife had been kidnapped and murdered? "Yes," I said.

"It's quite comfortable." The look he gave me said I'd answered the wrong question.

"Hmm." He speared some french fries, then spoke. "Did you know Dumond's business is having financial trouble?"

I set down what was left of my burger and wiped my hands carefully. Bean burgers tend to leak sauce and bits of bean, at least the good ones not made from preformed patties. "No, I didn't. But that's none of my concern."

He went on. "Did you know Dumond and his wife had been having marital problems?"

I pushed back from the table. "No," I said, trying not to show my anger. I had expected he would ask me questions, but I hadn't expected this. "And that definitely is none of my business. Why are you telling me?"

He smiled a humorless smile. "Things that perhaps you ought to know." He picked up his burger and took a bite. "Especially if you're involved with him."

I stared at him. "I'm not. But that's not the issue."

He said nothing.

"I cannot help what you believe or don't believe," I said with force. "But I can never and will never believe that Philippe Dumond ever did anything that would harm his son."

He shrugged. "Maybe that part wasn't supposed to happen."

Inhale, exhale. Inhale, exhale. This was too much like what Simon had said. I hadn't considered at the time that the police might actually believe it. The walls were shimmering and the room almost shifting around me. *Just keep breathing,* I told myself. Breathe in, breathe out. "I want to go," I said.

Without a word, Jameson paid the bill and followed me outside. Neither of us spoke. When his car stopped, I got out and didn't look back.

On the way home I stopped at the public library and talked the librarian into issuing me a library card based on a piece of Philippe's junk mail I'd brought along. To get a card you're supposed to have something with your name and address on it, but because librarians want you to have a library card sometimes they'll bend the rules. I checked out *Girl in the Cellar,* about an Austrian girl abducted at age ten, and requested three other books on kidnapping.

When I got back to the house, no one was home yet, so I went up to Philippe's office and plugged in my laptop to download my emails. Simon had emailed that he was home; I answered and told him I'd delivered his sketches. I didn't mention the conversation I'd just had with Jameson.

Next I tried to compose an email to Thomas. What could I say? *I don't miss you, so we probably should break up?* If I were home, we would probably just gradually stop seeing each other and find reasons not to make the drive between Lake Placid and Burlington. No one would have to say, *This just isn't working out* or *I think we should see other people.* Or the old *It's not you, it's me.* However true it might be.

But even I knew you couldn't break up via email. I finally wrote a brief note apologizing for being sharp on the phone, and said that being here was something I had to do.

Then I flicked on Philippe's computer. As it booted up, Madeleine smiled at me from across the room.

In this computer sat dozens of emails to and from Madeleine — just two clicks of the mouse away. They were like Blackbeard's forbidden room, taunting me. I wanted desperately to read them. I wanted to know something, anything, about the woman who had been Paul's mother and Philippe's wife, who nobody would talk much about.

One of these emails could have a clue that

would point the police away from Philippe. I could tell Philippe, *Hey, look, I accidentally downloaded your wife's emails* and turn them over to the police. But surely the Montreal police would have checked her emails on the server, and would have already read them. Still, they could have missed something. I could read them and if I found anything promising, send it anonymously to the police here.

I opened Outlook Express. I opened Madeleine's identity. I looked at the email headings. My fingers hovered over the mouse. One double-click and an email would be open on the screen in front of me, and I would be reading words written by Paul's mother, by Philippe's wife.

But that would be incredibly intrusive. And I couldn't be sure that my main motivation wasn't just nosiness, wanting to know more about Madeleine.

I shut down the program and switched off the computer.

CHAPTER 27

Then Paul and Philippe were back. Paul was almost bubbling, talking in a mix of English and French about school and the children he had met and the lunch he had had, not so bad, but not nearly as good as Elise's. He seemed amazingly normal, like any child excited about a school visit.

Paul went off to see Elise, and Philippe told me he was pleased with the school: the teachers were attentive, the classes small, and the security measures impressive. Quite a few diplomats' children attended, and the grounds were gated, with several guards. They'd done some testing and made arrangements for enrolling Paul, including outfitting him with the school uniform. Paul would start school Thursday, giving him two more days to rest before then. This, I realized, was Philippe's concession to my concerns.

Philippe would drive Paul to school before

continuing to work, and Elise or I would pick him up. And when the regular school term ended soon, Paul would continue in a summer session to catch up on what he'd missed and work on his English. But I still felt uneasy about all this.

And now, Philippe said apologetically, he did need to go in to his office, and would I stay with Paul?

"Of course," I said. This was, after all, why I was here. After his father left, Paul flung his arms around my waist. I hoisted him up, and he wrapped his legs around me, leaning back.

"So, kiddo," I said. "It's just you and me for now. *Seulement nous deux.* What should we do?"

He cocked his head to one side, thinking. "First," he said seriously, "we must play that game, the little men on the machine, *l'ordinateur,* eh?"

I laughed; I couldn't help it. He had picked up far more English than I had realized, maybe from hearing English television through the door when he was locked up. Or maybe in Montreal he had had some English-speaking friends whose homes he visited. "You've got it," I said, swinging him to the floor. I'd brought along the CD with the game he liked, and we played it on his father's computer until I called it quits. He, apparently, could have played until his fingers went numb.

"Now for some quiet time," I said, and led him to his room. He didn't argue, and fell asleep quickly. He still tired easily.

I was walking down the hall to the library when Elise called me to the phone. "It's Monsieur Dumond," she whispered as she handed it to me.

"Hello?" I said, figuring he was calling to check on Paul.

"Troy, it's Philippe. How is everything?"

"Good. Paul and I played computer games, and now he's taking a nap."

"Troy, I don't think I've mentioned that Madeleine's brother, Claude, works for me."

Ah, the mysterious uncle. "No-o-o-o," I said. "But Simon said something about him." I didn't point out that Philippe had scarcely mentioned Madeleine, let alone her brother. Or that it seemed odd I was just hearing about this brother.

"Claude manages things when I'm gone; he's the only employee, in fact, who moved with me from Montreal. He's very eager to see Paul. But I'm not sure if it would be good for Paul to see him, to be reminded of his mother just yet."

I listened to the faint hum of the phone line. There had to be a reason Paul hadn't seen his uncle as soon as he got home. I chose my words carefully. "Were they close?"

"No. Claude came over for dinner occasionally, but he's single and doesn't have children." *And isn't crazy about them.* He didn't say it, but might as well have.

"We could ask Paul." I stopped, feeling out the words. "But, Philippe, Paul only mentioned his mother the one time, when he told me what happened. He didn't want to talk about it."

Silence for a moment. "He was the same with the police. Apparently he blurted it out and wouldn't talk anymore." Philippe paused. "I'm going to put Claude off. I'll tell him Paul's doctor has advised against it for now. Excuse me a minute." I could hear him conferring with someone, then he was back. "I have to go. I'll see you soon, Troy."

See you when you get home, dear. I knew I was in a pseudo-wife, pseudo-mom, pseudo-governess role here, and I knew I was falling into it a little too easily.

I went looking for Elise, hoping she would tell me something about this uncle. I found her leaning stiffly against the kitchen counter, and just the fact that she wasn't in

253

motion told me something was wrong.

"What is it?" I asked, my voice sharp with concern.

She pointed to the laundry room. I took a step forward. I could see several pairs of small underwear and socks, damp and wrinkled, laid out on the dryer. Clearly Paul's. I gave her a puzzled look.

"They were hanging in his bathroom." Her voice was so low I could barely hear her.

We stared at the damp clothes. "He's been washing them out," I said. He could have been bedwetting, but that wouldn't explain the socks. Then I remembered the clothes Paul had worn when I'd found him: shirt, underwear, and socks had all been gray and dingy. And then realization dawned, and I felt cold. While Paul was captive he must have been washing his clothes in his bathroom sink. At age six. Either his kidnappers had told him to, or he'd figured it out on his own.

And since he'd been doing it for months, he'd kept on doing it here, despite the stacks of clean new clothes in his dresser.

It took a moment before I could speak. I cleared my throat. "I think he's forgotten that you use the washing machine. I think he had to wash his own clothes while he was gone." I couldn't make myself say *while he was captive. While he was kidnapped. While he was imprisoned.*

Elise looked at the clothes, and tears slid down her cheeks. I blinked hard, so there weren't two of us standing there crying.

"Just put these in the wash," I said. "I'll talk to Paul after his nap and tell him you like washing clothes in the machine, and ask him to put them in his hamper for you. And I'll tell Monsieur Dumond about it tonight."

So when Paul awoke I pointed out his hamper and told him how much Elise liked using her big new washer, hoping I wasn't instilling a lifelong belief that women loved doing laundry. I showed him his stacks of clean things in his dresser, and said his papa would be happy to buy him more when these were worn out or too small.

After Paul went to bed that evening, I talked to Philippe. It was hard to tell him and hard for him to hear, but this was when I began to understand the significance of my role here. Elise couldn't cope with these painful reminders; I could. I was the path between the old life and the new.

I could see Philippe file this away: something else to ask the psychologist about.

Claude had been upset he couldn't see

Paul immediately, Philippe told me, but had said he understood. "I'd wanted to tell him in person about Paul coming home, but the police contacted him before I got the chance," he said.

Philippe had been right, I thought, to want to break the news to Claude in person. Learning that your nephew had returned but not your beloved sister would be bitter-sweet — an odd mix of emotions for anyone. Personally I couldn't imagine not being on my nephew's doorstep if he'd just gotten home from being kidnapped, but then I like my nephews a lot more than I like my sisters.

After I went to bed I started reading the library book about the ten-year-old kid-napped Austrian girl, who'd been kept in a cellar much of the time before escaping when she was eighteen. People wondered why she hadn't tried to escape sooner, because she had sometimes been out in public with her captor, but not until she'd been imprisoned a few years. Like the Dug-ard girl in California, who was kidnapped and kept for eighteen years. People don't understand how completely children rely on the adults around them, how quickly they recognize that their survival depends on the person in control of them. And how vulnerable they are to whatever the kidnapper tells them.

The envelope with my copies of Simon's drawings lay on my desk. I pulled them out and looked at the faces — these men had been Paul's only contact with humanity for five months.

After I crawled back into bed, I couldn't get their faces out of my mind.

CHAPTER 28

In the night I awoke suddenly, completely. Thoughts sprang into my brain with the clarity that arrives only in the middle of the night. If I had taken Paul to the police as soon as I found him, maybe they could have gotten sketches that day, better ones, while the images were fresher in Paul's mind, before he'd blanked them out, replaced them with happier memories and friendlier faces. The police could have searched for the men right away, before they had fled far from Vermont and New York, in who knows what direction.

If they don't find them, it's your fault, that insistent voice said.

I looked at the bedside clock: 2:16. I know that logic doesn't work at these hours, but I couldn't escape the cold truth I'd been dodging up until now: I'd had no business deciding not to take Paul to the authorities. *You just wanted to keep him to yourself,* the voice said. I reached out to stroke Tiger's warm fur. She stirred only slightly.

With a groan, I swung my legs out of bed. I wish my conscience would come alive during the day, when the distractions of daytime life help obscure those sharp, prodding thoughts. In the middle of the night, there are no gray areas — it's all black and white. I decided I'd look for something light to read to help shut out that insistent little voice.

On the way down the hall, I heard something from Paul's room. The door was ajar, and I pushed it open gingerly. By the glow of the night-light I could see him, curled on his side, facing away from me. His covers were in a knot at his feet, so I tiptoed forward to pull them over him.

I'd just bent over the bed when I heard movement behind me. I started to turn and saw a dark shape, large, coming at me, and then my arms were immobilized and a hand over my mouth. I began a silent, desperate struggle, kicking blindly backward and trying to wrestle my arms free. The whisper in my ear took a moment to penetrate: "Troy, Troy, stop, it's me, it's Philippe."

I stopped struggling, relief making my legs weak. The hand on my mouth disappeared, and Philippe was backing me out of the room, then leading me down the hall to the kitchen.

"What were you *doing*?" I demanded after he flicked a light on.

He scratched his head. He was barefoot, in a white T-shirt and blue-and-white striped pajama bottoms, his hair tousled. "I'm sorry, I didn't mean to frighten you. I was dozing and saw someone moving toward the bed. Then I realized it was you, but didn't want you to scream and wake Paul. What were you doing, anyway?"

"I couldn't sleep and I was going to get something to read. Then I heard a noise from Paul's room, and I was going to fix his covers. But . . ." I was confused.

"Why was I there?" Philippe sat at the kitchen table and began rubbing his shin through his pajama leg, where I'd kicked him with my heel. He looked like a small boy with his hand caught in the cookie jar. "I've been sleeping in there."

"Sleeping in there? What, in the top bunk?"

"No, in the armchair."

I stared at him, and he added, "Just until early morning, and then I go up to my room. But I can't . . . I don't want to let him out of my sight."

I leaned back against the counter, trying

to rearrange my features from my accusatory stare. I could still feel my heart hammering. "I think that's normal. I mean, you
can't spend every night in his room."

"No, of course not, but for now . . . I just
can't . . ." His voice trailed away. He ran his
fingers through his hair, almost angrily. "I
let him get kidnapped once; I didn't keep
him safe. I almost lost him forever."

I moved toward him, kneeling beside the
chair where he sat, and put my arms around
him. Without hesitation he folded his arms
around me. He was warm, smelling vaguely
of fresh laundry, a crisp cologne.

"It's not your fault, Philippe," I said into
his ear. "You can't always protect people."

His shoulders moved in a single compul-
sive silent sob; I rubbed his back, warm
through the T-shirt. He must have sensed
that kneeling on the floor was uncomfortable for me because he stood, pulling me
with him, and we clung to each other, swaying a little. After several long moments he
shifted, and I could feel him through his
pajama pants, hard against me, and my
body pulsed in response. I didn't move. Our
hearts were thudding, almost echoing in the
quiet kitchen.

"I don't want to be alone now," he said.
His face was stark, drained, tired.

I could only guess how I looked. The pull I felt toward him was almost palpable. It seemed that if I left the warmth of his arms I'd break into a hundred tiny pieces, shatter on the kitchen floor into shards that could never be put back together again.

"Philippe, I can't . . ." I whispered. "Your —"

Your wife? Your child? I wasn't even sure what I was going to say.

He put his finger on my lips. "I know." Maybe he did and maybe he didn't. He pulled me with him, toward the library, and sat me on the sofa. He knelt by the fireplace, opened the damper, and lit the stacked firewood with a starter from a slot beside the hearth. He closed the mesh screen and then moved toward me, pulling a thick afghan off the back of the sofa and sitting beside me in one easy motion. We swung our legs up and he draped the afghan over us. He pulled me toward him and I lay in the circle of his arms, my face against his chest. My heart was pounding crazily. He was stroking my back under the afghan, short, comforting movements, and gradually I relaxed. He kissed the top of my head once, and we lay quietly for five minutes, ten. Neither of us spoke. His hand started moving more slowly. I shifted slightly, but his breathing deepened and then his hand stilled. He was asleep. I wanted to stay conscious, to savor the warmth of his body against mine, the sound of his breathing. Come morning, I knew we'd almost certainly act as if this had never happened. But I couldn't keep my eyes open, and slid into a dreamless sleep.

CHAPTER 29

Paul woke us, pouncing on us, giggling at finding us asleep in the library. *"Pourquoi dormez-vous dans la bibliothèque?"* he asked.

Philippe reacted quickly, pulling his arms from under the afghan and reaching for his son. "Because," he said, pulling Paul up on the sofa and tickling him lightly, "we woke up s-o-o-o early there was no sunlight and it was chilly, so we made a nice fire to watch instead."

I disentangled myself, stiff from sleeping in one position. "And the fire made us sleepy, so we fell back asleep," I added.

"But it's time to get you dressed, little one." Philippe scooped Paul up and carried him down the hall, giggling, under his arm.

I headed to my room, grateful it was Paul who had found us and not Elise. I pulled on running clothes, called Tiger, and on the way out told Elise I'd be late for breakfast. Maybe it was just my conscience that made the look she gave me seem odd.

As my feet pounded rhythmically on the pavement, scenes from the past week cycled through my head. Me in Philippe's arms. Madeleine's emails downloading onto the screen. Jameson warning me about Philippe. The flicker of concern I'd seen from Simon when he'd first seen me with Philippe and Paul. The look Elise had just given me.

Of course I knew this was dangerous territory. Of course I knew I should leave before I let my heart get broken, by Paul or Philippe.

Of course I wasn't going to.

When I got back I toweled off and pulled on a sweatshirt and shorts, then slid into my seat just before the others finished.

Philippe looked up with a smile, an errant lock of hair falling on his forehead. I could see a pulse thumping in his throat, a small patch on his chin not shaved quite as closely as the surrounding area. I could, without much effort, imagine his cheek against mine, his breath on my neck, my fingers in his hair.

But that wasn't the way this script was written. I was his son's temporary substitute mother; last night I had been a pair of comforting arms. I knew the type of woman Philippe liked — stylish, fashionable, sophisticated. Like Madeleine. There had been a spark between us, but one we couldn't let ignite for many reasons, the most important of which was sitting at this breakfast table with messy hair, finishing his sausage.

"You went to run early," Paul proclaimed.

"Yes, I did," I said, patting my tummy. "I've been eating so much of Elise's good food that I needed some exercise before breakfast."

For some reason Paul found this very funny — I'll admit I don't always get six-year-old male humor.

Philippe smiled, and in this moment I could forget the ugly facts of kidnapping and murder and the looming threat of kidnappers. I could forget that this wasn't my life and that all too soon I would have to begin the painful process of extricating myself from it.

Paul was happy. For now, that was all that mattered.

Philippe went off to work and I left Paul playing with his racetrack and joined him after my shower. Piles of his old clothing were still lying about, and I tentatively suggested boxing up some that were obviously too small. He surprised me by agreeing.

He took it seriously, as he did most things,

trying on each piece of clothing and handing me the ones that didn't fit. He had far more preppy clothing than I knew a small boy could possess, all fine quality and showing almost no wear. I wondered if his mother had picked them out, or if she and Philippe had done it together. Or maybe this was something a nanny did.

Paul watched me letter PAUL'S OUTGROWN CLOTHES on the boxes and fold down the lids.

"When you want," I told him, "you can give these things away for someone else to wear, someone smaller than you."

He nodded. "Pete," he said, naming Baker's youngest.

"You're right." I was surprised he had thought of it. "These would be great for Pete, or maybe Rick." Of course Pete and Rick then would be the best-dressed kids in Saranac Lake, but it might be a welcome change from hand-me-downs. And it wouldn't take long for them to make these clothes look lived-in. "When I go back I can take them to them."

"When you go back," he repeated, his dark eyes luminous, almost tearful. It was too easy to forget how fragile he was.

I reached out and touched his cheek. "I can't stay here forever, sweetie. I have my

267

house, remember, and Zach and Baker —
and Tiger needs her lake to swim in. But
we'll be here awhile, and I can always visit.
It's only a few hours." I translated into
French as best I could.

He wasn't quite happy with this, and I was
annoyed with myself for upsetting him. I
grabbed him up and tickled him lightly;
then we heard Elise call us.

Zach was standing in the front foyer grinning, next to a beaming Elise.

"What are you doing here?" I asked, aston-
ished.

"Philippe th-th-thought you'd like to have
your bicycle, so he asked if I could bring it
up. Dave let me take his car."

I was almost speechless. Then I turned to
Elise. "Elise, have you met my roommate
Zach?" She nodded, and her smile told me
she'd been in on this.

"Zach, Zach!" Paul squealed, grabbing
Zach's hands and launching into a burst of
excited French.

I laughed at Zach's expression. "Paul, he
doesn't understand French — *Il ne com-
prend pas le français.* Zach, Paul says he has
a new room and lots of toys and is starting
a new school and has clothes for Baker's
children and maybe you can take them."

Zach blinked and nodded; this was way

too fast for him.

Elise scurried to set out thick sandwiches for us while Paul chattered to Zach as if he were a long-lost brother. After lunch Paul showed Zach his room and his toys, and we talked Paul into a nap, a very, very short one, while Zach and I unloaded my bike and gear. He had brought along my tool-box, bike stand, the crate with my helmet, bike shoes, shorts, and gloves — plus an armful of clothes on hangers and some folded jeans from my closet. This wasn't like Zach; I figured Philippe must have suggested it.

"Are you staying for dinner?" I asked.

"Sure. Fried chicken. Elise told me."

After Paul got up we played endless computer games, and then Philippe was home, looking weary but pleased. I caught his eye and mouthed *Thank you.*

At dinner Zach ate so much that Paul watched in awe. Elise, bringing refills from the kitchen, began to look worried, and I kicked Zach under the table. Philippe asked Zach if he'd like to stay over, but he declined, saying he needed to get the car back to Dave. After dinner Elise packed a box with sandwiches and fruit for Zach, plus a bag of pastries he promised to share with Dave.

I tried to give Zach cash for gas and the bridge toll, but he said Philippe had taken care of it. Men apparently are more adroit about these things.

I eyed the carton of food on the seat beside Zach. "Think you have enough chow there?"

"I'm a growing boy," he said, flashing his smile. He'd probably have half of it eaten before reaching the bridge to New York. He drove off, car sputtering.

I went to thank Philippe, and found him in the library.

"I hope you didn't mind," he said. "I wondered if you might want Zach to bring something specific, but I wanted to surprise you."

"No, that was fine. And Zach did bring up some of my other stuff." I didn't mention that I knew Zach wouldn't have done it on his own.

We sipped coffee and nibbled shortbread cookies. The psychologist had okayed Claude visiting, Philippe said, as long as no one mentioned Paul's mother and there were no emotional scenes. Which I thought would have been obvious. I also thought it obvious I didn't fit in at a family reunion, and said so.

"No, no, I think it's better for Paul that you're there," Philippe said.

And *kid-needs-you* trumps *you're-going-to-be-miserable-meeting-mysterious-uncle.* How could it not be painfully awkward, with Paul, his father, and uncle — but no Madeleine, and me there instead?

"Does Claude know about the, uh, ferry and rescue?" I asked.

Philippe shook his head. "He knows you found Paul and that you came here to help him settle in, but I wasn't comfortable telling him about Paul in the lake. Claude likes to dig at things, and can't leave them alone."

"But wouldn't the police have told him?" Something along the lines of *Someone tried to drown your nephew* and *Do you have any idea who?*

"Probably." He paused, weighing his words. "But if I haven't told him, then he won't discuss it here."

So if the host doesn't acknowledge the pink elephant in the room, the other guests can't either. I could see this being a useful standard — not that any of my friends would ever follow it.

At least Claude wouldn't ask me questions about the ferry incident. I wished Philippe could have avoided telling him I was the one who had found Paul, but he had to explain my presence here. And maybe the police had told him anyway.

So Madeleine's brother would be coming to dinner tomorrow night.

That night my thoughts tumbled together as I lay in bed: Paul and Philippe and kidnappers and Claude and Madeleine and Elise and Jameson. How quickly I was becoming entrenched here and how these people were weaving themselves into my life, and I was weaving myself into theirs. But this wasn't my world. I wasn't used to not being in control, not living in my own space, not making all the decisions.

It was a sensation I didn't particularly like.

CHAPTER 30

This morning Philippe was taking Paul to another psychologist's appointment. I watched Elise cooking chocolate pudding — I'd been in college before I realized pudding could be prepared any way other than instant. To me cooked pudding still tastes oddly smooth and creamy.

I wanted to ask her questions. I wanted to ask what Paul's mother had been like and what kind of mother she had been. I wanted to know what her marriage to Philippe had been like. I wanted to know how and why Philippe had abandoned his old home and life and seemingly so readily blocked out everyone but Elise and his brother-in-law.

But of course I couldn't.

I needed to go for a ride. My bike is the one place I'm fully comfortable, where I own my space in a way I don't on two feet, where the rhythm of pedals turning and wheels humming along the pavement lets my brain work smoothly and I can work out my problems. Usually.

I went out to the garage and lifted my bike into the work stand. It was gritty from my last ride down River Road at home, where sand spread for traction lingers long after the snow melts. I cleaned the frame, wiped the chain, scraped crud from the derailleur pulley wheels, and lubed the pivot points. I had disconnected the cables from the derailleurs and was dripping Tri-Flow into the housing when I heard a car door. When the connecting door into the house opened I looked up to see Jameson, wearing jeans and a shirt open at the neck.

I stood up and wiped my greasy hands with a rag. "What are you doing here?" As I said it, I realized it sounded rude. He held out something black — the daypack I'd left on the Burlington ferry.

"How did you get this?" I asked in surprise. I had thought about asking Thomas to retrieve it, but that would have required explanations I hadn't wanted to make.

Jameson reached out and lightly spun the front wheel of my Cannondale. The *tick-tick-tick* sound it made echoed against the walls of the garage. "We sent someone to Burlington. It was in the lost and found department."

I nodded. "I left it on the deck when I jumped in." So the Ottawa police were checking into things in Burlington. I unzipped the pack and peeked inside, wincing at the thought of policemen looking through my notebook, my toiletries, my change of clothes.

"You were on your way to see your boyfriend."

"Yes. Well, the guy I was dating." I didn't try to explain why they weren't the same thing. Or why I'd used the past tense.

"And you saw no one with Paul."

I shook my head. "No. I told your guys. I just saw him falling toward the water. I never looked up toward the deck. I just dived in."

He was watching me closely. "And Paul was where?"

I frowned. "He was on the back of the ferry going to Port Kent."

At first I couldn't figure out why he was asking, and then I got it: He thought Paul had been thrown in from my ferry — *and that I had seen it happen.* He thought I was shielding someone who would try to drown a child. For a moment I couldn't speak.

"Look," I said finally. "I was on the ferry to Burlington. Paul was on the ferry to Port

Kent. I didn't see anyone."

He waited a long moment, and when I didn't speak again, he pressed the button that opened the garage door and walked out.

I returned to my bike, moving by rote, reconnecting the cable housing and checking the shifting. So the police thought I'd happened to see Paul being thrown in and refused to tell them what I'd seen. Or that I'd been involved with the kidnappers. I could see the logic: Kidnappers want to dump the kid, soft-hearted female accomplice revolts. Paul would have told them he hadn't seen me before, but he was only six. And in theory I could have been involved without him ever seeing me.

So I was in cahoots with the kidnappers — but had rescued Paul and cheerfully returned him home? And now was living with father and kidnapped child? This made my head hurt.

I put the tools in my toolbox, washed up, and climbed the stairs to Philippe's office. I turned his computer on. Maybe the police had read these emails, and something in them had made Jameson suspect Philippe. Or maybe something in them would help clear him.

I needed to know.

I took a deep breath, opened Outlook

Express, and went to Madeleine's emails. I clicked on the first and oldest one, and started reading. By the time I had read the first half dozen, my stomach began to roil, but by then I couldn't have stopped, like not being able to look away from a car crash. Because many of the incoming emails quoted her emails and her Sent folder held outgoing emails, I could read ones she had written as well as those she'd received. Only about a third were in English, but I could read enough French to understand the gist of the others. I skimmed them, one by one, with a growing sense of nausea.

I couldn't tell Philippe about these, not now, not ever. I hoped he had never seen them. Some of the emails, the ones written to people on committees or in Philippe's business circle, were professional and polite, with a touch of humor. But the emails to her personal friends were entirely different. It almost seemed like reading a teenager's diary. She spoke scathingly of Philippe and never mentioned Paul; she talked of shopping and vacations and made crass sexual jokes. Her tone with male correspondents was coy and suggestive.

I couldn't reconcile these emails with the elegant, graceful woman looking at me from across the room.

How could Philippe have been with a woman like this? Had he known this side of her?

And the next thought followed immediately: *If he did, how could he not have wanted to get rid of her?*

I wanted to try to forget I'd ever seen these emails, to hit Control A and the Delete button and empty the trash so they'd be gone for good. But they weren't mine to delete.

Neither had they been mine to read, but that was done. And there could be something in these emails that would lead to the kidnappers: a name, a date, a hint of what Madeleine had done her last few days. Maybe the police had seen them, maybe not; maybe they had missed something in them.

I printed them out. I ran the French ones through an online translation program and printed the translations. I turned the computer off and went down and hid the stack of paper in the bottom drawer of my dresser, my stomach churning. I had crossed a line I'd thought I would never cross.

I went to ask Elise for something to quiet the turmoil in my gut. She gave me some Gelusil, a crunchy tablet that tasted like a Di-Gel. Then I went for my ride, and I rode hard.

■ ■ ■ ■

Paul and Philippe were back from the psychologist visit and in good spirits when I returned. It had gone well, Philippe told me. The psychologist had said that Paul washing out his clothes and his reaction to napping showed he was processing what had happened to him and adjusting to his new environment. And Paul seemed okay with the idea of seeing his uncle tonight. Just not eager.

Part of me wanted to meet a relative of Madeleine's, but part of me didn't. Maybe Philippe had had the right idea moving here: new house, new town, new school, new friends — even new language. Let the past go. Unfortunately the part of Philippe's past known as his brother-in-law had moved with him.

After lunch Philippe headed to work, and Paul went off for a nap. I agonized over what to wear. Shopping is one of those girl skills left out of my DNA. This is where I need friends like Kate, who can effortlessly find great clothes at bargain prices and could have had me outfitted in no time. I settled on my cord slacks and a pullover from among the stuff Zach had brought up. I tried to iron the slacks, but Elise appeared and took the iron from me. Whenever I try ironing, whatever I'm working on ends up more wrinkled than when I started. I should call it wrinkling instead of ironing.

"So Paul's uncle lives here in Ottawa," I said as Elise deftly wielded the iron. She gave me a quick look that somehow said that Claude wasn't her favorite person, then nodded.

"He and his sister were very close?"

Another nod. "Mostly," she said, and the tone of her voice told me she wasn't going to say more. Good nannies did not gossip, and she was a good nanny.

"So does Paul have other aunts and uncles?" I asked.

This Elise answered readily enough. "No, Monsieur Philippe is an only child, and there were only Claude and Madeleine." She handed me a crisply pressed pair of slacks, and I thanked her.

Philippe got home a scant fifteen minutes before Claude arrived, with just enough time to greet us and go change. By the time he reappeared, Claude was there. My heart was hammering — I felt as if I were going to meet a part of Madeleine.

But if Claude resembled his sister, I couldn't see it, except his hair color. His features were indistinct, and he was good-looking in a careless way, with wispy blond-ish hair and a diffident manner. He was flawlessly polite, shook my hand briskly, and presented Paul with a small stuffed dog that talked when you squeezed it. Paul accepted it with equal politeness and said in careful English, "Thank you, Uncle Claude."

Not even a hug, for a child who had been gone for months. But somehow I wasn't surprised.

It wasn't a scintillating evening, to put it mildly. Paul was dressed neatly with his hair carefully combed, and Tiger banished to the kitchen. The food was exquisite. But Paul was listless and answered in monosyllables. Philippe's manners were impeccable, but he wasn't what you could call relaxed. Me, I'm not that comfortable in new social situations in the first place, and this was particularly awkward. You couldn't discuss Madeleine or what had happened to Paul, and you could only say so much about the weather and how good the food was. It didn't help that Claude occasionally lapsed into French he assumed I couldn't understand, although Philippe steadfastly responded in English. The meal dragged interminably, and Paul asked to be excused before dessert.

"He starts school tomorrow," I offered, trying to fill the silence.

Claude was taking tiny precise bites of his cheesecake when Philippe rose. "Excuse me for a moment, please. I just need to check on Paul." I nearly panicked that Philippe was leaving me alone with Claude, whom I disliked without entirely knowing why.

Then Claude turned to me, and my hackles went up. "I'm rather confused about your connection," he said pleasantly.

"Connection?"

"To the family." He sipped his coffee and eyed me, almost mockingly. "Are you working here?"

"Oh, no, just staying awhile, until Paul is settled in. Just to help out."

"How amazing that he turned up, so long after he was taken. So you found him?"

I nodded. "Yes, I did." I watched for a reaction, but his face remained blank. I know statistically it's usually family members who commit violence against each other, and Claude made me uncomfortable.

He went on. "My little nephew seems very attached to you."

"Yes, well, I'm very fond of him."

"And Philippe, too." He smiled.

The innuendo was apparent now. Gloves off.

I reminded myself this man's sister had died tragically. I reminded myself he was Paul's uncle. I forced a smile. "Yes. Philippe, too."

Philippe returned at last. "So sorry it took so long. Paul's rather excited about school tomorrow." He and Claude chatted about work, while I tried not to let my eyes glaze over. At last Claude rose to leave, and on his way out said something in French I didn't catch. After the door shut behind him, I sighed. Philippe laughed.

"I'm sorry." I was aghast that I'd made my relief so apparent.

"No, no, it's all right. Claude isn't a wonderful conversationalist, unless it's a business deal, and he was beside himself trying to figure you out. And losing Madeleine has been very hard on him. They were very close — they lost their parents when they were quite young. I'm sorry it was uncomfortable for you."

Of course sitting at a table with his brother-in-law, nephew, and me, with his sister gone, had been difficult. Of course it was worse because they had no other family, and I felt a pang of regret for my lack of compassion. For Claude's first meeting with Paul, I should have been absent. On this, I think, Philippe had been wrong.

But this was the most I'd heard Philippe say about his wife.

That evening Paul had a nightmare, screaming, *"Non, non, non!"* Philippe was doing some work in his office; I was reading in my room and reached Paul first. He was still screaming when I grabbed him into my arms.

"Baby, baby, it's okay, everything's all right," I murmured, rubbing his back while his cries died away into a damp whimper against my neck. *"C'est seulement un . . . nightmare . . . un cauchemar."*

"Maman," he whispered brokenly. I felt a sharp pain. He wasn't mistaking me for his mother — he was calling to the woman who would never hold him again. I'd been wrong to assume that he hadn't been missing his mother.

"Paul, Paul, Paul," I said, rocking him back and forth. By then Philippe had arrived, and I handed the limp, teary bundle to his father. I went off to read until I could numb my brain enough to go to sleep.

CHAPTER 31

The next morning Paul had dark circles under his eyes, but he was excited about starting school. I admired his book bag and his blue slacks, polo shirt, and blazer, and snapped away with my little camera. Because of course you have to have first-day-of-school pictures. If I were Philippe, I think I'd be fighting the compulsion to lurk in the back of the classroom for the next few days.

After they left, I wandered back to my room. I felt down, and wasn't sure why. It was almost starting to seem that Madeleine haunted this house, and not just because of Claude's visit. Madeleine somehow seemed more present than if the house still held her things: her clothes, her photos, her knick-knacks, her magazines. Maybe her ghost couldn't be vanquished until people stopped acting as if she'd never existed.

Or maybe it was just me, and those emails

I'd downloaded.

I made myself read the printouts of them again, line by line. A few were confusing — probably personal jokes or idioms I didn't get — but nothing gave any clues.

Dead end.

So I went upstairs to see what I could find out about Madeleine and her brother on the internet.

Usually you can learn amazing amounts about people online, even if they've never used sites like Facebook or MySpace. You can find public records, newspaper articles, group memberships, reviews posted on Amazon, comments on other sites.

With some simple Googling, I confirmed the spelling of Claude's last name, Lemieux, and assumed Madeleine's had been the same. I knew their approximate ages and where they'd been living the last decade. This should have been plenty. It wasn't.

I did find a few mentions of Madeleine in society pages, and some references to business accounts Claude had represented. I found a brief wedding announcement, and learned that both sets of parents were deceased. With concentrated digging I found records of the marriage and of Paul's birth, and simple math told me he had been born less than nine months after the marriage. But without accidents, many of us wouldn't be here, me included.

I sat back. I'd never done so much research with so little result. No graduations, no previous jobs, no arrests. No photos, no comments, no book lists, no petitions signed, no donations given. It was as if Claude and Madeleine hadn't existed before they met Philippe.

Claude hadn't been what I'd imagined. I'd expected either austere, like the furniture in parts of this house, or openly grieving. Instead he was almost sly, as if he was secretly amused by something or knew things other people didn't.

Of course I wondered if Claude could have planned the kidnapping. Dumond said he had been very close to his sister, but close relationships can go wrong. And from the tone and brevity of Elise's comments, I'd gathered that brother and sister hadn't always gotten along. Or Claude could have set up a fake kidnapping that had gone bad. But if he had been involved, would he have followed his brother-in-law to Ottawa?

And could Paul be in danger from him?

Maybe I was being paranoid, or going off on this tangent because I disliked Claude. Or maybe there was good reason to distrust him. But surely the police had checked him out.

I emailed Simon from my laptop, telling him I'd met the mysterious brother, who wasn't precisely warm and friendly. I phrased the next line carefully. I couldn't ask Simon to check out Claude, but if I let him know my concern, his brain wouldn't let it drop. I wrote: *What if Claude planned the kidnapping and he knows the kidnappers can link him to it — where does that leave Paul?*

With that done, I opened Outlook Express and reread the last dozen incoming emails in Madeleine's account. All offered some variation on *Where are you and why haven't I heard from you?*

None of these people had heard of Madeleine's kidnapping or death: Philippe had let everyone think she was wintering in Florida. When he moved here, they would have assumed she'd moved, too, or stayed on in Florida. No one had notified these people of her death, and this seemed horrible.

If they think she's alive, I could send them emails from Madeleine's account.

I couldn't let the thought go. How would someone involved in her kidnapping or death react to an email apparently from

Madeleine? Not well, that was for sure. But they would react.

I composed a generic email: *I've been away, and lots has happened! What's up with you?* I copied it to each of her most recent correspondents, and clicked Send for each one. I had just sent the last one when a *ding* told me a reply had come in.

I took a deep breath and clicked on it.

Hey, girl, where have you been? It's been for-evv-ee-rr. How are things shaping up? Did you go to Florida? Fill me in! Gina T

This was no help, and it was abominably cruel to let this woman think her friend was alive. I'd jumped into this without thoroughly considering it, and now the damage was done. To buy time, I hit the Reply button and typed: *Too much to tell now — more soon. How R U?*

What had I been thinking? I had stepped over a line, and there would be no stuffing this genie back in the bottle.

My face burning with shame, I closed the program, shut down the computer, and took myself off to the library to pick up the books I'd requested about recovered kidnapped children: *I Know My First Name is Steven, I Choose to Live,* and *Invisible Chains.* So it didn't look quite so strange, I picked up Ruth Rendell and Michael Robotham novels as well. Which, on second thought, probably didn't help.

On the way back I stopped at a chip wagon and ate poutine while driving, miraculously managing to avoid dribbling gravy down my front.

As I took the books to my room, I heard Paul and Philippe come in. I joined them in the kitchen, where Paul was digging into a snack Elise had prepared, and discovered that school was great, the kids were fun, teachers nice, and lunch not so great — and that Philippe had, in fact, spent the whole day at school.

He gave a little shrug. "It's his first day."

So Dad had stayed in the back of the room for the entire school day. Which I thought was perfect for his son's first day back. It made me realize that Philippe wasn't confident about any of what he was doing — which I think was a strange place for him to be. Like the rest of us, he was just forging ahead as best he could.

After Paul went off for his rest Philippe went upstairs to do some work, but was back in a few minutes.

"I can't find a file I've been working on," he said. "It's driving me nuts — do you think you could take a look?"

I followed him up to his office. He was

using the remote access program I'd told him about, which let his work computer's desktop appear on the screen in front of him. I did a quick search. Nothing. "Was it a new file, or one you'd just resaved?" I asked.

"It came in an email today," he said.

"You opened it directly from the email?"

He nodded.

Now I knew where it was — in a temporary folder where the Search function doesn't penetrate. "You need to save files attached to emails before you start working on them," I said. "Just show me the email it came with." He pulled up the email. I clicked on the attached file, found the temporary folder it would have been saved in and the missing file, and showed Philippe how to save it to a new location.

"Ahhh," he said. "You make it look so easy." Which it is, but I'd lost plenty of files myself before I figured it out.

"Wait," he said, as I started to leave. "Could you show me how to set this up so it shows the file extensions?"

The default Windows setting hides doc, exe, pdf, jpg, and other file extensions, which I think is insane. So I showed him how to set folder options so you can see the file type at a glance.

"Back up a minute," Philippe said, looking over my shoulder. "That has to be a mistake. That says the date on that file is today."

"That would be the date you last saved it, not the date you wrote it."

"But that's the point. That's today's date and I haven't used it today — and no one should be using these files but me."

"Maybe your work computer somehow got set to the wrong date," I said. I ran the cursor over the file name and idly double-clicked, and a message popped up: *This file is currently being used by another user. Do you want to make a copy?* "Hmmm," I said. I tried a different file, which promptly opened. I closed it and went back to the first one. Still not available. "Houston, we've got a problem," I muttered under my breath.

"What is it?"

"This file won't open. Which means either it's been corrupted, or it's in use." I closed the file manager and reopened it. The file now showed a different time. I clicked on it, and now it opened. I turned to look at Philippe. "Someone's accessing your files. Would your secretary be looking at these?"

"No. Not my secretary and not anyone. I left my computer on, so I could use the remote program, but no one should be using it." He glanced at his watch. "Excuse me while I call the office." He pulled out his cell phone as he stepped out of the room, and I could hear a low murmur. When he returned he told me his receptionist had been away from her desk, and he had asked her to lock his office.

"Your files aren't password protected?"

He shook his head.

I made a face. "You need to install a boot protection program, Philippe, so no one can get into your files — and you should check to make sure no one has installed a keyboard capture or remote access program."

He looked at me the way Paul does when he wants something. "Could you . . . ?"

Of course I could, but his was a professional office that needed an office-wide daily backup system and professional-level security on each computer. "You don't have a computer person to do this stuff?"

He shook his head. "I should, but I don't. Could you do it? I'll pay you, of course."

It amazes me that people entrust their entire businesses to computers with no one on-site who really understands them. A friend who does computer installations told me about a big organization whose computers were set to back up at midnight every day — but when everyone went home at six, *they all turned their computers off.* So when a virus struck, months of files were lost.

I told him I'd come to his office tomorrow and do a basic security check and cleanup on his computer, if he would start looking for a pro to do company-wide security and backup. I wouldn't let him pay me, but he could take me to lunch.

CHAPTER 32

The next morning Paul went off cheerfully to school. Today Philippe would stay for only the first half hour, which Paul thought was fine. Apparently the routine of school and being around other kids appealed to him. Philippe had made a good decision enrolling Paul in school.

No reply yet from Simon, but I knew he was thinking on it. He might even call Jameson, although he wouldn't tell me about it.

I opened Outlook Express and found one reply in Madeleine's account, chat about what so-and-so was doing. It had been a dramatic notion to have sent out emails supposedly from Madeleine, but not, I realized, a particularly useful one. It would have been far smarter — and less nerve-wracking — to have pretended to be a mutual friend. Then I could have asked if anyone knew what had happened to her or who she had been hanging out with her last week or so, or if she had mentioned being followed or seeing someone suspicious.

It would seem too coincidental to suddenly get in touch with all the people the fake Madeleine had just emailed, especially if any of them communicated with each other. But I'd try it with a few. I signed up for an anonymous email address and sent emails to the three women who seemed to be her chattiest friends: *Hi, I'm a friend of Madeleine's — haven't heard from her and I'm wondering what's up — do you have any idea?*

Then I headed off to Philippe's office to do the work I'd promised to do on his computer. I wondered if Philippe's receptionist would remember me and my odd story about the misdelivered FedEx envelope, but if she did, she was too well trained to show it. A few other employees walked past as she buzzed Philippe and waved me back to his office.

He set me up at his desk, and went off elsewhere while I got to work. I checked for keyboard capture programs or remote access programs other than the one he'd installed, but didn't find any. Either what we'd seen had been an obscure blip, or someone had been using his computer.

I updated and ran his internet security program, ran Advanced System Care, defragged the hard drive, and installed a boot protection program. If he left his computer running, the screen would go blank, and couldn't be accessed until the password was typed in. Then I set up his small backup drive to do automatic document backups near the end of every workday. Most people don't seem to realize that it's not a question of *if* your hard drive will fail, but *when*. A better system would back up the entire hard drive regularly, but this would do for now.

I realized I was starving, and glanced at the clock — it was nearly noon. I'd been here more than two hours. Computers can be a huge time sink. As I stood, the door opened.

It was Claude, and the look on his face wasn't what you would call welcoming. "What are you doing here?"

"Just helping Philippe out."

"What do you mean?" His vehemence was startling.

"You can ask Philippe." I thought for a moment he was going to grab my arm. But he let me pass, and followed me out of the room. Philippe was speaking to the receptionist and by the time he turned to us, belligerent Claude was gone and suave businessman Claude was in his place — a Jekyll and Hyde moment so perfect I couldn't help but be impressed.

"Are you ready?" Philippe asked. I nodded, and we headed for the elevator. At a nearby bistro we had soup-and-sandwich combos — when you're eating Elise's dinners, you need a light lunch — and I briefed him on what I'd done on his computer. I didn't mention how annoyed Claude had seemed. I assumed he just didn't like me on his home turf.

I glanced at the time. I needed to get home in time to let Tiger out before going to pick Paul up from school.

Yes, I was starting to think of it as home.

At the school, cars were lined up to pick up children. Security guards checked license plates against a list before letting you through the gates, and if they didn't know you on sight, you had to show ID. It was laborious, but not so bad when weighed against the risks of having your child kidnapped.

Until this became routine, Paul would be waiting inside the classroom with his teacher. He was quiet when I retrieved him, in stark contrast to the bounciness of the other children. "How was it?" I asked after he had climbed into the booster seat we'd strapped into my backseat.

He sighed. "It is difficult to speak the English all day."

"Ah, sweetie, it will get easier very fast. *Ça deviendra vite plus facile.*" I knew he would pick up English quickly, and soon the summer term would start and classes would be smaller. If nothing else, this would give him an idea of what to expect of regular classes in the fall, so it wouldn't be new and scary, and would let him meet most of the children who would be in his fall class.

In the kitchen Elise gave him yogurt and fruit, and he chattered about his day in French. Philippe wanted him to speak English at home until he became fluent, but I thought we'd agree that all day at school was enough for one small boy. Especially his first few days.

When I took him off to change his clothes he pointed to his hamper. "Look, I put the clothes in my . . . my . . . *mon panier à linge,*" he said with pride.

"Laundry hamper," I told him. "That's good — it will make Elise very happy. Then when she has enough dirty clothes, she can run the washing machine."

He nodded, happy with this.

Philippe seemed more relaxed that evening, maybe because Paul was in school and handling it well. Over after-dinner coffee — I'd decided to take it easy on desserts until I started biking more — I told him about Jameson bringing me my bag from the ferry, and asked if he had heard of any progress.

He shook his head. "They told me they sent someone to Burlington, but that's all they told me."

It was hard to fathom that no one had noticed that two men were keeping a child prisoner, but the news is filled with stories of people kept prisoner in basements, in backyards, in secret rooms that no one finds. And Paul could have been kept anywhere within driving distance of that ferry.

Philippe saw me glance at the piles of paperwork in front of him. "Just going over some things from work," he said. "Some cost overruns I didn't expect."

At my concerned look, he shook his head. "Nothing major. You're always going to have overruns or estimates that are too low, but it averages out." I thought about Jameson's comment about his company's financial problems, but saw no point in mentioning it.

"Did you find out who was accessing your files?" I asked.

He shook his head. "No, but that's part of the reason I'm going over all these, to look for discrepancies. But I wanted to ask you about this." He pulled a thick envelope from his briefcase and handed it to me.

"What is it?" I turned it over, curious.

"One of my clients is having a thing Saturday evening to celebrate his company's twenty-five-year anniversary. Open it."

It was a heavy cream-colored card, like the ones extravagant people send out for weddings. It was an invitation to a party at the Château Laurier near the Parliament buildings, a hotel that resembled a castle. "Sounds pretty fancy," I said.

"Yes, these people never do anything in an ordinary fashion. Do you want to go? I know it's very late notice, but it slipped my mind until now."

I blinked. "Go? Me?" I asked, almost in horror.

Philippe laughed. "Yes, you. The invitation's for two, and most people bring someone. It's good for business for me to get out and about, and if I go alone I'll have to fend off too many people. It helps to have someone along."

Troy, the human buffer. Maybe having me

there would keep people from asking him about his home life. I assumed his office staff knew he was a widower, but maybe not everyone did. I picked up the invitation again. "What would you *wear* to a party like this?"

"I'd wear a suit. You'd wear a cocktail dress." At my blank look, he smiled. "I can assume that you don't have one with you?"

"I don't have one with me or anywhere."

He raised one eyebrow. "Would you like to go? You can find a dress here."

I almost said an emphatic *no*. But that's what old Troy would have done. I wavered, then took the plunge. "Okay. But I'm going to need help with shopping — a lot of help."

He agreed, and at that moment I loved him for not laughing at me. The next morning we took Paul along as we trekked into women's shops.

Philippe was good; I have to hand it to him. He found the right shops and the right clerks to steer us to the right clothes on the marked-down racks, knowing I was on a budget and knowing better than to offer to pay for it. He looked through them and indicated ones to try on, which Paul thought great fun. At the third dress at the second shop, a place on Sparks Street, he stopped me.

"This is it," he said.

It wasn't anything I would ever have considered. It was long-sleeved and off the shoulder, and I thought I'd look ridiculous in it. But I tried it on, and when I looked in the mirror a different person looked out at me. For a moment I didn't breathe.

I stepped out, tentatively, and from Philippe's expression I knew I'd been right. This was a Troy I'd had no idea existed. It was an odd feeling, like having a whole other self you've never happened to catch a glimpse of. Paul clapped his hands. I twisted around to look at the price tag, and winced. I took a deep breath. "Okay."

Looking good, even at a discount, doesn't come cheap.

We postponed shoe shopping until the next morning, and left Paul with Elise. I hoped she didn't think Philippe was buying me clothes; I hoped she knew this dinner thing was entirely platonic.

This was not fun. I think most women's shoes are apparatuses of torture, designed to deform — the modern-day equivalent of old Chinese foot binding. I flat-out refused to wear spike heels or pointed-toe shoes. But finally we found a pair I could wear, more or less comfortably.

After lunch I ventured on my own to a department store. I'd called Kate, who knew about makeup, and she'd told me what to buy and what to do with the stuff.

I ended up giving the list to a saleswoman and buying what she handed me. Then I stopped at an ATM and got more Canadian money. I could charge most things, but for some things you need cash: a candy bar, a bag of chips, poutine.

I had reservations about leaving Paul at home — we'd never left him with just Elise, except for this morning, but evening seemed more ominous. But of course the house was secure; of course Philippe would check with Elise throughout the evening. Nothing would happen.

Paul was more excited than I about the party. He kept popping into my room when I was getting ready, and by the time I emerged he was jumping up and down. I couldn't help but wonder if he'd done this with his mother, if it was a routine they'd had when she'd gone to functions.

"Pretty, pretty, pretty!" he declared.

I'd pulled back the sides of my hair loosely and secured them with combs Kate had told me to get. My hair springs into long curls if I don't tie it back, and even I knew it looked good. The eyeliner made my eyes stand out, and I began to understand why women used this stuff. I rummaged through my toiletry bag for the one piece of jewelry I owned, a birthstone necklace my parents had given me when I had turned sixteen.

When I came out Philippe smiled. "You look wonderful," he said.

To say that I was nervous would be a vast understatement. Cinderella didn't go to the ball every day of the week. But when I stepped out of the car at the Château Laurier, I made a conscious decision not to let my nervousness rule the evening. We chatted with people Philippe knew, nibbled hors d'oeuvres, and drank dry wine. And danced. "Philippe, I don't know how," I hissed as he moved us toward the dance floor.

"Don't you go dancing in Lake Placid?"

"Yes, but not *real* dancing. Not party dancing. Not steps or anything."

"It's easy. I'll show you." And he did, urging me onto the dance floor and leading me until I was moving without conscious thought.

"See? I knew you could do it." He smiled at me, and I swear I felt my heart move. Clichés exist for a reason.

On the way home, I relaxed into the leather seat of his car. "Thank you," I said.

"For what?"

"For taking me tonight. For a fun evening." I waved my hand. *For treating me like a girl. For showing me I can do this.*

He smiled but didn't speak, and I fell asleep before we reached the house. I woke up to tiptoe in to give a sleeping Paul a good-night kiss, hang up my beautiful dress, pull on a T-shirt and shorts, wash my face, and fall into bed.

At breakfast Elise showed me an *Ottawa Citizen,* folded to the society section. "Look," she said happily. "A picture of you and Monsieur Dumond." There we were, caught as we were entering the Château Laurier. Philippe looked handsome and natural, and for a moment I didn't recognize myself. I couldn't help but remember the photo of Madeleine from the Montreal magazine I'd seen an eon ago. *You are no Madeleine,* that unpleasant little voice said to me.

Which of course I knew. But neither was I the Troy I had been.

After everyone was done with the newspaper, I cut out the photo and tucked it away.

CHAPTER 33

Monday morning we began the new weekly routine, and I was living the most regimented existence I had since high school.

After a cheerful breakfast, Philippe drove Paul to school and went on to his office. I worked, read, ran or took a bike ride, and visited with Elise. Then I would pick up Paul, and after he had his snack, take him out to play with Tiger, Philippe and I having agreed that it seemed safe for Paul to be out with me and a large German shepherd–looking dog. Then he rested or played until his father got home, and after Happy Family Dinner came a quiet evening with homework or a game until his bedtime. Claude came for dinner regularly, and I got used to parrying his ripostes. I began to think of conversations with him as a game where I tried to turn the tables on him. Occasionally I succeeded.

I didn't do any cooking or cleaning or

even grocery shopping, except once in a while when I was going out and Elise asked me to pick something up or when I had a hankering for something she didn't normally get. I tried to do my own laundry, although Elise had become adept at finding it either just before or after I did it, and ironing all the things she thought needed ironing. So I was looking significantly tidier than usual.

If this were really my life — if not for un-caught kidnappers and suspicious police-men, and if I wasn't going to bed alone every night — it would have been wonder-ful.

But I was aware of the fine line I walked. I was part of their life, but not quite. Paul had his father, and he had Elise. He was going to school five days a week, and after another week or two, it would be time for me to head back to Lake Placid and a life that seemed no longer my own.

The thing was, I had plenty of spare time to spend on the internet.

Crimes have been solved by people being recognized from a Facebook account, so I decided to put up the equivalent of a personal ad on Craigslist. I resized the jpgs of the two men, and under the Vermont Personals, I wrote: *Looking for two French-Canadian men, who may be from the Mon-*

308

treal area and likely lived in or near Burlington recently and were fluent in French — any info appreciated, and uploaded the drawings. I used the anonymous email address Craigslist provides, and didn't list my name anywhere.

When I checked emails I saw that one to my fake identity had arrived from Gina: *Yeah, I've been wondering, too. Just got an email from her but that's all.*

Okay, go for broke. Mouth dry, I wrote back: *Want to meet for coffee or lunch and chat?*

Gina must have been sitting at a computer, because I had an answer within a minute. *I'm free tomorrow at 11:30, how about you?*

I took a deep breath and emailed back: *Sure, where would you like to meet?* She suggested a café on this side of Montreal; I pulled up MapQuest and saw it was about two hours away. Yes, I could do this. I emailed a confirmation.

I couldn't even pretend I was doing this just to try to find the kidnappers. Yes, I wanted clues, but I also desperately wanted to know more about Madeleine, to meet someone who knew her and would talk about her.

■ ■ ■ ■

Claude came for dinner that evening. I honestly wasn't sure why he came, unless he thought he was supposed to — or just wanted to torment me. Or maybe for Elise's cooking. Tonight he made only token attempts to engage Paul, and when Philippe left the room briefly, Claude nodded toward Elise, who was just leaving the room after refilling the coffee cups.

"Elise is very good," he said.

"Yes, she is," I said brightly.

"And devoted to Paul."

"Yes, she's fond of Paul."

His tone matched mine in blandness. "Perhaps a trifle too fond."

He knew I had to react to this. What was he implying? Or did he just want to rile me? "How would you know that?" I asked.

This wasn't quite the reaction he wanted. Something flashed in his eyes. "My sister told me."

I didn't have to respond, because we could hear Philippe returning. Later that evening I brought up Claude, asking Philippe how long Claude had been working for him.

Philippe thought for a moment. "Nearly six years now. He wasn't living in Montreal then, but he wanted to be closer to his sister, so I suggested that he come to work for me, and it's turned out quite well."

I couldn't quite hide my look of surprise.

"Oh, Claude is very good — he's phenomenal at closing deals. But I know he likes to tweak people. For a while he was giving Colette, the receptionist, a hard time, until she learned to ignore him. But that ability that lets him see how to tweak people makes him a superb salesman."

I suppose if you know how to annoy people, you probably also know how to please them. "I guess moving here was a big adjustment," I said. Surely Claude had had friends in Montreal; surely he had had a life there besides his sister.

"I think he wanted a change," Philippe said. "He'd been starting to see someone, and apparently it ended suddenly and badly. Starting up the business again here was a challenge, and it kept him busy. But I think since he's spending more time managing the office and not working as directly with clients he's getting a little bored."

A bored employee, I thought, is a dangerous one. But I didn't say so. This was Philippe's brother-in-law, and would be a part of his life forever. For better or for worse.

The next morning two responses had come in to my Craigslist ad, one an ad for a dating service and the other from someone who had interpreted my ad as a come-on. I decided it was time to try something more specific. I posted a message on Twitter: *Anyone know these guys? May have been involved in abduction of a 6-year-old boy last December,* with a link to the Craigslist posting. This would go out to my hundreds of followers. Some would repeat it so all their followers would get it, and so on — like a virtual, endless chain letter. You never knew who might see it.

Then I checked Madeleine's email account. There was one new one, from a sender called Gaius: *Julia o Julia, what game are you playing?*

I reread it. This was the first person who had used the name Julia, which implied a certain intimacy. Maybe this was someone Madeleine had been involved with — and perhaps was irate because he hadn't heard from her. This was tough; I didn't know how to respond. But if this person knew Madeleine well, maybe I could ferret out something. I typed, *What do you mean?* and hit the Send button before I could think better of it.

Now I had to leave to meet Gina.

If I cut things close, I always get lost, but if I leave plenty of time I'm fine. I arrived at the café in Montreal fifteen minutes early, and in fumbling French ordered iced tea.

I'd dressed in black — jeans, stretchy T-shirt, and blazer, with my recorder in the pocket. Gina had said she would be wearing red. I had no trouble spotting her when she arrived, ten minutes late. She had long fluffy hair and more eye makeup than I'd seen outside Nashville. I'd had plenty of time to practice my pitch: *I hadn't heard from Madeleine for months; I was worried, I happened to find your email address in an old email.*

It turned out I didn't have to talk much. In fact, it was so easy I might have felt guilty if it hadn't taken all my energy to keep up with Gina's discourse. All I had to do was introduce a topic, and she was off and running. Where could Madeleine possibly be? *Probably in Florida or on a cruise, she does like to travel, you know, and I wish I could but I just never can get away, but she said she would take me sometime and of course she'd pay for everything, I'd just have to buy my airfare.* Could she have gone off with someone?

Well, that husband of hers is at work all the time, but sometimes her brother went with her and who knows, maybe she had a boyfriend, but she never talked about it and I never saw her with anyone except her brother. She did meet some woman, I can't remember her name, she brought her into the salon to have her nails and hair done and even paid for it, but of course she always had plenty of money. What about her son? *Yep, he's a real cutie, but awfully quiet and spent most of his time with that old woman, the nanny.*

Oddly, I found myself liking her.

Somewhere in all this she squeezed in talk about her job as a hairstylist — which was how she'd met Madeleine — and ate a hearty sandwich and drained two glasses of white wine. And then I took a chance on our sudden camaraderie and leaned close and said, "I'm not so sure that Madeleine really wanted children, you know."

This started her off: *Yes, if you want to know the truth of course you know the boy was sort of an accident but like on purpose to help Philippe along with the idea of getting married because some men you know just will never take that step unless they have to and it's no wonder really that Maddie doesn't care for kids because she was surrounded by them you know and some really awful ones some-*

314

times growing up in all those foster homes and I'm pretty much sure that in some of those homes the dads took liberties you know because of some things Maddie said, in fact she got pregnant really young but the baby was born dead, and you know she was really gorgeous even when she was really really young, I've seen pictures.

I was glad I had my recorder — this was so fast I was barely following it. She paused and I murmured, "Sounds like she had a really tough time."

She nodded. "Yep, and it was worse, you know, after what had happened to her parents, and she was the one who found them when she was just eleven." She leaned close and spoke in a low voice: "One of them killed the other, you know, I'm not sure which." I blinked.

Suddenly she looked at her watch and stood. "Say, you know, it was great to meet you, but I've got an appointment and parking is awful, so I'd better run." She waggled her fingers at me and was gone before I realized that she had left me with the check.

Which I deserved. I'd encouraged this woman to talk about a friend she had no idea was dead, and had discovered details of a horribly sad past — dead parents, bad foster homes, lost baby. It didn't help that I had two hours of driving to mull it all over.

I went straight to pick up Paul, calling Elise on my cell to ask her to let out Tiger. As I neared the school I was newly aware of every car around me. On the way home I checked the rearview mirrors so often I almost didn't hear what Paul was telling me about his day.

When he was changing clothes, I checked Madeleine's email. Gaius had replied: ten short words that gave me a chill. *A game where you disappear, but the boy comes back.*

My brain stuttered. This person didn't know Madeleine had been kidnapped, *but somehow knew Paul had returned.* How could he know one of these things and not the other? I reread the initial email: *Julia o Julia, what game are you playing?*

I had to turn this over to the police, but I really didn't want to give them all Madeleine's emails, just in case the police hadn't seen them. I also didn't particularly want them to know what I'd been doing.

What a mess I'd gotten myself in. Simon would have told me this was why civilians should never dabble in these things.

But because I seemed so close to finding out something, I'd send one more message. I thought hard, and wrote back, *What did you think had happened?*

And then I began to research. This time I used Madeleine's and Claude's first names only, with the words *Québec, parents,* and *murder.* And I found the story.

They indeed had been nine and eleven when their parents had died in an apparent murder-suicide, and had been the ones who found them dead. They'd had a different last name then; perhaps they'd taken the name of one of their foster families. I wondered if Philippe knew all these grim details.

I clicked off the computer.

I felt thoroughly ashamed. I was ashamed for meeting Gina under false pretenses. I was ashamed I'd been so intolerant of Claude, who had had such a terrible childhood. And I was ashamed for having been foolish enough to think that I could succeed where the police had not.

I'd never realized how dangerous hubris could be.

CHAPTER 34

It didn't help that tonight Philippe had asked me to an annual affair for local businesses, where his company had been nominated for an award — he had an extra ticket because Claude had canceled. Even I knew not to wear the same dress, and on my own I'd found a simple black dress that had been marked down. Fortunately I could use the shoes I'd gotten earlier.

This was your standard awards buffet dinner, with pompous speakers and jokes not as funny as the tellers intended. It was fancier and bigger than dinners I'd attended for my small newspaper, but not all that different. Philippe had graciously accepted his award and we were at the post-dinner socializing part. He had gone to get us wine when I heard someone speak beside me.

"Hello," the voice said, and I jumped visibly. At first I didn't recognize the man standing there. It was Detective Jameson, shirt neatly ironed, tie closed, hair tidy.

"Hello," I said. "What are you doing here?"

He didn't answer. We could see Philippe across the room, in a three-way conversation with a shrill woman and a stout man, glasses of wine in his hands, gracefully trying to get away.

"So you're dating now," he said abruptly.

"No," I said. "No, we're not."

"What about the boyfriend in Vermont?"

I turned to look at him, but his face showed nothing. "I just told you that I'm not dating Philippe. Just because I am at a function with him doesn't mean we're dating. Look, you're here, I'm here, and we're not dating."

He shrugged. "How long have you been sleeping with him?"

For a moment I couldn't believe I had heard correctly, and then I was suddenly so angry I could hardly speak. "I can't believe you said that."

"You haven't answered."

With an effort I controlled my temper. "My private life is none of your business."

He shrugged again. "Maybe it is, maybe it isn't. When you have a puzzle to solve, it helps to have all the pieces." He looked at me placidly. "It's an easy question."

I stared at him. "I am not involved with Philippe," I said. "I am not dating Philippe. I am not sleeping with Philippe. But, *one,* this has nothing to do with anything you're investigating, and, *two,* you have no idea if I'm telling the truth."

The crowd jostled around us, and then he was behind me, and I could see Philippe detaching himself and beginning to move toward me. "One, I never ask anything without a reason," Jameson said, almost in my ear. "And, two, whether you're telling the truth or not, your answer tells me something." Then he was gone.

Philippe had to go to work early the next morning, so I drove Paul to school. When I got back, I went up to check Madeleine's email, feeling nervous and more than a little guilty. One reply from Gaius: *That maybe someone has gotten even with you — someone you cut off, like me?* I read the words once and then a second and third time. This sounded like something from a jilted lover. This had to go to the police, without a doubt.

I went off on my ride, and on the bike I worked out how to do it. I would print the incoming Gaius emails with the coding revealed to show IP addresses, and fax them to the police station anonymously from a Jiffy Print. The police could trace the sender. It would be out of my hands. I'd stop tinkering, now. No more emails. No more Craigslist ads. No more meeting friends of Philippe's wife.

Decision made.

When you've ridden a bike as many miles as I have, you look for trouble on a subconscious level. Without realizing it you watch for a car door suddenly opening, a dog bolting, a driver about to heave a can or bottle. When something happens, you have to react, and react quickly.

What crept into my consciousness now was a car, a big dark one, coming toward me and suddenly turning left directly across my path. Whether the driver was blinded by the sun, had fallen asleep at the wheel, or had had a sudden homicidal impulse, I didn't know and didn't care. A couple of tons of metal were bearing down on me, and if I didn't get out of the way I'd be dead. No time to reverse direction, and I knew I couldn't accelerate enough to get out of its path. Without conscious thought, I jerked my front wheel hard right in an almost impossibly sharp turn.

The car just cleared my rear tire, nearly knocking me over from turbulence. Had there been nothing in my way, I could have ridden it out or just run into the curb. But there was a line of cars parked along the side of the road, and nowhere to go. I crunched hard into the bumper of a shiny red car, and while I was airborne had time to consider how much better it was to hit a static object than be hit by one coming at you. Not for nothing did I make As in physics.

That was the last thing I knew until I opened my eyes and saw people leaning over me. I could hear a siren keening in the distance. "She's moving," a voice said. But moving hurt, so I stopped. It can seem surprisingly restful to lie on hard pavement. The sun was bright overhead, and too many people were staring at me. I could feel a wetness on my knees and elbows. I closed my eyes again. I kept them closed, ignoring the buzz of voices. But I heard an ambulance arrive, and felt the jostle as I was placed on a backboard. I didn't want to get in an ambulance, which wouldn't be cheap, but neither did I have enough energy to protest. I felt a tear trail from beneath my closed eyelids.

As they lifted the stretcher, I called out, "My bike, where's my bike?"

A murmured reply I didn't catch.

"I'm not leaving without my bike," I insisted, although in truth I wasn't about to try to hop up.

More murmurs. "Someone will watch your bike," a voice said near my face. "But we need to worry about you right now." I thought about trying to sit up, but something seemed to be holding me down. I heard the ambulance doors close, and we started to move.

CHAPTER 35

I don't recall much of the ride to the hospital. I do remember insisting I could walk when the ambulance doors opened, and they compromised on a wheelchair. I hurt all over, but by now I could tell that nothing was broken. I'd had plenty of bike wrecks in my teens, when I rode harder and faster than I should have. But I'd forgotten how much it could hurt.

A man standing at the front desk turned as we came in. He looked like Detective Jameson. I blinked. It was Jameson.

"What are you doing here?" I asked as I was wheeled past.

He surveyed me. "I could ask you the same question."

By the time I saw him again, the nurse and doctor had prodded for possible breaks, checked for concussion, and cleaned and dressed my wounds, a not comfortable process. I'd catapulted over the car, tucked and rolled, then slid to a stop. When you slide on pavement, you leave behind bits of clothing and skin, and grind in dirt and germs that must be removed. My padded bike gloves were ruined, but they had saved my palms.

"What are you doing here?" I asked again, sitting on the edge of the bed.

"Apparently you blacked out and couldn't answer questions in the ambulance. You had my card in your wallet, and someone called me." He thrust a plastic shopping bag at me.

"What's this?" I opened the bag and saw a T-shirt from the hospital gift shop. My confusion must have showed.

"To wear home." He gestured toward the hospital gown I had on.

"Oh, yeah," I said, remembering that my T-shirt had been shredded. I was taken aback that he had thought of this. "Thanks." I couldn't think what else to say.

Silence for a moment. "What happened?" he asked.

I shut my eyes, seeing it again. "Someone turned right toward me," I said slowly. "A big car, making a left turn across traffic, and there was nowhere to go. I veered right, and I hit a parked car." I opened my eyes. He was watching unblinkingly. "I was on

Cumberland, going north, and he was going south — and then turned left in front of me."

"You were lucky," Jameson said, and held up my bike helmet, scarred and with a prominent crack.

I winced. I was going to need a new helmet, and good ones aren't cheap.

"Do you know who it was?" he asked.

"Who what was?"

He looked at me as if I were an idiot. Maybe I was. "Who almost hit you."

"*No,* I don't know who it was. Why should I know who it was? It was some jerk who was half blind or who thought I was moving so slowly he'd clear me, I guess." I was too annoyed to mince words.

"You said *he.* Was a man driving?"

"I don't know, I just meant he, it, the driver."

"You didn't see the driver?"

"No. The windows were tinted. I couldn't even see if it *had* a driver." I knew my voice was testy.

"What kind of car was it?"

"It didn't stop, did it?" I'd had this happen once before, with the driver continuing on after forcing me off the road.

He repeated, slowly, enunciating each word, as if to a not particularly bright child:

"What — kind — of — car — was — it?"

"God, I don't know." My head hurt. "It was something big, with a big grille in front. A dark car, black or really dark green. All I saw was that grille, coming at me too damn fast."

His lips quirked. "Plates?"

I shook my head. "Didn't see 'em. I don't even know if they were Canadian."

"Do you have a routine, a certain time and place that you ride?"

I blinked. "Well, yeah, I do the same route just about every day, at roughly the same time." Silence. "You think someone tried to run me down deliberately." My voice was sharp.

He stood up. "The doctor says you can leave. Get dressed and I'll drive you home."

"You think someone tried to run me down, I mean, me in particular?"

Jameson didn't answer, just looked at me. Cripes, this man was frustrating. How about asking me, *Gee, Troy, would you like a ride home?* Or saying, *I'm so sorry you were hurt; we'll do the best we can to track this guy down.* But he had bought me something to wear, and I did need a ride, so I got dressed while he waited outside the room. It hurt to move.

It was icky pulling on my sweaty torn bike

327

shorts. But at least the new T-shirt covered the parts that were shredded. I tossed my torn shirt and gloves in the trash. I'd keep the helmet; sometimes companies let you trade in a broken one. I padded out of the room in my socks, with my cleated bike shoes and helmet in the plastic bag. The nurse pushed discharge papers and instructions at me, and handed me bandages and packets of Polysporin.

At Jameson's car I stopped. "My bike. I need to get my bike."

"It's in my trunk. You were so worried about it that someone brought it to the hospital."

Thank heaven for Good Samaritans. I didn't ask to see it — I didn't want to know what shape it was in. I leaned back in the car seat and kept my eyes closed all the way to the house.

Jameson insisted on walking me in. Elise was frantic when she saw us, and I wished I had thought to call ahead to warn her. "This looks lots worse than it is, Elise. I had a little bike accident; it's just some scrapes." I turned toward Jameson: "My bike . . ."

He nodded. "I'll get it."

"If you could put it in the garage that would be great. I'm going to get into the tub. Elise, you'll need to pick up Paul. Tell him I've had a little accident but that I'm fine." She nodded and trotted off. I must have swayed on my feet, because Jameson grasped my arm, adroitly avoiding the bandaged areas.

"You *did* hit your head, you know," he said mildly. He walked me back to my room, and turned to go. As he reached the doorway, without conscious decision I said, "Wait."

Maybe I should have thought about it more, but all my instincts were telling me to do this, now. I fumbled to the bottom of the dresser where I had hidden Madeleine's emails. He stood, watching, eyes narrowed. I held out the sheaf of papers.

He read the first words on the top sheet, then looked up at me sharply.

"They're hers," I said. "Madeleine's." I didn't like the look in his eyes. I went on, my voice thick. "I found her email program on Philippe's computer and accidentally downloaded them. The ones on the bottom, those are ones . . . some that I sent out, from her email address."

"You sent out emails pretending to be her." His voice was flat.

"Yeah, and I met with one of her friends in Montreal, a woman named Gina. But Philippe doesn't know any of this. Look, can we talk about it later?"

He nodded slowly, but sat down on my bed. I left him there and went into the bathroom. I ran hot water into the tub and eased myself in. I could hear Jameson turning pages. I closed my eyes and lay there until I could no longer hear him. Then I sat on the side of the tub and poured hydrogen peroxide from the medicine cabinet over the scrapes, watching it bubble. It's pretty much the best way to prevent infections, a trick I'd learned from a kayaking friend.

I added smears of Polysporin before applying the bandages, the nonstick kind that doesn't adhere to broken skin. I eased on loose shorts and T-shirt, ran cold water into the tub, and tossed the bloodstained towel in to soak. I popped some Advil and limped to the kitchen for a sandwich and orange juice.

Jameson was gone, but he had stayed until Elise returned with Paul. Somehow Philippe was there as well. Paul exclaimed over my bandages, seeming more impressed than dismayed. I had to explain that he wouldn't be able to hug me for a week or so.

"You broke your *vélo,* your bike," he said.

"Yes, but I can fix it. Or get it fixed."

He put a tentative finger out and touched a bandage on my arm. "You put medicine on?"

"Yes, I put medicine on it, and it will get well very soon."

He patted my cheek. If I could have hugged him, I'd have probably halfway crushed him. I settled for leaning over and kissing his forehead. I could tell from Philippe's expression that he wanted to talk, and we left Paul in the kitchen with Elise.

"It's no big deal —" I started to say, but I stopped at the look on his face. For a horrible moment I wondered if Jameson had told him about the emails.

"Someone tried to pick Paul up at school," he said.

For a moment I couldn't catch my breath. "You mean . . ."

He nodded. "Someone called the school and asked to have Paul released. They said I'd been in an accident and that a driver would be sent to pick Paul up."

My eyes widened. The school had called Philippe immediately, and when he couldn't reach Jameson, another detective had met him at the school. No one had actually shown up to try to get Paul.

My head was spinning. "So someone tried to hit me — it wasn't an accident? And the same people threatened to snatch Paul?" My voice was rising. "But who? The kidnappers? And why? I never saw them; I can't

331

identify them."

"Yes, but they may not know that. Maybe they think you were on the same ferry as them, and saw them get on or when Paul went overboard." Like me, he couldn't say the words. *When they threw Paul in the lake. When they tried to drown Paul.*

"This could have been an accident," I insisted.

"But, Troy, you got hit and no one stopped."

"I've had things like this happen. People don't pay attention or just don't care about someone on a bike — sometimes they don't even notice. Or they try to run you off the road for the heck of it."

He pursed his lips. It would have been a huge coincidence that I was nearly run over the same day someone tried to pick up Paul at school, and we both knew it.

"Does —"

"What —"

He gestured for me to go ahead.

"Is Paul safe?" I blurted.

"Safe?" Philippe waved his arm violently. "He's safe here, at least as safe as I can make it without putting up bars. He's safe at school, if someone doesn't show up and gun down the guard and force his way in." He was talking faster, sounding more

French than I'd ever heard him. "I can't protect him completely. Anytime he's in the car, he's at risk. A fender bender, something to force the car off the road. Boom, they could grab him. Anytime we take him out, someone could snatch him. But there's nothing to do, unless I hire a bodyguard. And I've thought of that. But what kind of life would that be for Paul, to always be reminded that life isn't safe, that someone is out there who could snatch him, that his own father can't protect him?"

He stood, his breathing loud.

I'd forgotten the rage Philippe had shown when I first met him, and I hadn't realized the amount of anger he was still carrying. He was coping, but barely.

I cleared my throat. "We can vary our routine, drive different ways to school. Limit the times you're in public with him, make sure it's never just one person out with him. Until these guys are caught."

He looked up with a bitter half smile. "If they ever are."

"We have to believe they will be." My voice was sharp. "We have to."

He nodded absently. "If you don't mind, as soon as you can get around, I'd like you to always pick up Paul from school, not

Elise. For now, I'll take off work early and do it."

"Sure," I said, but Philippe seemed far away.

I was stiff the next morning, but I knew the following day would be even worse. I might as well face Jameson now. I'd give him the recording I'd made of the conversation with Gina and also that first conversation with Paul. That, at least, had simply slipped my mind. And copies of the Craigslist ad and the replies I'd gotten.

Full disclosure — supposedly good for the soul.

At the police station I followed a uniformed policeman in, and no one tried to stop me. I tapped on Jameson's half-opened door.

He looked up without expression. "Something I forgot to give you," I said, holding up the tapes. "From when I talked to that friend of Madeleine's in Montreal, and when Paul told me about the kidnapping. And a Craigslist ad I did. Madeleine's password, if you need it, is her first name backward." He made no move to take the tapes or the pages. I set them on a corner of his desk, atop a pile of papers.

"I read the emails," he said.

I waited, but he said nothing else. "I'm

sorry I didn't give them to you sooner." My voice almost cracked. "But I knew they would make you suspect Philippe, and I didn't want him to know about them. I wanted to . . . I wanted to see if anyone knew anything, so I sent out some emails."

Silence. "I know you think I'm stupid," I said, and limped away. It wasn't a dignified exit.

My bike frame, I discovered when I'd gathered the courage to look at it, was scratched but not bent, but the front wheel was pretzeled. I bought a new rim and spokes at a nearby bike shop, and began building a new front wheel.

I hummed softly as I threaded spokes into the rim, standing to stretch when I got too stiff. Every other spoke hole is offset a little, and once I'd carelessly laced an entire wheel with the spokes through the wrong holes. I began truing it, adjusting the spoke tension bit by bit, then pushing the wheel against the floor sideways to seat the spokes and nipples. It's slow work, but I like it. Next I moved on to cleaning the derailleurs, brakes, and drive train. I love getting all the parts clean and working smoothly.

I thought about the car that had almost hit me. I thought about someone calling the school about picking up Paul. I thought about Philippe and the strange limbo he lived in. I wondered if Claude had been different when Madeleine was alive, and when he'd been dating someone. I wondered if Jameson was finding out anything from the emails. I wondered if I had turned them over sooner, whether my accident and the threat against Paul would have occurred at all.

Had I somehow led the kidnappers back here? Had they seen me, followed me to Lake Placid? Or had my emails or my postings about the kidnappers somehow alerted them? I couldn't figure out how.

Or maybe my crash was an accident and someone had simply played a cruel prank on Philippe and the school.

I was moving slowly, so it took the better part of two mornings to clean the bike and true the wheel as well as I could without a truing stand. I'd emailed Simon, and he called. He was worried, but didn't try to talk me into leaving. He asked if I minded if he talked to Jameson, and I didn't. I didn't confess all the snooping I'd done, but Jameson could tell him if he chose. "Be very careful, Troy," my brother said, and I agreed. I couldn't do much else.

A response to my Craigslist ad came in:

these look a lot like 2 guys I met in a bar in burlington near the university, they had funny accents & said they were from montreal. one was named jock i think.

I took a deep breath. I looked up Jameson's email address at the Ottawa Police Service and forwarded it to him.

CHAPTER 36

The next morning the call came — the one everyone had been dreading. Elise brought the phone to the breakfast table, and Philippe's face turned white as he listened. He stood and turned, as if to shield us. When he clicked off the phone and faced us, he was working hard to appear normal.

"Troy," he said, too casually. "There's something I need to ask you about on my computer."

I winked at Paul and said, "Back in a flash, cowboy," and followed Philippe upstairs. In his office he turned and leaned against the desk.

He spoke immediately. "They found a woman's body, Troy, just outside Montreal. They think it's Madeleine."

My breath caught, and I made a sound.

He went on. "It was in her car, in the woods, and matches Madeleine's description. They're checking dental records now."

I found my voice. "But, Philippe, it couldn't be her, not in Montreal. Paul said he heard her shot, after they'd been moved." My throat was dry.

He shook his head. "He must have been wrong." He tapped his ring, and cleared his throat. "Wedding ring. We had them engraved." His face crumpled, and he sat in his desk chair, his back to me.

He sat for a long moment, face in hands, and then straightened, back in control. "I have to go to Montreal to identify the body and meet with the Montreal police. Jameson will go with me."

"What are you going to tell Paul?"

Philippe shook his head, picking up the phone on his desk and punching in numbers. "I'm not going to tell him that it's her, not until I'm sure, but I'll have to tell him something because Jameson will be here soon." He spoke into the phone, telling his receptionist he wouldn't be in. I wondered if he'd tell Claude or wait until the identity was confirmed. Or if the police had already called Claude.

I went downstairs and gulped coffee, almost burning my mouth. I smiled at Paul and nibbled at a muffin. Philippe followed moments later, and Paul looked up curiously.

"Paul, Papa is going to go off today with the police, to help them," Philippe told him.

"To look for the bad men?" Paul asked, putting a blueberry from his muffin into his mouth.

"Well, yes." Philippe shifted in his chair. "And perhaps to find out what happened to your mother."

Paul looked at him calmly. "I heard the bad men shoot her."

We both froze. It was the first time we had heard Paul voluntarily say anything about the kidnapping.

"Yes, I know, Paul," Philippe said. "But we would like to try to find her and if . . . if we can, bring her back and have a funeral."

"When you die, your inside . . . *votre esprit* . . . goes away." Paul waved one hand as if it were a small bird in flight.

Philippe couldn't speak. I answered gently. "Yes, your spirit, your soul, goes away and your body is left behind, like a shell."

"And you put the shell in the ground?"

"Yes. And then you put up a marker, or a stone, with the person's name, to respect and remember them." Paul nodded, and took a bite of the muffin he'd been picking the blueberries from.

The doorbell rang. Elise ushered in Jameson, and he stopped in the doorway. "Would you like coffee?" asked Elise, her eyes worried. She knew something was very wrong.

"No," said Jameson, shaking his head. His eyes moved around the room, taking in the breakfast remains, moving past Philippe and Paul, stopping on me. He nodded brusquely. I nodded back, a tight knot in my throat. "We need to go," he said to Philippe.

Philippe nodded, and set down his coffee. He gave Paul a hug, telling him that I would drive him to school today. "I'll call when I can," he told me.

The body was Madeleine's, Philippe told me when he called a few hours later, but it would be much later before he could tell me more. Jameson got on the phone and told me to be at the Ottawa police station with Elise by two thirty.

"But I have to pick Paul up from school."

"Monsieur Dumond will be able to pick his son up," he said.

"Okay." As I hung up I met Elise's eyes. "They found Mrs. Dumond's body," I told her. "They want us at the police station at two thirty."

She muttered something in French I didn't understand, and switched back to English. "Why do they want to talk to us?" Twin strands of gray hair had escaped from her hair and were framing her worried brow.

"To find out if we know anything, I guess. Maybe if you remember anything from before, about people Madeleine knew, maybe."

We busied ourselves, her scrubbing kitchen cupboards, me taking Tiger for a walk, and when it was time I drove us to the police station. A police officer took Elise somewhere, and a few minutes later Jameson appeared and waved me back into his cluttered office. I sat.

"Do you own a gun?" he asked, shuffling some papers at his desk.

"No."

"Have you ever owned a gun?"

"No."

"Have you ever fired a gun?"

"No. Well, not since I was a kid — a shotgun, at a target. Just once." I had been about eight, and the recoil had nearly thrown me to the ground.

He watched me closely. "Did you ever meet Madeleine Dumond?"

"No. I mean, no, I don't think I ever did, if I did, I didn't know it." I was babbling, and couldn't help it.

"Were you aware of the manner of her death?"

"Paul said he heard her shot."

"Were you aware of the whereabouts of Madame Dumond's body?"

"No. From what Paul told me, I'd thought she was shot in Vermont, or wherever he was kept."

He scribbled some notes on his paper, ignoring me, and then looked up blandly. "All right, thank you, Miss Chance."

I hesitated. This was it? I met his stare, and knew he was baiting me. I stood up. "So I can go?"

"Yes," he said, and I left without looking back.

Elise's questioning had been along the same lines, I supposed, but with more specific questions, as her interview took longer. She didn't tell me, and I didn't ask. I caught sight of Claude in the waiting area, face ashen, looking as if he had crumpled in on himself. I hesitated, wanting to say something to him, but I didn't think anything I could say would bring him any comfort. But I couldn't not try.

I walked over to him. "I'm so sorry," I said. He lifted his head, and it shocked me; I've never seen a face so ravaged with pain. He tried to sneer at me but couldn't manage it, and somehow the attempt — and maybe the failure as well — made me like him more than I would have thought possible. "I'm so very sorry," I said again, and he nodded. I left him alone.

Philippe was questioned extensively, he told me that evening. The body had been in Madeleine's car in a ravine in a deeply wooded area outside Montreal. It wore the wedding ring and a leather coat and a pair of boots Philippe recognized. Apparently she had been strangled or garroted, not shot.

It took me a moment to digest all this, and to work out that Madeleine had been killed before Paul was taken to wherever he was kept captive — so what he had thought was his mother being shot must have been a horrible charade to get him to cooperate. And Jameson questioning me about a gun apparently had been to see if I'd slip and say something revealing like *But she wasn't killed with a gun.*

Philippe told Paul that evening that his mother's body had been found and would eventually be put into a grave. Paul seemed to take the news calmly, and my eyes met Philippe's. *Surely this can't be a normal reaction,* we were both thinking. But what did we know? Yet another question for the psychologist.

The police had asked Philippe if he had owned a watch like one they had found near the car with a broken pin (yes, it looked like one he'd once had, but hadn't worn for years). They'd asked him a lot more, I could tell, but he, like Elise, didn't want to talk about it.

I called Simon.

"Do they have any clues, any suspects?" he asked.

"They . . . I think they're suspecting Philippe," I whispered, sounding as miserable as I felt. "They found a man's watch near the car they seem to think was his."

"Have they traced it to him?" Simon's voice was sharp.

"No," I said, shaking my head, never mind that he couldn't see me. "At least not that I know of. But he says it does look like one he used to have."

Simon was quiet for a long moment. "Even if it is his watch, Troy, this was his wife, it was her car. She could have had the watch with her for some reason; she could have been taking it to be repaired."

"I know." I was crying quietly by now, and I think he knew it.

"This doesn't mean anything," he said, and his matter-of-factness calmed me. "The killer could be anybody who knew Philippe had money. It could be a complete stranger; it could be someone he used to work with. It could be Madeleine's brother. It could be someone trying to frame him."

It hurt even to get the words out: "What do you think?"

"I think you should trust your instincts, Troy. The one thing I can tell you is that I don't think that Philippe would ever hurt Paul, or do anything that could hurt him."

Philippe knew the police considered him a suspect, but having his wife's body found apparently provided him some closure. He seemed calmer. Paul seemed no different, but Claude took several days off work, and stopped coming for dinner.

Claude, I realized, must have been clinging to the hope that his sister would be found alive. Which I suppose hadn't been much more unlikely than Paul's coming home as he had.

They held a funeral service in Montreal. I didn't know if the body would be buried or if the police had to keep it until the case was closed, and didn't ask. After some thought, Philippe decided Paul should attend, and we took him out to buy a tiny suit. Elise and Claude went to the service. I didn't. I hoped Jameson had notified Gina — it seemed that Madeleine should have at least one personal friend there.

It was a long day for me in Ottawa. I took a bike ride. I worked. I cleaned my bike. I walked Tiger for an hour. I emailed Baker. I thought. And then I called Thomas. It was a short and pained conversation. I told him I didn't see a future ahead for us. He thanked me for calling, and that was that. I hung up, and then I cried.

CHAPTER 37

In some ways I can be dense. Very dense.

I knew Philippe liked me. I knew he had found me attractive those two evenings we'd gone out. But I had thought it was attractive in a distant sense, like a cousin or sister or someone you're fond of who happens to be devoted to your child. And except that one night on the sofa, we'd been living together for weeks with nothing more between us than if he had been Zach or one of my other housemates. I'd tamped down the attraction I'd felt for him because, one, it wasn't appropriate, and, two, I'd learned long ago how painful it is to want someone you can't have. But somewhere along the line things had changed, and I had been too stupid to see it. It hadn't occurred to me that the discovery of Madeleine's body had set Philippe free in some ways. Although I had noticed he'd stopped wearing his wedding ring.

We were in the library after dinner, as usual, with Paul asleep and Elise off in her apartment, and Philippe was showing me an old photo in a book about Montreal. I leaned in close to see it, never mind that I was pretty damned close to him, because we had been playing this platonic thing so long that in my brain that's just the way it was. And then suddenly he turned my face toward his and the touch of his hand on my face was like fire. And then his lips were on mine and his tongue in my mouth, and I was feeling things I'd only ever dreamed of. It was nothing like kissing Thomas, or anyone else I'd kissed, for that matter.

At a certain point you have to come up for air, and we did, and I became aware he was speaking.

"Troy, we have to talk," he was saying. "There are things I need to tell you, things about Madeleine."

I was shaking my head without realizing it. For weeks I'd wanted to know more about Madeleine, but not now. She was dead, in the past, gone. I wanted to let her and everything about her stay buried. "I don't want to know," I said, and the words were thick and awkward.

He shook his head. "No, I need to tell you. You need to know."

If I could have stopped him I would have. I had thought I was all for truth and straightforwardness, which shows just what a hypocrite I can be. "Okay," I said, and shifted a few inches away from him. And he told me.

Most of it I could have predicted, from the emails I'd found, from talking to Gina, from the dates of Paul's birth and their marriage, from what Elise had said and not said about Madeleine — but mostly from Paul's and Philippe's reactions. Yes, people deal differently with loss, but who doesn't occasionally say, *Mama used to . . .* or *When Madeleine and I . . .*

Madeleine had, it seemed, targeted Philippe, although he didn't say that. Maybe he didn't even realize it. He had met her at a party; she was gorgeous and charming and by the end of the night they were together. Three months later she was pregnant, by accident, he thought *(yeah, right)*. So they got married, and things seemed fine until Paul was born. Madeleine had no interest in the baby. Philippe thought at first it was postpartum depression, but her attitude toward Paul never changed, and Elise had taken over Paul's care. Madeleine had played the corporate wife, hosting parties and chaired community events, but in the last couple of years she'd gradually done less and less and had seemed increasingly discontent. She spent a lot of time shopping and lunching with people he never met; she suggested selling the house and buying one in a fancier neighborhood. She spent more time in Florida and began to go on trips with friends or alone. She started spending hours in internet chat rooms. They argued frequently; she refused marriage counseling.

"She couldn't bond with Paul," he said. "But I knew she'd had a terrible childhood, and she'd done her best to look out for Claude. I knew she'd lost a baby when she was very young. I thought she would work it out."

And then one day she was gone.

"I didn't want her to come back," Philippe said, his voice toneless, staring at the floor. "I was relieved she was gone. I thought she'd gone off to make a point, so I'd give in to whatever she wanted next. I thought she'd taken Paul just to annoy me, and that she'd send him back as soon as she got tired of him — which I thought would be very quickly. And that she wanted to embarrass me by having me raise a fuss. So I didn't report her missing. And we lost the time when they could have been found."

I could have pointed out that Madeleine

was almost certainly dead by the time the police would have investigated. I could have cited the statistics I'd found, that three-fourths of kidnap victims are killed within three hours. I could have pointed out that the kidnappers clearly never had any intention of returning Paul.

But none of it would have helped. Philippe was carrying an enormous amount of guilt, which he'd have to work through at his own pace.

We held each other. I rubbed his back, as I had that night in the kitchen, and tried to ignore the painful knot in my throat. As much as I would have loved to have believed in a fairy-tale ending, Philippe and me together — the computer-loving bicycle-riding girl happily ever after with the handsome executive, raising the child they loved — it was just that, a fairy tale. At least for now. We both had things to deal with. Philippe blamed himself for his wife's death. I had kept his son when he may have been able to help the police find the kidnappers, and I had dabbled with those emails, which Philippe still didn't know.

And there were kidnappers and murderers out there who knew that Paul could identify them.

■ ■ ■ ■

The next morning, while Paul was playing in his room, I went up to Philippe's study.

"Philippe, I need to go back to Lake Placid." My eyes were hot. I hadn't slept much.

He nodded, as if he had been expecting this. His eyes held so much pain that I almost tried to convince myself that we could keep on. But I knew we couldn't. We couldn't ignore the attraction between us, but neither could we act on it.

I would stay through the weekend, and Philippe would bring Paul to Lake Placid to visit the weekend after next. It was heartrending to tell Paul, and he cried as I'd expected and threw his arms around me, but I remained determinedly, falsely cheerful. That afternoon we carried out the other part of our plan — surprising Paul with a black Lab mix puppy from the Humane Society. Child and puppy both were ecstatic. "You must take good care of your dog," I told him, and he promised. He named the puppy Bear, following the logic, I suppose, that had led me to name my dog Tiger. We made a trek to PetSmart, and selected a collar and leash, dog bed, and toys we thought a puppy named Bear would enjoy.

I knew I had to tell Jameson I was leaving, but I waited until the last minute. I left a message at the police station after what I supposed were his normal work hours, but he called back an hour later.

"You're going back to Lake Placid."

"Yes, tomorrow."

"I want to take you to lunch."

I laughed harshly. I couldn't help it. "I don't like going to lunch with you. In fact, I don't like being around you." My nerves were raw. I couldn't stop myself.

Silence. "Can you stop by on your way out of town?"

"Is this an official request?" I asked.

"Can you stop by on your way out of town? Eleven thirty."

I took a deep breath. "Eleven," I said, and hung up.

My leave-taking with Philippe was deliberately brief, and then he went off to work and I drove Paul to school. Paul clung to me before getting in the car, but I didn't let myself break down. "Hey, I'll see you soon," I said, tweaking his nose gently, smearing his tears away with my thumb. "Less than two weeks. And then you and Bear and Papa will come see me, and I will see how much Bear has grown and how much you have taught him." I drove him to school, and he snuffled most of the way. As he got out and ran in the school door, I tried not to think, *This is the last time.* But the pain I felt was so intense it took my breath away. When I took the booster seat out of my backseat and set it in the back of the garage, tears ran down my face.

It didn't take long to finish packing and load everything in my car. I lingered over coffee with Elise, and then it was time to go. She hugged me hard, as she had the day I had met her, and like that day, could not speak. This time I couldn't either. She handed me a large bag of pastries, her parting gift.

Jameson was waiting for me in the station's parking lot. "Why not just meet in your office?" I said. He shook his head. I wasn't up to arguing, so I followed him to the restaurant. Tiger likes hanging out in the car, and it was cool enough that she'd be comfortable with the windows partly opened. We sat in silence at an outdoor table until our food arrived.

"So is there a problem with me going home?" I asked, bluntly.

"No. No problem." Jameson buttered a bit of bread and popped it in his mouth.

I began mechanically to eat my salad.

"There's nothing I haven't told you."

"Isn't there?" he asked.

"No. I've told you everything. And I wish you would say what you mean. Is it me you suspect? Or Philippe?"

A cool level gaze. "I suspect everyone. I can't afford not to."

I turned my attention back to my salad. It was good, with different types of greens, bits of nuts and rich cheese, and a tangy dressing.

"So why did you decide to leave?" he asked.

I looked off at the skyline. He didn't need to know that Philippe and I had stepped close to the romantic involvement he'd always suspected. "Paul is settled in school; he needs to make the break from me. Philippe and Elise can take care of everything he needs. I need to get back to my life."

"Your work, your house, your friends."

"Yes." I speared another forkful of salad.

"It's not over yet, you know," he said. I narrowed my eyes as he spoke. "It won't be over until we catch the kidnappers."

"Do you think I don't know that? Do you think I don't *want* them caught?" I dropped my fork and stood without realizing I was going to do it. My voice was shrill. "Of course I do. I think about it all the time. I think about what they did to Paul. I think about how they almost drowned him. I think about the fact that *they are still out there* and someday I may turn around and there they'll be. Every face I see I wonder: *Is that one of them?* I dream about them, for God's sake."

Tears were blinding me, and I groped behind me to move my chair, but Jameson was faster. He pulled my chair out and threw money on the table, and took my arm and guided me out onto the sidewalk. We walked several blocks. I blinked tears away and sucked in enough air to calm myself. When we stopped we were at a fenced corner overlooking a park below.

"I'm sorry," I said, without looking at him.

"Don't be," he said. Surprised, I turned toward him. He pulled a handkerchief from his pocket and, instead of handing it to me as I expected, stepped forward and quickly, gently wiped the tears from my cheeks. Then he tucked the handkerchief in my hand and stepped back, so swiftly I could have thought I'd imagined it.

I was staring at him. "You've always acted . . . you've always treated me like a criminal. Or an idiot."

A crooked smile. "A child had been kidnapped, a woman killed. You were a suspect,

Troy. You were a suspect living with the victim and another suspect. What I thought personally didn't and couldn't enter into it."

He had never used my first name before. He leaned forward against the fence, looking sideways at me. His shirt was rumpled as usual. He was just an inch or two taller than me, his hair disheveled. As usual.

He had used the past tense. "So now I'm not a suspect."

"Unofficially, no. Not now."

"Mmm."

"We're still looking. We'll keep looking."

"What was she like — Madeleine?" I asked suddenly.

He didn't ask why I wanted to know. "You've read the emails. You talked to her friend. She was exactly like what you think she was like."

After a moment I spoke into the silence, saying what I hadn't been able to say to Philippe. "I've always thought if I'd taken Paul to the police right away, maybe you would have caught them by now. But I didn't . . . didn't think that he could handle the police or foster care at that point. Or maybe I just didn't want to give him up. So I didn't. And now I think that was a really awful mistake."

"Maybe so, maybe not," he said. "You'll

never know."

We stood there a full minute longer, leaning on the fence, looking at the view, feeling the breeze on our faces. He hadn't said anything I didn't already know and hadn't tried to comfort me. But I felt better. I pushed away from the fence.

"You know where to find me," I said. He looked at me. I had disliked this man; he'd been rude and accusatory. But his eyes held a compassion I hadn't expected, and something else I couldn't read.

We both seemed to be waiting for something, and in the end I was the one who moved. I stepped forward, almost without volition, and brushed his cheek with my lips, and then I was gone, heading down the street toward my car. If I walked away quickly enough, we could both pretend it hadn't happened.

By the time I reached Lake Placid, I knew what I was going to do. I cleaned the house thoroughly — the guys either hadn't noticed or cared how grungy it had gotten. I found a roommate to replace Ben, who had moved in with his new girlfriend; produced a special summer section for the newspaper; and wrote a batch of press releases for some quick cash. Paul and Philippe came down with Bear for their weekend, and we picnicked with Baker and her family and Holly and John and their kids.

Parting was only slightly awkward. Paul was sleepy from playing and didn't protest, although he clung to me after I settled him in his seat. Philippe kissed me lightly, just before he got in the car. "See you soon," he said in my ear.

Three nights later the phone rang, when I was almost asleep.

"Hello, it's Alan," a voice said. At my long pause, he added, "Jameson, Alan Jameson."

"God, I'm sorry." Now I was completely awake. "I didn't know your name."

He gave a short laugh. "You thought my first name was Detective, right?"

"Something like that, yeah."

"How are you doing?"

"Okay." I sat up in bed. My heart was thumping audibly. "Paul and Philippe came down this weekend; Paul seems to be doing fine." Silence. I went on: "Do you . . . I mean, how are things?"

"Things are fine. I wanted to check on you."

"I'm fine." This was awkward. I plunged on. "Look —"

"Troy," he said, cutting me off. "I just wanted to see if you were all right. And to remind you that you can call me. You have my numbers?"

"Yes." The card was in my wallet, where I'd put it the day he'd given it to me.

"All right, then. Good night."

"Good night," I whispered, and hung up.

Jesus. I wasn't sure if I was praying or cursing. Every encounter I had with this man confused me in one way or another.

The next day I left for Burlington.

■ ■ ■ ■

PART III

■ ■ ■ ■

"Don't think too much about it —
we all have instincts to survive."
— *from a Learn to Swim blog*

CHAPTER 38

I had delayed the search for Paul's kidnappers. I had kept Madeleine's emails to myself. And it was possible that I had somehow led the kidnappers back to Ottawa.

I had to do what I could to make things right.

What could I do? Baker asked me. All I had were some details from Paul, the sketches, and a Craigslist response suggesting the men had lived in Burlington. All of which the police had as well.

"I can try," I said. The police couldn't devote full time to this case, and they couldn't be as motivated as I was. How much investigating would the Montreal or Ottawa police do in Vermont? How hard would the Burlington police work to solve a crime from Québec, with one victim recovered and the other dead?

Baker didn't try to talk me out of it. She

knew it was something I had to do.

Philippe and I emailed daily and talked often. Paul chattered about his puppy and what had happened at school, speaking English except when he got excited. Philippe had found discrepancies in several work files compared to older hard copies, and had brought in an outside firm to do an audit and, as promised, a computer firm to set up company-wide security. No more incidents had occurred, so whoever had tried to run me over and made the phone call to the school was presumably gone. It seemed to have been a one-time thing — maybe to scare me off. In a way it had.

I didn't tell Philippe I was going to Burlington. Or Simon.

Thomas, surprisingly, was supportive. We hadn't spoken since I returned from Ottawa, but he called one evening and asked how things were going. When I told him I was coming to Burlington, he said, "You should stay here."

"Tommy —" I started.

"It's okay," he said, cutting me off. Since we had broken things off we hadn't talked, and staying at his place seemed strange even for me. But it would be easier and cheaper than anything else, and I could bring Tiger. We could talk about it when I got there. If nothing else, he could keep Tiger and I could find a cheap room to rent.

I drove up on a Wednesday, late in the afternoon. The bright sun and crisp air seemed incongruous with thoughts of kid-napping and murder. I drove south and took the bridge across, because the ferry was expensive if you drove on — more than thirty bucks round-trip. I tried not to think about the what-ifs: *What if I hadn't had that play to review back in May?* Then I would have planned to stay in Burlington the entire weekend, would have taken my dog, wouldn't have taken the ferry. And Paul would have drowned.

I was there almost too quickly, pulling up to Thomas's apartment. He must have heard my car, and came out to meet me. Tiger greeted him eagerly, and he petted her absentmindedly before reaching in the back of the Subaru for my bags.

I made a halfhearted attempt to stop him. But I was tired, and didn't want to start a discussion on the street, so I let him take the bags and followed him in.

"You can use my study," he said, pushing the door open with his foot. "I've set up the futon for you." Thomas lived in the front half of a spacious old home that had been divided into two, like many of the old homes

367

near the university that had been carved into apartments. He had the best part of the house, with a big front porch. I stowed my bags in a corner of the study, where the futon couch was already unfolded into a bed, and in the living room sank into an easy chair.

"Would you like some tea?" Thomas asked. I nodded, and started to get up. "No, no," he said. "I'll get it." He disappeared, and Tiger ambled after him.

It felt good just to sit, and I shut my eyes. I felt drained. In a few minutes Thomas was back with a steaming pot of tea, two mugs, and a plate of cheese and crackers and apple slices. "I thought you might be hungry," he said.

I hadn't thought about eating, but I drank the tea and ate most of the food. Thomas turned the television to what seemed to be the second part of some Jane Austen adaptation. The English accents were heavy, and I had trouble following it.

I became aware that Thomas was speaking. "Troy," he was saying. "Troy!" I opened my eyes. "You're falling asleep. I've taken Tiger out. Why don't you go to bed?"

I looked at the clock on his mantel: only 9:10, but I didn't protest. So much for having a heart-to-heart. I crawled between the sheets on the futon. They were crisp, and smelled new. I slept hard, with no dreams for the first time in a long time.

I awoke feeling logy; it was tough to drag myself out of bed. The apartment was still. Thomas had left for work, and had left a note and spare key on the kitchen table. I ate some crunchy earthy type of cereal I found on the shelf, putting the box back exactly as I'd found it, because Thomas liked things just so. Then I walked Tiger briskly around the block and took a quick shower.

Time to get started.

What did I know? That there were two men, French Canadian, and roughly what they looked like. The Craigslist email suggested they had been seen in a bar near the university and that one of them might be named Jock, or more likely Jacques. They had stayed in two different apartments, at least one a basement apartment. And had kept a small boy no one knew about.

I drove to the post office on Elmwood Street and rented a post office box for the minimum six months, in my real name but also listing "Terry Charles" so I could get mail in both names. Next I headed for Ra-dioShack, where I bought a prepaid Trac-

Fone, feeling like a kid playing spy.

At Thomas's kitchen table I wrote out an ad:

WANTED: info on 2 French-speaking Canadian men, dark hair, 1 w/ mole on rt cheek, 1 maybe named Jock or Jacques, maybe w/ small boy.

I added the box number, TracFone number, and my alter ego's email address. Presto, a new identity. I called the *Burlington Free Press* and placed the ad for two weeks. The bored woman on the phone didn't react — I supposed she had heard far stranger. Then I posted a longer version on Vermont's Craigslist. I wrestled with my conscience only slightly before digging out the Craigslist response I'd forwarded to Jameson and answering it, asking for details. But I didn't sign onto Madeleine's account to check emails; that I was done with.

It took less than ten minutes to design a full-page poster with the two sketches, a brief description, and contact information. I printed a color copy on Thomas's printer, made adjustments, and printed two more before I was happy with it.

My stomach was growling. I had peanut butter on a slice of bread with a glass of milk, and ate an apple in the car on the way to Kinko's. Less than half an hour later I was leaving with two hundred copies, a fat roll of masking tape, and a container of thumbtacks. By six that evening I'd stuck my poster up on bulletin boards, in grocery stores, and on telephone and light poles.

I knocked lightly on the door of Thomas's apartment. No answer, so I let myself in with the key he'd left me. A neatly folded index card sat on the kitchen table: *Having dinner at the Pacific Rim Café on St. Paul Street with friends at 7:00. You can meet us there or help yourself to anything here.*

I wasn't up to meeting anyone, let alone going out, so I rooted around in the fridge and heated some leftover spaghetti, then had a bowl of Ben & Jerry's Chocolate Fudge Brownie. Like any good Vermonter, Thomas always had a couple of pints of Ben & Jerry's in his freezer, with at least one variety of chocolate, I suspected for my benefit.

While I ate, I scanned the classified ads in the *Free Press,* looking for basement apartments. If the men had left town after they'd dumped Paul, the apartment could still be unrented, because of the high rate of summer vacancies in university towns. I marked down a few that seemed like possibilities.

■ ■ ■ ■

I went to bed early and was only vaguely aware of hearing Thomas come in, and didn't see him in the morning.

The public library on College Street opened at 8:30, and I was there at 8:34. The reference librarian steered me to the reading room, where the older back issues of newspapers were stored on microfilm. I selected reels dating back to four weeks before Paul was kidnapped, and began to search classified ads, feeding the filmstrips through the machine, cranking away at the handle, peering at the grainy print. Then I switched to reels from the following months.

It took the entire day to make a list of addresses and phone numbers of apartments that might fit. I'd eaten a Clif Bar, but my head was aching by the time I headed back to the apartment.

Thomas's car was out front, and I could smell something cooking when I let myself in. In the kitchen a pot was steaming on the stove and he was sliding bread into the oven.

"This should be ready soon," he said without looking up.

"Tommy, you don't have to cook for me."

He peered at me through glasses that had

steamed up from the oven. "I know," he said pleasantly. "But we both have to eat."

So we ate pasta, salad, and garlic bread, and had a glass of Merlot each. I looked at Thomas and his sandy hair, wire-framed glasses, neat pullover and slacks, and thought, *How much simpler life would be if I could love him.*

"Thomas, we should talk. About us."

He blinked, and sipped his wine. His face was blank, although he never showed much expression. He spoke deliberately. "I think what's happening with us is that we dated for a while, and we've moved away from that and are, I think, becoming friends."

He was watching me, levelly. I did care for him, but there was no flicker of desire, nothing pulling me toward him. A pain grew in my throat, sharp and palpable. "I don't . . ." I said, almost choking.

He put his hand over mine on the table, scarcely touching me. "It's okay, Troy. I know you've been balancing a lot of things."

I made a sound, half laugh, half sob. "You could say that. But I'm not . . . nothing happened, you know, with Philippe."

He nodded, sitting back. "It doesn't matter. I already knew we were going in a different direction than I had hoped."

A tear fell down my cheek. If I could have

changed how I felt about Thomas at that moment, I would have. But you can't create emotions. You can fake them or pretend they don't matter. But I've tried both, and it never works.

We quietly cleaned up the kitchen, and he turned on the television. I went off to bed, leaving him in front of it. I couldn't tell if he was watching or just staring at the screen.

CHAPTER 39

In the morning we went for a run, easily matching each other's pace. On the way back we picked up bagels at a bakery on Church Street, and ate them with peach preserves. While Thomas read the *New York Times* on the front porch, I sat at the kitchen table with my list of apartments, marking locations on a map, and began to make phone calls.

First I made appointments to view basement apartments available for rent. Then I called the number for an older ad for a basement apartment listed before Paul was kidnapped.

"Hi," I said blithely. "I understand that you have an apartment that you rent out."

"Yeah, it's rented now."

"Well, I was trying to track down some friends of mine, but I've been out of town for a long time, and they were moving and I know they were going to look at your apartment. They're two guys, Canadians from Québec, and they speak French."

"Nope," the man replied. "Not here. Never had no Canucks here."

I kept this up until nearly lunchtime. I was amazed that not one person I reached refused to answer, asked the names of the guys I was looking for, or wondered where I had gotten their phone number. People are amazingly trusting, and love to talk. One lady kept me on the phone for ten minutes telling me about the time she had gone to Niagara Falls and how nice the Canadians were and how much she and her husband Harry had enjoyed seeing the Falls and how they were always going to go back, but never did, and now it was too late because he died last year, cancer, you know, because he smoked for so long.

But none of them had rented to dark-haired French-Canadian men.

I packed a sandwich and banana to head off to the first of my apartment-viewing appointments. On the front porch, Thomas looked up. "Do you want me to go with you?"

"Nope. I'll be fine." Better to slog through this alone. "But would you look after Tiger?" He nodded.

I thought the first apartment I saw was

bad, but they got worse. Maybe my time living in Philippe's house had spoiled me, but *basement apartment* seemed to be a synonym for *dark and dingy* — and often *musty* as well. I scribbled notes in my little spiral notebook and drew sketches of the layouts as if trying to figure out where my furniture could go, and promised I'd call back if I decided to take it.

None of the places fit Paul's description. Paul had said the first room had one of those grainy cubed windows that let some light in but didn't let you really see out, and a small attached half bath. His second room had been tiny, not much more than twice the size of his single mattress, with no windows.

It was dark when I got back to Thomas's apartment. On the way back I'd called to tell him I'd grab something to eat on the way home, and had gotten a tuna sandwich at Subway. He had been going out to a movie, something more complex and artistic than I could handle right now. I dialed my phone in Lake Placid to see if I had any messages.

Philippe had called. I called him back on my cell phone; I'd kept the Canadian cell plan. He answered on the first ring.

"Hey," he said.

The sound of his voice was hugely comforting. I could picture myself in Ottawa, finishing off one of Elise's dinners.

"How are things?" he asked.

"Good. I'm in Burlington for a few days." A pause. I could tell he was framing a question, so I answered before he could ask. "I'm . . . I'm doing some looking around, Philippe."

A pause, then he asked, "What do you mean?"

I took a deep breath. I wasn't sure I could explain this. "I'm looking around to see if I can locate one of the apartments Paul was kept in. Or if I can find out anything about the men themselves."

A longer pause. He was considering if he could talk me out of this and how to phrase it. "Troy, that could be dangerous. And I'm sure the police have checked all that out."

"Yes, but it's not going to be the highest priority," I argued, "especially with Paul home."

"Look, I could send a private investigator down there, or hire someone there if you feel it has to be done. I don't want to worry about you. You don't have to do this."

"Yes," I said, my voice almost cracking. "Yes, I do."

He was quiet. Maybe he did understand

— he was struggling with his own guilt. "Why don't you come back up here for a visit?"

"No, no, I can't, not now." My voice rose, and he changed the subject. He told me how Paul was doing in summer school, that Bear was now housebroken. I promised I'd increase my allotment of cell phone minutes, and gave him Thomas's number. I agreed to email and call regularly, to be careful, and to alert him if I even thought I'd found out anything.

If Philippe were free, I thought, he'd be doing this. But he had Paul, his job, his employees. Me, I had nothing to hold me down.

All Sunday I called about apartments and went to look at ones for rent. Thomas offered to put up some posters around campus, and took a stack of them to work Monday. I continued to look at apartments. By dinner Wednesday, Thomas looked at me with concern. "Troy, you have to slow down."

I grinned. "I look pretty bad, huh?"

"Well, tired, anyway."

Making phone call after phone call was dreary, but looking at the apartments was worse. If so many of the owners hadn't been happy to have someone to talk to, I would have felt bad about wasting their time. I'd hear in detail how grandson Johnny had been such a sweet boy until he started taking that cocaine. How daughter Martha had breast cancer and the doctors thought it was too late to stop it even after they'd taken both off, poor thing. How dear Lillian died in bed, just like she was sleeping, and she looked as sweet as she had the day they got married. And how all the kids were too busy to come visit and how taxes kept going up and how medicine was so expensive sometimes they only took half as many pills as they were supposed to and wondered if they should try to buy it from Canada like they'd heard some people do.

It made me want to go find the grown kids who didn't come visit and bang their heads together, and go buy the damned medicine myself.

Seeing these apartments made me think of Paul stuck in rooms like these for so long — nearly half a year, one-twelfth of his life. No parents, no nanny, no school, no home. Alone and lying near the door so he could hear the television. Washing his clothes in the sink. Happy to get a plastic McDonald's toy. Trying to dig a hole in the wall to freedom.

Thomas spoke up. "One of the professors

at work, Vince Thibault, saw your poster and asked me about it. You've met him once or twice, I think."

I searched my memory bank, and then I could picture him: a friendly man, on the short side, almost stocky, with a tennis club tan and wrinkles around his eyes when he smiled. I'd met him when I'd stopped by Thomas's office.

Thomas went on. "He told me about a French club he runs, a group of people who speak French and who meet every few weeks."

"A French club?" My tone must have suggested what I was thinking: that these guys wouldn't have joined a French club, or any club for that matter.

"Yes, he was thinking that maybe someone French-speaking could have run into these men or noticed them somewhere."

A long shot, but it couldn't hurt. And it was nice of Vince to have thought of it. "Sure. It's worth a try."

"There's a get-together Friday night at six, a wine-and-cheese thing. I can introduce you and then sit quietly in a corner and drink wine while you talk French." For Thomas, this qualified as outright humor, which meant he was trying to cheer me up.

"Sure," I said.

On the futon that night, I felt desperately lonely, with an ache deeper than I'd ever experienced. This was, I supposed, what happened when you let people into your life — when they were no longer there you felt an aching, grating loneliness. I reached out and stroked Tiger, who obligingly rolled over for a belly rub. I wished I could be back in Ottawa, with Paul and Philippe and Elise. I wished I could pretend everything was okay, that the kidnappers had gone far away and would never come back. I wished I could convince myself that this was all best left to other people, that it was foolhardy to be meddling here, that I should back off.

But I couldn't.

I had to try to right things. I had to do my best to ensure that Paul wouldn't be looking over his shoulder for the rest of his life. I had to finish what I'd started when I dived into Lake Champlain after him. You can't just do one thing to save a child and then walk away — you have to stick with it.

Or you may as well not have started.

CHAPTER 40

The French club gathering was at a meeting room in a church near the university, and when I arrived, Thomas was waiting for me near the door. He looked good in his professor clothes: crisply pressed slacks, neat blue shirt, tie, sport coat. I'd worn my trusty cord slacks and pullover.

A table in the corner held bottles of wine, plastic cups, and grocery store platters of cheese, crackers, veggies, and dip. A half dozen or so people were chatting. Most looked like university personnel, but some seemed to be students. Across the room, a compact man looked up as we entered, and I recognized him as Vince. He smiled broadly, excused himself, and walked toward us.

"Thomas," he said, pumping Thomas's arm and smiling at me. "So glad you could make it. Troy, so nice to see you again." Then he shook my hand.

I don't usually like people this hearty, but his friendliness was engaging. The crinkles at the corners of his eyes when he smiled made him look like a genial older business-man, like Robert Loggia, the head of the toy company in the movie *Big,* who danced across the giant piano keyboard with Tom Hanks.

"So how are you enjoying your stay in Vermont?" His accent was more British than French.

"Fine," I said. Because you could hardly say, *Awful, I'm frustrated trying to track down murdering kidnappers who dumped a small boy into Lake Champlain.*

Thibault continued. "I saw your poster and Thomas told me of your little problem. You are trying to locate some people, cor-rect?"

I had just opened my mouth to reply when a woman grasped his arm lightly. *"Vincent, mon cheri, tu parles anglais, mais c'est le club français ici!"* she said, in lilting French so precise it almost sounded affected. The woman was slender, with a slightly upturned nose and short auburn hair in a stylish cut I suspected was quite expensive. She made a *tsk-tsk* sound.

"Ah, Marguerite," he said in delight. "Yes, yes, you are so right, I should not be speaking English, but my poor colleague Thomas here unfortunately cannot comprehend a word of French, and I don't want to leave him out of the conversation."

She smiled at me with a touch of curiosity, but none of the rancor sometimes evident when wives find their husbands talking to other women.

"Troy, this is my wife, Marguerite. Maggie, dear, this is Thomas's friend Mademoiselle Troy Chance, from Lake Placid, and you remember Thomas Rouse from the history department."

She nodded and smiled and we shook hands, hers slender and elegant with silvery nail polish and several sparkly rings. I knew I hadn't met her, but I tried to remember if I'd seen her around campus. I didn't think so.

Thibault turned to his wife. "Dear, Troy is the one who is looking for the men from the poster, the ones who are French-speaking, Canadian, I believe, who have been living in this area." I nodded, and he continued speaking to Marguerite. "If you don't mind, perhaps, keeping Thomas company while Troy and I circulate?"

She raised her eyebrows, in apparent good humor. "Of course. I'd be happy to keep Mr. Rouse company." She somehow made it sound ever so slightly risqué. She took Thomas's arm and led him to a set of chairs in the corner of the room.

So I went off with Thibault to meet the club members and fumble with my French. The number of people in the room swelled to perhaps two dozen, people coming and going, with more arriving who weren't affiliated with the university. No one showed a glimmer of recognition of the drawings of the men, but all were friendly and willing to help. Most were American, a few from France, and only one was Canadian, from British Columbia. From time to time I glanced over to check on Thomas, who seemed delighted by Marguerite's company, which somehow amused me.

"Any luck?" Thomas asked when I rejoined them.

"No, but it was worth trying."

"Who are these men you are looking for?" Marguerite asked.

I told her the half-lie I'd decided on. "They tried to abduct a friend's child, and we had heard a rumor they were living up here." At her half gasp, I added, "Oh, the child is fine, but of course they'd like to find the men."

"But surely the police . . ."

I shrugged. "They do what they can."

Thibault had rejoined us. Some unspoken communication passed between him and his wife, and he said, "Thomas, my friend, we haven't had much time to visit. Would you and Troy join us and some people for dinner this Monday at our house? I know it's short notice, but we would love to have you. We will speak English, I assure you." He chuckled.

Thomas looked at me, and when I nodded slightly, replied, "Certainly, we'd love to."

"It's casual," Marguerite added. "Just a few other couples, some friends I think you'll like. We'll be dining around seven, but do come earlier. Do you know where we live?"

Thomas shook his head. Thibault pulled a card from his pocket, wrote an address on it, and handed it to him. "It's easy to find. We'll look forward to having you."

We thanked them as we headed out the door. "I hope that's okay with you," Thomas said as we climbed into his Toyota.

"It's fine; they seem nice. And, hey, a free dinner, right?"

He laughed. I wondered if the Thibaults thought we were dating, and if that would be awkward. But if Thomas wanted to set them straight, I figured he would. I found it curious that he seemed enchanted by Marguerite, who was so different from me. But maybe he was branching out. Maybe his next girlfriend would be elegant, with precise makeup and carefully lacquered nails. I closed my eyes. It had been wearying to try to think and talk in French for nearly two hours.

The next morning I drove out of town to see two apartments in the surrounding semi-rural area, but they clearly weren't what I was seeking. On a whim I decided to take the afternoon off, and looked up movie schedules. The latest Gerard Butler movie was playing at the Roxy on College Street, and I could make the next matinee showing if I hustled. I took Tiger out, left a note for Thomas, and set off at a fast clip, eating a yogurt on the way.

I'd been a Gerard Butler fan since some friends had talked me into watching the TV movie *Attila* from Netflix. Never in a million years would I have thought I would enjoy a three-hour movie about Attila the Hun, but, hey, it was Gerard Butler. Next came *Dear Frankie* and *300,* and even *P.S. I Love You* and *Nim's Island* — but I did draw the line at his screwball romantic comedies.

I love going to the movies and prefer going alone, because then you don't have to worry if the other person is enjoying it and can just lose yourself in the film. After the final credits, I sat in darkness a minute or two before emerging, blinking, into the sunlight.

I'd once seen an old Albert Brooks movie about writers who required a muse for inspiration, and theirs was Sharon Stone. Mine, I thought, would be Butler, unshaven, rambling, gorgeous.

"So, Gerard," I would say. "I'm getting kind of stuck here. I'm not finding anything out."

He would look at me with that sideways grin and say in his delightful Scottish brogue, "Well, Troy, I think you need to try something new."

I was striking out with the apartments and the posters. Nothing had developed with the French club, and I'd gotten no replies to my newspaper or Craigslist ad or email. The only other possibility I could see was asking around at the Burlington ferries. Surely the police had already done this, but it couldn't hurt to do it again.

"Ferries," I said to the imaginary Gerard. "I'll try showing pictures and asking questions down at the docks."

He grinned and winked, and disappeared.

That night I slept soundly. Maybe there was something to this muse thing.

CHAPTER 41

The next day, I borrowed Thomas's old three-speed, pumped up the tires, and rode to the docks and locked it to a nearby fence. I wouldn't leave a decent-looking bike locked outside in a university town, but this one was decrepit enough that no one was likely to cut through a cable for it.

I had planned to show the ticket seller the picture and ask if she had seen the men, but when I saw her downward-turning mouth and dead stare, I chickened out. Instead I just bought a round-trip ticket.

I watched the incoming ferry chug in between the pilings. When it docked, the ferry workers moved quickly, securing the boat, lowering the ramp, and motioning the cars off while the foot passengers walked off.

I boarded, handing my ticket to a blond kid, and went on deck to wait while the cars drove on. Today was a clear day, not misty and drizzly like the afternoon I had found Paul. This wasn't the boat I'd been on that day or the one Paul had been on either. Ours had had a separate section below deck for cars.

When the ferry was under way, I walked about, trying to get up my nerve to ask questions. The first worker I tried, a thirty-ish tanned guy with a black brush cut, neatly snubbed me. "I wouldn't know," he said, sneering, and hustled off as if he had something important to do.

I turned, flushed, and the blond kid who had taken my ticket winked at me. "Don't mind Horse. He just likes to throw his weight around."

"Horse?" I thought I hadn't heard right.

He grinned widely. "His name is Horace, but we call him Horse. He hates it. What is it you need?"

I pulled out the folded paper with the kidnappers' pictures on it. "I'm looking for these two guys. They were on the last ferry going to Port Kent on the last Sunday in May." This was a long shot. But it had been the first week this ferry route was open — ice on the river kept it from running year-round — so maybe it would stick in some-one's mind.

The kid took the paper and squinted at it.

His snub nose was sunburned and peeling, and he looked like a grown-up Dennis the Menace. "Why are you looking for them? Are you a PI or something?"

"No, nothing like that. They snatched a friend's kid, and we're trying to track them down."

"Wow, a kidnapping. Or a custody thing, maybe, huh? Are these guys local?"

"They're French Canadian, from Montreal, I think, but they may have lived here."

"Which boat was it? We have three that sometimes run this route — the *Adirondack,* the *Champlain,* and this one, the *Valcour.*"

"It wasn't this one," I told him. "It had a long lower deck for cars."

"Hey, Jimmy," someone yelled to the blond kid.

He looked up. "Be right there!" He started to hand the paper back to me. "That sounds like the *Champlain.* I don't recognize these guys, but I can do some asking around and find out who was on that shift. Can you come back tomorrow?"

"Sure, but keep the picture, I have a bunch."

Finally I'd met someone willing to try to help. Emboldened by my success, when the ferry docked I approached the ticket seller in Port Kent, who was younger and friendlier than the one in Vermont.

"Hey, I'm looking for these guys who ran off with my sister's kid, who were on the late-afternoon ferry from Burlington the first week the ferries ran," I told her. "I'm wondering if you've seen them."

She looked at the picture. "Wow, that's really tough. Nope, sorry." As I turned away, she called out, "I hope you catch the bastards." I thanked her and reboarded as the waiting cars filed onto the ferry.

The blond kid, Jimmy, took my ticket. "You again, huh?" He winked.

It did feel strange to cross to New York and then cross right back, spending an hour on a ferry and then heading back where you started from. I sat out on the deck, leaning back against the rail and feeling the wind on my face. I tried not to think of the last time I'd been on a ferry to Burlington. Another worker came by, this one with dark reddish hair, also young and tanned.

"Hey, I was probably on that shift," he said. "You want me to take a look at that picture?"

I pulled a fresh one out of my daypack and handed it to him. He studied it and shook his head. "Don't remember 'em. But that was one of the first trips of the year and I think Dwight was on that shift with me. If anyone will remember them, he will. He has an incredible eye for people and cars."

I perked up. "Dwight?"

"Yeah, he's not on today, but he'll be working this boat tomorrow. I'll give him a heads-up when I see him in the morning, if you wanna come back."

"Yeah, sure!"

"Just be sure you get on the right ferry. Check the name." He pointed it out, painted on bow and stern, and rattled off the departure times. I scribbled them down. If I missed it, it would be a two-hour wait before it returned.

You wouldn't think a six-block bike ride followed by two hours on a ferry would be exhausting, but it was. I pedaled up the hill toward the apartment, wishing for a lower gear. Or a lighter bike. I'd left my bike at home so I'd concentrate on this — not that I ever would have left it at the dock. It would have been stolen in a flash.

I threw rotini on to cook, and cut up some apples I found in the back of the fridge, mixed in oatmeal and cinnamon, dabbed butter on top, and popped it in the oven. I cooked green peppers and cauliflower, then added Ragu from a jar.

Thomas sniffed appreciatively when he

came in. "Apples?"

"Yeah, I made an apple crisp with those old Granny Smiths."

Maybe it should have seemed odd eating dinner with him, but it just seemed like dining with an old friend. It had been a lifetime ago that I'd dated Thomas. I'd been someone else then.

He reminded me about dinner at the Thibaults' the following night, and said he'd like to leave around 6:10. We'd be the first ones there, I figured, but these were his friends, so it was his call. I wished I could bow out of the whole thing, because I thought it might be awkward and almost assuredly a waste of time. But I didn't want to let Thomas down. And maybe it would be good for me to get out.

From my futon I called and talked to Paul, and then Philippe. We chatted about Paul, Elise, the weather, about anything but what I was doing in Burlington. The computer firm had set up office-wide backup and security, he said, and the accounting firm had turned up a steady flow of discrepancies, with figures altered to show more expenses than had actually occurred. Someone in his office had been skimming.

My vote would have been on Claude, but it would be stupid of him to bite the hand that fed him. Claude, I suspected, was many things, but stupid was not one of them.

Riding to the ferry the next morning in the brisk air felt good, and on the way I stopped at a bakery and got a selection of fresh pastries. I bought another round-trip ticket and boarded, double-checking the ship's name.

Jimmy must have pointed me out, because Dwight came to find me about ten minutes into the trip. He was a big guy, older than Jimmy and his red-haired friend, with scruffy brown hair that stuck up, a thick neck, and scars from what looked like a bad case of acne. Jimmy had given him the by-now dog-eared picture. He gestured toward the faces. "Yeah, I remember these guys. They had a van, an older Plymouth Grand Voyager, maybe a ninety-six or ninety-seven. Sort of a dark green."

Hope rose in me, tightened my throat. I'd never expected someone to have remembered this much. *Could it be this easy?* How could the police have missed this?

He grinned. "Doesn't look like much up here," he said, pointing to his head, "but I remember faces and I remember cars. I thought maybe they didn't know much English, because the driver seemed confused when I told him where to put his car."

"Do you remember the license or anything else about the van?"

"Nah, pretty ordinary looking. A Vermont plate, I think, but I couldn't swear to it."

I could barely get out my next question. "Did you see a child with them, a little boy?"

He shook his head. "Nope. But you couldn't see in the back of the van. They could have had half a dozen kids in there."

"You didn't see which direction they drove when they got off the ferry?"

Another head shake. "Nope, once they're off, I don't look."

"Did the police show you this picture?"

"Nope. They probably only talked to the bosses. Or maybe asked on a day when I wasn't here. I had a few weeks off a while back, when my sister was sick."

"Well, thanks. I really appreciate it." I handed him the bag of pastries. "I thought you might like these."

He peered inside and sniffed. "Hey, great, the guys will love these. But don't you want one?"

I reached in and took one without looking. "Thanks, Dwight."

"No problemo!" He took off, bag in hand.

I looked down. I'd pulled out a chocolate-filled croissant. A good omen.

I'd finally found something.

The last thing I wanted to do now was go to a dinner party, but I'd promised. It didn't take long to shower and change, and Thomas had already walked Tiger. I was neglecting her, but she was happier than if I had left her in Lake Placid. And I needed her, especially at night.

I put on a colorful silk shirt Kate had talked me into buying last summer and the cord slacks again. I was going to have to break down and buy another decent pair of pants.

We found the house easily, an imposing brick three-story with large white columns in front. We were shown into an ornate entryway, near an elaborate curving stair-case. Thibault was well-off for a university professor, even a department head. Family money, I supposed, his or hers.

We'd arrived what I thought was early, but we weren't the first ones there. A couple in their late thirties, dark and slender, was ingratiating themselves with their hostess, and greeted us perfunctorily, which suited me fine, because even from across the room I didn't like them. I'm beginning to learn to trust first impressions. I sipped the oaky red wine Marguerite had delivered into my hands, and Thomas went off to greet Vince.

"Your house is gorgeous," the woman gushed to Marguerite. "I adore your color scheme."

Gack. Burlington high society, I suppose, or the edges of it. I walked around. The rooms were decorated in golds and whites, with furnishings to match. Not my taste, but striking. My eyes were drawn to a huge photo on one wall, an artful shot of an attractive boy and girl with shiny brown hair and bright faces, holding tennis racquets and wearing immaculate tennis whites.

"That's nice, isn't it," Marguerite said, noticing me looking at it. "The twins had just turned eleven." She started to say something else, but as the doorbell chimed she excused herself.

The other two couples were more congenial than the first, but all the women wore dresses and heels. Their definition of casual was clearly very different from mine.

Marguerite came over to me. "How absolutely lovely your hair is," she said, almost touching it.

"Thank you," I said brightly, making myself not move away. If I don't tie my hair back, it automatically springs into curls. I never do much with it, and don't own a hair dryer. Although I've discovered that when you go out in an Adirondack winter with wet hair it freezes into brittle little sticks, which probably isn't particularly good for it.

The food was excellent: lamb and vegetables in a cream sauce, served with fluffy hot rolls. Vince told amusing stories about his escapades as a child in England, where his father had been a French attaché. Marguerite was his perfect counterpoint, feeding him lines and laughing at just the right moment. It seemed a routine they'd perfected years ago. I made a comment or two, but mostly just watched and listened. Thomas was clearly enjoying himself.

The first couple, who I'd gathered were both bankers, excused themselves before dessert. "We're terribly sorry, but our sitter just couldn't stay any longer, and we couldn't find anyone else," the woman said. "You know how difficult it is to get good sitters these days." Marguerite made commiserating noises and went to show them out.

"Speaking of children, how are Ryan and Rebecca?" asked a jovial red-haired man, who owned a real estate firm.

"Oh, they're doing marvelously," Thibault said, waving his arm. "They're spending the summer with their grandparents in France, and working on their French accents."

"They attend school in Connecticut, don't they?" Thomas asked.

Thibault chuckled. "Yes, the twins long ago decided that they wouldn't be caught dead in high school here. They're in their second year now and doing wonderfully. Becca's decided to be a doctor and Ryan still wants to be a photographer."

Dessert was chocolate mousse, served with coffee in thin china. I prefer my chocolate not so airy, but it at least was chocolate. Afterward we retired to the living room for after-dinner drinks, which seems an odd practice, considering that most people drive themselves home. I wasn't driving, but didn't care for liquor, so I sipped more wine. I let myself relax, and for the moment forget about kidnappers not found. I sat next to the wife of the real estate man, a sturdily built woman with a blond pageboy and a hearty laugh, who asked intelligent questions about writing. Marguerite was showing Thomas a painting behind one of the sofas, listening to him avidly. Vince was telling another funny story, and I gave it half my attention. After he finished and the laughter died away, Thomas caught my eye.

"We should get going," he said. The other couples simultaneously decided it was time to leave, and we thanked the Thibaults and made our farewells.

The air was cool as Thomas and I walked to his car. "That was fun," he said cheerily.

He was being great for letting me stay with him and helping out with Tiger, so I made an agreeable sound and commented on how good the meal was.

Before Ottawa, I would have been supremely uncomfortable at this dinner. While I did like Vince and maybe the real estate man's wife — and Marguerite was all right, if maybe a little too carefully polished — to me these people mostly seemed like actors playing roles, reciting their lines, acting like they were having a good time whether they were or not.

It made me long to be somewhere I felt I belonged — either home or Ottawa. Just not here.

CHAPTER 42

I slept heavily, and awoke with a slight headache, probably from the wine. The note I found in the kitchen said Thomas had gone for a run with Tiger. My dog had abandoned me. Illogically, this made me cross.

I drank two glasses of water and swallowed an aspirin, then had a slice of whole wheat toast spread thickly with crunchy peanut butter. I brewed tea, and thought as I sipped it. Now I had information to turn over to the police, but I wasn't going to waltz into the police station. I didn't know how the police would view the type of nosing around I was doing, or even if it was legal. I plugged my laptop into Thomas's modem and looked up the Burlington Police Department website, but it didn't list email addresses or fax numbers. I wasn't going to leave all these details in an anonymous phone call, so I'd have to resort to regular mail. I wrote:

*Concerning the kidnapping of Paul Du-
mond, age 6, a Canadian citizen from
Montreal: The kidnappers, who threw the
boy off the 3:20 Burlington ferry the last
Sunday in May, were driving a green 1996
or 1997 Plymouth Grand Voyager, accord-
ing to a ferry worker named Dwight.*

I used Thomas's printer to print out the
note and an envelope. Then I emailed the
details to Jameson. Of course he could tell
the Burlington police about me, but I wasn't
going to keep this from him. If the police
here tracked me down and I got in trouble,
so be it.

I dropped the letter in the drive-by box at
the post office, then went inside to check
my box. It had been empty except for an
advertising circular the last time I'd looked,
so hope flickered when I saw several envelopes stuffed in it.

After I'd looked them over back at the
apartment, I realized some people have
nothing better to do than read personal ads
and compose replies. And apparently a lot
of them are crackpots. The pile included
cryptic notes that said things like *All foriners
are devils and should be sent back where they*

come from, and a long letter in crabbed handwriting warning me about the end of the world and how to save myself. The saving process apparently involved much praying and copious donations to the included address.

Thomas, back by now, glanced over my shoulder and raised an eyebrow.

"Apparently classified ads bring out the nutcases," I said. When my TracFone in my pocket rang, I jumped. I gave Thomas a look before pulling it out to answer it. He knew me well enough not to laugh at me.

"Hello," I said.

The voice on the other end was female, young, decisive. "Hello, this is Alyssa Cox from the Burlington *Free Press.* Is this the number to call about the two Canadian men?"

My pulse quickened. I got up and walked into my room. "Yes-s-s. Do you know their whereabouts?"

"No, but I'd like to talk to you about them."

I was automatically shaking my head. "No, no press coverage."

"Does this have anything to do with a young missing Canadian boy?"

My brain did a stutter stop. "Why do you think that?"

"Is your name by any chance Troy Chance?"

I should have said a quick "No," but I wasn't thinking fast enough. Where could she have gotten my name? I had sent an email to the news desk at the *Free Press* the day I'd found Paul, but hadn't used my name or real email address. But somehow she'd connected that email with me.

"Look," the woman said, "I don't mean to upset you or anything, but I'd really like to talk to you. Do you think we could get together?"

It didn't seem I had a choice. We agreed to meet at a coffeehouse in the Church Street marketplace, a four-block area of shops with streets closed to traffic. Before I left I looked her up on the newspaper's website, and read several of her stories. She was a good writer, her stories well sourced and rich with details.

She was waiting for me in front of the coffee shop: a slight woman in her mid- to late twenties, with wiry brown hair in a French braid and a skin color that at first seemed to be a deep tan. But her features weren't quite Caucasian. Part Filipino, I guessed, plus maybe Mexican or even African. Or all three. We ordered coffee and sat in a corner.

She pulled out one of my posters from a

voluminous bag and slid it across the table. Next came a copy of my classified ad, then a printout of my long-ago email, a screen shot of my eBay identity with the same email address I'd emailed the newspaper from, plus the same page with the coding revealed. She'd highlighted the URLs of the photos on my eBay page, which were hosted on my home page under my real name. She was thorough. The only thing she hadn't found was the Craigslist posting.

For a moment I looked at the papers on the table. I wasn't used to people being as smart as me, let alone outsmarting me. Who traces email addresses to eBay accounts and looks at page coding to see where photos are stored? I would, but I never would have anticipated someone else doing it.

"What's going on?" she asked. "This looks like a hell of a story."

"It is a hell of a story," I said slowly. "But it isn't my story, and if anything is printed it would endanger the child."

"Has he been kidnapped?" She leaned forward.

I grimaced. "If the story gets out he could be in danger. Like, real danger."

She nodded. "I'll agree not to print until the boy is safe, and I always keep my word. I'll give you names of people you can call and ask." She scribbled names and numbers on a page from her notebook, and pushed it at me. She handed me photocopied pages from a folder, saying, "These are some articles I've done recently, so you can see the type of work I do."

I took them. I didn't mention that I'd already read some of her work. "Let me think about it. I'll let you know."

"I can help," she said. "Whatever you're trying to find out, I have a lot of sources."

The coffee wasn't as good as Elise's, but I sat there until I finished it, and thought hard. This woman could put together a story based on what she had so far — the poster, the ad, a missing child — which would send the kidnappers into hiding, if they weren't already. If she found out Paul's name, and I had no doubt she could, we could kiss his chances of a quiet and safe life goodbye.

At Thomas's kitchen table I read the articles Alyssa had given me, and then I called her references, people she'd written about. None of them had anything but praise for her.

I called her back an hour later, with the phone set to speakerphone and my recorder running. I told her I was taping the call, and she reiterated her promise not to print anything until it was safe. I told her the basics: the kidnapping, the murder, the attempted drowning.

"The police are looking for these guys, but it doesn't seem that they've even come close," I told her. "And if there's any news coverage, they'll almost certainly track the boy down and try to kill him. Somebody already tried to run me over, and to pick him up from school."

She was a good reporter. She listened intently and asked pointed questions. "I won't print anything until the kidnappers are caught. But I'll do some checking for you if you promise to give me the first interview."

"His life may depend on this, Alyssa."

"Yes, I realize that." And I thought she did.

I gave her the description of the van, and the date Paul had been kidnapped and when I'd found him. We promised to keep each other updated.

I hoped I hadn't just made a serious error. I hoped I wouldn't see headlines in tomorrow's newspapers about a lurid murder and an unsolved kidnapping.

It shook me that a tiny, forgotten act like a random email and an eBay account using photos stored on my personal web space might have jeopardized Paul's life. It reminded me that I had no idea what I was doing. I was going to have to be very careful, more careful than I had been. And I had to stop underestimating people.

I drove to the apartment-viewing appointment I'd made for that afternoon, in an older part of Burlington. Another dreary apartment, another dead end. I had four more appointments booked for tomorrow, back-to-back.

I'd looked at so many apartments that it was becoming almost routine — so routine that at that third apartment the next day, I almost missed it. The middle-aged owner handed me the key, telling me to look around and that she'd be down in a few minutes. The smart ones did this, let you look around alone so you could envision yourself in the apartment, see your furniture in the rooms, imagine your posters on the walls. This apartment had three rooms, all a bright off-white. As I glanced around I noticed a faint smell.

The rooms had been freshly painted, I realized. I walked into the smallest room. I went to the corner where a mattress could have lain, and ran my hand over the wall. My fingers found what I hadn't seen: the

411

slight unevenness of well-sanded patching material.

I felt as if I had just stepped into a freezer. This was where Paul had scratched and dug into the particleboard with his little plastic toy, and kept the hole covered with his pillow. It had been a small hole, leading to nowhere, and had been spackled over neatly.

Now I heard the woman's footsteps, and I straightened quickly. "This is nice," I told her. "You've just painted it."

"Well, yes. It was so dark down here the way it was, and it really needed painting, too."

"Has it been vacant long?"

"Oh, not long," she said vaguely. "A few months. We took over when my mother-in-law had to go to a nursing home. She had it rented to some people who left without telling her, and she didn't notice until she went down to see about the overdue rent. They left it a real mess, too, let me tell you. You wouldn't believe how some people live." She shook her head.

"Did you know them? I thought I might have known the people who lived here." I kept my voice casual.

"No, no, I just saw them once from across the yard, two men it was, foreign, I think. Some kind of accent, anyway."

My pulse quickened. I forced my tone to be casual. "Yeah? It could have been the guys I knew."

"We'll never know." She made a face. "Granny didn't take references and she let people pay in cash, and now she doesn't even remember their names. I'll tell you, I'd track them down if I could, and make them pay what it cost to clean and paint this place and haul off their trash. They left it like a pigsty."

"Did they leave furniture?"

She nodded. "It was all junk. Some old mattresses, an old sofa. We had to cart it all to the dump."

I looked around the small rooms. Through the faint aroma of fresh paint and cleaning products, I thought I could smell evil. Suddenly it was difficult to breathe. I told her I didn't think the apartment was quite right for me, and made my escape.

As I drove back to Thomas's, I couldn't shake a crushing sense of depression. Yes, I'd made a big discovery — but how did it help? The apartment had been cleaned so thoroughly the chance of any clue remaining was infinitesimal.

But perhaps the police could find clues that I couldn't, and they could interview the landlady and the neighbors. I emailed details to Jameson, as promised, and wrote another note to the Burlington police and went out to mail it. I called Alyssa at home, and left a message when her voice mail clicked on.

That night I dreamed that I saw the green van drive slowly past. As it went by I saw Paul's forlorn face in the back window. I yelled and started running, chasing the van, banging on its side as it pulled away. I ran as hard as I could, but the van was pulling away from me.

I awoke in a cold sweat.

CHAPTER 43

Alyssa was a fast worker. When she called the next morning she had already talked to the police. "So you found the apartment?" she asked.

"It's the second apartment where Paul was kept, I'm pretty sure, but I think it's going to be a dead end."

She whistled. "Hey, good going. But why a dead end?"

"The apartment's been painted and cleaned from top to bottom, the guys paid in cash, and the owner is in a nursing home and apparently doesn't remember their names."

She groaned. "You're kidding. You've got to be kidding. You couldn't have luck that bad."

"Yep. I talked to the daughter-in-law. I sent a note to the police, for what it's worth."

"Unbelievable. Hey, I've read the police

reports and asked around. You're right, they basically know zippo, but they did get your note about the van. I suggested that they go have a chat with Dwight and maybe check out the apartment address you left on my voice mail."

"You told them about me?" My voice rose.

"No, I just told them someone had mentioned those things to me. I get anonymous tips all the time; they're used to it. They'd know by tomorrow, anyway, when your note gets there. Hey, somebody's calling, I've got to go look something up. I'll be in touch." She broke the connection.

When I checked my email, I saw a note from Alyssa's home account that read, "Hi, you can email here; more private than work address."

I also had an email from the editor at *Women's Sports and Fitness* about the article on gender testing in sports that I'd finished while in Ottawa. She'd attached a copy of my piece, with questions and suggestions typed into the text. Easy changes, but they'd take a while. I wasn't in the mood, but I wouldn't get paid until the piece was accepted. Might as well get it done.

Alyssa rang me back in the afternoon.

"Listen, the police have talked to Dwight, and he confirmed the identification. They've also had the daughter-in-law take the pictures of the guys to the old lady in the nursing home, and she said that it could be them."

"*Could* be them?"

"Well, she's old and doesn't see that well. Poor old coot. I talked to her for a while; she was happy to have a visitor. She never saw a kid, but she thought she heard a child crying once, but the guys convinced her it was just the TV. And here's the clincher: the daughter-in-law says she found some little toy figures in the room when she cleaned it. They were those little McDonald's toys, and sometimes adults collect them, so she didn't think anything of it. But it all means the police for sure are buying the story that the kidnappers were here, and may still be here."

"But would they hang around after dumping a kid into the lake?"

"No one knew they had him, so how would it make any difference? Unless that's the only reason they were staying here. But I can't believe they were here so long and didn't have contact with *somebody*. I mean, these are guys, scumbags at that. I doubt they spent every evening at home watching the telly. I'll take a girlfriend and go out tonight and ask around in the bars near that neighborhood."

I wished her luck, and rang off. It was strange to have someone helping, someone who could dig in places and ask questions where I couldn't, and who thought of things I didn't. But it was a relief to know she was working on this while I was revising my article. Alyssa wouldn't be at this newspaper long, I thought — she'd be off to bigger and better things.

I polished off the article Sunday night and sent it to the editor before I went to bed, wondering how Alyssa and her friend were doing on their bar-hopping jaunt. Monday I started calling about rentals again and checking out apartments to see if I could find the first place Paul had been kept. I hadn't gotten any email responses to my ads or posters. In the afternoon Alyssa and I compared notes.

Three days later my personal cell phone rang, with a number I didn't recognize — from a 613 area code. I answered it.

"Troy?"

This time I recognized his voice. "Detective Jameson. What a surprise." I'd never given him my cell phone number.

"You've made some contacts in Burlington."

"Not really. I've just been looking around a little." My mouth was dry.

"You found the apartment; you got a description of the van. Sounds like more than a little looking around."

"I found the right person to talk to on the ferry. It was luck."

"And just stumbled across the apartment."

"Mmm. I checked out some basement apartments. Actually, a lot of basement apartments." If it hadn't been Jameson, I'd have thought what I heard was a muffled chuckle. "I haven't been doing anything illegal. I mean, I didn't break in or anything."

"These guys aren't Boy Scouts, Troy." His voice was serious.

"I know."

"They may still be there, and they may not have worked alone."

I didn't say anything. He sighed. "Troy, someone kidnapped two people, murdered a woman, and tried to drown a child — and tried to run you over. You have to be careful. And if you know anything or even suspect anything, you can't keep it to yourself." It was the longest speech I'd heard from him.

"I won't, I promise. I mean, I'm not. I'm telling you and the local police everything I know. Really."

"Next time you find something, call me, Troy. Don't just email."

I agreed, and we hung up.

He hadn't told me to stop looking around. Either he understood I had to do this or he was happy that some progress was being made on the case.

On my way back to Thomas's I stopped at a McDonald's to use the bathroom, and once back in my car it dawned on me: one of these guys had routinely bought Happy Meals for Paul. Maybe an employee would recognize the guy, or if he'd gone through a drive-through someone might remember the car, as the ferry worker had. But this area had several McDonald's, with large and probably ever-changing shifts of workers. No doubt proprietors wouldn't look kindly on me coming in and showing my poster to all their employees, and I'd find myself making explanations I didn't want to have to make.

Maybe the Burlington police had thought of this, but maybe not. I could have Alyssa ask them, but I thought it would have more weight coming from Jameson. Once I got back to the house I emailed Jameson and asked if he could check to see if the local police had shown the pictures of the kidnappers to McDonald's employees.

For good measure, I set up a new Craigslist posting looking for a guy driving a Voyager who had bought Happy Meals regularly.

Jameson emailed back: *We're on it.* This, for some reason, made me smile.

CHAPTER 44

The next morning my cell phone rang early. The police, Alyssa told me, had located a broken-down van that had been abandoned near the tiny town of Chazy in upstate New York. It matched Dwight's description, and had been registered to a phony name and address.

She had an interview to do in Essex Junction, a few miles east of Burlington, so we met at a wine and cheese shop where she said the owners made stupendous sandwiches. Alyssa had called ahead, and huge, wax paper–wrapped sandwiches were waiting when we got there.

"So how does it help to find the van?" I asked. I took a bite of the sandwich, which was stuffed with green and red pepper, roast beef, cheese, and other things I couldn't identify. It was incredible.

"Forensics," she said, pushing a bit of escaping salami into her mouth. "You'd be surprised what clues they can find from an empty van. Maybe not enough to locate the guys, but things that will help convict them when they're found."

I tried to imagine it: kidnappers found, Paul safe. My own guilt dissipated. To celebrate, we had slices of rich chocolate cake.

Alyssa was going cruising for information the next evening, and I agreed to go along. Bar crawling isn't my forte, but I figured I'd follow her lead.

We met near one of the bars, and she seemed to have morphed into another persona altogether. She had made only a few alterations in her appearance, wearing her hair loose and extra makeup, with jeans and a top that seemed to have shrunk slightly. But she seemed a different person, more sensual and slightly trashy.

And it got results — fast. Men lit up as soon as we walked in the door. Like clockwork, a minute or two later, two men ambled over and said, as if in a bad movie, "Can we buy you ladies a drink?"

Like my conversation with Gina, it was almost too easy. They sipped beer and I sipped Diet Coke, and Alyssa adroitly brought up the mysterious French-Canadian men, one possibly named Jacques.

This was my cue to pull out the poster and show it. Eager to please, they took us around the room to talk to their friends and show the pictures. No one had seen or heard of the men, and after a few drinks and a few games of pool, we said goodbye to our increasingly inebriated new friends. On to bar number two, and an almost identical scenario. I discovered I wasn't bad at pool.

At bar number three, where I switched from Coke to wine so I'd have a chance of getting to sleep tonight, a friend of one of the men who had just bought us drinks squinted critically at the picture.

"I think I've seen this one guy," she said. "Yeah, he looks like the guy my friend Tammi went out with a couple of times."

Alyssa and I exchanged looks.

"So do you think we could talk to her?" I asked.

The woman shook her head. "Tammi moved away and I don't know how to get ahold of her. She didn't have her own place even then, just stayed with friends."

"What was the guy's name?"

Again she shook her head. "I don't know that she ever said. I just saw them together here a few times; didn't really talk to them."

Alyssa asked a few more questions, and had the woman write down Tammi's name and the names of some of her friends. By the time we left the bar to walk back to our cars, my head was spinning from the smoke, the Coke, and the wine. Not a great combination.

"Damn, girl," I said. "This is rough work."

Alyssa laughed. "Yeah, and you never know if any of it is going to turn into anything. I'll call some of these people and see if any of them knows anything about Tammi or this guy, and I'll pass on the info to the police."

When I let myself into Thomas's apartment, Tiger sniffed me disapprovingly. I'd promised to call Jameson if I found out anything, but this didn't seem to qualify, so I just emailed him. I stood under the shower a long time. At last it seemed I was getting somewhere.

The weekend slid past. Alyssa hadn't turned up anything, and apparently the police hadn't either. I kept doggedly searching for the second apartment, putting up my little posters, and updating my Craigslist posting. I went to another French club function, without Thomas this time. No leads, but it was good to get out. Marguerite was there, but not Vince, who had had to attend a faculty meeting. She was congenial and convivial, managing to greet every person who entered the room, while still chatting with me. She had a talent for noticing or remembering something about each person and working it into the conversation.

I did have to turn aside a clumsy pass from a graduate student, one I didn't see coming until almost too late. Just what I didn't need, although maybe it was good for my ego. I emailed Alyssa, weaving it into an amusing tale, but ending on a disgruntled note: *I know this is probably just a letdown after feeling like we were starting to get somewhere. But this is really frustrating.*

She must have been at her computer — or else she had a smartphone — because her reply arrived moments later: *Don't despair! Remember, the lull comes before the storm. Genius is one-tenth inspiration and nine-tenths perspiration. And all those other clichés. Hang in there!*

She was right, but this was getting tedious. I'd been poking around — and imposing on Thomas's hospitality — for what seemed like forever. Thomas had been great about it, but he needed to get on with his life. While he seemed to have adjusted to us not dating, having an ex-girlfriend staying with him couldn't be the best thing for his social life: *Who's that at your apartment? Oh, some woman I used to date who's living with me for a while.* Maybe I'd ask Alyssa about bunking with her, if she didn't think that would infringe on her journalistic integrity.

That evening while I was out walking Tiger, Philippe called my cell phone. The audit was nearing completion, and it seemed evident the culprit was Claude. I couldn't pretend to be shocked, although it seemed unlike Claude to do something so clumsy. Maybe he had assumed Philippe was too busy or too grief-stricken to realize someone was cooking the books. As he almost had been.

"Be careful," he said, just before he hung up. *Careful careful careful.* I'd been careful my entire life. It had never gotten me anywhere.

Suddenly I desperately wished I could unburden myself, talk about my fear that none of this was actually going to resolve anything, tell someone that I had no idea what to do next. I thought about calling Baker, but I wasn't going to dump this on her. I wished I could talk to Simon, but I couldn't, not this time.

And I couldn't face Thomas's bland politeness. I couldn't pretend to be interested in a PBS special; I couldn't make polite, meaningless conversation. So I kept walking. The only movie within walking distance was a Kenneth Branagh flick, and that I couldn't handle either. I tried calling Alyssa, but she wasn't home.

I pulled the card Jameson had given me out of my wallet and turned it over, where he'd written his home number in bold black letters. Without letting myself think about it, I punched his number in my cell phone. It rang once, twice, and then he answered, a gruff "Hello." I opened my mouth, but nothing came out. A long second, and I hung up. I turned my phone off so he couldn't call back.

Tiger and I walked for what seemed like hours more, until I found a bench and sat with her beside me, my face buried in her fur. It wasn't the contact I longed for, but it was better than nothing.

I didn't go back until I knew Thomas would be asleep.

Chapter 45

Marguerite had asked me to meet her for coffee, so the next afternoon we met at a little pastry and coffee shop, where we had brownies with our cappuccinos. A triple hit: chocolate, sugar, and caffeine. She was wearing a crimson dress that shouldn't have worked with her hair color, but somehow it did. We chatted about the university and my work, and I found myself relaxing and telling her more about myself than I had intended. I could see why Thomas was drawn to her: she had a talent for focusing on you, and seeming genuinely interested in what you were saying.

"So have you found those people you were looking for?" she asked.

"No, but it's looking up. I think things will wrap up soon."

"And then you'll head back to — where was it, Lake Placid?"

I nodded.

"The four of us should get together before you leave," she said. "I'll check with Vincent tonight, but let's plan on doing something this weekend."

I made noncommittal noises. I wasn't going to commit Thomas to anything, and it seemed that doing something with just the four of us, as if we were two couples, might be awkward. I knew Thomas wouldn't misunderstand, but the idea made me uneasy.

On the way back, I stopped to check my mail at the post office. My mailbox held two envelopes. One was junk mail, but the other was a handwritten note I read twice before its significance sunk in. It said:

One of these guys looks like a guy I was with a couple of months ago. He was cute but a real asshole and didn't speak English very good. He lived near Pearl St, but I'm not sure where because I never went there. My phone won't be hooked back up til Monday, but you can call me then 555-4636.

Shawna

Bingo. The apartment where Paul had been kept had been one street away from Pearl Street. Maybe this woman would have enough information to help lead the police to these guys, or at least this one.

Back at the apartment I scanned the note from Shawna, emailed a copy to Jameson and one to Alyssa, then left her a phone message. I printed a copy of the note with *Concerning the people who kidnapped Paul Dumond* typed on top to mail to the Burlington police.

Between the van and this woman, surely the police would be able to track those guys down. Kidnappers would be caught, ghosts laid to rest. I'd be able to move on.

By that evening we had an invitation to spend Saturday on the lake on the Thibaults' sailboat, a forty-two-footer. We would spend the night on the boat and return in the morning. Thomas was as enthusiastic as I'd ever seen him.

"Yikes, that sounds pretty fancy," I said, none too sure about this. I wasn't eager for this much socializing, especially this close up, and overnight.

Thomas clearly wanted to go. "It'll be fun. You'd be amazed how much room there is on board — they'll have their own separate room, and there'll be bunks for us."

This would be more than a little awkward, I thought. But I owed him, and I knew he wouldn't go on his own. I was sure Alyssa

431

would take Tiger for the night. If nothing else, this would be something to tell her and Baker about — another new experience.

I tried the phone number the woman Shawna had sent, just in case. As she'd said, it wasn't hooked up yet. I'd call Monday.

Saturday dawned bright and clear, and my spirits began to lift as we headed to the marina. For the first time since this had started, I had the feeling it would all be over soon: kidnappers behind bars, murder solved, Philippe cleared, Paul safe. Chapter closed. Time to start the next chapter, whatever it would be.

It turned out to be one of those unexpectedly magical days. The weather was perfect: sky clear and sunny, the air with that crisp feel that makes it seem that something wonderful is just around the corner. Vince and Marguerite were experienced sailors and Thomas had done some sailing as well. For me it was brand new, and I loved it. I loved the sound of the sails crackling, the feel of the wind, and the warmth of the sun on my skin.

We docked at a small marina at Malletts Bay, poked around in a few shops, and stopped for lunch in a small restaurant and had mouth-watering fresh trout. The meal was relaxed and easy, the conversation witty and light, and Vince smoothly picked up the bill. Back on the boat, I sat at the bow, basking in the sun and feeling one with the boat as it moved through the water. We anchored before dusk in an open area. The wind had died down before we could reach the bay where we'd planned to anchor, but Vince said we'd be fine, even this far out, as this was a little-traveled area.

Dinner was a picnic the Thibaults had brought along, unlike any I'd ever had: delectable little sandwiches whose contents I could only guess at, fruit salads, and a variety of individual baked desserts. We ate until we could eat no more, and packed away the rest. We watched the sun set, and went below to sip wine and chat.

Vince and Thomas began playing gin rummy, with Marguerite watching and hanging onto Vince's arm, Thomas chuckling at her witticisms. She shook her hair back in a way that seemed familiar. Something about her reminded me of someone, maybe an actress I'd seen on a TV show. She must have felt me looking at her, because she glanced up.

Suddenly my meal seemed heavy in my stomach. I'd eaten too much, I thought. I set my wine down, murmuring that I wanted some air, and slipped away to go topside.

It had been good for me to get away from town, to be out on the water and away from everything. The day had provided a bookend for my time in Burlington. I'd done what I could to catch the kidnappers, to make up for my mistakes, to work through my guilt, and I'd given Philippe space to start working through his.

Things would work out. Life would go on. I would head back to Lake Placid and take up my life again. I'd figure out if it still worked for me, and change it if it didn't. Philippe and Paul, I knew, would always be a part of my life, some way or another. Some people you can erase as if they were characters on a canceled TV show, but others are with you forever.

The boat was rocking gently, and I leaned against a stanchion as I stared up at the sky. It was a rich dark blue, the stars brilliant slits of light, the moon luminous. I breathed in the cool night air. *This is the same sky Philippe looks at, the same one Paul sees at night.* I could imagine them here with me, standing beside me.

I'd been up there probably a quarter of an hour when I heard a faint noise. I turned to see Marguerite approaching, quiet in her deck shoes.

"Oh, hi," I said brightly, to cover my annoyance at being interrupted. "It's a nice night, isn't it?"

"Yes, it's lovely," she agreed. "Did you enjoy the day?"

"It was great," I said, and meant it. "You were wonderful to ask us."

"I'm glad you enjoyed it."

Silence. "You got tired of watching the card game?" I asked.

"Yes," she said with a smile, "I got tired of watching." She tossed her hair back in that curiously familiar gesture, giving me an odd look.

"Do you take the boat out often?" I asked, because it seemed rude not to make conversation.

"We've tried to get out every nice weekend this summer, and we'll keep it up until it gets too cold. We do love the water." She turned and looked directly at me. Her eyes, I saw, were brown, a little too dark for her auburn hair.

I blinked. She again shook her hair back, with a smile that seemed almost taunting. Her posture and the way she held her head had changed subtly, making her seem somehow quite different.

My heart skipped a beat. Suddenly I realized what that movement reminded me of: the way Paul shook his hair back when it fell into his face. I looked at her and suddenly I was looking into Paul's eyes.

CHAPTER 46

It was like looking at a movie right after the focus has been adjusted. The hair wasn't long or blond and the nose was more rounded and upturned than in the photos I'd seen. But it was her, or her doppelgänger. The things that had seemed hauntingly familiar, the toss of the head, the shape of the eyes, were Paul's. The face I was looking at was the one that had stared across the room at me from the photo on Philippe's desk: Madeleine.

Or her twin sister, I thought. I blinked. It was like the old TV show *Sliders,* where the characters kept sliding into parallel universes and running into their doubles, with different hair and a different life, but the same face. Just like now. This was Madeleine, but somehow not her.

She smiled, a graceful Mona Lisa smile. "Madeleine?" I whispered.

"I thought you figured it out downstairs."

She sounded amused, as if I'd made a joke.

My mind was reeling. *Had she escaped the kidnappers and taken a new identity? Had she had amnesia?* "You're not dead," I said stupidly.

"Of course not." She laughed, and it was so like Paul's happy trill I couldn't keep from shuddering.

"But you're married to Vince — you have the twins." I'd seen the portrait on the wall of their home: the beautiful shiny-haired boy and girl, off at school in Connecticut.

"Oh, we're married all right. It's been more than six months now." Her tone was pleasant, what you might use chatting to a friend at a party. "But the twins aren't mine; they belong to Vince and his dearly departed first wife."

This was a bad dream come to life, one of those where bizarre things happen that couldn't possibly be happening.

"But your body was found. In your car. The dental records matched." Even to me my voice sounded flat.

She smiled at me indulgently, like you'd smile at someone who's a bit slow. "Troy, getting the name changed on dental records was simple — men are easy to manipulate. Of course the body wasn't me; she was just someone who was getting in the way of things, and needed to disappear. She looked like me, so it worked out wonderfully." She said it as if it all made perfect sense, and in a way it did.

And that was the moment when I realized — while standing on this gently rocking sailboat on a lovely moonlit night — that I was talking to a psychopath. Who had been married to Philippe, who was still married to Philippe, who had given birth to Paul. Who had adroitly and convincingly pretended to be dead for the last six months, and who seemed to be telling me she had killed a woman in her place.

Suddenly I was calm. My breathing evened out and my brain clicked into survival mode. As I was forming my next sentence I was analyzing the distance between us, how composed she was, what her next move might be, what options I had. This woman was placidly telling me about killing her double or having her killed; I doubted she intended for me to leave this boat alive.

"So you were never kidnapped." I kept my voice steady.

"Of course not." Her hair was perfect, the strands falling evenly. Her outfit and makeup were immaculate.

Somehow I knew I needed to keep her

talking. "If you wanted out, why didn't you just leave?"

She laughed. "The prenup I'd signed would have meant I would have hardly gotten a dime. This way I ended up with quite a stash, more than enough so that Vince didn't think I was after his money." She seemed proud of a game well played.

"You convinced everyone — even Claude." I watched to see her reaction.

Her eyes flickered. "So Claude believed it was my body?"

"Yes, I think so. He was very upset."

Something shifted in her then, and I could almost see two people within her: one angry and resentful, one who felt something like regret at having abandoned her brother. "Claude wasn't as indispensable as he thought he was," she said at last.

She altered her stance, and her tone became almost mocking. "Poor Claude — I'm sure he was shocked when I cut off communications with him, especially after he picked up the ransom for me. But then you came along with Paul, taking him to Ottawa, going out with Philippe as if you thought you could take my place." She laughed at my stunned expression. "Oh, yes, I saw the newspaper photo, and I came up there. I missed running you over, but this is even better, getting you down here."

She watched my face as I took this in. *She had wanted me here in Burlington, away from Paul and Philippe.* I had played right into her hands. Somehow she had lured me here. Something clicked in my head, and then I knew she had been the one who had sent the Craigslist response about the kidnappers having lived here. She had played with me, setting up meetings, waiting for this moment when she could watch me learn the truth.

Sweat trickled down my side, despite the coolness of the evening. I had blundered along and ruined part of her intricate, brilliant plan, so she had needed to prove she was smarter than me. And she just had.

Then she reached into the purse on her shoulder and pulled out a small gun that glinted in the moonlight.

I couldn't keep the disbelief from my voice. This was a scene from a bad detective novel. "You're going to shoot me? And what, tell the guys you thought I was a burglar?" Even as I said it, I was figuring how fast her finger could pull the trigger, calculating how quickly I could drop to the deck or if I could leap overboard before she could adjust her aim and fire. And how loudly I would have to yell to bring Vince and Thomas above deck.

She raised an eyebrow. "I won't have to tell them anything. They're out cold from the Rohypnol I put in their wine, but they'll just think they drank too much and fell asleep. If you had drunk yours, I could have just walked you up the stairs and pushed you overboard."

I couldn't imagine how she thought she could get away with shooting me. But she'd pulled off everything so far, so of course she thought she could. And not that it mattered — I'd be dead whether she got away with it or not.

I had to ask one more thing: "What about Paul?"

She knew what I meant. "Oh, I had him kept as long as Philippe continued paying, and when that was over, *zut,* time to get rid of him." She waved the gun theatrically.

The one truly crazy thing I'd done in my life was diving off the Burlington ferry, and I'd done that without a moment's thought. This woman had a gun pointed at me, and I knew enough about guns to know it's hard to miss something vital from such a short distance. But when I heard her speak so casually about getting rid of her son — a child I'd loved probably since I'd seen the look on his face when he was beginning to

442

drown in Lake Champlain — something exploded within me.

I lunged without thinking.

She fired, but not before the force of my body had swung her arm into the air. The shot went high and I felt a burning pain in my left shoulder. I grappled with her gun hand, banging her arm against the mast. The gun fell from her fingers and skittered across the deck.

She was smaller and older and less fit than me. But she was vicious and acted without hesitation. She twisted one arm away from me and hammered at my bleeding shoulder, sending waves of pain through my body. She kicked at my shin while I was still reeling, and I fell to the deck. *Get up, get up, get up,* a voice was telling me, and I was forcing myself to my feet when something hit the arm I was using to lever myself up.

There was a sickening snap as the bone in my right forearm cracked, and the arm was instantly numb, a dangling dead weight. As I fell forward I saw Madeleine coming at me again, swinging a fire extinguisher at my head. Simple physics told me it could likely crush my skull. I spun on my butt, scissoring my legs and knocking her off balance. She fell heavily, and I heard the fire extinguisher thud to the deck and roll away.

She dived after the gun and I flopped after her desperately, pushing myself up with my left arm, ignoring the pain in my shoulder. She was twisting, reaching out for the gun, her fingers inching closer to it. I hesitated momentarily and then lunged upward desperately, slamming her throat with the edge of my left hand.

I think I pulled the blow at the last moment, with awful visions of crushing her larynx. I'd never hit anyone before, and it's more difficult than you might think. It made a horrible thwack and she gagged, but as I fell back she got her hands around my neck, those immaculate nails digging into my throat. I couldn't pry her fingers loose. I slid on the deck, desperately pushing with my heels to get away from her, but she came with me. Part of me slid under the bottom cable of the railing and over the slight lip at the edge, and she was pushing against my broken arm with her body weight while choking me. I felt wave after wave of pain. I couldn't get a full breath. She banged against my broken arm with her torso. I wrenched back, pushing away from her, trying to escape the pain, and toppled into space. Her hands were still around my throat, and slowly, horribly, she tumbled with me.

As we fell, I swung my left arm and hit her jaw with my elbow as hard as I could. Her hold broke, and I hit the water alone.

It seemed I went down forever. It wasn't as cold as when I had dived after Paul, but it was darker, and I was almost numb with pain. Finally I stopped descending. I was tired, so tired, and part of me wanted to let go, to drift off into nothingness.

But I saw Paul's face, and I thought of the nightmares he would have if I drowned. I thought of the other people who would miss me. And from somewhere I found the will to toe off my sneakers and force myself to kick, softly at first and then harder, bracing my broken arm against my side. Up and up I went, as if something were pulling me along.

I saw her then, a few yards away, lit eerily by the moonlight shining through the water. Her eyes were open, looking straight at me. Her hair was floating above her as Paul's had, with one hand at her throat where I'd hit her. She pirouetted slowly, reaching her other hand out toward me. I hesitated, then stretched out my left arm. Our fingertips brushed as I rose and she sank.

Chapter 47

I dived down once, awkwardly, but she was gone.

The movement of the water had pulled me away from the boat. I was oddly calm. I knew this lake flowed north; I knew it had been glacially formed and that the water was around sixty degrees this time of year. I knew the ladder on the side of the boat hadn't been extended, and I wouldn't be able to board. I shouted, in case she had been lying about Thomas and Vince, but there was no response.

I rolled onto my back. My shoulder was bleeding and there must be something I should do to stop it, but I couldn't think what. I was grateful my shirt and shorts were lightweight synthetic that I'd chosen in case I got wet on the boat. Heavy cold cotton would have dragged me down.

I began gently kicking, aiming where I thought shore might be. I think I eventually fell asleep, or may have passed out. I came to, sputtering, when water washed over my head, a wake from something far off or long gone. Then I floated on, fluttering my legs gently, letting the water carry me where it would.

I thought about Paul and I thought about Philippe. I thought about little blond Janey at the children's shelter, and wondered if she had ever found a home where she was loved. I thought about all the things in life I hadn't done yet. I thought about when I'd learned to swim at age fifteen, alone at night in the pool of a neighbor who was out of town, pushing myself off into the deep end and making myself learn to tread water. I thought about an evening swim at the beach I'd taken a few years ago, where the darkness of the night and the immenseness of the ocean had triggered the release of some of the emotion and pain bottled up inside me, which was when I'd discovered that you can't swim and cry at the same time.

But when you're floating on your back, you can, in fact, cry quietly.

A long time later my head nudged against something. When I twisted around, my grasping fingers found the dark, wet wood of a dock piling. I could smell the creosote that coated it. When I peered upward, I saw one odd large figure standing on the deck. "Help me," I whispered, trying to shout. I tried again, my voice a hoarse squawk, and slapped at the water with my left hand. The figure separated eerily into two. It was a pair of students, I found out later, who had thought a 1:00 a.m. stroll at the waterside would be romantic. Probably I took the glamour out of moonlit strolls for them forever, but very likely they saved my life.

The boy pulled me out, with help from his girlfriend, but I screamed when they took hold of my right arm, and fainted dead away.

I awoke in a hospital bed. The room was nearly dark, and it took a moment to recognize the hanging curtain and the controls on the bed and realize where I was. My broken right arm was heavily wrapped, and I could feel a thick bandage on my left shoulder. There was a phone beside the bed. With some effort I pulled it to me with my left hand, lifted the receiver, and pressed zero. I licked my lips. "Collect," I croaked out. "From Troy."

Philippe answered on the first ring. "Philippe," I said, "you need to come here."

"Where are you? I can barely hear you." His tone was sharp.

"In the hospital, in Burlington."

"What's happened? Are you hurt?"

"Please come." I dropped the receiver.

I always will maintain that I didn't faint that second time; I just fell asleep. At that point, I thought later, Thomas and Vince were likely just beginning to wake up from the drug Madeleine had given them, and wondering where the two of us were.

I awoke once more, and pulled open the drawer of the bedside table. There was my bedraggled wallet, sitting atop a plastic bag. I needed to stop jumping into lakes with my wallet in my pocket — it wasn't going to survive another dunking. I pulled it open and fumbled out the card from one of its compartments. Wet but readable. I punched in my phone card number, concentrating to get the numbers right, then the number from the business card.

"Alan Jameson, please," I whispered.

"He's not in. May I take a message, please?"

It was difficult to think. "Tell him . . . tell him Troy is in the hospital. Tell him Madeleine is dead."

"Hello? Who is this calling, please? Hello?"

"This is Troy," I said, and hung up. I realized it was late Saturday or, more likely, very early Sunday, and fumbled the card over. Now I punched in the home number, concentrating to place my finger squarely on each button. A machine answered, with Jameson's terse voice.

"It's over," I said to the machine, tears beginning to stream down my face. "It's over. She's dead now. She's really dead. She drowned."

I let the receiver drop into the cradle and cried until I fell asleep.

CHAPTER 48

Jameson got there first. He'd been at home and heard his machine record my message, and had called his office and my cell phone. Somehow he'd tracked me down, and then gotten in his car and driven through the night, undoubtedly faster than someone without a police badge could have.

When I opened my eyes, he was sitting by the bed.

"You picked a helluva time to call me at home, Troy," he said. "The first time I've had a woman in my house in a year, and you leave a message like that."

I tried to force a smile. "You said I could call you anytime." My throat hurt, and my voice seemed to be coming from a long way away. "Did they find her? Did they find Madeleine?"

"Divers are looking now. So she drugged Vince and Thomas and, what, threw you overboard?" It wasn't quite a question.

"We both went over," I whispered. "I hit her in the jaw to make her let go of me. I saw her drowning."

He looked at me, eyes narrowed. "Troy," he said, almost harshly. "You were shot. Your arm was broken. What, you were supposed to let her drown you?"

"I don't know," I said, hot tears running down my face. He grasped my left hand roughly, and held it until I stopped. I wouldn't have thought of Jameson as the hand-holding type, but the warmth of his hand was a connection to life, pulling me back from yesterday's nightmare. I hung on as if it were a lifeline, lifting me out of the lake.

"So what happened to your date?" I asked, finally.

He shrugged. "Put her in a cab and sent her home. Guess she's pretty ticked."

I smiled weakly. "Flowers. Flowers are always good."

He gave me a look I couldn't interpret, and handed me the box of tissues from the bedside table. I wiped my face and blew my nose and then, without prompting, I talked. I told him every word Madeleine had said on the boat, every move she'd made. I told him about the moment when I realized she was Madeleine, and about our battle, move

452

by move. I could have been recounting a bad dream to a therapist. He pulled out a small notebook and scribbled notes, then went off to talk to the local police. And presumably to let the Montreal police know the body they had found was not Madeleine Dumond's.

A nurse checked my temperature and pulse, and a doctor appeared. He told me the bullet had passed through my left shoulder and they needed to let the swelling subside in my broken arm before casting it, probably tomorrow. I was grateful for their briskness and efficiency — I couldn't have handled compassion at this point. I'd never felt so adrift, so not quite human. My emotions seemed to have frozen.

Jameson returned with two members of the Burlington police, and sat in a corner of the room as they talked to me. They were far less skeptical than they had every reason to be. I knew it was because Jameson had known the right people to talk to, the right things to say, the right things to be done. No one seemed amazed at my story that the Burlington professor's wife had really been the Canadian businessman's wife who had faked her own murder and had her son kept captive and dumped off the side of a ferry. I had to repeat parts of it several times, but they seemed to believe me. And no one admonished me for having poked around looking for kidnappers as I had. Maybe they figured I'd been punished enough. I'd seen myself in the bathroom mirror; I knew how bad I looked. And how bad I felt.

Philippe was on his way here, Jameson told me, and would be in by early afternoon. I didn't ask how he knew.

I'd done all this for Philippe and for Paul — okay, maybe some for me, so I could stop feeling guilty about having delayed the search for the kidnappers — but this wasn't what I'd envisioned. I'd been foreseeing a tidy wrap-up, with anonymous kidnappers handily caught and locked up. Troy exit stage left, to enthusiastic applause.

Instead, Philippe would be finding out that his wife had murdered someone, that she had tried to drown me and likely tried to drown their son. And that she was only just now dead.

In a bizarre way I felt guilty, which even I knew didn't make sense. Most of this had happened long before I appeared on scene. Without me, Paul would have drowned. But without me, Madeleine wouldn't have. It was too much for me.

But I wasn't looking forward to seeing

Philippe.

It was early afternoon before I did. He appeared in the doorway of my room, looking more drawn than I could have imagined. Jameson nodded curtly at him and left us alone.

"I'm sorry it took so long to get here," Philippe said. He spoke like an automaton, probably the same way I was talking. "I waited until dawn to leave, and then the police here wanted to see me."

"So . . . they told you?" What I meant was *They told you Madeleine is dead?*

He nodded. "They found the body," he said, and by his expression I knew he'd seen it. Maybe he'd wanted to, or maybe the police had asked him to identify her. Of course he'd already made one misidentification, but maybe there was a specific feature he could point out — a scar, a birthmark. Although I suspected that this time they'd be doing DNA testing as well.

We didn't talk long. I was exhausted and he was in shock, and it seemed clear that he would rather have been in denial. If he hadn't just seen the body of his wife and if I wasn't swathed in bandages in a hospital bed, I don't think he would have believed any of it.

Before he came in I'd pulled the collar of

my hospital gown up around my neck. Because no one's last memory of their wife should be the marks of her fingers around someone's throat.

He kissed my forehead before he went, telling me he was going to check into a nearby motel and make phone calls.

Then Thomas stopped in, so soon after Philippe left that he might have been waiting in the hall. He'd brought my toiletries, some clothing, and my cell phone, and for once I greatly appreciated his methodical nature.

He was still gray with shock, horrified that he had introduced me to a woman who had tried her best to kill me. But when he tried to say something, to start to apologize, I cut him off. He couldn't possibly have imagined that his friend's wife was the mother of the child I'd rescued — although I wished he had happened to mention that Vince had married this woman less than a year ago. Not that I would have guessed she was Madeleine, although maybe something in my brain would have kicked into gear fractionally sooner. But I doubt it.

Vince, Thomas told me, was grief-stricken, incredulous, finding it difficult to believe that the beautiful, charming Marguerite he'd met in an online French-language chat room had faked her own kidnapping and death. And had not, in fact, been his wife at all, because her own husband was alive and well.

I imagined Vince was more than a little relieved that his children were safely off at boarding school.

Philippe called to say that he was tied up for the rest of the afternoon. I supposed I'd realized he would have some arrangements to make. He was, after all, the widower — previously the prime suspect, now just a widower. I thought about calling Alyssa, but the idea exhausted me. Thomas would be picking up Tiger from her, and would fill her in and tell her I'd contact her tomorrow. The news couldn't be released yet, so she wouldn't miss her story.

I spent the rest of the day alone. I didn't mind. It suited me to lie in this hospital bed, in my hospital gown, and let my mind run.

Maybe a shrink would have told me to block it all out for now, to accept the pill the nurse offered and just sleep the afternoon away. But I needed to think it through. I tried to imagine Madeleine in Montreal, carefully plotting her exit and her new life here, planning to have her own child kept captive as long as it suited her. I relived every encounter I'd had with her when I thought she was Marguerite, and every moment afterward with her on the boat and in the water. I wondered about her relationship with her brother and why she had abandoned him. I wondered about the woman she had killed, her doppelgänger. I thought about when and why she had decided to leave Paul and Philippe, and I thought about the nature of a psyche that had been compelled to invent a whole new persona and inflict as much pain and damage as possible before moving on.

And I couldn't help but think of the eight-year-old boy I'd read about at the beginning of all this, whose mother had driven down from Montreal and tied him to a boat mooring in a tiny Vermont town — where he had drowned, in the same lake where Paul had nearly died.

Then I slept.

CHAPTER 49

Before I opened my eyes in the morning it all seemed like a ghastly dream. Then I heard the wheels of the cart in the hall, and a cheery assistant brought in a tasteless breakfast. I ate it, because I was ravenous — I couldn't even remember if I'd had dinner. I called Alyssa and told her voice mail where I was, but not what had happened. I knew she'd show up or call when she could. I wondered how Philippe was doing.

Jameson arrived carrying a fragrant McDonald's bag, and sipped his coffee as he watched me eat two Egg McMuffins, one after the other.

"Do you want to hear what's going on?" he asked. I nodded.

So he told me.

It was a mess, of course: a multi-jurisdictional, cross-border mess involving law enforcement from two countries, two states, and two provinces.

459

The Ottawa police were interviewing Claude, who had had the news broken to him that his sister had been living here and had just died. I supposed Claude could have tried to deny any involvement in the kidnapping, no matter what Madeleine had told me. But maybe he figured the police would find some evidence, or maybe he was just in shock and needed to unburden himself. But he was talking and talking fast. He admitted picking up the ransoms, and had thought Paul would be sent back to Philippe at that point. He reconsidered the sketches of the "kidnappers" he'd barely glanced at before, and after an artist had regressed their ages, said he thought they might be two brothers who had been in foster care with Madeleine and him. The police had located the two in a small town north of Montreal and had them in custody. If the Canadian police had been slow to get results on the kidnapping, they were making up for it now.

"So Claude didn't know Madeleine was here?" I asked.

Jameson shook his head. "He'd thought she'd gone to New York, and that he would join her there. But the accomplices were already living here. We're still finding out details."

No wonder Claude had needled me so

much — when I'd shown up with Paul he must have been hugely confused, wondering if I knew Madeleine or was involved somehow.

"Gaius," I said suddenly, thinking of the emails I'd seen. "Claude was Gaius."

Jameson gave me an odd look, and nodded again.

"And the . . . the body?" I said. "The dead woman in Montreal?"

He paused before he spoke, and seemed to be sizing me up to see if I could handle this now. "It's off the record until it's confirmed and family notified, but they think it's the woman Claude had been dating."

This took more than a moment to digest. Madeleine had killed her brother's girlfriend and stashed the body in her car — a woman who resembled her enough that six months later Philippe had identified the body as his wife's. And presumably Madeleine had called in the tip herself so the body could be found when she chose.

Jameson could see me working on this. He cleared his throat. "Troy," he said. "The Roman emperor Gaius was also known as Caligula. And two of his sisters were named Julia."

The puzzle pieces started sliding into

place. Even I knew that Caligula had been closer to his sisters than a brother is supposed to be, and if I'd known my Roman history better, maybe I would have figured it out sooner. But maybe not, because I can be astoundingly naïve.

"Does Claude know who the dead woman was?" I asked finally.

"No," he said. "Not yet."

I felt more compassion for Claude than I would have thought possible.

When Philippe came to see me later that morning, he looked infinitely better. He had reverted to efficient businessman mode, where he was perhaps most comfortable. He'd talked to Elise, who knew some of what was going on, and to Paul, who didn't. He told me Claude had supplied a copy of Madeleine's birth certificate and Québec child services had located her fingerprints, so they wouldn't have to wait for a DNA match. Of course at this point no one could be sure whose dental records were whose. I didn't ask what had become of the person Madeleine had gotten to change names on the records.

Claude had assumed someone local was keeping Paul, and hadn't known about the Burlington accomplices or about Vince. To

Claude it all had seemed a clever and relatively harmless ploy to bypass the prenup, and this I could believe. Philippe, too.

"It's just the sort of thing that would appeal to Claude," Philippe said. He'd known his brother-in-law's strengths and weaknesses. I didn't ask if he knew about the Gaius-Julia thing, or if he thought it was anything more than a particularly tasteless joke between siblings. Some things you didn't need to know.

Alyssa arrived around lunchtime, and was smart enough to have brought me a thick deli sandwich. She took one look at me and said, "Ah, Troy." I think if not for my bandages, she would have perched on the side of the bed and hugged me. As it was, she did what Jameson had, and held my hand lightly. It opened the floodgates, and I cried again.

As I expected she would, she had already talked to the police. All she needed to write her article was the interview with me.

"Are you sure you're up to this?" she asked.

I wasn't, but I'd promised, and maybe it would be good for me. Alyssa turned on her tape recorder and asked questions, taking notes as I talked. Then she flicked off her recorder and put away her pen.

Then I told her more: how Madeleine sounded, the look on her face, how I had reached out for her as she sank. She listened, which is what I needed. I was starting to get the hang of letting people be there for you, of not keeping everything to yourself.

We both had trouble wrapping our minds around Madeleine killing a woman, then using her like a set piece to frame her husband for her own murder. It was Alyssa who pointed out that Madeleine had in essence killed her old self in effigy, so Marguerite could emerge.

We both had brains that liked to work at things. We knew Madeleine could easily have found the photo of Philippe and me in the paper online; she could have had a Google Alert set up for Philippe's name. And that photo must have been like a match lit under her — I was willing to bet she'd driven up to Ottawa the same day. It made me ill to think of Madeleine watching the house, following as Paul was driven to school, seeing me leave for my bike ride.

My name from the newspaper photo would have led her to my Twitter account and Craigslist posting, and luring me here had been simple. I'd reacted with Pavlovian predictability, coming to Burlington and going to the French club, the dinner, the sailboat outing. All along she had been taunting me, waiting for the moment when she would reveal just enough for me to figure it out.

"I knew this would be a heck of a story, but I never expected anything like this," Alyssa said. She put her things in her bag — she had a story to write — and on the way out the door gave me a half salute. "Hang in there," she said.

The story made the front page of the paper, with a sidebar on Madeleine/Marguerite — the death of a prominent faculty member's wife, who hadn't been his wife at all. Philippe had talked to Alyssa, figuring that if he gave one interview the press might leave him alone. Alyssa had written the pieces well, but even handled with restraint, they were lurid. The wire service picked them up and they ran nationwide, and in Canada as well.

Alyssa had given me advance warning that the stories would be hitting the wires, so I called Simon for help with familial damage control. He said he'd alert our parents and sisters so they wouldn't go berserk, and asked if I wanted him to come up. I said no. He didn't say a lot, but I thought he knew pretty well what I was feeling. Philippe called Zach and Baker for me; I wasn't up to talking to them yet.

By now I'd acquired a shiny cast, and I was glad I'd been faithfully paying my monthly health insurance premiums. My shoulder wound had avoided getting infected — washed clean by the cold water of that glacially formed lake, I supposed. The doctor pronounced me ready to leave. I had one last brief interview with the Burlington police, and Jameson stopped in before he headed back to Ottawa.

He told me the accomplices seemed stunned by the murder. They had been the ones who had driven Paul across the border, curling his small body inside their wheel well — and that image made me shiver. But they'd thought he would be turned loose eventually. When Madeleine had ordered them to get rid of him, they'd moved to another apartment instead, and sent a ransom demand of their own. But she'd seen one of them at a McDonald's — buying a kids' meal — and had confronted him.

They fled town, planning to abandon a drugged Paul on the New York side of the lake. But she'd followed them onto the ferry and taken Paul from the van's backseat. They insisted that's all they knew. No one could prove if Madeleine had been on the ferry, and it could have been them who dumped Paul overboard. But I thought I knew the truth. I'd seen it in Madeleine's eyes.

Jameson promised he'd keep me up to date, and left.

Philippe wouldn't hear of my returning to Lake Placid. I would go back with him to Ottawa to recover, and he would have my car brought up. I didn't object. For now it felt good to have someone else making decisions.

Philippe drove me to Thomas's apartment, and loaded the bags Thomas had packed for me. I couldn't hug Thomas goodbye because of my injuries, but he patted my good shoulder, awkwardly, and knelt to pat Tiger before she jumped in the backseat.

"Thank you, Tommy," I said. His expression was blandly pleasant, as usual. But as if watching the scene from afar, I saw from the twist of his mouth and how his eyes didn't quite meet mine that his feelings for me had been more intense than I'd ever imagined. It was a shock, as if he, too, had

had a secret identity.

I couldn't have spoken again if I'd tried. This was like losing something I'd never had. Maybe my near-death had jolted Thomas enough to let his feelings show. Or maybe I was only now truly paying attention — and this was an even more unsettling thought.

Through the windshield I saw Thomas and Philippe cordially shaking hands. Then Philippe got in and we drove off. I forced my mind into blankness and closed my eyes.

CHAPTER 50

Four hours later we were pulling into the driveway of the Tudor house.

Paul had filled out; he seemed taller and his cheeks plumper. He danced around the room and presented me with a huge get-well card Elise had helped him make, signed "Paul and Bear," with an accompanying muddy paw print.

I blinked back tears when a beaming Elise served dinner, a steaming pot roast surrounded by vegetables, along with her homemade rolls.

So this was what home felt like.

Philippe and I told Paul only that I'd had an accident on a boat. Perhaps we would later tell him more, when he was older. Somehow I thought he would take the news calmly; he had to have known his mother hadn't loved him.

For now, we told him only that the bad

men who had kept him had been caught, and that Uncle Claude had taken money that wasn't his and had to go away for a while. For now, we let him continue thinking the body in Montreal had been his mother's, although it had been officially identified as the woman Claude had been seeing. Somewhere, a woman's parents were weeping at the news their daughter was dead.

I called Baker and filled her in, and even she was shocked. We'd known the world wasn't what we wanted it to be. We just hadn't realized it could be quite this bad.

During the days, life was good. Paul was loving his summer classes; he had friends over and went to their houses, like a normal, happy boy. Bear was growing fast, and gradually learning a few manners. Philippe was working hard, but often came home early, and laughed more often. He got down on the floor to play with Paul, something I realized I'd never seen him do. Zach and Dave took a trip to Burlington and brought my car to Ottawa, and stayed for a raucous dinner before heading back to Lake Placid.

But at night I lay awake. I thought about the brothers who had kept Paul captive, but in a way had treated him decently, getting him Happy Meals and little cartons of milk.

I thought about Claude, who had lost both girlfriend and sister, all because he had tried to break free of Madeleine. I thought about the woman who had made the mistake of loving Claude and trusting his sister enough to drive down a deserted road with her. I thought about Madeleine, so warped that her brother's perceived defection had triggered a deconstruction this complete and awful.

When I did sleep I dreamed of being in the lake, unable to breathe. Sometimes I grasped Madeleine's hand and saved her; sometimes she pulled me down with her. And sometimes I held her under.

Always, I awoke gasping for air.

I told Baker none of this; I didn't want her to share my nightmares. Alyssa I told a little more.

It was Jameson I talked to the most. We met every few days for lunch, takeout on a bench in a park overlooking the Rideau Canal. Some days we just ate. Some days he told me about developments in the case. Some days I just talked, and he just listened.

Claude had been the one who had embezzled from Philippe's company, which at this point seemed almost innocuous. The misdelivered ransom demand had been just that, courtesy of Canada Post: a mail carrier had stuck it in the wrong box. And it was the watch under the body that had led the police to suspect that Philippe was being framed — it was one touch too many. Madeleine had tried too hard.

I asked Jameson if he thought Claude had ever suspected that the body might have been his girlfriend's. He shrugged.

Maybe, I thought, it had been easier for Claude to have believed it was Madeleine — because otherwise, he would have had to realize whose body it was, and that his sister had killed the woman who happened to resemble her.

It was an overcast afternoon when Jameson told me that Madeleine had been nine weeks' pregnant when she died. Vince hadn't known. It didn't take a rocket scientist to work out the math: when she knew she was pregnant, she had decided to get rid of Paul. And maybe in six years or so, she would have gotten bored with her current life or angry at someone, and started the cycle over again.

Jameson knew my brain would go to the unborn baby that had drowned with Madeleine. He spoke before I could: "Who pushed you into the water, Troy? Who shot you? Who broke your arm?"

Of course he was right. Would I have done

anything differently had I known she was carrying a child? I could never know. But I did know that if I had hesitated at any point during our struggle, I would have been the one who ended up dead, not Madeleine.

I told Jameson, and only Jameson, how it had been on the boat with Madeleine, that the evil emanating from her had been nearly tangible. I told him about agonizing over having failed to guess that Marguerite wasn't who she pretended to be, to sense the dichotomy of someone living a life that wasn't theirs. It was true I hadn't warmed up to her initially, but I'd assumed that was my usual discomfort around immaculately groomed and dressed women. But I had recognized her appeal; I'd watched her charm people and make them feel important.

Jameson took a long breath and launched into the longest speech I'd heard from him. "She fooled everyone, Troy. Her friends, Philippe, Vince, even her brother. She was a pro — a professional psychopath, a professional liar, a professional actor, a professional killer. Don't be egotistical enough to think you could possibly have recognized or comprehended that." He turned my face toward him. I blinked tears back. "And, Troy, you stopped her. You won. You saved

Paul. You saved yourself. You gave all these people the chance to begin to put their lives back together. Even Claude. You did a good thing." Without seeming to realize he was doing it, he reached forward and tucked a strand of loose hair behind my ear.

And then my tears did fall. I felt shaky afterward, but better.

I stayed in Ottawa six weeks. We hiked in the Gatineaus. We saw every new movie suitable for Paul, and occasionally left him with Elise and went to some on our own. We tried out restaurants, and laughed when Paul made faces at foods he didn't like. We sorted through his clothes again. We selected an iMac for him, one with games even better than the one with the little round men — and let him know that when I recovered, Tiger and I would be returning to my house in Lake Placid. Baker and family came up for a weekend, and all the boys insisted on staying in Paul's room, cramming two to a bed and giggling much of the night.

Eventually we told Paul, casually, that his mother hadn't died last year as he had thought, but had died not long ago, in Burlington.

"When you were there?" he asked.

I nodded. He thought a moment and then

said, "Well, I am glad you are here now," and went off to play.

His psychologist told us this wasn't an unusual reaction at his age, especially since Paul hadn't been close to his mother and she had been absent from his life so long. She advised us to answer other questions as they arose, as honestly as we could without being brutal. I privately wondered how much Paul would ask, and how much he had already figured out. I hoped he hadn't seen the face of the person who had dropped him into Lake Champlain.

Eventually while we were walking around the neighborhood after dusk, I told Philippe the details of what had happened on the boat — I didn't want to talk about Madeleine in the house and I didn't want to see his face as I told him. He listened, and when I finished, he pulled me toward him and held me tightly. And then we walked on, and never mentioned it again.

We did have several talks about us, late in the evening after Paul had gone to bed. We'd been through too much to be coy with each other, but we both had things to work through. I wasn't the person I'd been at the start of all this, but I wasn't quite who I wanted to be yet either. Philippe had spent years living with a wife who had turned out to be a murderer, and I suspected he was having bad dreams of his own.

Maybe someday I would transplant myself into a new life, but it would have to happen when I was ready, and I wasn't yet. And I wasn't going to leap into Paul's life full-time and let him consider me a permanent fixture, then have him lose me because Philippe and I had jumped into something too soon.

I didn't know if I belonged in Lake Placid any longer, but it was my home for now.

It was time to go.

I hugged Elise, and then Philippe. "Come back when you can," Philippe said, and folded me in his arms. I hugged back, hard. Then I knelt and gathered in Paul and held tight, and shushed him as he sobbed.

"I'll see you soon," I whispered to him, but he wouldn't look at me.

I was having trouble getting enough air. I felt dizzy, as if at high altitude, and had to concentrate to move my body into the car. I put a half smile on my face and waved goodbye. I knew this was what I had to do; I knew this was right for me, for all of us.

I drove away, seeing Paul in his father's arms in my rearview mirror until I turned the corner. A mile or two away I stopped the car and cried, great gasping sobs, until my breathing evened out and I could drive. Tears trailed down my cheeks until I reached Cornwall and started across the bridge into New York.

Sometimes you know you've made the right decision, simply because of how hard it is.

ACKNOWLEDGMENTS

Thanks to:

Meg Waite Clayton and Mac Clayton for their help and encouragement; early readers Dee Dee O'Connor, L. K. Browning, Kimberly McCall, and the now-defunct Nashville Writers Group; Mike Modrak and Linda Yoder for their support; Linda Allen for telling me to rewrite the middle.

Michael Carlisle, Ann Close, Leslie Daniels, Sands Hall, Sue Miller, and others from the Squaw Valley Writers Conference; readers Sandy Ebner, Carole Firstman, Cat Connor, Bevan Quinn, Amanda McGrath Anderson, Robert Smolka, Persia Walker, Steph Bowe, and Reed Farrel Coleman.

Jamie Ford, whose quiet assurance that I would do this was more help than he knew; Michael Robotham, who had me change the title; Persia Walker, who helped give me insight into the mind of a small child; Reed Farrel Coleman, who saved me from my worst writing instincts.

The RCMP, Ottawa Police Service, and Québec Police Service; Celine Temps, Gisele Grignon, Gaël Reinaudi, and Inga Murawski for translation help; Luke Ringrose, who breathed life into Paul simply by existing; Patti Gallagher, for being there; SFC, who titled this book and believed in it.

And my wonderful agent, Barney Karpfinger, and editor, John Glusman.

READING GROUP GUIDE

1. The novel opens when Troy dives into Lake Champlain to save a child she had only seen for a split second. Have you ever been in a similar situation? How did you react?

2. Troy describes her attachment to the little boy she rescues as quick and atavistic, and wonders if this is what her sisters felt like when they had their children. Do you think a maternal bond is instinctive and instant? Do you think a similar bond could be formed by people who share a traumatic experience?

3. Hoping to protect Paul from being put into foster care, or possibly being returned to a bad home situation, Troy keeps him at her home until she can track down his father. Why do you think she does this?

Was she right to keep the police out of it?

4. Troy thinks she will be able to tell immediately if Paul's father had anything to do with his kidnapping. Is it possible to be so sure about a person's motives based on a first impression or gut reaction? What did your instincts tell you about Philippe when he and Troy first met?

5. In Lake Placid, Troy doesn't really have to adhere to any schedules or be accountable to anyone, until Paul enters her life. Aside from her lifestyle, how else does Paul change Troy? Are these changes for the better?

6. No one in Philippe's household talks about Madeleine at all. What conclusions did that cause you to draw about her relationships with Paul and Philippe? Were you right?

7. When Claude learned that a body was found that matched Madeleine's dental records, he was devastated. Did this change how Troy saw him? Did it change how you saw him?

8. Vince, Marguerite, and Alyssa all gain

Troy's trust quickly, while it takes her a while to warm up to Jameson. Was Troy's trust always well-placed? Which characters did you find easier to trust than others?

9. Claude and Madeleine grew up in foster care after tragedy struck their family. What role do you think this played in their actions as adults?

10. There are several men in the book that seem to care for Troy deeply, especially Thomas. Does Troy treat him well? What do you think her feelings are toward the other male characters, and how well does she handle them?

11. The dogs in the story are all named for fiercer animals. What significance does this have? Could the characters be looking for protectors? What else was important about the animals?

12. How does the title illustrate the themes in the book? Troy has to swim for her life several times, but do you see any other significance to the title? What else does she learn?

13. At several key moments in the book,

Troy reminds herself that the best thing to do is usually the hardest thing. In the end, she makes a particularly difficult decision. Was this the right choice? What about her other decisions? When she responded with ease, did she usually make the right choice, or the wrong one?

14. What's next for Troy Chance? What issues or characters in *Learning to Swim* would you like to see explored further?

ABOUT THE AUTHOR

Sara J. Henry has been a columnist, soil scientist, book and magazine editor, website designer, writing instructor, and bicycle mechanic. *Learning to Swim* is her first novel.